MASKED MOSAIC

EDITED BY:

CLAUDE LALUMIÈRE AND CAMILLE ALEXA

READ ORDER

230	279	186 (11)	171	37
88	131 (7)		21	109
226 (4)	63		72	150
58	207 (9)		92	233
216	197			255
221 (5)	285 (10)			

CANADIAN SUPER STORIES

EDITED BY:

CLAUDE LALUMIÈRE AND CAMILLE ALEXA

TYCHE BOOKS LTD.

Published by Tyche Books Ltd.
www.TycheBooks.com

Cover Art by Steve Thomas
Cover Layout by Lucia Starkey
Interior Layout by Tina Moreau and Susan Huot

Library and Archives Canada Cataloguing in Publication

Masked Mosaic : Canadian super stories / edited by Claude Lalumière
    and Camille Alexa. -- Calgary, AB : Tyche Books, c2013.
    p. ; cm.
    Issued also in electronic format.
    ISBN 978-0-9918369-0-1
    1. Fantasy fiction, Canadian (English). 2. Short stories, Canadian
(English). 3. Canadian fiction (English)--21st century. I. Lalumière,
Claude. II. Alexa, Camille.

First Edition: February 2013

CONTENTS

INTRODUCTION

MARK SHAINBLUM

When Gabriel Morrissette and I launched our *Northguard* comics series in 1984, we were far from the first to try our hands at creating a genuinely Canadian superhero: Marvel Comics had recently debuted *Alpha Flight*, and Richard Comely had created the archetypal maple-leaf hero, *Captain Canuck,* back in 1975.

Going back even further, well before our time, scores of Canadian adventure heroes like *Johnny Canuck* and *Nelvana of the Northern Lights* flourished during World War II, when emergency economic measures restricted import of American comics. That said, by the 70s and 80s those comics were remembered by only a handful of scholars and hardcore collectors, and we knew them only in snippets and outtakes. We were influenced a lot by their existence, but virtually not at all by their content.

For their part, *Captain Canuck* and *Alpha Flight* were both great, innovative series that opened a lot of creative doors. Richard Comely and his brilliant collaborator George Freeman made great strides in illustration, colouring, and distribution, while John Byrne's *Alpha Flight* literally put Canada on the map in mainstream superhero comics, where it really hadn't existed before. However, I never felt that either series really confronted the essential contradiction at the heart of that innocuous phrase, Canadian superhero." Some people considered it an out-and-out oxymoron like "military intelligence" or "open secret." Canada, after all, was the land of "surviving," not "winning," or so Margaret Atwood told us: "Our stories are likely to be tales not of those who made it but of those who made it *back*," she wrote in *Survival*, her seminal 1971 critique of Canadian literature. "Back from the awful experience—the North, the snowstorm, the sinking ship—that killed everyone else. The survivor has no triumph or victory but the fact of his survival; he has little after his ordeal that he did not have before, except gratitude for having escaped with his life."

Does that sound like good fodder for a typical superhero adventure? Not so much. Superheroes are all about winning: order overcoming chaos, justice triumphing over injustice, or, at the most primal level, good defeating evil.

In the 1980s, Canada wasn't very good at primal. Pop music excepted, our culture was all about shades of grey and weighty moral complexity. Pop culture was by definition almost entirely American, imported, and—to the cultural elite, anyhow—*other*. If you were a Canadian author interested in, say, mystery or science fiction, you were constantly being put on the spot to (a) justify why you were wasting your time when there were great novels left to be written about prairie farmers during the depression and (b) prove that Canadian mystery or science fiction actually existed in the first place.

Comic books and superheroes, needless to say, were even a step below either of those on the ladder of cultural propriety, with an even greater burden of disdain to overcome.

With *Northguard*, Gabriel and I came to the conclusion that if we wanted to succeed artistically we'd have to cross this cultural no-man's land instead of simply skirting it or pretending that it didn't exist. We advertised the series with the tagline "Canada does not believe in heroes," and we opened the first issue with another Atwood quote: "Canadian history defeats attempts to construct traditional society-saving or society-changing heroes." It'll never beat "With great power comes great responsibility," but it makes the point.

Frankly, though, at the time I was a little unclear on exactly what the point was. I vaguely thought that by acknowledging the contradiction I could inoculate myself against it, but it didn't work that way; Atwood was right, Canada *is* different. It's not that we're incapable of creating our own pop culture or working with archetypes like superheroes, but if we're true to who we are they won't be like American superheroes. Or British superheroes. Or Japanese superheroes. And we shouldn't expect them to be.

After all, superstar comics writer Alan Moore—of *Marvelman, V for Vendetta, Watchmen*, and *League of Extraordinary Gentlemen* fame—turned the American superhero genre on its head in the 1980s by filtering it through his uniquely British sensibilities. I often say (tongue only partially in cheek) that I was the first North American comics writer to rip off his style, while all those other johnnies-come-lately waited till after his run on *Swamp Thing* or even *Watchmen*. (Hey, if you're going to steal, steal from the best!) A mature writer hopefully outgrows his superficial stylistic influences, but I think I learned something far deeper and more intrinsic from Moore: He didn't sacrifice who he was in order to write some of the greatest superhero stories ever told. On the contrary, Moore took what was perceived to be a quintessentially American idiom and made it into something entirely new.

And that's what *Masked Mosaic* is all about. In the old days, an anthology of prose Canadian superhero stories would have been almost unimaginable. Serious writers would have disdained it, and even serious science fiction and fantasy writers might have struggled with the premise. Thankfully, today, we've got Claude Lalumière and Camille Alexa. If you don't know Claude's previous work, he is, quite simply, one of the best authors and editors Canada has produced in the last twenty years, in any genre. In particular, he's rewritten the book on what Canadian science fiction and fantasy should look like. I don't know Camille as well, but it's clear from her published work that she knows speculative fiction backward and forward, and also has a keen editorial eye. Together, they've worked a rare kind of magic in *Masked Mosaic*.

Claude and Camille have recruited an awesome cross-section of Canada's speculative-fiction talent to write stories about people with superhuman powers and (in some cases) capes and tights. A decade or two ago, a book like this would have been a curiosity, a novelty item full of pastiche, broad parody, or exercises in candy-store-on-the-corner-where-I-bought-my-comics nostalgia. I doubt anybody would have had the guts to play it straight, to work within the genre to tell meaningful Canadian stories that stand on their own merits.

You can have meaning. It can be Canadian. It can feature superheroes. Go figure.

MARK SHAINBLUM was born and raised in Montreal, where he and illustrator Gabriel Morrissette co-created Northguard and the bestselling political parody Angloman, which later appeared as a weekly strip in *The Montreal Gazette*. Mark also collaborated on the *Captain Canuck* daily newspaper strip, *The New Original Captain Canuck*, and *Canadiana: The New Spirit of Canada*, a webcomic featuring the first Canadian flag superheroine with her own series. He recently moved to Ottawa with his wife and daughter. For more about Mark, go to www.northguard.com/mbs.

NOCTURNE

E.L. CHEN

My name is Doug, and I haven't been sleeping well lately.

When I do sleep, I dream of strange panoramas: clouds of sooty fluff, bird's-eye views of neighbourhoods as intricate as a computer motherboard, and a flinty-eyed man in grey who can fly.

I dream he saves the city a hundred times over. I dream that he's happy.

I think I'm depressed. I have all the symptoms: not eating, not sleeping, no motivation, no joy. I've been contemplating suicide. I mean, we all have to die sometime, don't we? This way you don't have to worry about retirement, or what your girlfriend is really doing when she says she has to work late again with Tyler, the one guy she didn't introduce you to at her office Christmas party.

I wonder—if I jumped off my apartment balcony, would the flying man in grey save me?

"So, Doug—where do you see yourself in five years?"

I hate that question. It's so irrelevant. Five years ago I was starting university and thought my degree was a ticket to a career, not a season's pass to a cavalcade of interviews for unpaid internships, between shifts at Starbucks.

I flash a smile at Dylan Gomi, the Motherf*cking CEO. That's what it says on his fucking business card. *Dylan Gomi, Motherf*cking CEO.* I suspect it's the alter ego for his real

3

identity, *Dylan Gomi, First-Degree Asshole*, the way Doug Wolochuk, Eager University Grad, is the alter ego of Doug Wolochuk, Perpetual Barista.

"Well," I say, "I'm really impressed with the work your startup's done. In five years I see myself as your head of Marketing."

Dylan throws his head back and guffaws. I can see the fillings in his back teeth. "Seriously, dude?" he says. "Seriously? You think five years straight outta school at one company qualifies you to be the head of a marketing department?"

"Yes," I say. *Smile. Be assertive. Be confident. Be Doug Wolochuk, Eager University Grad.* "With my passion and enthusiasm, it's possible."

Dylan taps his finger on my resumé on the table. It's only one page, single-sided. I wonder if he's actually read it. It wouldn't take him very long.

"Christ. You fucking kids," he says, although he can't be more than ten years older than me. "Your moms were wrong. Passion is worth shit in the real world. *Trying hard* doesn't win you a prize like it did in kindergarten."

I want to punch him. But Doug Wolochuk, Eager University Grad, doesn't punch people, and I may not have won the prize for *Trying Hard* in kindergarten but I do have one for *Getting Along with Others*.

Dylan suddenly sits up straighter and frowns. "You look familiar," he says.

I shake my head. "I don't think we've ever—"

He snaps his fingers. "You live in my building. The Majestic. The new condo development on Wellington."

He would know if I lived there if he had actually read my resumé. My address is printed at the top. I say, "Um, yeah. I do live there."

He raises an eyebrow, and I know he knows there's no way someone like me can afford a condo at the Majestic. "I'm renting," I add, lamely.

He smirks. "From your parents?"

"No." *From my girlfriend's parents.*

"Hey, let me ask you something," Dylan says, pulling his phone out of his pocket. "You ever the see the flying man in grey?"

My mouth goes dry. "Excuse me?"

"The flying man in grey. You ever see him around our building?" He swipes the screen on his phone until he finds the right photo. "This guy. I got up at, like, 3 a.m. last night to take a piss, and this guy streaks past my living room window. Twenty stories up. Managed to get a pic the second time he came around."

He shows me the photo on his phone. A grey blur in the shape of a man doing front crawl floats in the night sky.

I remember how the wind felt in his face in my dream last night. I remember his smile. A genuine, joyful smile, not like the one I'm wearing now.

"No," I lie. "I've never seen him before."

"What do you make of it? Some kind of wire? A marketing stunt?"

"Yeah," I say absent-mindedly. It was cold, I remember. Colder than he thought it would be, twenty floors up.

Dylan yanks the phone out from under my nose. I hadn't realized I had been staring. "That's all you have to say?" he says, and I remember that I'm interviewing for a marketing position. I should've offered some insight.

"Sorry, Doug," he says. "We're wasting our time here. I'll see you around."

His mobile chirrups on the desk. He snatches it up and barks, "I told you not to call me at work, Robin. This better be important."

He stands and offers me his hand, but his attention is on the call. The flying man in grey would have taken that hand and judo flipped Dylan Gomi, Motherf*cking CEO, onto the ground. Instead, I shake his hand, smile another Eager University Grad smile, and leave.

The man in grey flies above the city. He doesn't really need to stretch out his arms, but he likes doing it. It makes him feel like he's slicing through the air like an arrow, even though he's moving at a leisurely pace in order to survey the streets below.

He crosses off Toronto's neighbourhoods in his head as he circles the city. Chinatown. Koreatown. Greektown. Cabbagetown. Little India. Little Italy. The Annex. The Junction. The Beach (or Beaches, whichever you prefer). The Village. Liberty Village. Bloor West Village. Roncey. Leslieville. Parkdale. So many neighbourhoods, more than he can name, and so many opportunities for trouble on a mild spring night.

He finds it first in St. Jamestown. Voices carry from a playground tucked within a cluster of highrise apartment buildings. Someone shouting about wanting someone's phone in exchange for not kicking the shit out of him. He peers down with his razor-sharp vision, sharper than an HD camera. Three young men are using a fourth as a punching bag. It's a nice night, so they aren't alone. But those lingering outside on benches and motorized wheelchairs look away. They don't want to get involved.

The man in grey plummets to the ground like a shooting star, feet first, landing right in front of the muggers. "Holy shit!" one of them says. "Where the fuck did he come from?"

The others aren't so lucky. They don't get the chance to say anything. *Biff! Bam! Pow!* and they go flying through the monkey bars, collapsing like rag dolls around the swings.

The man in grey picks the phone off the ground and dusts off the sand. The glass screen is still glossy and intact, the brushed aluminum still unscratched. No wonder the muggers wanted it. "I believe this is yours," he says.

The phone's owner has sank to his knees. His lip and nose are bloody. He can't be more than fifteen. "Thankth," the kid rasps around the blood in his mouth.

The man in grey nods, raises one fist in the air, and leaps up to the sky from which he came. But not before the kid raises his phone and flicks on the camera.

I wake up to muffled shouting. I can never tell if it's in the unit above us or next door, or else I'd call the police. Chelsea says to ignore it, it's none of our business. I guess she's right.

I roll over, reaching for her—and my arm flails in nothingness. I've fallen asleep on the balcony again, on Chelsea's parents' wicker chaise longue, my old camp sleeping bag tucked damply around me. There's a soft thump from our fighting neighbours. A body has been thrown across a room. I know what that sounds like now, thanks to my dream of the man in grey.

I swing my legs over the side and trudge to the master bedroom, still cocooned in the sleeping bag. The shower is running; Chelsea's side of the bed is only slightly rumpled, as if she got in but changed her mind.

The shower turns off, and Chelsea emerges from the bathroom in her robe, a towel wrapped around her blond hair. "What time is it?" I say, yawning.

"Seven-thirty," she says. "I gotta get to the office."

"So early? When did you get in?"

"Late," she says. "Press release for a big client has to go out this morning. You were sleeping on the balcony again."

I frown. "I don't remember going out there."

She shakes her head. "You never do. I tried to wake you, but you were tossing and turning and muttering in your sleep. I swear, one of these days I'm going to take a video of you so you can see how weird it is. How was your interview?"

I sink onto the bed and watch her get dressed. "Okay," I lie.

"Do you think you'll get the job?"

"Maybe," I lie.

"That's good. You look like crap, babe. You really should think about going to a sleep disorder clinic."

"Yeah," I say, rubbing my eyes. My hand comes away sandy.

She pouts in the mirror above the dresser and applies her lipstick. She never wore makeup when we were in school. "Don't forget we're going out tonight with Nicole."

"Is it Friday already?" I yawn again.

"Yes," she says, rolling her eyes. "I'll text you where we're meeting."

I shrug off the sleeping bag and find that I'm wearing my grey hooded sweatshirt and jeans. The hoodie smells like clean sweat and ozone, as if I'd spent the whole night running a marathon in it.

"I'll see you later, babe." She gives me a quick kiss, and then wrinkles her nose and gestures at my clothes. "You really should do some laundry," she says, and then she's gone.

After working the evening shift I end up at some dive on Queen West or West Queen West or however far west the nigh-trendy stretch has shifted. We're so far west on Queen West we're practically in Vancouver. The bar's name consists of two randomly paired words that have nothing to do with the bar itself, like Pineapple Stalin, as if it's an indie band.

We're apparently here because some Toronto blog extolled the virtues of their organic beer and artisanal poutine. Nicole has brought her boyfriend Brandon, whom I've never liked. He wears hats too much, and the frames of his glasses are so dark and thick they suck in the light like a black hole. Knowing Brandon, they were probably designed in Japan and assembled by fair trade African orphans in an organic carbon-neutral facility. I've always thought that men shouldn't like accessories so much, but this past year has taught me that everything I knew while in school is wrong.

Nicole, I don't mind so much. She's a brunette version of Chelsea, also long-haired and banged and fond of thrifted men's shirts and patterned tights like she's an extra in a John Hughes movie.

"Did you guys see the Grey Hoodie video?" Brandon says when a table frees up in the back. Tonight he's wearing a straw fedora with a black ribbon, black as his glasses.

Chelsea and Nicole nod. "It was all over the office," Chelsea says. "How do you think he did it?"

"Did what?" I ask, putting on my guileless Doug Wolochuk, Nice Boyfriend, face. It's for Chelsea's sake; I know she wants me to get along with her new Toronto friends. "And who's he?"

"You didn't see it?" Nicole said.

"Oh, of course not. He was at work," Chelsea says.

"No computers behind the counter at Starbucks," I say, with a smile that doesn't reach my eyes.

"You didn't even watch it on your phone?" Brandon asks. "On your lunch break?"

"I was eating lunch," I say.

The irony is lost on him. Which is ironic, because I thought hipsters were all about irony. "So this guy comes out of nowhere," he says, "saves a kid from an ass-kicking, and then flies away. The kid posted a video online. Dude actually jumps in the air and flies away. Here."

Brandon pulls out his phone, taps it a few times, and then passes it over to me. I set down my beer and take it. Chelsea leans over my shoulder. "I've seen it a million times," she says, "and it still blows my mind. How does he do it?"

"He's a superhero," says Nicole. "He's an honest-to-God, motherfucking superhero."

"Do you think he's from another planet?" asks Chelsea. "I mean, he can fly."

"He could just have some high-tech gear," says Nicole.

8

"No way. He's definitely from another planet," Brandon says. "No-one from Toronto would ever step in to help a stranger." Brandon grew up in Montreal, if I recall correctly. "He probably dances at concerts, too," he adds. Nicole punches him in the shoulder.

Chelsea says something else, but I don't hear her. The video loads up, and there's the man in grey from my dreams, rocketing from the ground as if launched upward by invisible wires. There are no wires, though. I know that the flying man in grey doesn't need them.

"Why do they call him the Grey Hoodie?" I ask. They're arguing now about which Canadian city the superhero *could* possibly be from, St. John's, Newfoundland, being the top contender.

"Because he's wearing one. Duh," Chelsea says, and I remember the sweatshirt I'd woken up in that morning.

"And other reports of a vigilante in a grey hoodie came out of the woodwork after this video went viral," Nicole says. "Seems he was pretty busy last night."

I blink; and I remember other faces, other neighbourhoods besides St. Jamestown. That cabbie in the Financial District, and those girls in Kensington Market. And there were more, but it's all a dreamlike blur of cloud-shaped shadows and flying fists and the wind striking the man in grey's face.

"It's a genius costume," Brandon says. "None of that cape and tights shit. Sweatshirt, jeans and sneakers—dude can just land on the ground and look like everyone else. No need to find a phone booth to change in."

"Anyone see his face?" I ask.

Nicole shakes his head. "Nope. Had that hood over his head the whole time."

"I bet he's white," Brandon says.

Chelsea shoots him a dirty look. "Seriously? How can you tell?"

"Because, if he were black, someone would've shot him."

Nicole snorts. "In Toronto?"

"Okay, well—no-one would have stopped their cab to pick him up late at night," he says.

Chelsea laughs. "Does it look like he needs a cab?"

"Speaking of late nights," I say, passing the phone back to Brandon, "were you also doing work for that big client last night, Nicole?"

9

Nicole's brow furrows. Chelsea says, quickly, "She's staffed to a different project."

"Yeah," Nicole says, smiling. "I don't have to work crazy hours like Chels does, thank God."

My answering smile is just as fake. Doug Wolochuk, Nice Boyfriend, would never suspect his longtime girlfriend to be cheating on him. "Lucky," I say, and then a massive yawn overtakes my face. Chelsea frowns. "Sorry, I didn't sleep well last night."

"Doug *never* sleeps well," Chelsea says. "Always tossing and turning, and then he gets up and ends up falling asleep somewhere else, like the sofa or out on the balcony."

"Too much noise, I guess," I say. "I'm not used to the city. I should go." I yawn again, gulp down the rest of my beer, and set down the bottle.

"Really?" Nicole gives me a puppy-dog face. Brandon makes some kind of faux-protest sound. Chelsea's mouth thins.

"I have to work tomorrow morning," I say.

"He's no fun anymore," Chelsea says. "When he's not working, he's sleeping. Because he doesn't sleep well. It's a vicious cycle."

I stand up. Chelsea proffers her cheek. I dutifully kiss it.

"See you back home, babe," she says.

"Yeah," I say. *Eventually.*

The Grey Hoodie plans to save Toronto, one night at a time.

He saves cyclists and pedestrians from reckless drivers. He saves reckless drivers from irate cyclists and pedestrians. He swoops down to carry stalled streetcars out of the way. He hands out bottled water and Tim Hortons gift cards to the homeless.

On Friday and Saturday nights, he helps people find their housekeys when they stumble home at four in the morning. He stops women from going home with unsuitable men, and men from going home with unsuitable women. He breaks up bar fights. When someone pulls out a gun in the middle of the Entertainment District, he's there to melt it with his heat-ray vision.

When the guy behind you at the ATM peers over your shoulder to get your PIN, the Grey Hoodie is there.

When you stagger out of the Dance Cave and none of your friends have followed you out to hold your hair back when you puke on the sidewalk, the Grey Hoodie is there.

When you're walking your dog on Church Street and a group of drunken frat boys follow you around and call you a dyke, the Grey Hoodie is there.

The Grey Hoodie wants to save the city. The Grey Hoodie wants to save *you*.

❦

The neighbours are fighting again. I leave the sleeping bag on the chaise longue and plod into the bedroom, trying to listen to the ruckus over the sound of Chelsea's hair dryer. Mostly shouting this time; less bodily contact.

Steam puffs out of the bathroom as the door swings open. "Gross, you fell asleep in your hoodie again," Chelsea says. "You really should wash it. It smells. I'm almost glad you sleep outside. Have you taken up jogging again?"

"Um, yeah," I lie.

"That's good; the exercise will probably help you sleep better. Oh! I have something to tell you." She perches on the foot of the bed. "So Nicole and I went back to Mango Lenin for a quick drink last night, to take a break from the pitch, and you'll never guess who we just missed."

"Who?" I say.

"Guess!" She bounces excitedly on the mattress.

I shake my head. "I'm not awake enough to guess."

"The Grey Hoodie!" she says.

"The *what*?"

"The Grey Hoodie! The superhero, remember?"

"Oh," I say. "Right."

"Apparently there was this obnoxious customer who'd drunk too much and was hitting on a waitress. The Grey Hoodie just— *whoosh!*—appeared out of nowhere and dragged him outside."

"Did he beat the crap out of the guy?" I ask, rubbing my eyes. I don't remember that part from my dreams.

"No, just shoved him into a cab," she says. "It was pulling away when we got there. People were still standing on the sidewalk looking up. Videos are online already. Actually, there's a *ton* of them from last night. The guy was *everywhere*. He really gets around."

"He *is* a superhero," I say.

"Yeah," she says. "Isn't that exciting?"

She's never looked that excited for anything that I've ever done. "Look, Chelsea," I say. "I've been meaning to talk to you. . . ."

"Oh?" she says in an overly light voice, and I think, *You're afraid I'm going to ask you about your work BFF, Tyler.*

"I don't know how to say this . . . but *I* have a grey hoodie." I stick my hands in the kangaroo pocket for emphasis.

"I know. I bought it for you."

"It's not just that," I say. "I've been having these dreams lately. Dreams about flying—"

She laughs. "What, like you think you're the Grey Hoodie or something?" At the expression on my face, she laughs again. "Oh my God, you *do* think you're the Grey Hoodie!" She laughs so hard that she falls off the bed, which makes her laugh even more.

I don't know what to say.

Finally Chelsea picks herself up, but there's still laughter in her eyes. "I'm sorry, Doug. I love you," she says, which she hasn't said in months, "but you, an ass-kicking urban superhero? I don't think so."

"But the flying dreams," I say. "They're so real, so vivid."

"Everyone has flying dreams. And everyone's got a grey hoodie. I've got two."

"But you said so yourself—every morning I smell like I've been out jogging."

"Doug, your sleeping habits have you so mixed up you've probably forgotten when you last showered." She shakes her head. "Fine. Fly. Fly for me now."

"Okay." I take a deep breath and lift both arms in the air as if I'm about to dive into a swimming pool. I close my eyes and launch myself up on my toes.

Nothing.

I can tell Chelsea's trying hard not to laugh again. I sink back on my heels. She's right. Me, a superhero? Absolutely ludicrous. I'm Doug Wolochuk, Nice Boyfriend. I'm only good for pouring espresso shots and dozing off while waiting for her to come home from the office.

"Yeah, you're right," I say. "Anyway, you'd notice if I were out all night fighting crime."

Chelsea suddenly walks over to the mirror above the dresser and picks at a clump in her mascara. "Oh, Nicole says that Brandon says there's a marketing internship opening up at the agency he works at. You should apply."

"I don't want to work with Brandon. He's always telling me I should quit Starbucks and work for an indie coffee shop instead."

"Well," she says, turning back to look at me, one hand on her hip, "if you get the job, he won't be telling you to quit Starbucks because you'll have already quit. Anyway, he's a designer, you probably won't have to talk to him at all."

"I don't know—"

"Do you want to be a barista for the rest of your life?" she says.

"No, but—"

"Then I'll get the deets from Nicole."

"I don't know."

"What don't you know?" she demands. "What happened to all the plans we made together before graduation?"

"I don't—"

Chelsea throws up her hands. She huffs out the door, probably to run to Tyler and complain that she's saddled with a delusional sad sack of a boyfriend.

"I don't know," I say to the empty room.

I tell Chelsea I have to work an evening shift even though I actually finish at five. I don't feel like hanging out at home, waiting for her to text and tell me that she's going to be working late yet again. Instead, I wind through the streets between the coffee shop and home, waiting for night to fall, waiting for something to *happen*.

Kensington Market buzzes as the sun sets. It's the start of patio season. They say that in Toronto there are two seasons, winter and construction, but if you live downtown it's actually winter and patio. Even though the city hasn't thawed completely—it's chilly even in May—people happily shiver outside ancient mom-and-pop bars that woke up one morning and found themselves trendy. All the girls look like Nicole and Chelsea; all the guys look like Brandon.

Kensington spits me out onto Dundas. I continue on Spadina through Chinatown, weaving through tourists and locals. Surely any minute now I'll come across an urban misdemeanour, and either the flying man in grey will appear or I will find myself rising to the occasion. Someone will dine and dash out of a pho restaurant. Someone will threaten a streetcar driver. Someone will harass a dozing panhandler. And I'll know for once and for all whether my dreams have just been dreams or not.

I zip up my hoodie. I'm not that cold, but I pull the hood over my head anyway. I'm not the only one. Chelsea was right; everyone has a grey hoodie—and suddenly seems to have decided to wear theirs tonight in imitation of their hero. Men, women, even the few sleepy-eyed children being hustled home to bed. An apple-cheeked blonde wearing nothing but a grey hoodie zipped down to her navel smiles up at me from the cover of the *Toronto Sun*. Someone has spray-painted *Grey Hoodie 4 Mayor* over the window of an abandoned video rental shop. A man in an unzipped grey hoodie and Santa hat does pushups next to the giant thimble at Spadina and Richmond.

"Yes yes yes!" he shouts. The zippered edges swing against his muscular bare chest. He seems more likely to be a superhero than me. His face is all sharp angles and he's got that wicked movie villain goatee. Furthermore, he's got the alpha male swagger, like Dylan Gomi, First-Class Asshole. Even Brandon, being an alpha douchebag, would be a likelier candidate than me.

Me, I'm all sandy hair and soft edges, nondescript and inoffensive, like a Doug should be. When we first started dating, Chelsea used to say I was cute in a boy-next-door way.

But now that I'm twenty-three I'm no longer a boy. I don't know what I am.

Or maybe I'm still that boy.

It all seemed easier when I was a kid. Being a grownup seemed easy. Adulthood was going to be your secret identity, the time in your life when you would finally shine and that kid who used to rough you up behind the portables would be sorry.

I thought I was going to be a cop or a firefighter or mechanic, because I thought that's what men did. Fixed things. Saved things. Made things better for people. Instead I majored in Marketing and Business Communications at a second-rate university in a small Ontario town. Which qualifies me to steam milk and tell customers that it's *venti*, not *large*, and *would you like whipped cream with that?*

Night has fallen. Someone's shouting in the parkette down the street from the condo. I can make out two figures: one large, one thin. The larger one, of course, is doing the shouting. The thin one just stands there, still and small, as if he or she is trying to make themselves as invisible as possible. A small dog, like a Jack Russell, dances around their feet. Between its yaps I catch words like *worthless* and *stupid*.

The shouter raises his fist. I should do something. I should step forward and say something like—what *do* men say in situations like this? *You oughta pick on somebody your own size!*

Something like that. In a John Wayne voice.

I bet Chelsea's boyfriend-in-waiting, Tyler, would know what to say.

I bet the Grey Hoodie would know what to say.

I count to ten, expecting him to descend like an avenging angel. He'll step in. I know he will. I've *been* him in my dreams.

Nothing.

At least call the police, I tell myself. My hand curls around the phone in my hoodie's pocket, but the shouting man scoops up the Jack Russell terrier and slips into the shadows. The smaller figure scurries after them.

It's too late. At least I tried. I breathe a sigh of relief and disappointment and continue on my way home.

Then I remember, as Dylan Gomi, Motherf*cking CEO, had said, *trying hard* isn't enough to win a prize in the real world.

The flying man in grey isn't flying tonight.

He dashes faster than a cheetah through a warren of hallways, honing in on the noise with his super hearing.

There. A torrent of angry words floods from the penthouse unit. *You useless, no-good little bitch. You're nothing without me. Do that again and I will kill you, Robin. I mean it.*

The door splinters under the force of the Grey Hoodie's body. A thin young man bends backward over a rather nice mahogany dining table. It looks like a black eye is about to surface on his face. A larger man has his hands around his throat. A Jack Russell terrier circles them in a frenzy of barking, but whether it's protesting or egging the aggressor on, the Grey Hoodie can't tell.

With a flick of his wrist, the Grey Hoodie throws the large man across the room. He crashes into the kitchen island. Copper pots tumble off the granite countertop and clang on the floor. The thin young man, presumably Robin, screams.

"So you like to bully the weak," the Grey Hoodie snarls. The large man groans. The Grey Hoodie grabs him by his shirt collar and hauls him into a sitting position. "Just remember, there is someone stronger than—"

The large man looks up then, and his eyes widen.

"*You!*" the Grey Hoodie says.

"*You!*" Dylan Gomi says.

The Grey Hoodie lifts Dylan Gomi, Motherf*cking CEO, into the air above his head, ready to throw him across the room a second time. Robin yells, "Don't hurt him!" and suddenly he's clawing at the Grey Hoodie like a cat on fire. His attack is but a mere tickle to the Grey Hoodie, but it surprises him enough to drop Dylan back on the floor.

Dylan's foot shoots out and the Grey Hoodie trips and lands on top of him, the Jack Russell snapping at his arm, Robin whirling with clenched fists. The sleeve of his hoodie tears between the dog's teeth.

"Enough!" the Grey Hoodie booms, springing into the air. The two men and the dog fall off of him onto the floor. He hovers above them, boring holes into Dylan with his eyes, regretfully without his heat-ray vision.

"It's okay," Robin whimpers, clinging to Dylan's arm. "Don't hurt my husband. It's okay. I deserved it."

In the distance, the Grey Hoodie hears approaching police sirens. They'll sort this out. They'll take one look at Robin and haul Dylan off to jail.

The Grey Hoodie turns and soars out the ragged man-shaped hole he made in their door.

He hears Robin ask Dylan if he's all right.

Some people, the Grey Hoodie thinks sadly, just don't want to be saved.

The cold teeth of the sleeping bag bite into my cheek. I flip over on my back, squinting at the morning sunlight.

Something's not right.

It's quiet.

I yawn, shed the sleeping bag, and plod inside to the bedroom. The shower is running. I remember Chelsea's complaints about the smell so I grab a clean T-shirt from the dresser and peel off my sweatshirt. There's a tear in the right sleeve, about the perfect size for a yappy little canine mouth.

The shower turns off. I toss the hoodie onto the bed and quickly exchange my dirty T-shirt for the fresh one.

Chelsea emerges from the bathroom, towel wound around her head. "You missed all the drama last night," she says. "You know the noise and shouting we always hear? Guy upstairs got taken away by the cops for domestic abuse. Turns out he was beating up his partner."

A thin, forlorn face with a bruised eye flashes in my head. "Poor guy," I say. "I hope he's okay."

"What? How can you sympathize with the abuser?"

"No, no—I meant his partner."

"How did you know his partner's male?" she asks.

"I've seen them around," I say, truthfully. "They have a Jack Russell."

"I got in just as the asshole was being pushed into the back of a police car," she says. "He looked a mess. Apparently the Grey Hoodie got to him."

Her eyes flash with excitement. I sit up a little straighter, hold my head up a little higher. "Really."

"Uh huh. I can't believe you slept through it. There were police cars and news trucks and everything. Turns out the guy's some well-known local entrepreneur—"

"Dylan Gomi, Motherfucking CEO," I mutter.

Chelsea looks at me, startled. "That's the guy."

"Yeah," I say. "I interviewed at his startup last month. He's a dick."

"Good thing you didn't get hired then." Her mouth twists, and she turns away. She cocks her head to one side, towel-drying her hair in front of the mirror. I pick my hoodie off the bed and straighten out the sleeve. I didn't imagine it. The tear is there, as plain as day.

"Did Dylan Gomi say anything?" I ask.

"Other than *Get those fucking cameras outta my face*?"

"Did he say anything about the Grey Hoodie's identity?" I repeat, turning the sleeve over in my hands, pulse pounding in my ears. "Maybe he saw his face."

"Nope. If he had, I'm sure it would've been all over the internet this morning."

I glance up at her. She's still tousling her head. She doesn't notice me looking at her in the mirror. With her hair damp and pulled away from her makeup-free face, she looks like the girl who'd sat next to me in Marketing 101 when we were frosh, the archetypal faithful girl next door. Emphasis on the word *faithful.*

I don't think she's that girl any longer, even though I'm still that boy.

"Chels," I say.

She turns around, head still cocked. I put on the hoodie, zip it all the way to the top, flip the hood over my head—and *look* at her like Christopher Reeve taking off his glasses in front of Margot Kidder.

I'm Doug Wolochuk, Superhero. Motherfucking Superhero.

"What?" she says, and the moment is lost. I jab both my thumbs toward my chest and raise an eyebrow.

She frowns. "I don't understand."

"The Grey Hoodie!" I say, exasperatedly. "*I'm* the Grey Hoodie!"

She lowers the towel from her hair. "Doug, seriously?"

I show her my sleeve. "This is where Dylan's dog bit him—I mean, me!"

She rolls her eyes. "Doug—"

"*I* beat up Dylan Gomi. *I* saved his husband. Yes, they're married. Now, how would I know that?"

"Doug—" she says again, and there's something in her voice that isn't laughter, or contempt, or a protest. It's anger. "Doug, just stop. Stop it. You're being stupid."

"It's not stupid!" I protest. "I can fly! I have heat-ray vision and super hearing! I fight crime!"

She flings the towel down on the floor. "Grow up, Doug. I'm so tired of your mid-twenties crisis shit. I'm tired of waiting for you to man the fuck up and figure out what you want to do with your life."

How can I man up when I don't know what it means to be a man?

"You know," she continues, "I thought things were getting better when you went for that last interview, but then you regress into this fantasy—"

"It's not a fantasy! Look at my sleeve! That little dog—"

"Doug. You are *not* the Grey Hoodie. You just *want* to be him because you're—" She suddenly bites her lip.

"Because I'm what?" I say. "Because I'm *what*, Chelsea?"

Because you're a loser. She shakes her head angrily, but I know she's thinking it.

"Is *Tyler* man enough to be the Grey Hoodie?" I demand.

Her eyes blaze.

Then, to my surprise, the fire goes out in her face, leaving only sadness. She shakes her head again.

"The Grey Hoodie can't save you from yourself," she says, and she leaves the room.

My name is Doug, and I haven't been sleeping well lately.

When I do sleep, I dream of a man in grey who can fly. I dream he saves the city a hundred times over. I dream that he's happy.

Not like me.

Chelsea's late again coming home from work, but this time she hasn't bothered to text me. She must still be mad. Or she doesn't care. Or she's simply forgotten. Or she's in a passionate clinch with Tyler in a locked boardroom. It doesn't matter. Not anymore.

It's easier than I thought to hop up on the balcony ledge, almost as easy as it is in my dreams.

I push the chaise longue over and clamber up onto the cushions. Beads of light speckle the street below. Traffic on Wellington hums softly and steadily. The air smells crisp and clean, like spring, like quiet. The night sky is as black as Brandon's thick hipster glasses, sucking in all the light save for a tiny sliver of moon.

I pull the grey hood over my head. Instant anonymity. Another jaded twentysomething male who thought he was going to grow up to *be* someone with his sweetheart by his side.

Just one more step, one more leap, and I will slice through the air like an arrow. Will the Grey Hoodie save me, or will I save myself?

Only one way to find out.

E.L. CHEN was born, raised, and now works and lives in Toronto (AKA The Freakin' Centre of the Known Universe) with a very nice husband and their young son. Her superpowers include selling the occasional short story and sleeping on the subway without missing her stop.

Canadian Blood Diamonds

KRISTI CHARISH

Have you ever wanted to kill your minions?

No, seriously. Have you ever had the urge to grab them by the neck and inject some really nasty nanobot that will eat them from the inside out? Cause that's about where I was last night at three a.m., standing outside my generator shed in worn, pink bunny slippers, up to my ankles in freezing snow. I sipped my coffee and took in the two shot rotator belts covered in icicles—on the nuclear generator I bought last week for over a million dollars.

"Fuck me," I said. It was so damn cold I half expected my breath to form icicles. "So let me get this straight. The heat's off, the lights are out, and my diamond mine is offline. All because you two morons cheaped out on insulator?" I rubbed my forehead with the sleeve of my pink bunny bathrobe.

Tweedle Dum and Tweedle Dee shuffled their feet before Tweedle Dum spoke up. "Well, boss, when you say it like that—"

I held up my hand. "Yes or no."

Flustered, Tweedle Dee said, "Package says it's good through minus twenty, boss—"

"*Wind-chill factor,*" I said, emphasizing every single syllable. I tapped a bunny-slippered foot and stared up at the clear night sky. Well, at least the nuclear core didn't break this time. That counted for something. And the aurora borealis was still working.

I headed back inside to order yet another generator belt.

"What do you want us to do, boss?" One of the Tweedles yelled after me.

"Freeze to death, for starters," I mumbled under my breath, then yelled, "What do you think I want you to do? Clean it up!" I slammed the heavy chalet-style door behind me. This morning was getting off to a really fucking spectacular start.

Served me right, though. Of all the diamond mines in the world, why the hell had I picked one in Yukon? Why not a nice Aztec Mexican fortress? Could've done the world a favour and knocked off a few Mexican mob bosses in the process. . . . Hmm, I took another sip and mulled it over.

As soon as my laptop powered up I headed to the Super Villain Emporium. I had just pressed *submit order* when a message from Cyber Punk, my accountant and financial planner, flashed across the screen. *URGENT* was highlighted in the subject line. I sighed and opened it: *"Kelly, call me. Now."*

I groaned, picked up my laptop, and headed to my room. You know things are bad when the accountant to supervillains and superheroes everywhere schedules an emergency conference call.

Apparently there's no sleep for the wicked *or* supervillainesses tonight.

Cyber Punk slid into a swivel chair on my screen. He pushed a pair of yellow-tinted lenses up his face and scratched his head. He'd been trying the geek chic look out lately. It worked for him.

"Kelly, *what* the hell did you just try to buy?"

"A new generator band. I've got repairs to make, and I'm freezing my ass off in soggy bunny slippers. I'm also seriously behind on my laser satellite launch, and those small European countries aren't going to ransom themselves. Why?"

He pushed the lenses further up and frowned. "Supervillains wear bunny slippers?"

I pulled my bunny-slipper-clad foot into view of the screen.

"Hunh, learn something new every day." Cyber fidgeted in his chair. "Kelly, I'm just going to come out and say it. You're broke."

I choked on my coffee, spitting most of it out over my comforter. "Shit!" I tried mopping it up, but it was a lost cause. Great, another expense.

I lowered my voice. You never know when your minions are listening in the background. "What do you mean, I'm broke? I just gave you thirty million dollars worth of diamonds to launder—"

Cyber shook his head. "Kelly, no-one *wants* Canadian diamonds anymore. Everyone wants to buy diamonds from liberated blood diamond workers. Canadian diamonds just aren't sexy enough. The Kanuck Crusader really screwed you guys this time."

I closed my eyes and counted to ten. If it hadn't been for the Kanuck Crusader heading to Africa, of all places, I'd be flush with cash. Not even the goddamn American superheroes bothered with Africa. Why the hell the Kanuck Crusader felt the need to clean up the rest of the world's garbage. . . .

My diamond mine funds all my other projects: satellite death laser; my own nuclear reactor; trying to get an arms race going between Québec and the rest of Canada. . . .

"Only in Canada could I be sitting on a diamond mine and be broke," I muttered. Wait a minute. . . .

"Cyber, one sec." I minimized his screen before he could say no and pulled up Google. I don't care what anyone says, Google is a supervillain's best friend. Well, that and Dan Savage; we need all the relationship help we can get.

Supervillains differ from superheroes in many critical ways, but the biggest is that we're not dumb enough to give out names, not even one little itsy-bitsy supervillain name. It's all about outsourcing; let the media and fans do it for you. For example, my supervillain exploits are attributed to no less than four villains: the Lynx (I kind of like that one), the Minx, the Raven, and the Northern Cougar ... not so happy about that last one, but I'm not about to pipe up and start yelling, *Hey over here! All those crimes? I did them, one big supervillain, and I want you to call me the Lynx.*

Besides, it's a hell of a lot easier to evade superheroes when they're looking for four different villainesses.

In less time than it took to type in "I heart Kanuck Crusader" I had ten of his fan pages in front of me. Through their diligent reporting that borders on serious sociopathic stalking, all ten fan freaks are positive the Crusader is still stalking the unjust—hunh, I always thought it was *injust*—on the plains of Africa, righting wrongs, saving giant cats, freeing blood diamond workers, and fucking up my business model. Well, that last one wasn't there exactly, but the point is that courtesy of his superstalkers I was 99.9 percent sure the Kanuck Crusader was still fucking around in Africa.

And if you're wondering, yes, I do have a fan that keeps a web tab on me. Her name is Fiona, and she's a physics grad student in Montreal. It's a very respectful supervillain/fan relationship—I send her the odd tidbit, and she doesn't pry.

Healthy. Normal.

You ever see a superhero fan? Psychos, all of them.

Holy shit, this was going to work. I pulled Cyber's chic geek face back up. "Can you meet me here at noon?" I fired off the coordinates for the local pub. "I've got an idea."

"Make it three. I've got an emergency meeting with another client. Media lawsuit."

I laughed. "Let me guess, The Bayou Gator didn't want everyone to know he was moonlighting as a New Orleans drag queen named Caramel?"

Cyber groaned. "Sometimes I really hate working for superheroes."

I snickered. I'll tell you right now supervillains are light-years ahead in handling bad media. It's called dropping snooping reporters and fans in an ice floe.

I locked up the laptop and headed down to my lair to put something together before my meeting.

This might be one of my best schemes. Ever.

I didn't bother doing my hair or putting on makeup—I'm not that kind of supervillain. I pass for more of a hippie chick than a supervillainess. Damn good thing I'm in Canada; I'd never cut it across the border. The standards are different. A hell of a lot of surgery and waste of money, if you ask me. Plus, I wouldn't be caught dead in those heels.

Tweedle Dum and Tweedle Dee were still messing around with the generator when I stepped outside a little before three and had the pleasure of feeling my nose hairs freeze.

"Boss?" one of the Tweedles yelled.

"I'm heading to Mike's. They have heat."

This time of year the "road" from my place to town consists of a beaten path of dirty snow, and the "town" consists of Mike's pub. It's "rustic," which is redneck for "we mount animal heads on the wall." This late into winter it also doubles as a grocery store, so it's a nice excuse to meander in every few days for a beer.

"Mike," I said as I walked through the worn catch-spring doors. Mike Capshaw was the owner and bartender at Mike's, and I put him at a spry sixty or so.

"Heat out again, Kelly?" he asked. I nodded and he shook his head. "That's got be, what, the third time now?"

"Fourth."

Normally I sit under the Lynx head, but I headed right for the fireplace. It's under the cougar head, but, damn it, I'm cold.

Mike put a beer in front of me, no coaster. Classy. "Just suck it up and get hydro. Less mess than those generators you got up there."

Yeah. Right. Get a power meter. Let the government know exactly how much power I'm pulling. Best idea I've heard all day. "Thanks for the advice, Mike." I stretched in front of the fireplace and peeled off my gloves. I thought I could see the colour returning to my fingers.

"Anytime. You need help up there, you just let me know." He winked before heading back behind the bar across the room.

Now, I'll let you in on a little secret. I did my research before heading to this town. Mostly I was using every little dirty trick in my book to steal a diamond mine, but I also seriously investigated the locals. You never know when you'll accidentally trip over a rock and uncover a superhero. We tend to like the same middle-of-nowheres.

I found nothing too exciting; domestic violence, a few murderers, two guys who take some really weird vacations to South East Asia. . . .

Mike came up clean as a whistle.

My money's on him being the North Wind, the first real Canadian villain—the only one I'd call super. Rumour has it he retired right around the time of the tech revolution. If it's him, he wrote the book on supervillainy. Screw the Vegas Witch and the Californian Litch; they only wrote their how-to books to pass time in jail. The North Wind's got 'em all beat. He never got caught.

If it's him.

One things for certain, he's somebody. Nobody insulates their basement with lead if they've got nothing to hide. I'd never ask, though. Some things just aren't done in polite super society. Provided he leaves my lead-coated basement alone, I'll leave his lead-coated basement alone.

There was scuffling outside; the doors creaked opened a crack, before slamming back and hitting the person outside. "Ow!" came a muffled voice. The doors creaked open again, and Cyber's skinny frame spilled through.

He stamped the snow off his feet. "It is fucking cold up here," he said.

"Yeah, funny that. Yukon is cold."

Now, I don't know how the hell Cyber does it, but given five minutes notice he can meet you anywhere in the world. I know—I've tested it. I heard a rumour years back that he can turn into light particles and travel through fibre-optic cables.

"Friend of yours, Kelly?" Mike asked good-naturedly from the bar.

"Financial planner and accountant. He's really good," I added. Fucking expensive, but it doesn't pay to cheap out when laundering money.

Cyber looked over his glasses. "Yeah, if you ever need any financial advice," he said to Mike, "I'm always taking on new clients."

I glared at Cyber as he joined me. Son of a bitch had probably found the lead-coated basement, too. "Not above a little desperation, are we?"

He shrugged and placed a sound disrupter on the table. It was disguised as a phone and was guaranteed to make any camera, microphone, and satellite image unusable. Hell, it even blurs sound for the human ear.

"Yeah, well, sue me for trying to recoup upcoming and imminent voids in income," he said, and sat back. "Kelly, I *can't* sell your diamonds right now. The market is flooded. You're screwed. You can barely cover your new generator belt, or," he patted a package under his jacket, "your special order. The only thing hotter than cleaned-up blood diamonds is *actual* blood diamonds. So unless you have a hotline on the real deal. . . ." He shrugged. "My advice? Take a vacation, shelve your death ray, and wait till this blows over."

I took out the samples I'd been tinkering with and scattered them across the table. "Just take a look," I said.

He grumbled but pulled off his glasses and held the biggest diamond up to his eye. His pupil switched out, and the high-powered lens flicked in.

I cringed. I can't help it. I draw my line in the sand way before cybernetic implants. I waited while he checked three more diamonds.

"Well?" I said.

"Whoa, where the hell did you get unlicensed blood diamonds?"

I smiled. "They aren't. They're plain old Canadian diamonds. I dirtied up their geologic signal with a laser so they *look* like pretty, sexy, unsanctioned blood diamonds. Can you sell them?"

Cyber let out a low whistle. "Yeah, but Kelly, I was kidding! These hit the market from over here, shit is going to hit the fan. All new diamonds are tracked. They're gonna want to know where the hell these came from."

"So? Make it up. Tell 'em they're from a diamond mine in some really obscure mountain, preferably one with a few terrorists crawling around it."

Cyber gave me a hard stare. Or the closest thing he could muster. "Do you know what the Kanuck Crusader did to the last set of smugglers he found?"

"Yeah. In *Af-ri-ca.*" The look on his face was priceless as he caught on. Damn, I'm good. "These hit the market, I get cash, and the Kanuck Crusader stays in Africa hunting a master supervillain who doesn't exist. By the time he figures it out, I'll have my laser satellite launched and happily be holding Europe ransom."

Cyber let out a low whistle. "I already know three buyers . . . how many more can you produce?"

"Let me worry about that, just keep 'em moving."

Cyber put his disrupter and the diamonds away and stood. "As far as I'm concerned you're back in the black." He pulled out my special order and set it on the table. "By the way, what is this?"

"Oh, something I saw in a vampire movie. You know me, boots, a leather jacket, add a laser bow. How can I say no? It's a prototype I'm trying out."

He pulled his hand away quickly—the word *prototype* will do that—and glanced up at the cougar's head above the fireplace. "I don't care what anyone else says, Kelly; the Lynx, the Minx, and the Raven don't have anything on you."

I gritted my teeth and smiled, but I swear I was this close to ripping the damn cougar head down and tossing it into the fireplace. Why does everyone always think I'm the Northern Cougar?

I went and paid Mike for my beer. Time to go see how Tweedle Dum and Dee were doing on my fixing my nuclear generator.

All right, before you judge, hear me out.

It was an accident.

Besides, I said *prototype*. They were supposed to be professional minions.

Well, at least my laser arrow worked, that counts for something, doesn't it?

I pushed a torso out of my systems chair. Tweedle Dum's I think, though it was always hard to tell the two apart—more so now that they're reduced to body parts. Geez, there was a lot of blood. . . . I would've thought the laser would cauterize more. . . .

I pulled up the net on my blood-spattered screen and fired off an encrypted email to Fiona at my fan site. She paid the bills with a classified page for supervillains. Don't knock it until you try it. The dating section makes for a fun read on a Friday night.

I typed: *Wanted: Two Assistants for high profile supervillainess. Must perform odd tasks upon request.*

As an afterthought I added: *Preference given to applicants with university education in physics or computer science. Also will accept biology applicants—particularly pathogen specialties. Must be able to perform heavy lifting. Robotics acceptable.*

Five minutes later there was a response in my inbox. An email from my biggest fan, Fiona, with two attached resumées: hers and her twin brother Fijord's. No cover letters.

Astrophysics, robotics. . . . Damn. And her brother's was just as good—no, better. Not only did he have a background in virology, he was on the swim team. They'd both included photos, and man oh man I hadn't seen abs like that in, well . . . the brother was ripped.

What was I thinking? I can't hire my fans . . . that would be . . . just. . . .

Four little words at the bottom of the email made my finger pause over the delete button: *Come with postdoctoral funding.*

What was I supposed to do? Yeah, they were fans, but, hell, the government was willing to foot the bill.

I arranged for transport and sent two tickets.

Less than a week later I was back at Mike's pub reading plans Fiona had cooked up to get us into the power industry. I was in assistant heaven. Fiona was spearheading four separate website campaigns dedicated to my alter egos. It was so . . . organized. That Fijord often walked around the house without his shirt on didn't hurt, though Fiona hinted that he batted for the other team.

The point is, life was *good*. My badass diamond-in-disguise scheme was raking in millions. For the first time in my life I had assistants of above-average competence. The North Wind's mantra was paying off: don't do anything stupid. There I was, minding my own business under the Lynx head when a shadow moved over Fiona's plans. The voice was masculine with just enough gruffness to make it attractive without going into meathead land. "Can I buy you a drink?"

I didn't even look up. "Fuck off." Now, that might seem harsh, but keep in mind this is a redneck bar in the middle of buttfuck nowhere. *Fuck off* is a completely acceptable response from a young lady. Besides, the math in Fiona's plans was killing me. Shit, I was going to have to ask my assistant to explain three of these equations. How lame is that?

But then someone else cleared his throat. Deeper, more gruff, and older. Shit—Mike. Reluctantly I looked up. There was no way I was getting any reading done with both of them blocking my light.

Standing beside Mike was a tall and surprisingly good-looking guy.

"Hey Kelly, wanted to introduce my son," Mike said, his mouth set in an embarrassed line.

Good-looking extended his hand. "Hey, Alex Capshaw, pleasure to meet you." And with that he sat down. Without asking. I forced myself to smile and put aside Fiona's awesome laser plans.

No sense alienating Mike's good-looking offspring. Alex rivalled Fiona's brother in the looks department. He was a good foot taller than me, had really great blondish hair, and an awesome set of teeth. Okay, Fiona's laser plans could wait till later. Besides, Alex might be the North Wind's son, and Fiona was busy testing a new robotic arm.

"Hi," I said, extending my hand and flashing my best girl-next-door grin. "Pleasure's mine. Mike never mentioned he had a son." Keep in mind I'm only a seven most days—*maybe* an eight if I really put myself out there.

Mike cleared his throat again. "Alex here is back visiting from a university field trip."

"And helping out with the bar," Alex added.

Mike looked back at the bar as if something might have crashed or broken. "I'll leave you two to chat," he said, and escaped.

"So listen. . . ." Alex leaned across the table and lowered his voice. "I know who you are."

I sat up straight. Not that it was surprising, especially if Mike had been talking about me. But supervillains don't just come out and say it . . . it's rude. I was this close to getting up and leaving when he grabbed my hand.

"I have to admit I'm a huge fan of your work." His eyes took on a serious glaze. "I'm in the same business. The last thing I want is to jeopardize your identity. Is there anywhere more private we could go to talk?"

My god. Not only did Mike Capshaw, still my best suspect for the retired North Wind, have a son—but he was cute *and* a supervillain. Damn, who was he? Hmm, Cannon Ball? Wolverine's Revenge? Not Sasquatch; too pretty.

Have I mentioned how hard it is for supervillains to get a date? We're a cagey, paranoid bunch at best. And he was still smiling at me . . . with those perfect teeth. I started wondering what kind of abs were under that plaid lumberjack shirt. . . .

"I know just the place," I said.

Well, whoever Alex Capshaw was, he was going to make Fiona's blog tomorrow morning.

My alarm was ringing. And ringing. I sat up in bed and picked up my phone. Fiona's face flashed onscreen above a text message: *You need to get down here and see this now.*

I looked over to where Alex still slept. I admit I'd had a great time the last few days. Alex was more of gentleman than I usually went for, but, hey, I'd heard that was fashionable: the nice guy who's really deep, dark, brooding. We were still playing footsies with the supervillain identity, but that was normal. No-one reveals his or her identity till the fourth date—or that's at least what Savage Love said in his superhero/supervillain episode.

Fiona again: *Now, Kelly! Like five minutes ago get your ass out of bed and get down to the lair!*

A third message chimed in. It was Cyber Punk: *Kelly! You need to hold off on project European Vacation. Will explain in one hour at your place. Repeat. Do not send any more European Vacation Funds!!*

Two exclamation points. Shit, this had to be serious.

I threw off the covers and hopped out of bed. Alex rolled over and looked at me sleepily. "Just making coffee," I said, adding cheer into my voice I really wasn't feeling. I closed the door, flipped the coffeemaker on, and headed to my control room one floor down and hidden behind my fireplace. I know, how original is that? But think: what spot hasn't been used? Fridge, secret trapdoor, bookshelf . . . you name it, it's been done.

At least the fireplace is classy.

I dashed down the steps in bare feet. Fiona and Fijord were in a panic at the bottom of the stairs. Huge relief spread across Fiona's face, "Oh! I was starting to worry!" She ran to the control screen and pulled up a Google tab.

I pursed my lips at the Kanuck Crusader's fan page headline. *Shit.*

The Kanuck Crusader was back in North America to hunt down the Northern Cougar, alleged to be responsible for an influx of blood diamonds onto the world market.

Fiona read my face. "It gets worse. Much worse." She pulled up a series of hacked satellite images focused on my diamond mine—heat readings, geological overlays. Shit.

"Fiona, please tell me those are our satellite images." But I already knew the answer before she shook her head.

"Someone's watching us. I just finished breaking the encryption. Kelly, they've got everything—"

Damn it, I had to go and warn Alex and Mike. If the Kanuck Crusader was in town. . . . Maybe we could form a supervillain coalition or something. I wasn't big on coalitions; every time a group of us got together it seemed like everyone either got their coolest toys broken and/or thrown in jail after some spandex-clad superheroes spent a few hours beating the shit out of everybody.

But, hell, I was out of options.

"Kelly, wait! Please!" Fiona yelled up the stairs after me.

"No time, I've got to warn Mike and Alex."

She yelled something else, but I was already out the secret fireplace. I ran upstairs and checked my bedroom. The bed was made and Alex was gone. Damn it. I bolted back downstairs to find the coffee and one of my travel mugs gone. A note with very neat handwriting lay on my kitchen Island: *Headed home. Come by later, we need to talk.*

Well that was just great. Either I was about to be dumped, or get shit for bringing the Kanuck Crusader raining his righteousness down on our buttfuck nowhere town. Why the hell couldn't Alex just use text messaging like everyone else?

I threw on my coat and dashed through the snow. I slipped twice and was soaked by the time I burst through the pub door. Mike and Alex stood by the fireplace, both staring quizzically at my feet.

Shit, I was still wearing my pink bunny slippers. What can I say? Not all villainesses make fantastic entrances. "I've got something really important I need to tell you guys—"

Mike held up his hand, "I think we're past having to reveal our identities. We know who you are, and I'm betting you know who we are. So let's cut to the chase."

I stopped talking and nodded. Man, when the North Wind spoke, he knew how to command the room.

Mike cleared his throat. "I would've said something sooner, but I'm retired and Alex here is the hotshot now—"

The bar phone rang, "Give me one second, that's my contact," Alex said and headed off to answer.

My phone started playing the red alert alarm from *Star Trek*. I swore and glanced at Fiona's message. Instead of her picture, the screen was flashing a picture of Alex's passport with a visa. For Africa.

I fumbled the phone and swore. "Sorry, dropped my phone . . . ran over here. Emergency . . . be right back. . . ." I ducked around the coat rack. "Fiona? What the hell?"

"I've been trying to tell you! *Alex* is the Kanuck Crusader."

I didn't say anything. My god. I just slept with a superhero.

"Kelly, are you okay?" Fiona said.

"I just slept with a superhero named the Kanuck Crusader. Does that sound okay to you?" I was never going to live this down. "Fiona, do we know if Dan Savage takes personal calls?"

Fijord, bless his sweet Calvin Klein model heart, piped up over the line. "I heard this happens to the best supervillains, more often than you would think."

"Listen, they're coming, I'll call you back in a minute. . . ." I hung up. Shit, if Alex was the Kanuck Crusader, there was only one person on the face of the planet Mike could be. The biggest, baddest superhero to ever wander western Canada. . . .

"I'm so fucked." I ducked back into the main room. It was time to see just how much damage a phone could do to a skull. Damn, why did the nice guys like Alex have to be so messed up? And why the hell didn't I take the pocket explosives Fijord had left on the hall stand for me?

"We called you because someone is smuggling blood diamonds through the north," Alex said. "It's the Northern Cougar, just like I suspected, and the blood diamonds are from your mine."

Goddamn it. I readied my cell phone. Why the hell hadn't I paid more attention to that TV show where they turned phones into tasers. . . .

"And we need your help pulling her in."

Hunh? The expression on my face must have said everything.

Mike harrumphed. "Come on, Kelly, we agreed—no more games. Alex here is the Kanuck Crusader himself, I'm the retired Hudson Hawk, and we know you have to be the Ice Falcon. Really, Kelly, it's nothing to be ashamed of. You're our top female superhero. You're setting the example."

Alex added, "The Cougar has been intercepting diamonds from your mine and passing them off as illegal blood diamonds. She's been trying to frame you."

There was a knock at the door. Mike went to get it, and came back slightly perturbed. "Kelly, it's for you."

I went outside. Cyber was chattering in a bathrobe, holding a cup of coffee and carrying a parcel under his arm. "Kelly, I stopped by your place first, Fiona and Fijord told me to give you this, It's about Alex—"

"I know, I know," I whispered, "he's the Kanuck Crusader. I'm handling it." I took the parcel. It was a rocket launcher disguised as a ski pole. It brought tears to my eyes; my minions so needed a raise. "Listen, Cyber, those two think I'm the Ice Falcon—"

Coffee shot out his mouth, spraying the white snow a dirty brown. "What?"

I frowned. "Hey, it's possible."

Cyber just stared.

What would the real North Wind say? When the world gives you lemons, make really awesome hard lemonade. Besides, even though it was probably going to give me therapy-worthy hangups in the future, I had to admit I liked Alex.

Even if he was a lousy *superhero*.

"I need you to do me a favour," I whispered. "Go back and tell Fiona and Fijord to play along. As far as anyone's concerned, I'm the Ice Falcon. And tell them to hide all my supervillain stuff, like fast . . . especially my satellite."

Cyber nodded. "Geez, I hope you know what the hell you're doing."

So did I. I stood up a little straighter and headed back inside. "All right, gentlemen," I said in my best superhero imitation. "Time to work together to bring the Cougar down. We can use my headquarters."

Holy shit; I was going to be a superhero.

I palmed a bottle of tequila from the bar while Mike wasn't looking. I was going to need some serious alcohol to pull off lines like that.

So it's been a few weeks now and I'll bet you're wondering how I'm doing?

I think part of me will never get superheroes. Last week I called in to Dan Savage—well, I made Fijord do it for me—and told him about my dilemma. He had some really great advice, suggesting I hang in there and see it through. It's not like I'm marrying the guy, so why pass up a good thing?

Alex and I listened to the episode, but I'm pretty sure he didn't catch on. Besides, my laser satellite is still sitting locked in my basement.

Then, one night, *she* showed up.

She looked like a supermodel lounging in my favourite chair. Like, *really*. Beautiful ice-blue eyes peered at me over the top of a National Geographic with a falcon on the cover. She wore a perfectly coordinated ski outfit and two sets of feathers dangled from her ears. Falcon feathers.

Poor Fiona and Fijord were out cold and tied up on the floor beside her.

She put the magazine down when she saw me. "I'm Faradee," she said.

The falcon on the magazine, the feathers in her hair, the ice blue eyes—those *had* to be contacts. "Let me guess," I said, giving her the once-over. "You're the Ice Falcon?"

She nodded. "So, do you have anything to say for yourself?" she said, with a swish of her perfectly highlighted hair.

I cocked my head to the side. One thing hanging out with Alex and the Hudson Hawk has taught me is that superheroes really like to talk. It's tedious, but I'm slowly breaking Alex of that habit. "Yeah: did your parents name you after a fairy or something? I mean, what kind of dumb name is Faradee?"

She stood up, all five foot nine of her, crossed her arms and stared imperiously. "Well I have something to say to you, too. I'm marching you to the Hudson Hawk's bar, and you're going to confess everything to him and the Kanuck Crusader."

I hopped up on my kitchen counter. "What if I like being a superhero?" I said, and gave her my best supervillain stare. Trust me, I practice.

She laughed. "I don't care if you want to be a dancing bear. I'm the real Ice Falcon, and I know who you are."

I raised my eyebrow.

"You're the Northern Cougar," she said, and struck a pose.

Why the hell did everyone want to call me the Northern Cougar? I mean, is the Lynx or the Minx really too much to ask? Why is the go-to always Cougar? Talk about giving a girl a complex.

She tapped her foot. "Are we going to do this the easy way or the hard way, Cougar?"

I wasn't going to budge. "I like it here," I said, reaching for a knife.

She got into a crouching stance, ready to kick my ass. Her perfectly red lips parted, probably to say something heroic. I caught the slight movement of my fireplace as the lair opened and my laser bow peaked around the corner. I dropped the knife and dove behind the kitchen island as the laser bow sliced through her.

She toppled over, and one of the contacts fell out.

I knew it!

Mike stepped out in the open.

"You know," I said, "I never bought you as the Hudson Hawk. Always had my money on you being the North Wind."

He chuckled. "Never was one for playing black or white. Prefer to choose sides as it suits me."

I've said it once and I'll say it again; the North Wind was a genius.

"Saw her sneaking in. You've been doing a good job, kid. Figured I should help you out." He pushed the Ice Falcon over with his foot. "Besides, she was a stuck-up piece of work."

"So how the hell do you explain Alex?"

Mike shrugged. "He was always an independent one. Unfortunately, not the brightest apple in the bunch. Got a furnace down there, Kelly?"

"Yeah, but I have a better idea." I pulled the feathers out of her hair. "Upstairs closet, there's an old beat-up fur jacket." I went and grabbed some fake nails from my bathroom Halloween box and started filing them into sharp points. "Alex isn't coming over for another couple hours. Can you get rid of the blood before then?"

Mike nodded. "Got just the thing," he said, and headed back downstairs to my lair.

I finished dressing up Faradee as the Cougar and roused Fiona and Fijord.

"The Northern Cougar just met with a fatal accident," I told them.

"Oh! But, Kelly, it would be so much easier to knock off the Minx or the Raven," Fiona said. "The Cougar has the most popular fan site. . . ."

"No, we're getting rid of the Cougar," I said, maybe a little too quickly.

Fiona pursed her lips but didn't argue. Time to dump the body and get back to the lair in time to hook up with my superhero boyfriend.

Did I mention I love being a supervillain?

KRISTI CHARISH was born and raised in southern Ontario and now resides in Vancouver. She holds a PhD in Zoology from UBC, specializing in genetics and cell biology.

Iron Justice Versus the Fiends of Evil

SILVIA MORENO-GARCIA

Pepe Losanto had not set foot in the Arena Mexico in over three decades. He'd gotten rid of the red and silver luchador outfit long before that, but he kept the mask. It wasn't that he was nostalgic, or that he missed being Iron Justice—he'd left the ring at a young age and didn't regret it. It was superstition; the mask had been a part of him, had been him, and one did not just throw away a thumb or a toe into the garbage.

He kept the mask in a box above the old wardrobe, right by the typewriter—the other part of him, the remains of a journalism career—and Tito's photograph. Superstition had prevented him from opening the box before he tucked it into his carry-on. But now the duffel bag sat on his lap as the taxi made its way out of the international terminal, and he wanted to unzip it and look at the mask.

Because you always put on the mask before the fight.

Not that there was a fight. Yet. But if La Colorada was willing to spring for a round-trip ticket to Vancouver it was because she needed him, and if she needed him it was 'cause a big fight was in the cards.

She hadn't needed no-one, La Colorada. Big and strong and tough as hell. Pepe thought it was cute that she'd married The Canadian Wasp, a hairy little marshmallow, a lightweight with a fondness for poetry. He really was Canadian, though he had the uncanny ability to drink more mezcal than the locals and he swore worse than a verdulero from the Merceded. The only person who could outswear him was La Colorada. Maybe that's why they'd married.

A faint drizzle was beginning to fall by the time the taxi dropped him at La Colorada's apartment. She looked old, which he'd expected, and frail, which he'd never imagined.

"Come on over here, big man," she said, hugging him.

"Leti," he said, smiling.

"How was the flight?"

"Terrible. I still hate airplanes."

The inside of the apartment was plastered with posters of wrestlers from the seventies. A glass case with Leti's old mask and newspaper clippings testified to her numerous matches. On top of a little upright piano sat a bunch of photographs of La Colorada and the Canadian Wasp in their youth, and a few in their old age. "That's you in that one," Leti, said pointing at a photo.

Pepe squinted and frowned. It was the whole gang. He saw himself standing in the background, looking young as hell. "I don't think I even have facial hair there," he muttered.

"Ah, you were the cutie of the bunch. But Jules was the most *handsome*."

"How long has it been?"

"Three years since he passed away. Won't be too long for me now."

"Leti. . . ."

"Ah, don't 'Leti' me. You can't challenge cancer to Mask versus Hair. I've lost that match." She lifted the cap she was wearing and patted her bald head. "We can visit Jules later on. Right now I want to talk to you about the investigation."

"I warned you, I'm not good at that stuff," Pepe said.

"What are you talking about? You're a journalist."

"I was," Pepe said. "I retired last year. Besides, I worked for the sports section."

Leti shook her head. "You don't get to belittle yourself. You're a damn good writer."

"I'm a fat writer," Pepe said, staring at his younger, fitter self. He was hitting 110 kilos, and even at 6'3" that wasn't exactly lightweight category.

"Give me that." Leti snatched the photograph and placed it back on the piano. "I didn't have you come all the way to

Vancouver to wallow. We've got work to do. Got ourselves a monster to catch."

"Wait, let me guess," Pepe said, pressing his index fingers against his forehead. "Vampire? Aztec Mummy? No ... Inca Mummy!"

"Don't mock. Those vampire women were a pickle. They managed to seduce The Whip, remember? A little more, and he would have been a goner."

"I do remember. Deadly, half-naked vampire women. Good thing I'm gay."

Leti smiled. She grabbed two folders and placed them on a little table. Pepe sat across from her and opened one, looking through the photographs.

"What am I looking at?" he asked.

"Feet."

"Well, that's obvious," Pepe said. "Why am I looking at feet?"

"They've been washing up 'round Vancouver. Just feet. About a dozen of 'em in the course of a few years. Then a cartload: fifteen feet during the past seven months."

"Are they matching pairs?"

"Nope."

"That's fifteen people walking around missing a foot."

"Or dead."

"So who's your client? I imagine it's not one of the owners of the feet."

"The mother of a young missing man. That's one of his feet in that folder. She wants us to find who did that to him."

Pepe picked another of the photos and shook his head. "I have no idea what could've done this."

"I'm not sure who goes 'round cutting feet off. People are saying the Tcho Tcho are responsible, and Little Tamja is going to go up in flames if we don't figure out who is the culprit."

"What's a Tcho Tcho?" Pepe asked, coughing the word out.

"Southeast Asian people. The USA supported them during the Vietnam War. Guerilla fighters who fought the communists in Laos along with Hmong, Tai Dam, Khmu, and other folks. They came here as refugees in the seventies."

"Do they have a history of cutting people's feet?"

"No," Leti said, standing up and looking for something in her bookcase. She plucked out a book and placed it before Pepe. "Cannibalism."

"Really?"

"Well, they're a small group and kept very much to themselves back in Asia. They developed a bit of a reputation. Tales of cannibalism and bizarre cults."

"*Under the Ancient Stars: Oral Histories and Legends of the Tcho Tcho*," Pepe read off the cover of the book. He opened it, landing on a page with a black-and-white photo of a dagger resembling a snake's head. There was a mask on the next page, curvy lines etched on its surface.

"It's all in there. Probably nothing more than legends and old wives' tales, but people are looking for a culprit."

"And mobs form quickly."

"It could get pretty bad."

Pepe remembered that time they had been hunting a soucouyant; everyone thought it was an old bag lady. The hardest part of that adventure was stopping the neighbours from carving the woman a new asshole. Good thing they succeeded: it turned out she wasn't the witch.

"I've got a lot of reading to do," Pepe said, eyeing the folders and the book wearily.

"You've got until tomorrow. We're meeting with the mom of the kid around noon."

He pulled a packet of bubblegum from his breast pocket and began chewing.

Bao, the mother of the missing man, lived in Richmond, in a large house that Leti called a "Vancouver special." Pepe did not know what was special about it. It resembled a shoebox. They sat in the living room of the "special" house and Bao served them ice tea. All around were little framed photographs of the son: standing up in a crib, in a playground, as a lanky teenager, and finally as a young man.

"He was finishing his thesis," Bao explained as she handed Pepe a glass of tea. "He also had a part-time job. He didn't have much time to socialize. Any free hours he had, he spent going over his notes or working on the computer."

"Studying Asian folklore," Leti added.

"The Tcho Tcho." Bao made a face and shook her head. "I told him not to. There are stories . . . about demons and such. I am not superstitious, but still . . . why risk it?"

Pepe looked at the ice cubes floating in his tea. He knew enough about things that go bump in the night to agree with the sentiment. "Why was he interested in the Tcho Tcho?" he asked.

"His father, my ex-husband, he is Tcho Tcho. He used to tell Jun stories about his homeland. About his family, his eldest brother, Jaha, who'd brought them to Canada. Jun thought it was a way of getting in touch with his roots. We had not . . . my ex-husband remarried, moved away. It was a way for Jun to find himself and his father's side of the family." Bao looked down at her hands, then turned to Leti. "By the way, I found those tapes I was telling you about. Jun left them at his sister's house. She didn't even know they were there until she was . . . cleaning up the guest room where Jun stayed. I'll bring them."

Bao left the room and returned with a large cardboard box, setting it on the coffee table. Pepe opened the flaps, revealing several dozen cassette tapes and even some old reel-to-reels. He took one reel out and read the label: *Session 1: May 13, 1977.*

"What are these?" he asked.

"My son found old interviews conducted with Tcho Tcho elders in the university archives when they were moving into a new building and throwing out all kinds of stuff. Jun saw these and kept them."

"Who did they belong to originally?"

"Some researchers who worked at the university back then. Jun actually spoke to one of them."

"Ryan Gainseville," Leti said. "He's the guy who wrote the book you were looking at yesterday. He was something of a specialist in Tcho Tcho culture. I talked to him a couple of weeks ago, and he asked if we still had the tapes. We would have never found out about them if Ryan hadn't mentioned them."

"He wants them back," Bao added.

"Can I listen to them before we give them to him?" Pepe asked.

"I suppose," Bao said, staring at the tapes, a hand pressed against the hollow of her throat.

Pepe closed the flaps of the cardboard box.

♦

"What's that?"

"An e-reader," Leti said. "I've got the boy's notes and his thesis—whatever he had of it—loaded onto it."

"Leti, I can barely use e-mail."

"I'm not printing it out. There's a lot of notes."

Pepe sighed and took off his glasses, rubbing the bridge of his nose. He had spent most of the afternoon going through folders and was barely into the second chapter of *Under the Ancient Stars*. He wasn't sure he could stomach one more page of myth and folklore. "What did the Ryan guy tell you about Jun?"

"Jun gave him a call a few months back to get some information on Tcho Tcho culture. They were in touch a couple of times. Nothing more."

"Jun visited the Tcho Tcho in Little Tamja, didn't he?"

"He went several times," Leti said. "He seems to have talked to several people there."

"I should drop by tomorrow morning, see if I can meet some of the people he interviewed."

"I have therapy at VGH tomorrow."

"I can go by myself and pick you up when you're done. I can take the subway," Pepe said. If he could get around a city of more than twenty million people, he could get around Vancouver.

"It's called the Skytrain." She sat down, frowning. She was wearing a light grey sweater but he could tell she was cold. Leti rubbed her arms and shook her head. "Fine," she said. "Go see what you can dig up and we'll meet in the evening."

Pepe nodded. He wanted to pat Leti's hand but he knew she would interpret such a gesture as pity. He smiled, instead.

On the Skytrain, Pepe sat with the backpack in his lap, the mask stuffed in a side pocket. He felt like putting it on but knew that wouldn't go well in Vancouver. It had been different back in Mexico City. The seventies were full of crimefighting luchadores. Their pictures were published in the fanzines, and some of the most famous fighters starred in their own films.

Pepe had never been one of the famous ones, but he'd done all right. By eighteen he was a preliminarista. He worked as a tecnico, a good guy, and toured with wrestlers like La Colorada and Dozen Faces. They fought mummies in Guanajuato, the notorious lesbian vampire women, a group of chaneques. . . . When he wasn't fighting, Pepe was pounding a typewriter, churning out sports stories for the rag printed by the union of newsboys. Then he'd hurt his shoulder during a match.

He was with Tito by then, and Tito worried he'd be seriously injured if he kept fighting. Wrestling didn't pay much for a mid-level like himself, and Pepe was pretty sure he was never going to join the big leagues. So he packed the mask and retired. He wasn't sorry. Bad guys changed. These days it was drug cartels and mercenary killers prowling the streets, not crumbling mummies. Ah, what would Tito say today, if he could see what had become of the luchadores and the villains?

Pepe glanced at his reflection in the window of the Skytrain and saw an old man with thinning hair, and he was glad Tito wasn't here for that either.

He missed his station and had to go back. He walked around, struggling to find the right street. Sleek buildings of blue-green glass rose on each side, almost identical. A drizzle was falling by the time he stumbled onto Little Tamja, a network of a few streets dotted with squat little brick buildings. It contrasted with the polished, artificial downtown core, appearing darker, dirtier, and more used.

He paused to admire the graffiti in an alley: a large snake, crudely spray-painted in red and black, with a man next to it holding a stick. Something about the configuration made Pepe think of a stained-glass window he'd seen, picturing Saint George and the dragon.

Heroes don't grow old, Tito whispered in his ear.

Pepe passed a grocery store, a butcher, an apartment building. He didn't spot any stores for idiot tourists, or any of the Disneyesque banners that adorned some other parts of the city. Little Tamja did not seem like the kind of place you put on the visitor's guide.

He found the place he was looking for: a herbalist shop. When he opened the door, a bell jingled. He spotted lots of jars on the walls, shelves with neatly labelled boxes, and a glass counter. It reminded him of home, of downtown Mexico City, of a store on Tacuba which sold old-fashioned shaving instruments.

A young woman sat behind the counter, emptying a big bag full of a fine red powder into smaller plastic bags. She nodded at him when he approached. Her gray smock had the name *Rhammala* embroidered on it.

"Can I help you?"

"I'm looking for Mr. Thoa."

"That's my grandfather. What do you need?"

"I'm investigating the disappearance of a student."

"A lady already came about that," the young woman said, frowning.

"I'm helping her. I'd like to speak with Mr. Thoa myself, if it's not an imposition."

The young woman sighed and pushed back the stool. She motioned Pepe to follow her behind a flowery curtain, to what he imagined was the back of the store. The room they walked into was full of crates and boxes. In a corner was a large couch; an old man sat there, watching television. The young woman said something to the old man, a flurry of consonants with nary a vowel.

The old man tilted his head and looked at Pepe. "You are another private investigator?"

"Yes. I'm Pepe Losanto," he said, extending his hand.

The old man shook it and lowered the volume of the television. He nodded at the young woman, and she pulled up a chair. Pepe sat.

"What would you like to know?"

"Jun came to speak to you several times. What did you talk about?"

"Legends. Fairy tales. The kind of stories we'd tell around my village when I was a child," Thoa said with a shrug.

"Like what?"

"Oh, the spirit runner, or the hag that lies upon your chest when you try to sleep at nights. The great serpent at the womb of the world—tales for children."

"Any tale he liked in particular?"

"I cannot say. I didn't really pay much attention to what he was studying. Frankly I thought the Tcho Tcho had gone out of fashion, that there'd be some other group for the linguists and ethnographers to study."

"I have in my notes that you last spoke to him on July 30 over the phone. He disappeared a few days later. Did he say anything odd? Was anyone upset with him?"

"No," Thoa said. "He said he was going to spend the upcoming long weekend with his sister on the Island."

"He never made it."

Pepe asked Mr. Thoa a few more questions, mainly about Jun's disposition and appearance during the weeks before he disappeared. When he was done, he thanked the old man and Rhammala walked him out. "Were you with your grandfather when Jun interviewed him?" he asked her.

"Yes," she said. "For the most part."

"What do you think was the story he was most interested in?"

Rhammala hesitated, biting her lip. "The One Serpent."

"What's it about?"

"In the old days the Tcho Tcho had a protector, a great serpent called Lelukli. They fed it the corpses of their enemies, and the serpent gave them riches and kept them safe. It could grant life and death: *mikil* and *ryahku*."

He looked carefully at the young woman's face. He'd spent enough years as a reporter to know when someone was holding back. "You don't like the story?"

"No, not really. My grandfather doesn't like it either, but he says we carry our stories just like we carry our ghosts: from shore to shore. And so we must tell them."

Pepe grabbed his notepad and scribbled Leti's number on it. "If you remember anything else, would you give me a call?"

"All right," she said.

The little bell jingled as Pepe stepped outside. The drizzle had turned into full-fledged rain. He walked back to the Skytrain with his hands in his pockets and his head bowed.

Leti went to bed early. She didn't eat anything, even though he'd made a modest picadillo. He watched her from the doorway to her bedroom and felt his heart sinking. He recalled the announcer's voice booming across the Arena Mexico: ... *and in that corner, the fastest, most intrepid, most disruptive girl in wrestling. Ladies and gentleman, La Colooooooorada!*

Pepe closed the door and sat in the dining room, placing a reel-to-reel in the ancient Panasonic recorder. He unwrapped a piece of bubblegum and began chewing. The recorder whirled to life, forgotten voices bouncing around him. He played a couple of reels and was busy making himself a cup of coffee when he heard an interesting thing.

"... *the One Serpent which lives in the womb of the world,*" said a voice on the tape.

Pepe walked from the little kitchen to the adjoining dining room and replayed that bit. Someone said something in Tcho Tcho and then the translator spoke: "*In my land there is the One Serpent which lives in the womb of the world, and if you whisper to it the right words it will come to you.*"

"*What kind of words?*"

"*Ancient words written in stone.*"

Pepe grabbed *Under the Ancient Stars* and flipped through the black-and-white photographs of Tcho Tcho jewellery until he found the picture he'd noticed before: a traditional, hand-polished Tcho Tcho knife in the shape of a serpent. The caption read, *In Tcho Tcho myth, the snake, with its ability to moult, is regarded as immortal.*

He looked in the index for snake, serpent, One Serpent, and found nothing. The table of contents classified stories by type, but there was nothing about snakes.

Pepe turned on Leti's e-reader and located the file he was looking for. He searched for the word *snake* and found a whole bunch of passages in Jun's notes for a chapter on the One Serpent. He started reading.

"Are you sure you want to go by yourself?" Leti asked for the third time.

"Yeah, I've got the directions," he said, taking out a napkin from his front pocket and showing it to her.

Leti leaned against the door, frowning. "You could wait a couple more days until I feel up to it. I could drive you. Or you could phone the guy."

"You know phones are no good. You've got to look at people in the eye. Just rest, and I'll be back later. Anyway, I already spoke to him and he's expecting me."

Leti relented, and Pepe rode the bus to Kitsilano with his backpack in his lap. Gainseville lived in a house that was more like a mansion, with tall, ominous gates and everything. He wondered if teaching really was that profitable or if Gainseville had simply been born into wealth. A young man—quite tall, he surpassed Pepe—opened the door. The theme inside seemed to be oriental-Polynesian circa 1965, but on a grand scale. Pepe followed the man down a long hallway and through a set of double doors to Gainseville's massive studio.

Pepe paused in front of a large glass case with numerous figurines and some jewellery. A golden mask occupied the centre of the display, sinuous lines etched on it, like the trail of a snake.

"I see you are admiring my Tcho Tcho artifacts."

Pepe raised his head and saw Gainseville walk into the room, leaning on a wooden cane with a gold tip. His hair was all white, and his hands trembled a little. He smiled.

"They look expensive."

"Perhaps, but their value is really of another nature." Gainseville lowered himself onto an armchair. "You brought my tapes?"

"I'm sorry. I am not done with the tapes yet. I'll have to send them over afterwards."

Gainseville's displeasure was easy to read. "I fail to see why you'd want to keep them. My old interviews have nothing to do with your investigation."

"Those interviews, were those the ones you used for this book?" Pepe asked, unzipping his backpack and showing him *Under the Ancient Stars.*

"Of course. They were a major portion of my research."

"But you don't mention the One Serpent."

The old man leaned back and frowned. "No."

"Why not? This is probably the *only* book on Tcho Tcho folklore, and the One Serpent is an important element of the culture. Jun was writing a whole chapter on it."

"The One Serpent is sacred to the Tcho Tcho. I didn't think it should be approached lightly."

"Did Jun tell you he was writing about it?"

"He said so, yes. But most of his information came from a man named Thoa, a fellow with a poor reputation within the community."

"Do you know Mr. Thoa?"

"No, but Jun said he wasn't well liked . . . he was an outsider of sorts. This would have made them even more likely to voice an objection against his research."

"Do you know if they objected?"

Gainseville rubbed his chin, nodding slowly. "Not directly, no. I do remember him saying he was being followed, though he couldn't say by whom." He glanced at the clock. "If you'll excuse me, it's time for my medication."

"Please call this number if you remember anything else."

Gainseville nodded. As Pepe leaned to shake the old man's hand he noticed the thin, sinuous lines on the cane. And the gold tip ... viewed at the right angle, it might resemble a snake's head.

♦

The reel-to-reel spooled and voices spoke. A barrage of consonants. Tcho Tcho words, then someone translating.

"The One Snake is not meant to be seen by outsiders. The elders say so."

"Tell him I don't care what the elders say. Can he arrange it?"

The interviewer had been growing openly hostile. This didn't sound like scholarly research. It was an interrogation.

"He doesn't know."

"Let's clarify a few things—"

The reel went silent. The recording had been interrupted. Pepe sat in Leti's dining room, listening to static.

"Pepe, I found the stuff you needed," Leti said as she walked into the apartment, taking off the scarf wrapped around her head, sprinkling raindrops onto the linoleum. "It took me longer than I thought, because Gainseville stopped teaching in '84; the digital archives only go back a few years, and everything else is on microfiche or stuffed in binders."

"So what do you have?" he asked.

"Well, I went to the *Vancouver Sun* and then stopped at the city's archives. Ryan Gainseville started specializing in the Tcho Tcho in the early seventies. He published his book in 1981. Sometime in 1984 he came into a bunch of money and bought a large house in Kits. He said he was retiring, and planned to dedicate most of his time to restoring it. I also found this photo." Leti handed him her phone; she'd taken a photo of a newspaper page. "Zoom in and read the caption."

"'Ryan Gainseville and translator Nouvak Thoa stand with recent Tcho Tcho refugees outside the Vancouver Public Library,'" Pepe glanced up. "Those two sure as hell aren't telling us everything."

"Isn't that always the case?" Leti placed her hands on her hips. "You think that snake you're talking about is connected to this?"

"Somehow." Pepe pressed a finger against his lips. He unwrapped a piece of bubblegum with his free hand.

♣

Rhammala looked up as soon as Pepe walked in, shaking his umbrella. "Lots of rain, huh?" he said.

"Grandpa told you what he knew already," the young woman said, whip quick.

"I'd still like to talk to him. There's a bunch of dead people and missing feet floating around Vancouver. We need to find the killer."

"Cops are on the case."

"Are the cops going to stop the neighbours from burning down your business? I got off the Skytrain, and somebody had graffitied 'Tcho Tcho ate the missing men' across the platform."

"You're trying to scare me."

"I'm a realist," Pepe said with a shrug.

The woman sighed and took him to the back. Her grandfather was watching a game show. Rhammala leaned down and whispered into his ear. He glanced up at Pepe. "I should have known you'd be back. Heroes always come back."

"I ain't a hero anymore."

Thoa smirked, palming the remote control and lowering the volume. He nodded at Pepe. "You have more questions."

"You told Jun about the One Snake even though the knowledge is sacred. How come?"

"We talked about a number of things. I told him about Lelukli because he'd already heard stories from other elders. And he had a right to know. This was part of his family's history."

"What exactly did you tell him?"

"Jun's uncle, Jaha, was lahaglelulki. He died in a state of grace. I cannot say more."

"Whatever you know killed that kid. Make amends and tell the truth, Mr. Thoa."

The man's lips quivered and he shook his head. He said something in Tcho Tcho, and Rhammala placed a hand on Pepe's elbow, gently directing him out of the room. Once they reached the entrance of the store Pepe turned to her. "I'd like to hear more about the lahaglelulki."

"My grandfather says wishes are like bulls that dream of flying."

"I've seen bulls fly, Rhammala," he said. "Right across the ring. I've read Jun's notes. In the old days, in times of great need, the Tcho Tcho used to call upon the One Snake for assistance. They'd perform a special ceremony. They'd sacrifice someone and summon the snake that lived in a deep pit. But it took a great toll, and there had to be secondary sacrifices. They'd toss gold and carvings . . . but sometimes they'd also toss enemy captives into the pit."

The girl glanced over her shoulder, back at the curtain separating the store from the storage area. "That's kishaha, secret knowledge, only passed on to special people. Jun's uncle was lahaglelulki, and that made him of the bloodline, but I was never told what that meant because I'm a girl, and women are not instructed in kishaha. But I . . . .overheard bits and pieces when Jun was here."

"There were priests that participated in the Tcho Tcho ceremonies. Was your grandfather one of those priests?"

"My grandfather was a translator. That's all he did."

"How did he meet Ryan Gainseville? Don't say they don't know each other."

Rhammala shook her head. "They worked together, that's all I've heard about it. Will you leave now?"

The little bell jingled, and Pepe stepped out into the rain. He paused to look at the alley with the graffiti of the serpent, his eyes fixing on its red and black contours.

❦

"Mr. Gainseville, it's Pepe Losanto."

"Yes, you've been calling all day. Are you by any chance thinking of dropping off my tapes?"

Pepe was outside the Skytrain, standing at a payphone. Someone had scrawled: *The motherfucking Tcho Tcho did it.*

"Mr. Gainseville, what do you know about lahaglelulki?" Pepe asked.

There was a sour silence. He heard Gainseville breathing and waited.

"You're asking a lot of stupid questions, Mr. Losanto. This is not your city. Perhaps you should leave . . . while you can."

"I've heard that tune before. What happened to Jun?"

"Exactly what are you accusing me of?"

"You ain't no innocent, mister."

Gainseville laughed. "Mr. Losanto, you have *no idea.*"

There was a click, and the line went dead. Pepe hoisted his backpack onto his left shoulder, leaned against the telephone booth, and chewed his bubblegum.

Heroes don't grow old, Tito had said.

Ah, no. But sometimes lovers don't grow old either.

"Yeah, there's something very creepy about those reels," Leti said, placing a cup of coffee in front of Pepe. The sharp sound of Tcho Tcho words echoed across the dining room. It was grey and cold outside; the rain never stopped in this city.

"There's something creepy about this whole thing. I think I'm just too old for bad guys," Pepe admitted. "I can't believe you're still doing this stuff. Private investigator. Heroine."

"What I can say? I'm waiting for it to catch on again."

He smiled, curving his fingers around the cup of coffee. The phone rang, and Leti picked it up. Pepe thought it might be Gainseville, but it was Rhammala on the line. She wanted to meet them. Leti went to her glass display, pulled out her mask, and stuffed it in the purse.

"Just in case," she said.

"Leti, it's not like the old days," Pepe admonished, though he had his own mask in the bottom of his backpack.

They met at an all-night diner on Main Street. The decor was 1950s: polka dots, Bettie Page pictures. The usual quasi-alternative retro stuff. Pies glistened under glass domes; Pepe ordered a slice of the blueberry.

Rhammala arrived on time. The rain had washed away the colour from her cheeks. She sat across from them in the little booth looking miserable. "My grandfather's gone to see

Gainseville. Grandpa told me the whole story . . . and said I should tell you."

Water droplets slid down the girl's fingertips, pooling over a laminated menu. She curled her fingers slowly, into fists, resting them on the edge of the table.

"Gainseville went to Vietnam in the seventies, to research the Tcho Tcho. Grandfather translated for him. It started with stories, but Gainseville wanted to know more . . . he wanted to know the Tcho Tcho secrets. He'd heard about the One Snake and . . . he wanted to see it. Things were bad for the Tcho Tcho in Grandfather's village, and Gainseville had important contacts. But he wanted to see the serpent, or he wouldn't help. Grandfather was not a priest. He shouldn't have, but he sneaked him into the great serpent's pit. Afterward, Gainseville helped Grandfather immigrate to Canada. Grandfather thought that was the end of it."

"What happened?" Pepe asked.

"Nothing, at first. Grandfather translated for him. But, over time, Gainseville asked more and more questions. He kept pressuring. He said he could get other families from the village into Canada, if only they'd help him."

"What did he want?"

"To be a keeper of the One Snake." Rhammala rubbed a finger along the edge of the table's formica surface. "The One Snake cannot be summoned without sacrifice. A lahaglelulki was chosen, an acolyte. He shed his mortal skin, and upon his death Gainseville acquired the serpent—the One Snake."

"Let me guess," Pepe said. "The snake eats people, but it doesn't like feet. And it's very hungry."

"Lelukli is a manifestation of the divine. It is the darkness that coils around the world. The Tcho Tcho fear and respect it and do not invoke it recklessly. Gainseville respects nothing."

"What about Jun? How does he fit into this?"

"Jun's uncle Jaha was lahaglelulki. My grandfather thought Jun might be able to stop Gainseville. He thought Jun would not—could not—be harmed because he was kin. Grandfather gave him a Tcho Tcho ceremonial dagger, and Jun went to face the One Serpent. But he suffered the same fate as the others."

"So essentially Gainseville is controlling a supernatural—no wait, a deity—and the Tcho Tcho have let this go on unchecked for a couple of decades," Pepe said.

"The serpent was young, weak ... and Gainseville did nothing for many years. It is only now that he has awoken the One Serpent. My grandfather, he was an optimist ... he thought it might never awaken," Rhammala muttered. "Besides, my grandfather has gone to confront Gainseville. He said I should tell you that it was his fault. You should not blame the other Tcho Tcho. My grandfather knows that he shouldn't have sent Jun, and he knows you should have never gotten involved. He said it's not your fight. These are his ghosts ... he just tried to pretend they were not. He was a coward."

Pepe contemplated the remains of his blueberry pie. He unzipped his backpack and took out his mask. Leti opened her purse and did the same.

Rhammala looked at them in confusion. "What are you doing?"

"It's three fall matches and no time limits," Pepe said.

"What, you're just going to ... punch the One Serpent?" the girl asked.

"We'll see if it comes to that," Leti replied.

It felt weird jumping into Leti's little compact car and zipping through Vancouver with the mask on, but at least when Pepe looked into the rearview mirror he couldn't see the wrinkles on his face. He flexed his fingers. He thought about the old days, about the Red Hand and Mr. Diabolico. He thought about Tito.

"You're not going chicken on me, are you?" Leti asked.

"Over a snake?" Pepe scoffed. "Ask me when we face a golem."

The gates to the mansion stood open. A bunch of cars were parked in front, and all the lights were on. Leti got out of the car and cracked her knuckles. Pepe followed.

The vestibule was empty, but they could hear people chanting, dimly, far away.

"Always with the fucking chanting," Leti muttered.

"It reminds me of that time we fought against Brain of Destruction."

"Didn't you break your ribs?"

"Don't remind me," Pepe huffed.

The chanting came from a door that clearly led down into a basement. Pepe wondered why bad guys never committed their evil deeds in a nice, airy space.

The stairs were conveniently lit with torches, like in the cheap luchador films. The basement had been decorated in the same expensive, quasi-tacky pseudo-Asian style as the rest of the mansion, with liberal use of golds and reds. At the bottom of the stairs congregated maybe a dozen people, all dressed in some odd variation of a kimono. Gainseville was sitting in a golden chair, wearing the golden mask with the little marks. Another chair, painted in red, hung from the ceiling, with Mr. Thoa tied onto it smack over a pit. Pepe had met enough villains to imagine what the setup meant.

"Hey, Gainseville, we're here," Leti said.

Gainseville turned, his golden mask reflecting the light of the torches. "I've been expecting you."

"Yes, yes," Leti said, shaking her head and walking toward the centre of the room. "Let's skip the introduction and go to the part where you explain what you're up to. Why'd you kill all those people?"

"*Mikil* and *ryahku*," Gainseville said, using his gold-tipped cane to stand up. "You've heard that part? Life and death." The congregation was still chanting. Gainseville slid the mask off, revealing the face of a young man. At least, half of it looked like the face of a young man; the other half was still old and wrinkled . . . and peeling. "The snake sheds its skin, and so I am shedding mine. You are old. You grow ill. What if that could be fixed?"

"And all we'd have to do is kill a few dozen young men?" Pepe asked.

"And one old, stupid man who thought he could interfere," Gainseville said with a shrug. "But he's interfered enough. Now he'll die, just like that nosy student."

Pepe noticed that the attendants, except for three goons, seemed to be senior citizens. Probably friends of Gainseville who had been promised a demonstration of the power of the snake. Maybe that's how he'd gotten rich: promising eternal youth for a premium once the snake grew powerful enough.

"Wouldn't you like to be fighters again?" Gainseville asked.

"We are fighters," Leti said.

"Let's see about that."

The tall man was the first to head toward Pepe. It was different fighting a man without the ropes behind. The lack of a ring was distracting. On top of that, Pepe had not fought anyone in ages. He felt like he was standing on quicksand. When the man threw a punch, the best thing Pepe could do was wince as it hit him square in the jaw.

The man threw a second punch. This time he hit Pepe in the gut.

Man, he *hated* that. Pepe shook his head.

The young man was readying for a third punch, but Pepe dodged and countered with a sweeping kick, his old signature move, knocking the guy down. A second goon approached. Pepe jumped, dealing a massive dropkick before flipping to land on his feet, leaving his attacker barely twitching on the floor.

Meanwhile, Leti was evading goon number three. Just when he thought he had her cornered she swept around him, dealing a double knee backbreaker and ending with a mounted stranglehold that had the much younger man howling.

The tall man was standing up. If Pepe had been at the Arena Mexico he would have milked the fight for all it was worth. But he wasn't, and he was old and tired. So he curled his fingers into that famous iron fist of his and dealt the man a massive hit to the face, then another right in the gut, then the final finishing move: an Indian deathlock that left the young man unconscious.

The chanters had grown quiet, looking around nervously. Pepe turned to Gainseville, ready to make him into jell-o. Gainseville yelled something and an odd, deep rumble sounded as the ground began to tremble. Pepe didn't think this was an earthquake.

Leti rushed to his side, pressing a hand against her chest. Her voice was hoarse when she spoke. "Any brilliant ideas?"

"Sorry, I was never the main act," he muttered, trying to catch his breath.

A glint of gold attracted his attention; Gainseville was holding the ceremonial dagger. Pepe was about to formulate a brilliant plan when a gigantic red and black snake sprang up into the air, its voluminous body landing a few metres away.

The snake opened its massive jaws and let out an angry cry.

The congregants who had been happily chanting just a few minutes before rushed for the stairs. The snake caught one and slammed him against a wall. Gainseville yelled a command, and the snake turned. It hissed, showing Pepe and Leti several rows of nasty teeth.

Mr. Thoa's scream cut through the air. He yelled something in Tcho Tcho, then said, "Jaha! Jaha, Gainesville killed your kin!"

Pepe noticed the snake's eyes. They looked disturbingly human.

He shed his mortal skin.

Jaha, the uncle who'd died . . . only he hadn't died. No. *Sacrifice* may have more than one meaning.

"He's right!" Pepe said. "You killed Jun, Gainseville. You fed Jaha his own nephew!"

The serpent reared back, hissing even louder. It was going to strike, and Pepe thought that the only thing he might be able to do now was scream—

—until the snake turned. It flipped around with the speed of a whip, its tail knocking Leti down. It opened its mouth, hissing at Gainseville.

"You cannot!" Gainseville said, holding up the mask in one hand and the dagger in the other. "You cannot!"

"Yes, he can!" Pepe roared. He jumped over the snake's tail and delivered a punch straight to Gaisneville's face, tearing the mask from him.

"No, wait!" Gainseville shrieked, just before the snake ripped out half of his chest.

The golden dagger went flying through the air. Pepe caught it and gripped it tight.

Heroes don't grow old, Tito said.

Pepe nodded. He jumped, slamming the dagger down on the monster's head. *Iron fist of justice, iron fist of justice*, they used to chant, and he could still hit *hard*. The dagger tore through the snake's skin and skull and everything. The monster flailed, its tail rising and falling. It coiled on itself and rolled into the hole it had come from, dragging Gainseville's body with it.

Pepe slid to the floor and closed his eyes, trying to will his heart to slow down a bit. He could hear Mr. Thoa's sobs and Leti's soft groans.

❦

The Canadian Wasp's grave was more modest than Pepe had imagined it would be. He'd pictured a huge mausoleum befitting his antics. Instead, it was a quiet little tombstone that said: *Jules Guêpe 1940-2009.*

"Nothing about how he saved humankind from aliens in 1969," Pepe muttered. His arm was in a sling.

"It was a while back," Leti said. She'd injured her ankle and walked a bit wobbly, but otherwise she was fine. "You did well with this snake business. The whole Tcho Tcho community is grateful, and Rhammala has assured me nothing like this will ever happen again."

Maybe. Maybe not. The Tcho Tcho wanted peace and quiet, but there were always new evil fiends looking for blood and power.

Leti placed a hand on his arm. "Did you think about what I said? I ain't going to last too much longer, and the city can always use a hero."

"Heroes don't grow old," Pepe said. "I'm old, Leti. I can't be your replacement."

Leti was standing in the shadow of a great maple tree. From Pepe's angle, with the light filtering the way it was, she resembled La Colorada, the fighter he'd known. Then she moved, the light shifted, and she was an old lady wearing a black tuque.

"Well, maybe you'll go back to Mexico City and find your hero muscles again."

"Maybe I'll just move to Acapulco and tan," Pepe muttered.

Leti leaned down and placed a framed photograph on the tombstone. It was the one from her living room, showing the old gang together: Iron Justice, La Colorada, The Canadian Wasp, Pandemonium, The Whip, La Venus, and Dozen Faces.

They both stared at the black and white image as a drizzle began to fall. Pepe reached into his pocket and unwrapped a piece of bubblegum.

SILVIA MORENO-GARCIA was born and raised in Mexico but now lives in Vancouver. Her fiction appears in *Imaginarium 2012: The Best Canadian Speculative Writing*, *The Book of Cthulhu*, and other places. The latest anthology she has edited is *Fungi*. Her first collection is *Shedding Her Own Skin*.

NEVER THE TWAIN

JONATHAN OLFERT

The Akwesasne Mohawk reserve both straddles the border and ignores it, like a cowboy riding an invisible horse. I slip across the forty-ninth parallel in a truck carrying half a million counterfeit cigarettes, and, just like that, I'm home. I haven't set foot on Canadian soil in years. The Akwesasronon would say I still haven't.

The next best thing to an old friend is an old enemy, like Mariel Lazore. It's late at night when the old woman answers the door of a big, rundown house on the outskirts of Cornwall Island. The other residents are nowhere to be seen. She's expecting me. This is the first time we've seen each other since our fight over El Paso.

"It's nice to see you again, Doctor Lazore. I'm Jethro Carver." Stormcaller, my *nom de guerre,* has been long since unmasked, publicized, and almost forgotten; now I just go by my birth name. These days the magazines prefer supers— villains and heroes alike—who don't just take sides, they adopt the uniform. A flying arsonist in a Guy Fawkes mask or an Occupy shirt gets good press, but my generation remembers Vietnam; we'd rather resent a senseless world than support a dozen placebo causes. When I killed, I never advertised it, and I sure didn't use product placement.

The old Mohawk superhero shakes my hand. "I can't exactly say it's an honour."

"Honesty is a good start, I suppose."

She smiles without humour. "Start to what, exactly? Come in."

The house is battered, sparsely furnished, dusty, and cheap. It is, however, both large and anonymous. Mariel moves like any old woman in her own home might, with a slight distrust of her own decreasing faculties and thus a disconnection from long-familiar surroundings. A hotplate or broken mirror can badly injure; stairs and shower whisper threats of a broken hip.

Even if the years have blunted Mariel's powers—Sunflame used to throw radiation in an era favouring bravado and colourful tights—her attitude and the memory of her strength keep this place secure. I let myself relax a little.

"We don't accept fugitives," she says, pouring me a cup of tea at a folding table in the dingy kitchen. The metal chair creaks under me, and I'm not a large man.

"Really? The Underground Railroad waypoint for every super on the run since Arcanos dodged the draft?"

"The world is different now." She sips from a cracked teacup. "What's your legal status, Mister Carver?"

"In a nutshell? Canadian citizen. I'm not wanted for anything here. In America, sure, statute of limitations has yet to expire on a few minor peccadilloes, and one or two of their supers hold a grudge, but extradition—"

"Don't worry about extradition. That much, at least, I can guarantee for the moment. The Canadian government wouldn't touch Akwesasne."

"Sounds idyllic," I say, voice dry.

"Our own little utopia, yes. Such as it is." Sadness clouds her eyes, and I remember her as she was—so bright you could hardly look at her. But her gaze sharpens and refocuses on me. "So you understand my reluctance to accept you on any kind of a permanent basis. Why not apply for Schedule Five status?"

"Be a registered super? The tax breaks aren't what they used to be—besides, you're Mohawk. You tell me how 'status' worked out for you."

She grimaces. "You have . . . unique talents, Mister Carver. A man who channels the forces of entropy will be its victim, sooner or later. Whatever measure of stability and safety you find can only fall into ruin."

"I don't believe that," I say.

"Convince me, Stormcaller."

I shrug. "I make no defense of my life thus far. My choices have incurred their consequences. If I remain in a place like this, I have no doubt that I can be—"

"Rehabilitated?"

"—at peace."

That earned a thin smile. "Do you deserve peace? Those who live here have retreated from the world—tired old heroes and the chronically misunderstood. Not mercenaries, or murderers—"

"Please." It comes out as a snarl. "How much collateral damage is on your conscience, Sunflame? And the 'heroes' who live here—have none of them ever killed in anger? Don't judge me without applying the same standard to yourselves. Yes, I've broken my share of things that didn't ask to be broken—"

"Spines, hearts, promises, governments?"

"All of the above, but which super hasn't? I make no apologies, Mariel."

"Agency lies in the difference between accident and deliberate intent."

"Please. You go out, you do your job as a superhero, and people get 'accidentally' hurt. How are you not responsible for that?" It's an old argument, but it's one of the few things I believe. I know I'm shooting myself in the foot, but I can't stand self-righteousness.

I knew what I was getting into when I set out to take sanctuary here. I make myself calm down. Mariel is swelling with rage, preparing the kind of tirade that left Crimson Overlord's mansion a smoking wreck, back in the day.

"All I'm saying is, I'm a person, Mariel. Don't judge me because your crimes and sins and failures are less public, or at least less publicly memorable."

Mariel grimaces and deflates. She looks away. "Not so loud, you'll wake the others." It's an evasion, a capitulation; I guess I still have it in me to beat up an A-grade superhero, albeit one with cataracts and a cane.

When I was young and drunk on changing the world, I would have called this tasteless, pointless thing a victory. Now I've learned to see beyond the moment. But I've never been able to define the difference between knowing a thing and following it through.

I'm not out for redemption. Peace of mind would be nice, don't get me wrong, but it's not the sort of thing I think about. I have other concerns, functional concerns. There are death warrants out on me across sub-Saharan Africa, and in this hemisphere even the most incorruptible supers don't mind accepting a side job as long as *I'm* the side job.

I need to get in here. I really need it. A year or two off the radar, and I can have my pick of twenty consulting positions. Turns out Nigerian rebels really like people with a knack for breaking oil refineries. It's the sort of job I've taken my whole life.

But I'm tired. Maybe it's the way old Mariel is crumpling in on herself. She glances at me, her face a ruin of fatigue, sadness, even guilt.

"I'm sorry," I say at last. "We always tried to solve our problems the hard way, didn't we? Massive conflagration of light and power? Cue music. Cameras flashing. Big words." I run a hand through my thinning hair. "Where do we go from here? What follows naturally from what we are—and what we've said and done? It used to be I could fix anything with the proper application of entropy."

She laughs, or cries. It sounds like choking. "Violence."

"Violence."

Her hands clench and unclench, wiry claws. But it's a frustration without direction, not a threat. "I've burnt a lot of people, Carver," she says. "More than you've broken."

I snort. "And right now we're a stone's throw from the kind of competitive games we used to play. Who would win in a fight? Your powers, your weaknesses—how well do they stack up against mine? They used to list our temperaments and backgrounds in bullet points. And I hate the—what's the word, pillboxes? Niches? The little boxes they put you in."

"Stereotypes."

"Close enough." I snap my fingers. "Pigeonholes, that's it. I sang to their tune and let them define me, but now I find all I want is . . . what I used to have." And I mean it. I want the jobs in Africa, yes. I want freedom, of one kind or another. But if I get it, what will I do with it?

My guess is, if Mariel lets me stay, I might have a chance of finding out who I am, apart from a guy who wears black and breaks things really, really well.

A wry, tired grin steals over Mariel's face. "We can't turn you back into a child, Carver."

"You can give me a few months or, hey, a few years without worries. You can give me time to grow up."

"Careful. You'll lapse into cliché." She stands, visibly aching, her teeth clenched, and shuffles over to the dusty fridge. "Coffee cake?"

"At this hour? Certainly." Behind the fridge door, she's out of my line of sight. There was a time when two supers with our backgrounds would have taken a sight-line break as an opportunity or a threat—*keep your hands where I can see them* and so forth. I make myself relax again. I can do this. This is a real life.

Mariel hums to herself. She produces cake on little saucers in the same ancient gold-edged style as the teacups. The cake is heavy, moist, all chocolate and structural integrity. It's the perfect midnight snack between friends—or old enemies.

"Thank you for the cake," I say. "This is delicious."

"I thought I warned you about cliché."

"Look, I want to stay here. I want it more than—than I wanted Hawkmoon's head that time in Bogotá. You ever hear about that?"

"Yes."

"And because I want it so badly, Mariel, I feel the need to correct your . . . impression of me."

"By thanking me for coffee cake."

"It's what normal people do."

"You want me to accept you. Haven't you noticed? A super can never be accepted. Either you want to be just like everyone else, or you want to be special. Two paths to happiness, utterly contradictory." She examines her cool tea. "Carver, I don't even know what to say: I'm not sold, I'm not rejecting you, and yet I feel none of the tension inherent in fence-sitting."

"Then give me a grace period. I could use a little grace."

"Couldn't we all." She sighs. "You can stay, as long—" she holds up a cautionary finger "—as long as the others are fine with it. I hope you don't have history with them."

"If there's bad blood, it won't be on my side. I'll make every effort."

I'm a bad man. But even a bad man needs a home.

Born in Vancouver and raised in Calgary, **JONATHAN OLFERT** studies international relations in Ottawa.

Circe and the Gunboat

KEVIN COCKLE

"She's freaking out again," the agent said, letting his disdain show. There was a sound from inside the penthouse: a glass smashing against a sink.

Silas approached, a wall of man in his long black trenchcoat. He had a skull like a tiger's skull; teeth like a tiger's teeth. He felt his heart rate rise to an attack cadence; willed it back into a more acceptable range.

"So I hear," Silas said, his deep bass voice vibrating in the hallway, even at low volume. "Disgusts you, does it?"

"Sir?"

Silas stared down at the man—a good-sized specimen at six feet, two hundred pounds, give or take. "Don't editorialize, agent," Silas rumbled. "Ever. She distresses easily. It's part of her charm."

A disembodied voice spoke inside Silas's earwell: Ben Mainwaring on The Deck keeping watch from geosynchronous low Earth orbit, "You okay, buddy? Your adrenals are spiking."

Silas ignored Mainwaring for the moment, concentrating his inhuman gaze on the agent. Instead of eyes, Silas sported two bug-black HUD arrays designed in part to make the average person extremely uncomfortable.

The agent swallowed, fear-sweat pungent on his skin.

Silas pushed his way past the trembling man into the thirty-first floor penthouse apartment. *Note to self*, Silas thought, *have that man replaced.*

63

Another agent—a woman—stood by the door, the chemical scents of her hair and deodorant products masking the sweeter musk of her flesh. She glanced at Silas, maintaining her professional calm. "She's been drinking. Heavily."

Silas grunted. He could smell the bourbon in the air. "Tell you what: there's an all-night Starbucks down the block. Why don't you get us a tray of venti espressos?"

A shrill voice bellowed from the bedroom: "Is that my Gunboat?"

Silas said, "Go."

The agent left as Circe appeared in the bedroom doorway in all her frazzled glory. Twenty-nine years old. Five-foot-one-inch tall, standing as she was in bare feet. Dishevelled blond hair obscuring her left eye. Bra strap showing; her skirt torn. Even in such a state, Silas could not help but feel humbled by her—by the idea of her: the single most powerful human being since Alexander the Great.

"Where the hell have you been?" she said, voice cracking with emotion. Her clear blue eyes were red from tears.

"Securing the conference centre," Silas said, keeping his voice at a low, measured growl. "Remember? Your day job as saviour of the state and civilization, all that jazz. You've got a meeting with the Federal Open Market Committee in three days."

She strode toward him in a drunken reel, eyes blazing.

"Fuck you," she slurred as she approached. She slammed her little hands on his reinforced chest. Again she hit him, nearly losing her balance.

He took her by the arms to keep her from falling, willing his grip to be gentle. *I'm handling a bird*, he reminded himself. Teary-eyed, she grinned up at him through her bangs.

"Get yourself together," Silas said. "Have a shower. I'm having coffee brought in. We'll get some fresh air to sober you up."

"Where were you?" she mumbled, eyes rolling lazily back, lashes fluttering.

"I had drone coverage on you the whole time, Circe," Silas said.

"Fuck you," said Circe, head lolling.

❦

1:30 a.m., not a soul in sight: Circe and Silas stood on Calgary's ornate Peace Bridge, looking down onto the Bow River. The bridge's latticework glass covering changed colour, gradually progressing through shades of jade, to indigo, to crimson, then back to green again, the light playing on the benighted water. Circe leaned against the railing as a cool breeze drifted through lozenge-shaped openings in the glass carapace. She held a giant cup of espresso in her right hand—her fingers barely reaching halfway around. The bridge light shifted, washing her in monochrome green.

"Why did he leave?" Circe asked, her voice husky from all the booze-induced bawling. She was stable now—groggy from tears, jacked from the coffee and alcohol-suppressing beta-amphetamine Silas had given her. She hardly ever slept; to keep her from being restless, he often walked the nights with her, whichever city they were in. "Why?" she asked again.

"You feel very, very strongly," he said as the glowing bridge gently bathed them both in neon blue. "It's scary for boys, Circe."

"Doesn't scare you. Nothing scares you."

"Not true. There's always something to be scared of." Blue to violet, then to a moody merlot red.

Circe sniffed, turned her attention to the water again. "Do you honestly think I don't know? That I can't tell?"

"Of course you can tell; that's your gift."

"Stop paying for them, then. Stop manufacturing the 'boyfriend experience' for me and just let me find somebody on my own."

"You know we can't do that," Silas said, not unkindly.

"You can do whatever the hell you want."

"Circe, sweetheart. Grow up. What do you think would happen, if evidence of your behaviour tonight got around? Evidence of you most nights? You with your miraculous limbic system, Circe—the girl with the flawless intuition of 'price,' setting perfect monetary policy, providing the 'visible hand' to guide the economy through all its turbulence—what if markets got wind of your . . . instability? Do you understand that the very concept of 'government' is bound up in your credibility these days?"

"So you always tell me."

"Do you deny it?"

"No."

"Okay then. Will yourself to believe the fiction provided. Think of the alternative. I wouldn't want to see you alone all the time."

Circe crimped her lips, sipped at her coffee, stared at the changing hues of the water below.

Eventually they walked on, Circe taking Silas's elbow without even thinking about it; Silas slowing his stride to accommodate her. She looked like a child beside him. She still was, in many respects. And she was the only human being aside from doctors who ever willingly touched him.

They came to a bench on the north side of the river, looking back at the grand panorama of the city centre at night. They sat: Circe with her hands ringed round her knees as she brought her feet up; Silas sprawling with his right arm on the armrest, the other arm a protective tree trunk around the girl. The wood and wrought-iron bench groaned under the weight of Silas's battle-braced skeleton. Overhead, drone coverage assured Silas via his embedded heads-up display that no-one was approaching.

"I love this city," Circe said wistfully, gazing up at the illuminated glass towers to the south. "Wish we could come more often."

"It's changed like you would not believe. When I was a kid, the downtown was just coming into its own, just starting to flex its muscle. Now it's like something out of *The Wizard of Oz*— those big green towers. Look at that: like a wall of light across the river."

"How much of all this could you take out? Right now?"

"Jesus—bloodthirsty much?"

"Come on."

"In theory? Two or three blocks I suppose, but I'm only operating a three-drone pattern here, not a swarm. It's Calgary for Christ's sake, not Jerusalem. In a city, I'd use smart-bullets anyway—you know that. No reason to bring the whole place down."

"But you could, right? Bring buildings down."

"What's gotten into you?"

"Don't bullshit me. You think about the power all the time."

"All for you, kiddo, remember that. Without you, I'm nothing."

"Why do they call you a 'Gunboat' anyway?" Circe asked, suddenly seeming so young—twenty-nine going on ten.

"I've told you that before, remember?"

"You know I don't remember. Not exactly, anyway."

Silas nodded. Details were not Circe's strong suit. Her brain had been wired for other things. "In the nineteenth century," he began, "before internet and telephony and such—British sea captains had a lot of discretion on missions. When one of their warships showed up in a foreign port, the captain spoke for the crown; his ship was law. They called it 'gunboat diplomacy.' It's funny because it's ironic."

"So that's what you used to do? Before me, I mean. Gunboat diplomacy?"

"When I showed up, yes. It was time for people to do as they were told." The Gunboat program had started as a joint US-Canadian initiative but had eventually gone private, along with the SEALs and tactical nukes. He'd killed for governments and markets both; politicians and corporations; citizens and consumers. Yesterday, the terrorists had been anti-globalist radicals; now they were free-market radicals. He couldn't help thinking of the villages he'd razed. Smelled the smoke. Heard the screams. Felt the heat on his bulletproof skin.

"Oh my God," Circe said suddenly. "I'm so sorry!"

Silas was confused. "What?" he asked.

"I forgot your frigging birthday."

He chuckled. When she was little, Circe had wanted to know his birthday, and Silas had teased her by withholding the information. So she'd assigned him one and, invariably, would recall the date only after it had passed.

"It'll come around again," he assured her.

"How old are you? Like, really how old?"

Silas smiled. "I'm a hundred and two."

"Get the fuck out of here."

"I'm a hundred and two. I was an Air Force fighter pilot in the 1980s. They've been swappin' out parts ever since."

"Wow," Circe said. "Explains why you're so grouchy all the time."

"Guess it does," Silas agreed. He wasn't entirely kidding. He'd been feeling his age of late.

"A hundred and two," Circe mused. "You had, like, a normal face and everything back then, right?"

"Normal-ish, sure."

"Were you married?"

"Are you positive you don't remember any of this?"

"Humour me."

"Yes, I was married. Hannah was my wife's name. Two boys, Eric and Lanny".

"But they'd be super-old now too, wouldn't they?"

"They would if they were alive, yes."

"What happened?"

"Well, honey, things got bad before you came along. Nobody watched out for anybody else; everything just kind of ran itself. Lot of people thought that was a good idea and just decided not to see the corpses piling up. Hannah and the kids . . . they just didn't make it. I'm relieved though, in a way. They missed the worst of it."

"But you were there for all of it."

Silas nodded. "That I was."

Back and forth like that—Circe trying to forget who and what she was, talking to Silas like he was her grandfather and not her bodyguard. He'd played the role many times before, and to be honest he didn't mind. At first, The Deck hadn't been sure it was a good idea; thought maybe they should rotate Gunboats on Circe duty. In the end, psychologists felt the continuity and friendship would be good for her. They had never considered whether or not it would be good for Silas.

"You know what the worst thing about being me is?" Circe asked at last, something in her inflection catching Silas's attention. "Nothing seems real," she whispered. "I never sleep, but it seems like I'm always dreaming."

This was new. Silas started paying very close attention indeed.

"I feel like I'm . . . like I'm shredding apart. I feel so thin you could see right through me. Like a ghost." Her eyes began to shine: tears glistening in the moonlight. Silas felt his artificial aggression matrix kick in at the sight of her distress; he dialed back on the attack instinct, breathing deeply.

"You're not a ghost," Silas ventured.

"Sometimes. . . ." Circe whispered, then stopped. Silas was wondering if she'd start again when she said, "Sometimes I wonder what would happen if . . . if I just said something crazy at the FOMC. Like, told them interbank rates should be set at twenty percent. Said it live, on the air. And they'd have to do it."

Take that back, Silas pleaded in silence. *Take that back, Circe.*

She didn't take it back. She continued: "They'd have to set me free, right? If I crashed everything, I wouldn't be the hero anymore. If I were wrong, even just one time, they couldn't use me anymore. They wouldn't need me."

Was she asking him about her exit strategy?

"Silas," she said, "I think that would make me real. Then I could *live*. . . . I could find a real boy. It could be like you and Hannah. I could have that." She choked back her tears, unable to continue.

Silas tried to sound comforting. "No-one can ever love you the way that you can love, Circe. They just can't."

It was the wrong thing to say. Circe shuddered with sudden misery.

"I'm sorry," Silas continued, recalling Hannah against his will. He'd fallen out of the habit of thinking of her. "Trust me, you don't want that kind of hurt."

"Maybe I do," Circe sniffed. "Maybe that's exactly the kind of hurt I want."

"How long have you been feeling this way?" Silas asked.

"A while now. Years."

Silas nodded. He knew something of the weight she carried. He carried something similar himself. Under government, he'd been a soldier, and a citizen. He'd been Canadian. As a corporate troubleshooter, he was now a stateless employee. After all this while, it seemed as though there might be nothing left in the place where his "self" was supposed to be. He could only imagine the dissolution Circe felt, being connected at the cellular level, in some empathetic way, to every consumer on the planet. She was alone, adrift in a sea of desires not her own.

"You're tired," Silas said. "You're unhappy. It's late. I think we should get you back to the penthouse, lie you down, and get a couple hours meditation in before morning. I know it's hard, but your mind, kiddo, when it's racing like this . . . it's awfully hard to stop."

"I know," she agreed.

"What do you say?"

"Are we the same, Silas?"

Silas would have blinked if he still had eyelids. "What?" was all he could manage.

"Did whatever make you, make me?"

"We're not the same, Circe. You're special. I'm just a Gunboat, honey, here to keep you safe."

"But we are, a little bit, right? Same inside?"

"Maybe a little bit. But you are definitely an upgrade, kiddo. Gunboat 2.0. At least."

She looked at him again. "I wouldn't really do what I said before, you know. Crash everything. Not on purpose, anyway."

He stared at her with his shark's eyes, her biometrics playing out on his heads-up display as she spoke. She was reading him; he was reading her; both knew.

Don't bullshit me. You think about the power all the time.

He smiled, felt his plasti-flesh crinkle into lines at the corners of his mouth. He knew streetlight reflecting off his artificial skin would make him look something like a crash-test dummy in the near dark. "Of course not," he said, and gave her slender shoulders a reassuring squeeze.

After, when he'd seen her to her room, and set her meditation metronome to tick-tocking, Silas took himself back out to the Peace Bridge to stare at the water and let the changing lights wash over him.

She knows, he thought. *She knows what I will have to do. Was she saying goodbye tonight? How much control does she have left?*

"Hey, buddy, you there?" Ben Mainwaring, checking in. "Gettin' some weird readings from your. . . ."

"Yeah," Silas muttered, "I know. You're reading that I'm still human, or so close as to be nearly indistinguishable."

"So, what do you figure?"

"You catch it all?"

"Yep."

"She's cracking. She's cracked. She's going to crash the system. Eighty-seven percent chance she'll do it at this FOMC, but, if not, one hundred percent it'll be soon."

"What do you want to do?"

"You know what we have to do."

"Want me to task a team?"

"I'll do it. My call; my responsibility. What's the status of the new girl—what's her name?"

"Delphi. She's eight years old, but she's wired right. She's hitting ninety-five percent accuracy on her market tests right now. That's ahead of where Circe was at that age."

"Get her camera-ready, stat."

"How stat?"

"I need her right away, Ben. Better prep media-support as well. Full-spectrum coverage."

"Will do, Silas. . . . Silas?"

"Yeah?"

"I'm sorry. Really sorry, you know?"

"Thanks. Give me a little dark time will you? Tune out till six."

"Roger that, Silas. Talk to you soon."

The sat-comm went silent, leaving Silas alone with his thoughts.

Circe was like a God—an Olympian, and he her Prometheus. He could bring down fire from the heavens to destroy a village, but Circe . . . she could bring down a continent—a world, in these interconnected days. They had brought back Gods to save people from themselves, and the price of that power, for Circe as well as for himself, was well worth paying.

Wasn't it?

It was just one girl—and a handful of civilians, of course, but they hardly mattered compared to the death of a God.

Gunboats, Silas mused. *Should've called us Mamluks. The slave soldiers of Egypt who wound up ruling the joint. The hell did they think would happen?*

Markets had proven to be insane. Governments corrupt and incompetent. Citizens, soldiers, consumers, employees—it didn't matter. None of them could be trusted. All of them were rotten. Only heroes could save the world. Like Circe, before she was broken.

It had to be public, messy; there could be no doubts or mystery about it. He'd take out the top few floors of the penthouse apartment from the sky and blame it on freedom activists. Delphi would be activated, and all would be forgotten.

The Bow River glistened green, then red, then indigo, and a cool breeze brushed Silas's plastic face.

KEVIN COCKLE resides in Calgary, and the city often serves as both a physical and cultural backdrop for many of his stories. Author of more than twenty published stories, Kevin is currently developing some of the ideas in "Circe and the Gunboat" for a film treatment.

KNIFE FIGHT

DAVID NICKLE

Not many outside the confines of the political wing at City Hall
would guess it, but our new mayor is an expert with a knife.

He has been practicing since he was a boy—from the day he
first laid eyes on the eleven-inch bowie knife jammed hilt-deep
into a tree stump in the family's ancestral woodlot, and
withdrew it.

The concrete of his father's basement workshop floor is still
flecked with tiny, reddish-brown dots, a Jackson Pollock record
of the young mayor's apprenticeship, those nights when he was
too slow, or worse . . . too quick. Those days are long past, and
now the mayor is neither. He is merely bold. He is an expert.

Since the hour of his swearing-in, the mayor has kept the
knife in the desk drawer next to his chain of office, wrapped in
an oilcloth tied with thin leather straps. There it slumbers, six
nights in a week. The seventh—Thursday—the mayor carefully
unwraps it, holds it to the fading afternoon light to see that its
edge remains keen, and, in the company of his older cousin . . .
the one who oversees road repairs in the west district . . . the
mayor steps into the elevator that takes him straight to the
parking garage.

And so it begins.

❖

In the beginning, the waiting crowd had been small indeed—
comprised of a handful of senior staff and five city councillors,

72

each hoping to become the mayor's deputy and thereby enjoy the attendant perquisites and honours. They had been there since three p.m., stripped to the waist and greased with goose fat, not daring to speak, barely breathing. The mayor's cousin had reviewed the rules with each of them, which he called "Robert's Rules of Knife Fight." It is said that the city clerk, leaning against the planning commissioner's SUV, snickered at the procedure, and that this—not political differences—was the reason for her dismissal at the next meeting of council.

The mayor's cousin explained the rules then, as he has at each subsequent Thursday.

1. There are only ever two combatants in a knife fight, and each combatant is allowed a knife.
2. The knives are to be provided by the combatants, in a keen, clean condition free of rust. Other objects—scissors, hammers, axes, surgical instruments—shall not be considered knives for the purposes of the knife fight.
3. Combatants shall arrive stripped to the waist, and well-lubricated so as to keep the knife fight from becoming a wrestling match, which is unseemly.
4. Goose fat is considered an acceptable lubricant for the purposes of a knife fight.
5. Victory in the knife fight is usually decided by the drawing of first blood.
6. Combatants shall avoid their opponents' faces, hands, and throats, confining their strikes to parts of the body usually covered by appropriate business attire.
7. In the event that both combatants draw blood from one another in the same instant, the knife fight shall be considered a draw and entered into the Records as such.
8. To the victor go the spoils.

The knife fight remained a well-kept secret for many months. It is true, we wondered at the selection of the new deputy mayor—a stocky, dull-witted rookie councillor from the slaughterhouse district who was unable to finish a sentence without uttering a profanity and crumpled his briefing notes without reading them. And more than once we had seen a blossom of red erupt on the white blouses that the new budget chief wore to the committee meetings regarding capital allocations for the coming fiscal year. And we had wondered at the propensity of the new chair of the Transit Commission to press a fist to his mouth and shut his eyes during breaks in meetings—as though holding back tears at some awful recollection.

But who cared about such things, in the larger scheme? Not us, not at first.

The first year of the mayor's first term was successful by any account. The budget chief not only balanced the books but was able to deliver a modest property tax reduction for the elderly and lay down plans for a swimming pool and target range, creating the first two-thirds of a much-needed triathlete program in the underprivileged slums lining the west riverbank. Our editors wrote supportive editorials as the deputy mayor announced that the Association of Suburban Golf Courses would open up in the winter months, for the final third. The new light rail line servicing the old, blue-collar municipality of Smelt received all the funding it needed from a new federal grant program, announced the Transit Commission chair in tremulous tones.

So we filled our newspapers and broadcasts and blogs with triumphant stories of the mayor's success. We remained silent on the price that his council seemed to be paying for that success. Perhaps we intuited the truth: getting too close to the story might mean crawling too close to an edge.

A knife edge.

❦

Tabloid reporter Stan Bollixer broke the story. Nobody should have been surprised, yet we all were. For few outside the jungles of El Salvador knew it at the time ... but Stan also was an expert with a knife.

The carbon-steel butterfly knife Stan keeps in the pocket of his jeans has been with him nearly as long as the mayor has possessed his bowie knife. But Stan was a grown man when he first wielded his blade; when we asked him later why he kept it so close, he would say only that it had saved his life enough times that he owed it a good home.

No doubt: Stan was an old hand, with sound instincts. He'd come to City Hall during the election and had watched our mayor from the start of the campaign. In the newsroom, he'd predicted that the mayor would prevail, even when the polls placed him a distant fourth. Stan recognized something in the man's eye, in the way he handled metaphor in his speech . . . in the way he moved.

He recognized a predator, and he recognized prey.

So Stan went to work on the mayor, the way a reporter does. He started asking around with his police contacts and located an arrest report from twenty years earlier, when the candidate, then just a lad, was caught knocking over tombstones in the nearby town of Reamington. The story made the front page and sent the future mayor's campaign into a flurry of damage control that proved unnecessary: for who among us has not, in the naiveté of youth, mocked death with a well-placed boot and a war cry?

Stan pressed on. The mayor was but a lowly school trustee prior to his ascendancy. Stan dug up the mayor's voting record and discovered he had voted to ban several well-regarded texts from public school libraries, that he had voted for his own salary increase—not once, but three times. Stan discovered a formal complaint, alleging that the mayor had arrived inebriated and used salty language during a Parent-Teacher Association meeting to discuss the refurbishment of playground equipment.

None of it stuck. With each article, the mayor's public approval rose. The campaign stopped even responding to Stan's reportage, and the week before the election the campaign manager sent Stan a thank-you note on gilt-edged, embossed stationary that seemed very expensive, in gratitude for all his support. Stan wrote another story based on the note, questioning whether the mayor was operating within campaign spending guidelines, given the opulence of the gesture. Three days later, the mayor was elected.

Thus did Stan's permanent assignment to the press gallery at City Hall become an inevitability.

We liked Stan very much from the start. He was soft-spoken in scrums, but attentive. When he did ask a question, it would be the question that pierced the heart of the matter. When he filed his story, it would be the one that, if we were all to be honest, best described the nuance of the issue at hand.

When he watched something, before too long, he saw what it was about.

So it was that on the Tuesday after the announcement of the new light rail line to Smelt, he requested a personal, one-on-one interview with the mayor. No-one thought he'd receive it. Our mayor, as everyone well knows by now, is not a friend of the media. He prefers to speak to constituents directly, over the public address system on the subway or via skywritten aphorisms—or in person, descending upon the backyard barbecues, garage sales, and weddings of leading citizens for impromptu moments of bonhomie. He does not grant many interviews.

But he made an exception for Stan. The interview was scheduled for 12:05 and expected to last fifteen minutes. The subject was to be a retrospective of the mayor's first hundred days in office. The Mayor's Office was suspicious, for they had a sense that Stan was up to something. So the mayor didn't face Stan alone; his second-floor office was crowded with his press secretary, his deputy mayor, and his cousin in the Transportation Department, who had taken a lunch break from road repair to see what Stan Bollixer truly wanted.

Stan was not dissuaded. He smiled, sat down across the desk from the mayor, and reached into his pocket, as if to produce a digital voice recorder.

There was no recorder.

"This can be off the record," he said, as he flipped open his butterfly knife, turned it so it gleamed in the noonday light, and with a sudden, savage plunge drove its point deep into the mahogany top of the mayor's desk.

Tuesday comes but two days before Thursday, and there was much to be done. The mayor's chief of staff and communications director tried to talk the mayor out of it, but he was determined. So they set about devising political strategies, anticipating the worst possible outcomes. The mayor's cousin attempted to arrange to have coffee with Stan and see if he might be dissuaded, but Stan refused even to take his calls. Stan meanwhile whispered, to those few of us he'd come to trust, about the thing that he had begun. He spent time in his office, honing his blade with a whetted stone and recalling, again and again, the night in San Salvador—August, hot as a sauna, smelling strangely of cinnamon—when the one-eyed man from the jungle had appeared at his room and tried to kill him.

One thing he did not do was inform his editor. Neither did any of us.

Our mayor is a man of chiselled granite. This is not apparent when he appears in public, bedecked in his checkered blazers and generously cut trousers, the novelty ties that light up with strategically placed LEDs. Were his constituents to see him shirtless, the goose fat sliding down his torso in thick rivulets, highlighting tendons and veins and ropy, hard-won scars, they would not recognize him—and, worse, they would no longer recognize themselves. They might recoil, as we did, seeing him step off the elevator in the parking garage reserved for city councillors and senior staff, watching him meet each of our eyes in turn with his hard and fearsome stare.

The mayor's cousin allowed three of us to accompany Stan— on the condition that we left all recording devices, including pens and notepads, in a small organic recycling bin left over from the previous administration. The mayor was accompanied by his cousin, and his deputy mayor, and his budget chief. The interim city clerk sat in the passenger seat of his Citroen, an ancient portable typewriter in his lap, a stack of carbon paper by his side.

The interim clerk squinted at Stan as he came out from the stairwell, and in his lap the typewriter keys began to clack out a description.

Stan Bollixer glistened. He was stripped naked to the waist, polished with a thin slick of goose fat, which stained the beltline of his old cutoff jeans. His eyes were wide, and seemed a little crazed, and the interim clerk noted for the record that Stan might be under the influence of a performance-enhancing stimulant. This was true, in a way: he had downed a room-temperature extra-large cup of Colombian coffee from the commissary just prior to coming downstairs. The butterfly knife rested, closed, in his left hand as he walked out past the Works Committee chairman's Harley Davidson, and faced the mayor.

The rules were read, then—the mayor's cousin declaiming them in a slow drawl that was almost a song. When he finished, "To the victor go the spoils," the deputy mayor knelt beside his

Subaru, lifted the mayor's knife, and put it in the mayor's extended hand. Stan made a whiplash motion with his wrist, and the blade of the butterfly knife—less than a quarter the length of the bowie knife—flashed silver in the pallid light of the garage.

We all withdrew a more than respectful distance. For the knife fight between Stan Bollixer and the mayor was on—and no-one wanted to be caught in the middle of it.

There are rules for the knife fight, and those are written down. But there are also customs. The mayor knows them instinctively, for many are his own, but most of his opponents do not. We suspect that inwardly the mayor is saddened by these vulgar bumpkins, who enter combat with thin-lipped, badly feigned rage and leap directly for the mayor's midsection to end things at once with a slash to the nipple or a stab at the collarbone. The mayor finishes these opponents quickly.

Stan Bollixer was not one of those.

Eyes never leaving the mayor's, Stan drew a long, slow circle in the air using the point of his knife; and again, marginally faster—and so on, until he was looking through a circular blur of steel and arm, spinning as fast as a propeller on a biplane. Did we hear the crick-crack of a shoulder dislocating, the creak of sinew bending? Could any of us mark the precise instant that the knife shifted from Stan's whirling left hand to his right? Did any of us truly see admiration, respect, and perhaps a soupçon of fear, cross the mayor's implacable brow?

No, not truly.

But we did hear the mayor emit a long, low growl—the only appropriate response to such a fundamental challenge ... an alpha-male warning cry that came from the depths of our ancestry. The mayor bent down, pulled a dollop of goose fat from the fold beneath his arm, and dipped it into the dust of the garage floor. As he stood, he smeared the filthy grease in long black lines under his eyes, and over each brow, and then again at the edge of his jaw. Weapon clutched in his left hand, he raised both arms over his head like wings, the tip of his knife scoring the bottom of the blood-red EXIT sign. The effect was fearsome: no-one would leave without going through him.

Stan flexed his arm and spun the butterfly knife, handle clicking open and closed, and bent his neck first to the left, then the right.

The mayor drew his breath over his teeth in a serpentine hiss.

The butterfly knife solidified in Stan's fist.

The mayor bellowed, and the knife swung in a crescent of steel that shimmered in the fluorescent afternoon. It might have slashed Stan's left pectoral in two, but his own blade met the mayor's as Stan ducked low and drove his opposite shoulder into the mayor's stomach. Stan let out a cry and drew his blade down in a slice that might, on another day, have relieved the mayor of a kidney. The mayor skipped aside instead, then retreated and swung his free arm contraclockwise to create a deadly momentum. The knife plunged, and Stan shifted, and the blade squealed across the windshield of the mayor's truck as Stan whirled in a failed attempt to slice a piece from the mayor's shoulder. It was too much—Stan's shifting and whirling—and the mayor caught Stan with his free arm, hard in the chest, and Stan doubled over. The butterfly knife would have been airborne had Stan not hooked his pinkie through the handle. The mayor might have had it then—he brought his own knife about, holding it an inch above Stan's shoulder. It hovered there as Stan wheezed, then withdrew. The mayor stepped back, knife at his side, fixing Stan with an expression that may have been a grin of triumph, or simply a mask of exhaustion. The parking garage fell silent but for the increasingly frenzied clacking of typewriter keys from the Citroen's front seat.

By degrees, Stan Bollixer stood. The mayor raised his knife, and pointed it at Stan like a deadly forefinger.

"Next week. Same time," he said. "Same place."

It is rumoured that one of us—a new reporter with something to prove—filed a news bit about the battle. But her piece never saw print, nor appeared on the internet. Before a week had run out she had been transferred to the radio room where, it was said, she spent her nights listening to the police scanner for word of fires, and crimes, and other nocturnal catastrophes.

The rest of us kept to the pact, and the mayor kept to a busy public schedule. Stan joined us in following him—how could he do otherwise? Following the mayor through the wards of his city was Stan's job as much as it was any of ours. When time came for the mayor to declaim, Stan Bollixer's microphone had its place: in front of the podium.

Stan was a professional. If his eyes ever met the mayor's through the scrum, and if he ever felt the mayor taking his measure . . . well, he didn't let it show. Nor did the mayor. At least not in those moments.

But we wondered: did the mayor's frenetic activity that week—shielding him in the midst of the children of the Smelt Community Centre, Pool's Summer Fun Day Camp, or the Cannery District Seniors Snooker Club—indicate that his nerve was slipping? Or perhaps he was using the business and ceremony of his office as a kind of extended display, a demonstration that he, and not this cocksure pretender, was the leader of this tribe?

But if he was so shaken, we wondered, why hadn't he simply ended the knife fight the previous Thursday—taken his slice from Stan Bollixer's greasy shoulder, and called victory?

On the following Thursday morning, several of us came in late to work. We'd been called from our beds by frantic city editors to join the night team in covering an atrocity unfolding in the food court at Old Town Abattoir Mall. It was a terrible crime, a tragedy, but so immense that in those early hours—days, really—no-one could reliably determine what precisely had happened.

Early reports indicated a hail of gunfire, erupting from the rendering gallery, perhaps. But injuries did not bear this out, and the theory did not explain the smashed masonry at the base of the fountain, or the size of the holes in the ductwork. Although many had been knocked unconscious in the event, no-one was treated for bullet wounds. Descriptions of the perpetrators were similarly vague and contradictory: giant men, possibly of African descent, faces covered in cheap fabric, heads shaven, teeth emerging like tusks from their jaws. . . .

The Abattoir Atrocity, as our editors dubbed it, was an impossible story to tell; it would not make sense of itself. Those of us called upon to help wrestle it into a narrative came in late, exhausted and dispirited. The only thing that kept us going was the resumption of the struggle between Stan Bollixer and the mayor.

Although we knew we could never tell it, that was a story that at least we could understand.

The knives flashed ribbons of steel through the air as the combatants danced across the concrete floor of the garage where it was not smeared with long slides of goose fat and back hair. A fluorescent tube sent a snowfall of shattered glass as the bowie knife cut through it; the director of Community Services spent the second part of the fight huddled behind a Subaru, applying pressure to an accidental slash across his arm from the fine-honed blade of the butterfly knife. Although it was warm in the parking garage, the city clerk rolled up the windows on his Citroen and kept low as he clacked away on the minutes of the second instalment of the knife fight.

This one lasted longer than the first—the mayor's cousin called it at twenty-seven minutes, fifty-three seconds, standing over the mayor collapsed on his back, while Stan, similarly exhausted, propped himself against a cement pillar. The two may have been invulnerable that afternoon to mere steel—but middle age and the hot, dry, carbon-monoxide-rich air of the VIP parking garage were another matter.

"Why don't you call it a draw?" cried the director of Community Services, blood staining his fingers and necktie where he held it against his arm. "Haven't you proved enough?"

The mayor drew a wheezing breath and fixed narrow eyes on the bureaucrat, who looked away. The mayor turned back to Stan, who was coming out the other side of a long coughing fit.

"These are the end times," the mayor said, and sat still a moment, before gathering himself up and quitting the ring.

The words were prophetic. The following week's monthly city council meeting was attended by not only the mayor and all his councillors, but also the senior staff and their assistants, all of us, and delegations from wards across the city. This meeting had been scheduled to go long. Merchants from Abattoir Mall had come with a petition demanding greater police presence and the installation of video cameras. There was to be discussion of a cost overrun on the light rail line into Smelt, and a committee of residents were asking for additional stops to better service the rehabilitation hospital. The city's poet laureate had composed three new stanzas of an epic retelling of our amalgamation fifteen years ago, and there was to be a presentation no later than three p.m.

These things, combined with several dozen routine items, ought to have added up to a sometimes vigorous but relatively straightforward session, finishing no later than seven; meetings under the mayor were famous for running with brutal efficiency.

It was not to be.

The merchants were joined by a local civil liberties group shouting down the Abattoir Mall manager's deputation, requiring the services of the City Hall security squad and a recess to clear the chambers and restore calm. The debate continued for three solid hours after that, the matter becoming so confused with amendments that, on the clerk's advice, council finally deferred the item until the Christmas session.

Through all this, the denizens of Smelt hovered at the back, stoking their grievances one upon the other until their matter came up, and as a group they demanded that the light rail line be ripped out altogether and the remaining funds be reallocated to the restoration of the Smelt Arms Bijou—a cinema that had been derelict since the war, but held many fond memories for the elder Smelters. Despite vigorous lobbying by the mayor's staff, council sided with the deputants, and narrowly voted to kill the rail plan.

The poet laureate, meantime, had grown bored early in the meeting and, as poet laureates do, comforted himself with the contents of his hip flask throughout the afternoon. When his time came, he'd drunk himself into sufficient belligerence to substitute an obscene limerick in place of his more sublime stanzas. While some of us might have commented that the limerick was an improvement overall, the mayor obviously did not agree.

"This city is swirling into the toilet," he was heard to mutter, unaware, momentarily, that his microphone was still on.

❦

The third time nearly finished it.

Mayor and reporter went at one another savagely from the outset, crashing together, each wrestling the other's knife-arm with his free hand. The mayor smashed his forehead into Stan's, twice, and Stan at a point managed to loop his arm between the mayor's legs and so hoist him above his head, slamming the city's chief magistrate hard onto the hood of a mid-sized sedan. Had this been a wrestling match and not a knife fight, Stan would have won it.

The savagery grew. The parking garage onlookers gasped as one when the mayor missed slashing Stan's throat by scant inches—and again seconds later, as the tip of Stan's blade hovered an instant over the mayor's right eyeball.

In the third round, it seemed, the knife fight had transformed into a killing fight.

Yet, for the third time, not a drop of blood was shed.

On Friday morning, the Doucette Greeting Card Company held a press conference at which their president, Wallace Doucette, announced that they would be ceasing production by November; by year's end, they planned to have moved all remaining operations south of the border, where a more favourable tax regime combined with a more eager labour market in a city more attractive to executives and their families would ensure the company's survival. The workers received their layoff notices at the beginning of the morning shift.

The mayor spoke to reporters afterward, attempting to downplay the impact of Doucette's departure and deflect the suggestion that our city was no place an executive would want to raise a family. But he could carry it only so far; the Doucette family was the third-largest employer in the city, and as a boy the mayor had played Lacrosse with Wallace. The betrayal was both civic and personal.

On the weekend, it rained. The rains started early Saturday, coming down in thick, grey sheets reminiscent of flying knives, and did not relent until early Sunday. Creeks overflowed; storm sewers clogged; and unlucky householders found their basements filling with sludge as the sewer system overflowed. Three footbridges washed away in parks, and a great sinkhole opened at an intersection to the east of the downtown, all but devouring one of the city's two-dozen new ecofriendly buses.

The mayor did not immediately respond to calls from our weekend reporters.

How could he? He had other things with which to occupy himself.

He had to become better.

On Monday evening, Stan joined us for drinks after deadline. The storm had given way to awful humidity, and so we gathered in the pier district in the back room of a Czech pub well known to those of our profession.

As he had been since the fights began, Stan was quiet. Fortunately, drawing information from a quiet man is a hallmark of our profession. So we speculated—making note of the fact that the mayor's fortunes seem to have turned over the course of the long, stalemated battle between himself and Stan. We supposed that the stalemate may simply have sapped the mayor's confidence, although that, as we thought about it, didn't explain the rainstorm, or the drunken limericks, or the perversity of the men and women of Smelt on matters of public transit.

Stan smiled at that, and shook his head, and concentrated on the shape the foam took atop his ale.

And so we wondered: how was it that there wasn't any blood in the fights? How was it that Stan Bollixer and the mayor, both experts with the blade, could not land so much as a nick as they battled so energetically? The blades had cut cars, light fixtures, even a senior bureaucrat; what unknown agent so thickened the hides of the mayor and of Stan Bollixer?

Would this battle of titans ever end? To the victor went the spoils, said the rules. What if there was no victor?

And Stan shrugged, and smiled, and downed his beer in a single, long swallow. "Good question," he said.

We persisted. What if there was no victor?

"What if it stopped, you mean?" said Stan. He slid his glass across the bar and signalled for the cheque. "What if the long fight that has shaped the mayor—shaped the city—just came to an end?"

Yes, we said—what if no-one took the spoils?

"Well," he said, grinning a little, "I guess this city wouldn't go to anyone. I guess it would be on its own. I guess it might be free."

♣

The budget committee began deliberations three weeks later. This time it did not go smoothly. The city's treasurer had underestimated revenues, putting the city tens of millions of dollars in the red for the coming year. Flooding from the rainstorms had created an emergency liability that the city would have to cover through tax revenues, and the collapse of the greeting card sector meant a precipitous drop in assessments. While no-one spoke the words aloud, several of us found well-placed sources who hinted that the city could be on the verge of bankruptcy by Christmas.

Meanwhile, council members and senior bureaucrats quietly found other places to park their vehicles than the VIP parking lot—at least on Thursdays. For who, really, wants to leave their cars unattended on a battlefield?

Guided by the same principle, the audience grew smaller each Thursday; some nursing wounds from errant slashings; others sensibly retreating to their offices, or their homes, while the mayor fought his nemesis to a standstill, week after week after week.

Some of us stopped attending as well. Partly it was self-preservation, but also something more fundamental: work.

Termites rose up from the earth in the fashionable Palm District, devouring the stout oak-trimmed homes of our leading citizens. The garbage workers went on strike just before Halloween, and the bus drivers joined them in solidarity a week later. Three more atrocities followed the Abattoir Atrocity in quick succession, each incident delivering more mayhem and making less sense than the last, causing our editors to deem this The Year of the Atrocity.

On the Thursday before Christmas, none of us attended. How could we? The city was bankrupt, its homes crumbling to sawdust, the busways silent but for swirling snow, and garbage piled up in mountains outside the shooting range by the river. . . .

We had our hands full.

And then it was Christmas.

City Hall was not entirely empty, but near to it. Only a few of us came in to check on the place. Janitors and security guards patrolled the halls, and a handful of councillors wandered the political wing. But there were not many of those; most huddled in their homes, dreading the new year when, almost assuredly, the city would not be able to make its payroll.

Calls to the Mayor's Office went unanswered. Stan Bollixer's office was dark, the door locked. In the quiet of the Yule, we began to wonder: had there been a final battle? Had the mayor prevailed? Had Stan?

Had one or the other died? Had they slain one another?

"We ought to go see."

"What—you mean?"

"The garage. We ought to see."

"It's locked up."

"We ought to go see."

The conversation went in circles like that, and might have gone on forever had not the budget chief happened by. Unlike the mayor, she was a great friend of the media and sought us out as often as she could. After handing out her annual stash of candy canes, she asked us if we would join her on a tour of the VIP parking garage. Her pass card, so far as she knew, still worked.

The garage was empty but for an old convertible covered in a canvas cloth, rumoured to belong to the Works Committee chair. The floor had been swept; there was not so much as a smudge of goose fat on the ground, or along the walls. It was as though the knife fight had never happened here.

We asked the budget chief if she had seen the mayor recently. She said that she had not, but that wasn't unusual. "He seems preoccupied," said the budget chief, "and who can blame him?"

"What do you mean?"

The budget chief shrugged as we walked the wide circle of the garage. "It's tough times. You guys were all calling him on it; he couldn't miss it. And that's got to weigh heavy on him. I mean, a mayor's supposed to keep a handle on things. He let go."

And to no-one, we realized, went the spoils. We stood near to one another in the cold, empty parking garage, considering the implications of that. How had Stan Bollixer put it?

We would be on our own.

We would be free.

One of us wondered aloud if the budget chief thought the mayor's time might have come; if she might have thought that she, the budget chief, could do a better job of it.

But the budget chief didn't answer. She stopped, looking down at the base of one of the pillars—where a glint of steel emerged, below a hilt bound in old leather. The blade had been driven into the concrete, tiny cracks like capillaries branching off from it.

"Look at that," she said, and wrapped her fingers around the hilt.

DAVID NICKLE was born in Newmarket, Ontario, and left town almost immediately. Since then he's lived exclusively in Ontario—for the most part in downtown Toronto. He's published numerous stories and is the author of several novels, including *Rasputin's Bastards*. He works as a reporter, covering Toronto city politics.

On-to-Ottawa

DERRYL MURPHY

The earth shook when Iron Heel slammed his boot down onto the ground, and the oncoming train, the roofs of the boxcars riddled with the parasites who some days ago had refused the good jobs given them in British Columbia, jumped the tracks. Bodies scattered, men and even youth of undesirable backgrounds hit the parched earth, which eagerly drank the blood so many of them spilled.

The one slap of his heel upon the land was all that was needed, he was sure, and with his work now done Iron Heel stood back to watch as his team of Mounties rushed in to clean things up. The Marxist rabble would learn their lesson from his rare appearance, and their leaders, even this mysterious Hero who called himself Slim, would be soon brought up on charges and then unceremoniously dumped into the Super Wing at Kingston, as escape-proof a place as would ever exist for those with Powers who refused to use them for the common good.

But something was wrong. Police were suddenly shooting weapons, tear gas swirled into existence, and men who hadn't been hurt when the train had catapulted from the tracks were now falling, injured or dead. A large group of Mounties moved in on one particular knot of men; a rifle was fired, a man dropped, and it was clear even from this distance that the shot had torn a ridge through the top of the man's skull.

Marxists and revolutionaries though they were, Iron Heel knew that if many more were killed in this fracas he would lose even more public support. Secrets about this day would be spilled, causing even more damage than the splattered blood. He raised his foot. . . .

. . . but instead of hitting the ground with it watched as a young man reached down, placed his hand on the gaping wound in the other man's head, and with a gesture the wounded—dead, surely, but how was this happening?—man stood back up. A third man said something to the gathered Mounties, and without a second thought they all scattered, running as fast and as far as they could.

"You'll do no such thing!" Iron Heel barked, and once more he brought his foot down to the ground, harder this time. Buildings swayed, people screamed, and everyone for hundreds of yards around his personal epicentre stumbled and fell to the ground.

Except for two men. The young man who had healed the one who had been shot, and the one who had spoken the words that had sent everyone running. They held their balance, and then ran up the small hill toward him. He raised his boot once more, this time holding it back behind him, preparing to kick at the two men if they came any closer, hoping that he would be able to keep his balance; he wasn't the young Hero he'd once been.

But they stopped about five yards shy. Neither man wore a mask, which was very odd and quite strictly against convention. Even though most everyone in the country must by now know the former secret identity of Iron Heel, he still wore a simple mask over his eyes. Indeed, he kept a collection of them, each designed to match whichever jacket he was wearing that day. Today's was a basic grey with a hint of faded tartan, the colour he had deemed most suitable for this expedition to the dustbowl of Saskatchewan.

Before he could say anything, the first man turned sideways and seemed to disappear from his sight—it was Evans, whom he'd had removed at that angry meeting in Ottawa. Evans was Slim!—and before he could react he was thrown to his back, Slim having turned himself to an angle where he couldn't be seen and then snuck up upon him. Iron Heel lay there, the wind knocked out of him, and wondered why and how a Hero would cast his lot with Marxists, with unionists, with the lowest rabble of society. It was beyond his ken.

Not a Hero, then. A villain.

"Mr. Prime Minister," said the second man, now standing over him, careful to stay clear of his feet. He was in his twenties, with wire spectacles and with his hair parted along one side. He was quite small and lean, and Iron Heel did not doubt that he could take the youngster in a fight, even given his relatively advanced age, if only he could get up from his turtle-like position: on his back in the dust. But before he could make a move Slim reappeared beside the other man.

"Who are you?" Iron Heel asked. "You seem to have the better of me at the moment."

"The people around here call me Medicine Man," came the answer, and Iron Heel cast his memory back over briefing papers about any new Heroes that might have cropped up in these parts, but nothing came to mind. "But I make no secret of who I am, and you will find out soon enough. Next election, I stand for the Co-operative Commonwealth Federation in Weyburn, not far from here."

Iron Heel chuckled, though he felt appalled; how could anyone think a socialist in the House of Commons would be a good thing? King, that ever-irritating psychic Hero sitting across the aisle from him, was a Liberal, which was already too close to socialism for his liking. King would know how to use someone like this "Medicine Man" to his benefit, and Bennett couldn't have that. "You'll never win," he said.

"But he will," said Slim. "Your time has come and gone, Mr. Bennett."

"That's not my name today, Slim, just as your name is not Mr. Evans," said Iron Heel. He slowly pulled himself up to a sitting position, and the other men danced back a step or two, both ready if he tried anything with his Power. He shook his head. "I told you before, my government will not go in for your extortion racket."

"We only want what's right for these men," said Slim, and Medicine Man nodded in agreement. "The relief camps are no place for a man to earn his dignity, to say nothing of money to help support his family."

In the distance, high in the sky, something winked brightly and momentarily in the sun. Iron Heel sighed in relief. The Mounties were gone, routed by the remainder of the rabble who had come to town riding atop the boxcars, and he had not been sure if he was going to find his way out of here. But Transporter, one of his Cabinet ministers who had also once been a Hero, was on his way. He counted silently to himself, and at the right moment he quickly raised both hands into the air and called out in pain at the sudden jerk of being pulled up and forward into the sky at high speed. Transporter wasn't wearing a mask—it was his glasses Iron Heel had seen glinting in the sun, and his conservative tie and grey hair flapped and waved in the flurry. "Hang on, sir!" yelled the Hero, making sure his voice could be heard over the rushing wind. "I don't have the strength or endurance I had back when we were young and setting the world afire! I'll have to set you down very soon!"

But Iron Heel wasn't listening. Instead, he craned his neck and looked back at the two men receding into the distance, and wondered if he would indeed see Medicine Man again. He'd have to see what he could do about disallowing socialists from taking public office.

Provided he could convince King to cooperate.

DERRYL MURPHY is the author of the Aurora Award-nominated novel *Napier's Bones*. His newest book is the collection *Over the Darkened Landscape*. He was born in Nova Scotia, grew up in Alberta, lived in BC, and is now in Saskatchewan.

THE SECRET HISTORY OF THE INTREPIDS

D.K. LATTA

... it is during the darkest times that the brightest lights can emerge, as men and women of valour rise to the challenge and say to the darkness: 'No More!'
—From the unpublished memoirs of
Prime Minister William Bishop (1939-1948),
courtesy of the National Archives, Ottawa

Thunder cracked, and the car veered off the miserable road onto a pathetic strip of mud. Given the torrential rain and the blackness of the night, the young man had no idea of their destination. Then a flash of lightning revealed an unlit farmhouse up on a hill.

Earlier, three large men had dragged him from his apartment with no more explanation than flashing him a glimpse of the pistols they carried under their coats. They had shoved him into the backseat of this car, two squeezing in on either side of him.

The men didn't sound German, which was the first thing that had occurred to the young reporter: Nazi spies. Though why spies would want him he could not imagine, unless it was some tragic case of mistaken identity. Or unless it had to do with the story he was researching.

For a moment that gave him pause. But, no—how could it be that? He had barely assembled a few rumours and suppositions. If these guys knew enough about what he was working on to think he was worth kidnapping ... then they already knew more about it than he did.

He dreaded the jerk of the car skidding to a halt. As long as they were driving, he still had a future ahead of him. But now? The massive man to his right flung himself out into the night, and immediately a terrible wind sent the rain drumming across him.

"Out," growled the gorilla of a man.

He reluctantly slid off the seat, his shoes sinking ankle-deep into the mud. He glanced furtively around. The terrain was too open to offer hiding places, and there was even less chance he could outrun his abductors.

His escort caught his glance and snorted derisively. "In your dreams, chump." Grabbing him by the arm, the big man ushered him toward the house. It had appeared dark from the lane, but he realized heavy blinds had been drawn to block out all hint of light from a distance. Up close, glowing fissures lined the windows.

The big man pounded out a deliberate pattern on the door. Immediately it was flung wide. Standing dry and cosy on the other side was no Nazi spy, but a tall, lean fellow dressed in a traditional Native Indian regalia of buckskin. He looked at the young man with a penetrating stare.

The big gorilla nodded, "Archie, tell Intrepid we've got his pigeon."

He was left alone in a book-lined room, a fire cackling pleasantly in the hearth, the warmth soaking into his chilled bones. At least it wasn't a dungeon, or a torture chamber. Things looked marginally more optimistic than they had during the long, terrifying drive.

Without preamble, a door opened. Startled, he jumped to his feet.

A nattily dressed, middle-aged man entered. But it was the figure behind him that caught the young man's attention: short and somewhat portly, he sported a long brown cape and a loose, ill-fitting cowl that covered the upper part of his face. Suddenly the young man began to feel afraid again; his investigations had been onto something after all.

"Berton, isn't it?" asked the well-dressed man. He spoke with a mid-Atlantic accent: a tad British, a tad Canadian. "Dreadful night to be out. My name is William Stephenson."

"Intrepid," Berton blurted, then instantly regretted opening his mouth.

Stephenson was still smiling, but with ice in his eyes. "Now, where did you hear *that* name?"

"Around," said the young man, trying to affect a bravado he did not feel. "You're supposed to be a big deal in the war effort—though no-one's quite sure what you do."

Stephenson smiled wider. "Let's just say . . . I get things done. My friend—"

"—Is The Oracle." interrupted Berton. "I recognize him from eyewitness accounts. He's The Fighter with the Foresight, as the less reputable rags have dubbed him."

The flamboyantly garbed man put a hand to his head, as though concentrating. "Mother says—Mother says the boy *can* be trusted. And that I shouldn't skip lunch like—" He stopped, and frowned. "Sorry. That last was just for me."

Stephenson looked at Berton. "Your compeers in the fourth estate have it wrong. W.L. here doesn't have the insight—his mother does. He just communicates with her. Poor dear's been dead for years."

Berton glanced sceptically at the masked man, but the portly crimefighter said nothing.

"It's come to my attention you've been making a few inquiries, young man," continued Stephenson. "A cub reporter hoping to land a byline, eh? Well, I can admire that. I was a bit of a go-getter myself in my youth. So why don't you tell me what you know?"

Berton hesitated, but realized he didn't have much choice. "Not much—pieces of a puzzle glimpsed through cheesecloth, really. I was working in Vancouver, but recently moved to Toronto to be closer to the action. I'd started researching these masked adventurers that have been cropping up. I was even narrowing down possible secret identities for some. There's The Oracle here, and The Northern Lama—who I have good reason to believe is a medical doctor. And Powerhouse. But recently their activities have been less public, and I found indications that someone seemed to be organizing them—ever since the Nazis invaded Nova Scotia."

Stephenson stared at him a long while, the only sounds in the room being the crackle of the fire, the trampling of the rain outside as though a thousand giants were drumming their fingers, and a low murmur that Berton realized was The Oracle muttering, apparently to himself. Then the man called Intrepid nodded curtly, as though arriving at a decision. "I could have you locked up, of course. For the sake of the war effort. But I won't. Indeed, maybe having a journalist on hand would be good for posterity. They say keep your friends close, your enemies closer . . . and nosy parkers closest of all! Berton," he held out a hand, "welcome to the inner workings of Operation: Strong and Free!"

❦

The stately bookshelf creaked aside on hidden pulleys like something out of a Mary Roberts Rinehart play, exposing a hidden lift. Stephenson stepped inside, followed by The Oracle and, after a moment's hesitation, Berton. Stephenson pulled the cage closed and started them downward. The farmhouse was clearly just a disguise, Berton realized, like the mask sported by The Oracle, who was scratching at his clumsily homemade cowl, obviously finding it itchy in the humidity. The masked man glanced questioningly at Stephenson, who nodded. "After all," Stephenson remarked sardonically, "your own mother said we can trust him. . ."

The Oracle pulled back his hood with relief, revealing a plump face and thinning hair. He was much older than Berton would have expected. Then the young reporter's eyes flared. "Wait a minute—you're . . . William Lyon Mackenzie King."

Stephenson looked impressed. "Good lord, you *are* good."

Berton shrugged. "I happened to have read Mr. King's book, *Industry and Labour*, in school. And recently I was assembling background research for a staff reporter who was doing a piece on the history of the Liberal Party, and I came upon Mr. King's name again." He looked at The Oracle. "Some older party members figured you were headed somewhere in politics . . . then you simply dropped out."

"I *had* been pursuing a life in politics," admitted William Lyon Mackenzie King, "until a Gypsy woman seer I had been consulting, knowing of my interest in the afterlife, cursed—I mean, *granted*—me with the power to commune with the spirits all on my own." The portly man glanced upward. ". . . And Mother insisted my destiny lay in another direction."

"So even from the grave your mother tells you—" Berton stopped himself as Stephenson glared at him. Suddenly another face he'd seen this night struck a chord: "That Indian who answered the door . . . was that—?"

"Grey Owl?" Stephenson nodded, then winked. "The reports of his death were exaggerated, as a man from Missouri once said. Grey Owl was finding being arguably the most famous living Indian in the world a bit too much, so he faked his death. Thankfully, the current crisis persuaded him to emerge from hiding and offer his skills as a hunter and a tracker to the war effort."

Berton said, "He didn't look quite as, well, *Indian*, as I'd expected."

Stephenson shot him a condescending look. "And have you seen a lot of Indians up close?"

Berton was about to say, *probably more than you have*, but held his tongue. Instead he said, "So you've been gathering. . . ?"

"Let's call them 'Special Operatives,'" Stephenson suggested, "and yes. They had been acting as lone-wolf individuals, fighting street criminals, black marketeers, that sort of thing. And the government was content to let them do their part, in their own way—until it all went wrong, of course. The death of the American President Roosevelt rather scuppered our expectations of how things might unfold. And the election of President Lindbergh just made things worse. He's taken neutrality to an absurd degree. That's how the Nazis were able to land sufficient forces in the Maritimes—they used New England as a staging ground."

"I can't believe an American president is so pro-Nazi," said Berton bitterly.

Stephenson chuckled. "I'm not sure he is—he just fears the death and destruction that accompanies taking sides in a war of this magnitude. But some of us know the price of *not* fighting the fascists will be more costly by far in the end." The lift lurched to a halt and Stephenson yanked open the cage to reveal a long corridor illuminated by caged lamps strung along the ceiling. "I had been co-ordinating international espionage efforts between Great Britain and Canada and, unofficially, the

US. But when Lindbergh got elected I became persona non grata in the States, and when Nova Scotia fell . . . well, I rather felt a need to stay on this side of the pond and devote my energies exclusively to my homeland. I was born in Manitoba, you know."

"But we're holding them east, at least," Berton noted. "Prime Minister Bishop said on the radio that our soldiers are keeping them hemmed in 'like a dam around a lake.'"

Stephenson clucked his tongue. "William Bishop is many things. An aviation ace. A war hero. But his biggest attribute is that he knows how to spin a yarn or two. The Nazis are staying where they are, but that's because they don't seem to be interested in moving out just yet. They are content with Nova Scotia for the moment—and that absolutely terrifies me."

Before Berton could ask him to elaborate, they stopped before a wooden door braced by a heavy metal X bolted in place. It looked old and modern at the same time—like the door of a submarine, had submarines been invented by Vikings. Stephenson grunted as he jerked the handle, and the door swung inward. He ducked through, followed by the young reporter, with Mackenzie King bringing up the rear.

Beyond was a massive chamber with a high, vaulted ceiling. Soldiers in uniform moved about. Blueprints were being argued over at one table by men in suspenders waving slide rules. At another table, beakers frothed while a man and a woman in lab coats sidled nervously away. At the far end was the mouth to a massive cavern, and what looked to be train tracks disappeared into a darkness tempered with flashing lights, suggesting welding torches at work.

Striding purposefully from the organized chaos came the buckskin-wearing Grey Owl. "You have decided to take the boy into your confidence, then?" he asked.

Stephenson slipped his hands into his pocket, as though no more impressed with the sights before him than a father would be arriving home after a day at the office to find dinner in the oven and his slippers by his favourite chair. "Yes—we can't let him run around loose. But it would be a shame to lock him in a military stockade for the duration of the war. He seems a bright lad, and I prefer to have assets working for me."

Grey Owl's lips crooked in a suggestion of a smile. "Then welcome, little cub," he said to Berton.

The reporter was awed by the man's charisma. As an aspiring writer, he couldn't help but be impressed standing before such a wildly regarded author, though he still could not shake the vague feeling Grey Owl was maybe trying a bit hard, like an actor playing a role that even he had half-forgotten was a part.

"Where are the others?" asked Stephenson.

Grey Owl nodded behind them, and Berton glanced back. "Jehoshaphat!" he exclaimed. Right at his shoulder was a man wearing a domino mask over his handsome, moustached face, dressed in a kind of modified monk's robe white as a snow drift: The Northern Lama. "But ... but ..." Berton stammered, for behind them was nothing but a blank wall—no place from where the man could have appeared.

The Northern Lama glanced at him. "I learned many secrets from the Shaolin Monks of China."

Seeming oblivious to the exchange, Grey Owl pointed across the room. "Powerhouse is just finishing up in there."

A tall man, built like a circus strongman, emerged from the black tunnel. Perched on his shoulder, as though weighing no more than a sack of potatoes, was a massive iron apparatus that looked not unlike an oversized car engine. Once outside the tunnel, he shrugged the object from his shoulder and it hit the floor with such a heavy thud that Berton felt it through his shins even across the room. Powerhouse's mask concealed all his features, save his eyes, while his body was sheathed in form-fitting yellow and red—again, evoking a circus performer's costume. He even wore shorts on top of his leggings!

Berton's gaze was suddenly caught by a figure in a gondola overhead. At this distance, he could make out very little, save that the figure had a white beard. Looking down over all the activity, the old man seemed to occupy a position of importance.

"Come on then," said Stephenson. "Let's find the Apparition and make the proper introductions."

As Stephenson led the way toward a side door, the others fell in around him. Berton leaned toward The Oracle and, nodding at The Northern Lama, whispered, "Did he really just walk through a wall?"

"Don't get too enamoured." The Oracle leaned closer. "He's a Red."

✦

They settled in the mess hall, coffee and sandwiches already set out on one of the long tables. Without asking, Berton, still shivering a bit from the rain, immediately went to pour himself a cup. When he reached for a sandwich, a woman's hand was there ahead of him, slender and delicate—and eerily pale. He looked up to see the coquettish smile of a pretty girl.

"Oh, sorry," he said, "help yourself—" He stopped. She wasn't just pale—she was bone-white, even her hair. Even her clothes. "I . . . I'm Berton," he stammered.

She smiled radiantly at him, and spoke. At least, her delicate lips moved . . . but no sound came forth. Berton stepped back, then twisted as he realized another woman was next to him. Except it was the same woman, with the exact same deathly pallor. And behind her was yet another. They all smiled, moving their lips in silence. Unnerved by the eeriness of the situation, Berton dropped his cup.

The Northern Lama caught it and nonchalantly placed it upon the table, then stepped forward—literally through one of the ghostly women—as he helped himself to his own cup. The women wagged their fingers crossly at him and seemed to be chastising him—but still with no sound. "Ignore them—Mary just likes her little jokes. That's the trouble with the pampered bourgeoisie."

"Says the wealthy Bolshevik," came a woman's voice.

Berton spun around and saw the same woman again—only this time in flesh and blood hues, and capable of speech. As she stepped forward, her ghostly echoes flickered and vanished, and he perceived that she wasn't exactly the same. Though still a handsome woman, she was decidedly older than her projections by a couple of decades. She appraised Berton, a cocky grin on her lips. "So you're the writer, eh? But let me guess . . . you *really* want to direct?"

"He's not *that* kind of writer," said The Northern Lama.

The woman thrust out a hand. "I'm called the Apparition. Though you may have heard of me as Mary Pickford. I used to be a big to-do in the pictures."

Of course! thought Berton, taking her hand. She had looked familiar: the Canadian-born movie star who was once dubbed 'America's Sweetheart.' "You still are, Ms. Pickford—at least, by reputation," he finished lamely, realizing that her career since the advent of the talkies wasn't what it had been.

"My girls helped me make a lot of movies, back in the day." She shrugged. "But I'm afraid they weren't much use to my career once sound came in." She paused, then looked down. "You planning on keeping that for your collection?"

Berton realized he was still holding her hand. Embarrassed, he hastily released it. "Sorry."

She smiled knowingly, then changed the topic. "You've met Norman, of course," she nodded at The Northern Lama.

"Yes," said Berton. Determined to prove himself, instead of just gawking at them all, he added, "Doctor Norman Bethune, if my investigations are anything to bank on: pioneering surgeon, political radical, and veteran of the Spanish Civil War. Rumour was you almost died in China fighting the fascist Japanese."

"Yes," said the Northern Lama, "but I was ministered to by some kindly monks. They taught me a few of their more esoteric techniques. Techniques I realized I could use in the battle against the fascists—and, in time, in defense of the proletariat. Oppressors don't just wear swastikas, kid. The industrialist warmongers and the—"

"Yes, well," Stephenson stepped forward and clapped The Northern Lama on the shoulder, "one battle at a time, eh, Norman? Let's deal with the fascists, and then you can see about saving us all from capitalism, okay?"

The Northern Lama scowled. Sensing this was a longstanding source of tension, Berton cleared his throat and attempted to redirect the conversation. "So ... some of these people had already been operating as lone crimefighters. And now you've brought them together, Mr. Stephenson. And this complex—well, it's nothing short of amazing. But. . . ."

"The Nazis still control the East Coast?" Stephenson finished for him. "You're quite right. But preparations have to be made— one can't just blunder in without a plan. Though we're racing the clock; the longer the Nazis control Nova Scotia, the greater the likelihood the war will be lost—and the world will come under the dominion of the Ratzi bastards."

"You said something like that earlier. What's in Nova Scotia that could decide the fate of the world?"

"Something *very ancient* ... and something *very new*, young man," came a reedy voice he'd not heard before. Berton turned to see the old man he had glimpsed on the gondola totter into the room, leaning heavily on a walking stick. His long white beard reached to his chest, and his face was small and shrivelled. "And if the Nazis get to either one before we can stop them, it will mean the end of the world as we know it."

... the place itself was a marvel, with some of the best and brightest scientific minds at work. Intrepid, or Stephenson, was in charge of the compound, but the old man was the one everybody looked to. He was very aged; they called him "the professor," though his official code name was "The Operator." His presence was considered an even greater secret than that of all the others combined.

As for the others. . . .

I had at first taken Grey Owl and The Northern Lama to be drinking buddies, but I became aware that they simply liked to drink and so tended to sit next to each other morosely at the compound's afterhours bar. The Northern Lama could be an ugly drunk. Whatever he had learned from the monks, it wasn't inner peace.

Powerhouse claimed to be a medical doctor named Banting, and he told me he had been working on a cure for diabetes when he, instead, accidentally discovered a formula that bestowed super-strength. Unfortunately, he hadn't kept notes and so had been unable to duplicate it, otherwise Canada would have had an army of supermen. Still, if he had ever managed to find a treatment for diabetes—how different would the world have been?

As for The Oracle, he struck me as the oddest of the bunch. And perhaps the saddest. If the others sometimes seemed too alone, his curse was that he was never fully alone. More than once I came upon him muttering to himself in a dark corner, engaged in a conversation with someone only he could hear. . . .

—Excerpts from *Me & The Boys in the Capes:*
The Wartime Journals of P. Berton
(1974, out-of-print ed.)

The workshop—as Berton had come to think of the main hall over the last couple of weeks—was eerily quiet, the scientists and soldiers absent. It was just the eight of them: Intrepid, the old man (known as The Operator), Berton, and the five 'special operatives.'

Stephenson addressed the group: "According to our intel, the Nazis are on the verge of realizing what they call Project: Fafner!"

Berton frowned. Fafner was a dragon, if he recalled. That sounded ominous.

". . . I'll let the professor here explain."

The old man tottered forward, drooped over his cane. "To put matters succinctly, there is an ancient power buried deep in Nova Scotia that the Nazis seek to unearth. That was the sole reason behind their invasion."

He waited. No-one said anything.

"The available ancient texts are vague," he resumed, "and as much myth as anything we can remotely credit as fact. But the consensus among our researchers—and apparently among the Nazis as well—is that, centuries ago, Vikings encountered something . . . incredible. Perhaps it was what we would call supernatural. Perhaps it was something that fell from the stars. Whatever the case, it was deadly, and malevolent, and they brought it across the ocean and buried it . . . on Oak Island, off Nova Scotia."

Berton had heard of the legendary Oak Island treasure. A mysterious arrangement of traps and countertraps laid by persons unknown, which had, over more than a century, claimed the lives of many treasure hunters who had sought to uncover its secret. The common theory was that it was buried pirate gold, though no-one had quite explained why pirates would bury something so thoroughly that it seemed to defy all hope of ever unearthing it.

. . . Unless it was never meant to see the light of day again. Unless it was meant to keep something in as much as to keep others out.

"Half of you will head to Oak Island and attack the Nazi archaeological force there. The other half will come with me, on a slight detour."

"*You*?" said the Apparition. "But, professor, wouldn't you be better here, devoting your genius to—"

"To not dropping dead of a heart attack? No need to sugarcoat it, my dear. I know I am not ideal for combat. But there is no other way. This detour leads to another treasure the Nazis seek to uncover—secure in a largely impenetrable vault. I'm afraid I am the only one capable of leading this particular mission."

Behind him Stephenson looked unhappy, but resolved, implying all this had been decided already.

"Now, come—see what we've been up to, hmm?" the professor said, sounding for a moment like a giddy inventor, eager to show off his new project. The role of warrior was not one with which the old man seemed comfortable. With one hand on his cane and the other on Stephenson's arm, he turned and led them into the dark tunnel that had seen so much mysterious activity over the last few weeks.

The darkness closed about the eight figures. Gravel crunched beneath their feet, and gradually the slope of the land turned upward. They eventually rounded a corner and found themselves emerging into daylight. All stopped, collectively awed by the sight of a vessel unlike any other.

In his mind, Berton tried to find the words to describe it. But somehow saying it looked like a cross between a steam locomotive, a submarine, and an airship seemed inadequate. Accurate ... but inadequate, not correctly capturing the aesthetics of the thing: the trim lines; the keel plated with gold; the round porthole windows studded with great bolts which gave it an almost owl-like aspect, suggesting power and fierceness.

Yes, the professor—The Operator—was a man of vision, not a man of destruction. Yet even so, cannon-like protuberances jutted from its front, like horns from the brow of a primeval beast.

On its hull was painted its name: *The Isaac Brock*. The Oracle turned to Berton with satisfaction, "A proud name—a defender from the last time Canada was invaded."

"Didn't he die?" muttered The Northern Lama.

A gantry had already been lowered, ready for them. Stephenson caught Berton at the end of the procession filing up into the vessel. "I *have* to stay behind," he said, "because, frankly, there are other things I'm overseeing. And you, well, you have no obligation to go. You can write your story ... once the war is over, of course."

Berton looked at him, then up into the ship, then back again. "Every story needs a good ending."

Stephenson smiled, then nodded. "Good luck then, son."

Moving with an almost preternatural quiet, *The Isaac Brock* followed the coastline of the mainland for twenty minutes after secretly depositing Powerhouse, The Oracle, and The Northern Lama on Oak Island. Using one of the ship's many telescopes, Berton spotted a stately house on a cliffside overlooking the water. He zoomed in on the site. The property around the house was heavy with jeeps and uniformed soldiers, as well as men in plain clothes—Gestapo, most likely.

"Next stop . . . Beinn Bhreagh," muttered Berton to the old man.

An approving smile creased the professor's wrinkled lips, and he nodded in salute.

As soft as a baby's breath, the vessel landed behind some trees. The old man unstrapped himself and rose unsteadily.

"It looks so beautiful, so peaceful," Berton said, staring out the front window at the pastoral landscape.

Grey Owl stood beside him. "In Europe, there are forests that have been turned black with industrial soot," he said grimly. "Moths have changed the colour of their skins in order to match these new, stained hues."

Berton studied the tall man. Was that Grey Owl's motivation in fighting the fascists? The world's most famous conservationist was less concerned about politics and ideologies than he was about saving his beloved forests from the industrialized cancer already eating away at lands an ocean away. Berton realized they each had their own individual concerns in this war, their own motives. And who was he to say whose was the noblest?

The professor addressed the group. "Grey Owl and I will infiltrate the house. Rather, he will, and I'll follow his lead. Apparition will provide needed distraction. If something goes wrong, Berton, these buttons activate the sonic cannons—non-lethal, but they should get the enemy running."

Berton nodded grimly. It was difficult to stay behind, but he knew his limitations; he was a watcher, not a doer. And so he watched, with a prayer on his lips, as the Apparition descended the gantry, followed by Grey Owl and then the old man. All that was left for Berton to do was wait.

It did not take long.

Within minutes he heard shouting in German, then in heavily accented English—a call to halt. Using the various optical devices and telescopes at his disposal, Berton observed German soldiers running back and forth in the night after a succession of young, eerily pale girls who laughed silently and waved coquettishly, then ran away.

Berton next caught a glimpse of a shadow flittering from bush to jeep to tree. A feathered arrow clove the night and sent a lone remaining sentry pitching over. Hobbling through the darkness, the old professor followed in Grey Owl's wake, and the two disappeared into the big house.

After five minutes which felt like five hours to Berton, the pair re-emerged, the old man carrying something bulky in his arms. They were almost halfway back to the vessel when a clattering behind him caused Berton to spin around. It was the Apparition mounting the gantry, panting hard. "Jerry's figured out my girls are just projections. The soldiers are returning to the house. Are they back yet?"

Berton spun back toward the window as shots were fired. The old man and Grey Owl were running across the moonlit grass, German soldiers converging upon them. Grey Owl stumbled and went down, a bullet in his leg. The old man stopped, but Grey Owl waved him to go on. Berton flipped the switches The Operator had shown him and fired the sonic cannon. It made no audible sound, but every blast made his hair tingle and his teeth ache. Outside, the German soldiers in the cannon's path were thrown from their feet. But the old man was between the cannon and another clutch of soldiers. Grey Owl rose unsteadily and fired off a quick succession of arrows, and one after another the oncoming soldiers fell.

Then came a single shot, and the Indian collapsed.

The Apparition sobbed. The old man clambered up the gantry, his face unhealthily pale and sheen with sweat. "Go," he said hoarsely. "Go!" Berton, who had studied the old man piloting the controls all the way here, took the ship up into the air. They banked away, the sky behind them lighting up as the house on the hill exploded.

"What?" the Apparition exclaimed.

"I destroyed the rest of my workshop," said the old man. "The Nazis hadn't broken in, but they were close. And there were things that were too dangerous for them to get their hands on. Too dangerous ... for anyone." He glanced at the bulky object he had dropped by the entrance.

"... *Your* workshop?" she said.

Berton nodded, his suspicions confirmed. "Mary Pickford ... meet Alexander Graham Bell."

❦

"My experiments were becoming too ... problematic," Bell explained, seated once more in the pilot's seat. "There were potential dangers. I wanted—I *needed*—to pursue my research, but I couldn't continue in the public eye, or run the risk that untested devices might fall into improper hands. So with the aid of the Canadian government the fiction of my death was established. I have continued my studies and experiments untroubled for some two decades."

"At Beinn Bhreagh?" asked Berton, surprised.

"Why not? No-one suspected I was still alive, so no-one was looking for me—even at my own home. Once, when some nosy tourists came about, I even passed myself off as an actor hired to play myself—they told me I was not very convincing." He chuckled, but then grew quiet, his whimsy short-lived given the grim circumstances. "Even the Nazis didn't guess I still lived, but they did suspect my vault contained experiments and apparatus of value to them. Fortunately, it was securely sealed— another of my inventions. Though they would have found a way in, given sufficient time."

"And that?" Berton asked, nodding at the object by the door—the object that had cost Grey Owl his life.

"Something I experimented with in the last few years, based on new discoveries in the field of the radium sciences—an atomic explosive. It's a small prototype, but in theory a full-sized version could potentially destroy a city."

The Apparition said, "I've never heard of such a thing."

"God willing," said Bell, "you never will again."

They did not need to ask how the others were faring. As they approached Oak Island low across the water, they could hear the rattle of gunfire and see flashes of explosions.

Bell brought them down on the beach, but this time he did not unstrap himself. "You two, get the others—they've done all they can to slow the Germans. Tell them to fall back."

"Here—to the beach? You'll pick us up?" asked Berton.

Bell looked at him oddly, then smiled. "Yes—yes, that's the plan."

Berton and the Apparition jumped to the ground and raced into the woods toward the noise of the fighting. Suddenly there was a thunderous cracking sound. Berton futilely threw up his hands as a huge tree teetered as though about to pitch over. Then, impossibly, it seemed to hoist itself up a few feet into the air. Berton spotted Powerhouse at the base of the tree and watched as the strongman heaved it at a tank coming up over a hill.

A Nazi soldier erupted from the brush mere paces from Berton, machine gun poised. A white-garbed figure emerged spectrally through a tree and sent the Nazi down with a karate chop to the back of his neck. The Northern Lama solidified beside them. "The Oracle said you were here."

"How did he. . . ." Berton stopped, realizing he already knew the answer: informed by Mackenzie King's mother, of course.

The Northern Lama looked around. "Where's Grey Owl?"

"He didn't make it."

The masked man went pale, as though he had been shot himself. "Bastards," he growled, balling his fists. "Damn fascist bastards!"

It occurred to Berton that The Northern Lama had been fighting a seemingly never-ending chain of fascists since before most of them had even heard the term—first in Spain, then China, now here. With a very un-Lama-like roar, the man turned and raced back toward the enemy.

"Norman!" shouted Berton, but he was unheard—or ignored.

Powerhouse and The Oracle arrived at almost the same time. "The excavation pit!" panted Powerhouse. "There was something . . . *something* glowing inside it!"

"Come on," said The Oracle. "Mother says we've got to get behind some rock."

"Right. . . ." said Berton, still staring after the vanished Northern Lama. "The professor's waiting for us by the beach."

"No—he isn't!" shouted the Apparition, pointing up.

They all looked up just as *The Isaac Brock* flew soundlessly overhead like a great metal owl, heading in the direction of the excavation and the rest of the German troops.

"No!" shouted Berton, but it was useless. He found himself being ushered along by the unstoppable might of Powerhouse. The four of them went tumbling over a ridge, down into a gully.

"Oh," said The Oracle, "and Mother says 'close your eyes'!"

Berton did so almost instinctively, just as the night sky turned to day—it was so bright he could see it through his eyelids. The roar was the roar of the heavens being torn asunder. And underneath it, he could almost swear he heard a scream—the great, primordial dying scream of something malevolent and unspeakably ancient.

Much has been written and speculated about the East Coast Front over the years, from the identities of many of the participants to the precise nature of what occurred on Oak Island—most of it unproven and pure conjecture. What is known is that the German occupation was dealt a severe blow on the night of April 4th, 1941, with key commanders lost in the explosions at both sites. When Canadian troops poured into Nova Scotia two days later they found the opposition disorganized, and the province was retaken within days. Within a year, the bombing of Pearl Harbour dragged a reluctant United States into the war. Though most American historians tend to dismiss the potential danger a Nazi-occupied Canada might have represented for the United States had the Germans maintained such a foothold in North America, in Canada the liberation of Nova Scotia is generally regarded as a major turning point in the war.

—Unused voiceover script for the documentary
The Secret History of the Intrepids
(1981, National Film Board of Canada)

D.K. LATTA lives in Southern Ontario but at various times has had kin sprinkled literally from coast to coast and up into the Northwest Territories.

The Man in the Mask

EMMA FARADAY

Violet stood at the prow of the airship, which floated a hundred feet above the tallest spruce tree, and looked out at the Klondike River Valley and the mountains flanking it. As far as she could see, the world was forest, snow, and frozen river. Not a house to be seen, or a bank, or a blasted factory.

Uncle George would have a fit if he could see her now.

He had objected to her journey to the Yukon, refusing to give his blessing to her fulfillment of Felicity's last wish. Violet had fully expected to see an A'lle finder on her trail long before now. She had watched carefully, but once she left Upper Canada, she'd scarcely seen any of the strange beings. Nor had she seen any A'lle in Dawson City.

For the first time since Mama and Papa died, the sense of loss lifted somewhat and she felt free. Almost at peace. Even the air, cold as it was, smelled fresh, untainted by coal or oil.

With the beaver hat covering her forehead and ears, goggles covering her eyes, and the cashmere scarf attempting to keep her nose, cheeks, and chin warm, she might yet make it to the dredge without freezing to death. Some back home would frown to see the serviceable fur cap replace her black felt mourning hat with its veil and fashionable feathers, and they'd be positively aghast to know she wore woolen trousers beneath her full skirt. She had, however, kept the corset.

"Miss Stanhope!" Captain Frankel stood in the doorway of the so-called passenger lounge and stared at her. "Miss Stanhope, what are you doing out here? Come inside!"

She wanted to assure him that though she was from York she was not afraid of a little fresh air. Or, in this case, a great deal of fresh air. "I will, Captain. In a moment. You must allow me this." She waved a hand at the river valley, which spread out like a roll of rich green velvet on a bed of white satin. "For you, this sight is commonplace, but I have never seen anything half so grand."

The captain hesitated in the doorway, hatless, gloveless, and clearly cold. Only a sheepskin coat allowed him to brave the outdoors. "I am responsible for your safety," he said at last.

She smiled at him. "I promise I will not fall overboard. I would not like to crash, however."

His stubbled face grew ruddy. "Crash?"

She waved her fur muff at the enormous bag above them. "You are not piloting," she pointed out gravely. "I must assume that this is not a good thing."

He grinned at her, and in the grin she glimpsed the man she had met last night at the Dawson City airfield. "The *Eldorado* is as fine a ship as ever sailed the sky, for all that she looks rough. She'll stay aloft for many hours, as long as there's a flame to heat her." He looked up at the taut grey fabric above their heads. "Mind you come in soon," he said, and retreated back inside.

Violet smiled and turned back to the extraordinary view. Yesterday, at the Dawson airfield, she had stared doubtfully at the rusted metal framework and the stained sides of the ship, uncertain of his claim. The *Eldorado* was a tiny ship, with only Captain Frankel as pilot, mate, and stevedore. According to the hotel clerk, very few miners remained in Dawson City in winter and she was lucky to find even one airship still taking supplies to the far-flung mining claims.

A movement far below caught her eye. Was that a horse crossing the frozen river? No, its shape was odd, and its movements ungainly. And what was that on its head? Antlers?

She caught her breath. A moose!

She watched the creature pick its way across the river and found herself smiling with delight yet again. Then her joy dimmed. Felicity should be here, sharing this amazing sight, searching for a first glimpse of the mining dredge.

Violet's hand stole to her bosom, but between her heavy black great coat and the sheepskin gloves she had bought for the trip it was impossible to feel the bump of her sister's locket beneath her dress.

A sharp sound suddenly rent the stillness, filling the valley and startling her so badly that she clutched at the railing. As the echoes reverberated between the snow-clad mountains, she looked up. For a moment, the airship hung suspended, as though shocked by the noise. Then its airbag quivered as air began to rush out through a gash in the thick grey fabric.

Violet gasped and clung more tightly to the deck railing as the airship slowly tilted toward the ice-locked river below. Spruce trees reached up greedily, ready to impale the ship on spindly black fingers. Behind her protective goggles, she squeezed her eyes shut. The airship would crash in the forest, or, if they were very lucky, on the frozen river.

Then she remembered the satchel and opened her eyes.

Surely it would be too ironic, even for God, to allow her to travel all the way from York to this glorious land only to crash almost within sight of her goal. The thought of losing Felicity's ashes mere miles from their final destination snapped her out of her paralysis. Leaning against the tilt of the deck, she used the railing to haul herself toward the door. Far above, the sound of air rushing out competed with the whistling of the wind through the railings as the airship plunged faster and faster. The escaping air smelled faintly stale and old, and she glanced up only to bite her lip against a scream. The flame that heated the air in the bag and kept the ship afloat was exposed. Should the flame touch the sagging airbag, it would catch on fire.

Where was the captain? Was he trapped?

Her gaze caught on a movement on the frozen river below just as she reached the door. She looked down, expecting to see the moose, but saw instead a streak of gold crest the riverbank and disappear into the trees.

Violet tried to make sense of what she had seen, but there was no time. She had left her satchel inside the lounge rather than risk it on the open deck. She fumbled at the door handle with hands made clumsy by sheepskin gloves until at last the door fell open.

She fought her way inside against the pull of gravity. Smoke was beginning to fill the cramped room, and she peered through the goggles, trying to see.

"Captain!" she called, and immediately coughed as she breathed in smoke. Placing a hand over her mouth and nose, she looked around. The lounge was in reality a cargo hold with two hard wooden chairs bolted to the floor next to a series of small windows on the port side. In the centre of the hold, protected by a cage of metal strips with a gate, was a series of gears, pulleys, and levers: the machinery that made the airship run. It ran straight up through a hole in the ceiling and connected to the framework surrounding the airbag.

Beyond the machinery, at the stern of the ship, was the narrow staircase leading to the upper deck and the pilothouse. The clanking and grinding of the pulleys was usually overwhelming, but now the gears and pulleys were silent and still, and Violet could hear only the roaring of the flame far above her head.

Her heart hammered against her ribs, and she breathed in the acrid smoke and coughed again. Were they going to die here, alone in this wilderness?

Protected behind the goggles, her eyes remained open. She wanted nothing more than to get out of this room that might become her sarcophagus. The first tendrils of panic wrapped themselves around her and her breathing quickened, as did her coughing.

The ship lurched, toppling her off balance. She landed on one hip and slid down the rough, oil-stained wooden planks of the decking, her heavy woolen skirt catching on slivers. Scrabbling for purchase, she managed to catch hold of a strut to stop her descent. She *refused* to die here. Not after coming so far. She would *not* give Uncle George the satisfaction.

"Captain!" she called above the thin, dangerous whistling of the wind. She peered around the greasy gear array and saw the satchel on its side on the floor, prevented from sliding by one of the chair legs. It was only ten feet away.

She used the struts for leverage and crawled up to the first chair. Then she hooked an arm around one of the bolted legs and pulled herself to the second chair. Just as her hand closed on the satchel's handle, the ship gave another lurch, ripping her free from the chair. She tumbled the rest of the way to the far wall and slammed head and shoulder against the unforgiving strut.

Hold on to the satchel!

Pain filled her head. A noise like the end of the world swallowed her cries as the *Eldorado* crashed into the trees, sending her flying through the air to land against the metal cage.

Just before consciousness fled, she heard the sound of fabric catching fire.

When Violet opened her eyes, it took a moment to realize she was seeing footprints in snow and the back of the pair of laced hide boots making them. The shoulder pressing into her middle made breathing a struggle. Talking was out of the question. She glanced up as the roaring sound suddenly registered.

The airship was on fire!

"Stop!" she called, or tried to call. The sound came out as a wheeze. She slapped the back of the legs rising from the tall laced boots of whoever was carrying her, and the legs immediately stopped. She was flipped upright and dropped unceremoniously on top of something hard. She scrambled up, her head spinning, and reached for whatever she had landed on to steady herself.

It was a sled, perhaps ten feet long and low to the ground, with a waist-high hand hold to which she now clung. It was piled with canvas-covered boxes, and her satchel rested on top, its leather dried and blackened, but still safe. When she glanced at the other end of the sled, she momentarily forgot all about Felicity's ashes.

"Oh!" Seven golden creatures sat in the melting snow, staring blankly. They flickered with the light from the fire, which gave them a semblance of life. Violet backed away, but none of the beastly shapes moved.

She turned and gasped at her first clear view of the wreck. Flames shot high above the forest, devouring the *Eldorado*'s thick fabric, which sagged between the metal struts, drooping over the deck and snagging on the jagged ends of trees snapped in the crash. In moments, the fire would reach the last of the fabric, trapping the captain inside.

Almost tripping in the deep snow, she took a step toward the burning airship, but a hand on her shoulder stopped her. She whirled. A man stood before her. His face . . . it was ruddy and moved strangely. . . . No; he wore a golden mask that reflected the hungry flames.

She moved away from his hand. "The captain!" she said, raising her voice to be heard above the roaring of the fire. "He is trapped!"

With a terrible sound, the metal framework crashed to the deck, engulfing in flames and debris the erstwhile passenger lounge and the pilothouse above it.

"Oh, no!" cried Violet. She must have made a move, for he clamped a hand on her forearm to stop her.

The heat of the fire beat on her back, and the flames crackled as they devoured the remains of the ship. A smell half foul, half comforting reached her as the fire consumed metal and grease and the tops of nearby spruce trees. She turned to study the stranger. Granted, she was not a big woman at five foot two and a hundred pounds, but he towered above her by well over a foot, and the breadth of him intimidated. He wore a hood rimmed with a thick, dark fur that only added to his fearsomeness. Strangest of all was the golden mask, which left only his mouth and chin uncovered. It seemed to be made of the same material as the unnaturally still creatures waiting at the sled.

Through the narrow slit in the mask it was impossible to tell the colour of his eyes. What was wrong with his face, that it needed such an outlandish covering?

"There is no-one left inside. I made certain before pulling you out," said the masked man with a strong accent Violet could not place. "I did however see a man in a sheepskin coat jump from the airship with a parachute. Upon landing, he used a rifle to shoot a hole in the bag." He turned slightly to look at the burning ship. "It would seem, madam, that he meant to kill you."

Why would Captain Frankel want to kill her?

For the first time, Violet realized that the stranger's hands were bare and that his coat was open. A loud crack startled her: the fire dying down as it began to run out of fuel.

"We must leave this place now. In case he comes looking for you," said the man.

"You must be mistaken, Mr.. . . . . I'm sorry. My name is Violet Stanhope." She removed her glove and put her hand out.

The stranger hesitated, then shook her hand. His was large, callused, and, to her surprise, very warm. "Simon . . . Croix."

She noticed the hesitation but said nothing. Felicity used to read aloud from the letters Alvin, her betrothed, sent from the Klondike, in which he described some of the rough characters he encountered. It seemed that most of them were running from their pasts as much as they were seeking gold.

"Thank you for saving my life," she said. "But . . . why would the captain want to kill me?" And destroy his airship in the process? Not to mention leaping off into the middle of the wilderness in the frightful cold. It made no sense.

"I do not know, Miss Stanhope." The golden mask tilted down to her. "I know only what I saw. Perhaps he wants your satchel?" He nodded at the satchel on top of the sled.

This man might be a ruffian, after all, who thought she carried valuables. But he had saved her life. If he had wished her ill, he could have left her on the airship to die. Now that she'd had time to recover, she recognized she *had* heard something that sounded like a rifle shot just before the ship began to fail.

Violet shuddered at the thought of the death she had averted and drew the satchel close to her. "No," she said. "He would have taken the satchel before leaving the ship. The satchel contains my sister's ashes, and the captain knew it." She was surprised that grief could still close her throat, even a month after Felicity's death. "Her last wish was to have her ashes scattered over the dredge where her betrothed died."

The man stared down at her, so still that she began to worry. Finally he said, "Which dredge?"

"The *Rosario*." He seemed to have forgotten all about getting away from the crash. The airship had travelled a fair distance between the rifle shot and the crash. Even if the captain were determined to harm her, it would take him some time to reach the site on foot. She continued, "We were very close to the dredge, apparently."

"Yes." He turned his head. The light of the dying fire played on the side of his mask, revealing the fine filigree work etched in the gold.

Violet waited a moment more; when he said nothing further, she made her decision. "Mr. Croix." She laid a hand on his arm and was startled when he jumped. "Would your . . ." she glanced at the strange doglike figures standing still at the head of the sled ". . . conveyance be adequate to return me to town? I could pay you for your troubles, of course." That is, once she sold the factory and freed herself from Uncle George's meddling in her affairs.

As though shaking himself out of a stupor, he nodded and went to the tarp-covered boxes on the sled. "No need for payment." He worked at untying the knots in the rope that lashed the tarp tightly. His hood had fallen back to reveal thick black hair in dire need of a trim. "I was on my way to Dawson when I saw the crash. It will take several hours, but we will get there before nightfall."

"You live nearby, then?"

"Not far."

"Your dogs. . . ." She glanced at the golden creatures. She had seen them going up the bank moments after the shot rang out. She knew they could move quickly, though at the moment they resembled golden statues in a Chinese emperor's palace. "Did you build them?"

"I did," he said, and she sighed softly when he did not elaborate.

The *Eldorado* had left at first light, which meant that it could be no later than ten o'clock. Her gaze strayed to the south, in the direction of the dredge, as her hands tightened on the satchel. To be so close. . . .

Mr. Croix continued to rearrange crates and boxes, eventually removing a few from the sled to make room for her. The boxes must be very light, as they almost seemed to levitate out of the sled into his hands.

"You will be cold," he warned her as he worked. "I did not bring furs."

"No matter," she said. She had her hat, though she would miss her goggles, lost somewhere, probably when she was knocked out. For the first time, she realized she had lost her muff as well, and it was only after a moment that she found it hanging from its string at her back. She pulled it forward and gratefully slipped her gloved hands inside. "Mr. Croix, would it be a terrible imposition to ask that you take me to the *Rosario* first?" She held her breath while he stopped what he was doing and straightened, keeping his back to her.

"I realize I have no right, and you are being so kind to come to my rescue," she continued in a rush. "But I've come all the way from York. Eight days on a train and then to arrive in

Dawson to find only one airship available and willing to take me. . . . And now that one is destroyed and I must leave on tomorrow's train and I don't know when I'll have a chance to return here and honour my sister's wishes. . . ."

She trailed off when he turned to look at her. They stared at each other for a long time. Finally he said, "Why did you come now, Miss Stanhope? Why not wait until summer when travelling here would be much easier and safer?"

Violet studied the mask and controlled an urge to peel it off his face. She wanted to see with whom she was speaking. But that would be rude beyond measure.

A feeling of utter loneliness threatened to overwhelm her. First her parents six months ago in a car crash, and then Felicity. She had come now because she feared she would be unable to if she waited. She had access to Felicity's accounts for the moment, but Uncle George was fighting her for the right to the glass factory, since Felicity had died without a will. If Violet lost in court, she would be at the mercy of Uncle George's questionable generosity.

"I had very little choice in the timing," she said.

He looked down at her. "It is not safe. I should return you to town. There is a contingent of Northwesters stationed there. They can protect you."

"Of . . . of course," she said at last. "I see no reason why a man I met only yesterday, a seasoned airship captain, would want to harm me, but I will not impose any more than I already have, except perhaps to mention that the captain is on foot, while we have a sled with mechanical dogs."

The motion of the mechanical dogs was almost hypnotic. Each one moved in harmony with its mate, as though they were one. The golden plates that comprised their bodies slid over each other smoothly, allowing the bodies to stretch and contract. Their haunches bunched as in real dogs and only careful scrutiny assured her that the "muscles" were in truth overlapping miniature plates. How Mr. Croix guided the dogs, she could not say, for he stood on the skis that protruded behind the sled and, as far as she could tell, spoke not a word to the mechanical wonders.

Tree shadows dappled the dogs' golden surfaces as they found narrow passages on virgin snow between the black spruce and aspen.

Violet pulled up her cashmere scarf to cover her nose and cheeks, but still the narrow band between scarf and hat grew numb with cold as she huddled under the tarp. And yet, Mr. Croix's coat remained unbuttoned and his head uncovered.

The dogs suddenly plunged down an embankment, and Violet grabbed the sled's sides in sudden fright.

Then they were in the open, on a snow-covered, frozen river. The mechanical dogs stretched out, their golden paws a blur against the pristine white. Only the shushing of the sled's skis could be heard above the thin whistling of the wind in her ears. Beneath her scarf, Violet's mouth was parted in wonder; before she could stop it, a delighted laugh escaped her.

This was not the river the airship captain had been following; it was much narrower. The mechanical dogs slowed as they reached a bend in the river. Once they were past the bend, the dogs came to a complete standstill. For a moment, the world was filled with utter silence as she and Mr. Croix stared up at the carcass of the dredge looming over their heads.

It had once been a massive construct, perhaps three stories tall, judging by the charred metal structure that jutted into the sky. It was easily as long as three tram cars and as wide as a Pacific National passenger car. Or it had been. All that remained was a blackened hulk frozen into the river, with only the bow and stern untouched by flames.

She struggled with the tarp, and Mr. Croix hurried around to free her from its folds. She gratefully accepted his hand and allowed him to pull her up. Really, there was no graceful way to emerge from one of these things.

She approached the derelict slowly, her feet plunging through deep snow. She was immensely grateful for the sheepskin-lined boots the hotel clerk had insisted she borrow.

This, then, was where Alvin McAvity had perished.

Violet barely remembered Alvin. For her, he was a memory of kindness and jocularity. She was eight when he left to find his fortune in the Klondike, with a promise to return within the year and wed Felicity, who was eighteen at the time.

The first inkling they'd had that something was wrong was when Alvin's letters stopped coming. At last Father sent a telegram to the Royal Northwest Mounted Police in Dawson

City and learned that Alvin had been killed in an explosion on the dredge. The news had devastated Felicity. For a year they feared she would die of grief, but at last she rallied. She never looked at another man and devoted herself to helping Father run his business.

Then, six months ago, Uncle George, Father's brother, had returned from India barely ahead of his debtors, weeks before Father and Mother died in the automobile accident, leaving Felicity in charge of the factory. Violet had wanted to help, but Uncle George had insisted that she finish her studies.

And now Felicity was gone, too, after a long illness that had baffled her doctors.

"Did you wish to go aboard?" asked Mr. Croix, startling her. He had come up behind her.

"No." She turned from the derelict, intending to retrieve the satchel, but Mr. Croix had brought it with him. He handed it to her silently.

She smiled her thanks. All at once, the unreality of her position caught up with her. What was she doing here, five thousand miles from home, on a nameless frozen river in the Klondike, with a man who wore a golden mask and drove a sled outfitted with golden dogs?

He pointed to the riverbank against which the derelict sagged. "If you go up there, you will be close enough to honour your sister's wishes without risking your own life."

She studied the bank, and saw that his suggestion would work. She took a deep breath and immediately regretted it as the frigid air seared her nostrils. The sooner she did this, the sooner she could leave this place.

Mr. Croix held out his hand, and she took it. Holding on to the satchel and her skirts with her other hand, she allowed him to lead the way to an opening in the trees where the dredge butted up to the riverbank. He took short steps, and though she tried to walk in his footprints, more often than not she ended up with snow in her boots. By the time she stood on the bank, she was breathing hard and her feet were thoroughly chilled, while the rest of her was warm from exertion.

The wreck rose above the bank, black against the achingly blue sky beyond it. To her surprise, there was no smell at all emanating from it. Ten years of wind, rain, and ice had scoured away the scents of charring and death.

She frowned. There was a hole in the upper structure, as if a giant had tossed a huge stone at the dredge.

"What caused the fire?" she asked slowly, staring at the hole. She looked closer. Whatever had caused the damage had not come from outside. It looked as if something *inside* the dredge had exploded.

Next to her, Mr. Croix remained silent, staring at the hole, too.

"We cannot linger," he said at last. "Do what you came to do, then we must be on our way."

Something about his tone worried her. She immediately set the satchel down in the snow and opened it. She pulled the etched brass container out and unwrapped Felicity's favourite scarf from around it. The urn was dented but otherwise unharmed. Ten years, Felicity had waited to join Alvin.

With a small shake of her head, she unscrewed the heavy cap and without hesitating tossed her sister's ashes into the air.

They hung there for a moment, then the wind caught them and swirled them toward the dredge, Alvin's final resting place.

Goodbye, she thought. The tears caught her by surprise. She hadn't thought she had any left to shed. She quickly blinked them away as they began to freeze to her eyelashes.

"How did your sister die?" asked Mr. Croix suddenly.

Violet looked up at him in surprise. "She was ill for a long time. The doctors could not tell what it was."

His head lowered slightly, as if he were in thought. Then he raised his bare right hand, palm out. At once, the ashes began to swirl together like a miniature tornado, hovering before the hole in the dredge.

Violet gasped, then clamped a hand over her mouth to keep from screaming when the tornado shaped into a ball, still hovering unnaturally.

"Felicity!" she cried, her voice choked with horror. She turned to Mr. Croix, ready to set upon him with her fists to make him stop whatever he was doing to her sister's ashes.

A shot rang out and a bullet struck the tree next to her.

The ball of ashes dispersed as Mr. Croix leapt on Violet, knocking her to the snow.

"Stay down!" he ordered fiercely. Not waiting for her response, he sprang back up and disappeared, crouching into the trees as more shots rang out. Violet risked raising her head slightly to look around. Though at first she didn't see anything, she caught a movement out of the corner of her eye and looked more closely. Two men stood at the foot of the bank, less than twenty feet away, their attention trained on the spot where Mr. Croix had disappeared. One of them, bearded and tall, was a stranger to her, but the other man was Captain Frankel.

She must have made a sound because they both turned, their rifles raised and aimed directly at her.

Mr. Croix was right, she had time to think, before the rifles rose straight up in the air and out of their clutches, as if pulled by invisible strings. Captain Frankel and his accomplice stared open mouthed as the rifles travelled unaided through the air and into the trees overhanging the bank.

A moment later, Mr. Croix emerged from the trees, training a rifle on the two men.

"Who the hell are you?" demanded the stranger. "How—?"

"Be quiet," ordered Mr. Croix. "Miss Stanhope?"

She stood and brushed the snow from her coat. "I am well," she lied. Her hands trembled, though she could not tell if it was from anger, or from shock at what she had just seen.

"Please make your way down to the sled."

"Of course," she said, annoyed at the quaver in her voice. She clambered down the bank, less than ten feet from the two men, who stood as if frozen into the river ice, their hands in the air.

As she came abreast of the captain, she stopped. "Why?" she asked, her voice carrying on the cold air.

The captain's gaze dropped at her question, and he shook his head. She thought he was refusing to answer, but then she saw the sidelong glance he gave to his companion. The bearded man, unlike the captain, looked her in the eye. There was a coldness about him that had nothing to do with the temperature.

Anger suddenly filled Violet with strength. "I asked you why," she said deliberately. "Why try to kill me? Until yesterday, we had never met."

The captain raised his head, his look full of misery. "I had no choice," he began. "He—"

In a whirl of movement, the bearded man smashed his fist against the captain's temple. Captain Frankel's neck snapped audibly. Then the bearded man stepped back and raised his hands again as Captain Frankel's body slowly slumped to the snow, his unseeing eyes staring at nothing.

Her pulse throbbing in her ears, Violet looked up at the bearded man. There was no mistaking the amusement in his eyes. For a moment, she feared she would be sick.

A shot rang out, and the man ducked.

"Get down," said Mr. Croix. She could not see him from her vantage point but apparently the stranger could, for his gaze lifted to the trees above the bank. "I do not wish to kill you," came Mr. Croix's calm voice, "but I will shoot you in the leg if I must."

Without a word, the man sank to his knees in the snow.

"All the way," said Mr. Croix. "Keep your hands over your head."

Reluctantly, the man lay down full length in the snow and laced his fingers over his head. He must have removed his gloves to shoot, she thought. His body sank into the snow a few inches and she wondered if he would be able to breathe.

"Miss Stanhope," said Mr. Croix. He emerged from the shelter of the trees to stand on the bank, one rifle slung across his back, the other pointing at the stranger's back. "Please make your way to the sled."

She swallowed hard and nodded. When she realized that she was nodding too much, she stopped. She gave the murderer and Captain Frankel's corpse a wide berth and made her way to the sled. She sat in the little nest Mr. Croix had made for her and waited.

Mr. Croix scrambled down the bank. He handed her one of the rifles, and she trained it on the prone figure in the snow. The man didn't move.

Mr. Croix lifted a hand, gave it a slight twist, and the mechanical dogs padded in a circle, until they faced back the way they had come. After a moment, the dogs set off running.

Minutes later, they came across a team of huskies left unattended on the ice by the shoreline. The attempt on her life had been well planned: the captain had parachuted off the airship and shot the balloon, his accomplice waiting for him in the woods with a sled. The crash was meant to kill her, and if not the crash then the cold. When her pursuers arrived on site and realized she had been rescued, all they had to do was follow the tracks.

Mr. Croix stopped his team as the dogs from the other sled barked wildly, jerking at their harnesses. They were beautiful creatures, much smaller than she would have expected, had she ever given it any thought. There were eleven of them, almost all with ice-blue eyes and grey and white coats. Their frantic barking and jerking slowed and ceased as Mr. Croix approached. They allowed him to remove their harnesses, during which time Violet stood by, keeping watch on their trail and the riverbank, rifle at the ready. She hoped she would not have to use it.

As each dog was freed, it promptly sat on the frozen river to watch Mr. Croix's movements. He proceeded in eerie silence, with Violet and the dogs watching him, until the last dog was unharnessed.

He clapped his hands sharply together. "Go!"

As though his command freed them, they rose and bounded up the bank and into the dark Yukon forest without a sound. Mr. Croix turned to Violet. The sun glinted off his mask and the slits for his eyes revealed nothing but blackness.

Violet pointed the rifle at the ground. "Mr. Croix," she said, "I owe you my life; I will never be able to repay you for that. But. . . ." She forced herself to slow down. "But I must know: how did you draw the rifles out of their hands?" She waved in the direction of the sled with its golden dogs. "How do you command the mechanical dogs?

He glanced over his shoulder, as if to see if anyone were within earshot, but the river was empty of all save snow and ice bracketed by thousands of miles of forest.

"I am sensitive to metals," he said.

Sensitive? What was that supposed to mean?

"And Felicity's ashes?" she took a step closer. "Are you sensitive to ashes, as well?"

His chest rose under the heavy coat and his breath expelled slowly, creating vapour in front of him. He shook his head.

"No, Miss Stanhope. Only metal."

Violet's mind went momentarily blank.

All at once, the precariousness of her situation struck her. She was a continent away from her home in York, hours from the nearest Northwester, alone in a frozen wilderness with a man who wore a golden mask, built golden dogs, and could command metal to do his bidding.

He remained still, allowing her to work it out for herself.

"Mr. Croix," she said gently, "I would consider it a great courtesy if you were to remove your mask."

They stared at each other as long seconds ticked by. A wind sprang up, swirling the snow about her skirts, and still they stared at each other. Her hands were so cold that she could barely feel them, yet he stood before her, hatless and gloveless.

At last he raised his hands to his face. When they came away, the mask came with them.

Violet stared at him and felt even colder. She should have known. His incredible endurance to the cold should have told her.

"You are A'lle," she said through numb lips. "You were sent to find me." She expected the rifle to fly out of her hands but it remained still, pointing down.

Mr. Croix blinked furiously against the dazzling light. Like all A'lle, his eyes were unnaturally large, the iris almost filling the eye. Unlike any A'lle she had ever seen or heard of, however, his eyes were green, not blue. A beautiful green somewhere between grass and moss, mixed with cream. But like all A'lle, his hair was so black it looked almost blue in the dazzling sunlight.

When the blinking finally slowed, he moved toward her, his gaze fixed on her face. She raised the rifle but still did not point it at him. He had saved her life.

Twice.

"You have seen others like me?" There was a note of incredulity in his voice.

"Of course I have seen others like you. Or almost like you." She frowned. None of this made sense. "Why do you ask? We both know my uncle sent you to find me."

The confusion on his face did more to convince her that she was wrong than his words. "I do not know your uncle," he said gravely.

They stared at each other in silence. Like all the A'lle, he was very attractive, if strange looking.

"Please," he said intently, "where have you seen others like me?"

Violet lowered the rifle. "There are many A'lle in York. Our factory employs several. Though their eyes are blue. I've been told that there are even more in Lower Canada. Why is your last name Croix?" she asked. "Every A'lle is named after the ship that brought them here."

"A'lle," he said softly. "A'lle." An expression like grief swept over his face. She could not tell his age, but suspected he was at least ten years older than she was. Perhaps more.

"Croix is the last name of the man who rescued me," he said. "He was a miner. A hermit."

"Rescued you from what?" She was confused. Why did he seem so alarmed? Or perhaps that wasn't alarm. It was hard to tell.

He laughed, but not from amusement. "You asked what caused the hole in the dredge," he said. "It was me. I came here to learn if the . . . A'lle ship had found safe harbour on this planet, but something went wrong and I lost control of my own craft."

Violet forgot her frozen cheeks and hands, forgot to worry about frostbite.

"In all of this vast wilderness, you happened to crash into the dredge and kill Alvin?" It beggared belief. And then she remembered the metal curling away from the opening. "But wait. . . . The hole. . . . It wasn't made in a crash—something inside exploded and caused that damage."

Now the grief was clear on his face. He nodded.

"I could barely control my entry into the atmosphere and was going much too fast. I had time to see the town and the river, and aim for the river. I saw the dredge and tried to steer away from it, but the pull of metal within the dredge was so powerful that I drew it all to me. It surged out of the dredge, causing the damage you saw and starting a fire. The ore wrapped around my shuttle, and I dropped into the river."

He looked up at the top of the trees, as if he could see the shuttle there. "There was still snow on the ground, or the forest might have caught on fire. Mr. Croix found me, found the shuttle sinking in the river. He managed to get it open and pull me out. I was unconscious. He took me to his cabin and told me what had happened. The townspeople believed a meteor had struck the dredge."

Violet remembered her scarf and pulled it up to cover her nose and cheeks. Immediately the skin of her cheeks began to burn.

"We must leave now," said Mr. Croix—or should she call him A'lle?

"Why the mask?" she asked.

He stepped through the snow until he reached her side, then took her elbow to help her back to the sled. As he tucked the tarp around her, he explained.

"Mr. Croix had never seen anyone like me. He had never heard of the . . . A'lle, as you call them. He feared for my life should anyone see me."

Violet shook her head. "And you have been living in hiding for ten years?"

He nodded. "Mr. Croix would go into town and buy what I needed for my projects." He nodded at the mechanical dogs. "But he died a few weeks ago and I decided it was time for me to go, as well."

"I see why you wanted a mask, but why gold? Why not choose a less conspicuous material? And a team of golden dogs? You will cause a riot when they arrive in Dawson City."

He looked at her, then at the mask. "It is the metal that comes easiest to me," he explained. "And it is abundant here. Mr. Croix was always happy when I found more. But he did warn me to keep the dogs out of sight."

"Did he tell you how much the gold was worth?" asked Violet.

"You mean money?" She nodded. "My people do not use money. Did not use money." A shadow crossed his face, but he continued before she could ask about it. "He provided everything I needed, taught me to speak your language, taught me to read. He was my friend."

How desolate. . . . Ten years of living in fear of discovery, with only an old man for companionship. "Mr. A'lle. . . ."

He raised a hand. "A'lle was the name of a ship. It is not my name."

"Then what is your name?" she asked. He told her, but it was incomprehensible to her ears, and certainly not something she could pronounce. "What was the name of your ship?"

He smiled, understanding her reasoning. "The shuttle was named Aj'adde."

"Aj'adde," She repeated, trying out the name. "It can work, unless you prefer to keep Croix. . . . Let's get back to town," she decided. "We can finish discussing this in warmth."

He walked to the back of the sled and mounted the skis. She glanced over her shoulder and saw him wave. Immediately the dogs began to move.

"I am taking the train back to York tomorrow. If you like, you can come with me."

There was a long silence and she thought he would not answer, but at last he said, "I would like that."

Violet nodded, wondering if they could bring the golden dogs back with them.

❦

"We found Frankel's body right where you told us," said Sergeant Willoughby the next morning. "The other one holed up in the dredge and made a small fire. He's thawing out in the back as we speak." He nodded toward a closed door, behind which the Northwesters detachment kept its cells.

Violet nodded but did not speak. The desk clerk had alerted the Northwesters when she did not return as planned, and she and Mr. Aj'adde had run into the patrol long before they reached town the night before.

Sergeant Willoughby dwarfed the desk behind which he sat. His broad shoulders and barrel chest were barely contained by the red serge of his uniform jacket, and his short blond hair—more silver, really—was still tousled from him having removed his hat. A thick mustache, blond like his hair, graced his upper lip.

He glanced at a piece of paper on the desk. "The other fella's name is Pete Larssen. Well known to the Royal Northwest Mounted Police. Splits his time between Dawson and Forty Mile."

For the moment, the sergeant and Violet were alone in the detachment, a small wooden building on Dawson City's Front Street. It boasted three desks behind a counter that ran almost the width of the room. A barrel stove kept the place warm, despite the frost rimming the windows. Although she had taken a hot bath the night before and slept under a half-dozen blankets, she still felt chilled.

"Why did he wish me dead?" she asked.

"He's a ne'er-do-well," said the sergeant grimly. "We suspect him of jumping claims and threatening placer miners into giving up their claims to him—or to whoever hires him." He shook his head and sat back. The chair squeaked beneath his bulk but he paid no heed. "The detachment at Forty Mile wants to question him about a couple of murders. He admitted that he was hired to kill you. Says half the money was wired into his bank account, with the other half to come when he sent proof of your death." He smiled humourlessly. "He was to send your locket."

Violet's hand strayed to her neckline. She always wore the locket beneath her clothing; she had taken it from Felicity's room after she died, and kept a few of her sister's ashes inside. Whoever had ordered her killed knew about the locket.

"My uncle," she said flatly.

"I'm afraid so," said Sergeant Willoughby. "We've sent word to the York constabulary and they will investigate. I understand you're leaving today?"

Violet took a deep breath. "Yes. It's time I returned home."

"Perhaps you should consider staying here until charges are laid and he is arrested," said the sergeant. "It may not be safe."

"I will not be travelling alone," she hurried to assure him.

Sergeant Willoughby's blue gaze sharpened. "The A'lle?"

She nodded, choosing not to correct him.

"I've been here almost three years," said the sergeant. "I've never seen him in town." His voice was very carefully neutral. She did not think it would accomplish anything to tell him that the crash of Mr. Aj'adde's spacecraft had destroyed the dredge and killed Alvin. It would not bring Alvin back.

"Mr. Aj'adde was staying with Mr. Croix," she said, "who convinced him that the townsfolk would attack him if he showed himself." She stood. The train would be leaving in an hour and she still had to get her bags from the hotel.

Sergeant Willoughby stood as well. "Croix," he said musingly. "The old man was . . ." he hesitated, then clearly thought better of what he was going to say, "eccentric."

She smiled. "So I hear." She held out her hand. "Thank you, Sergeant Willoughby. I appreciate your help."

Willoughby shook her hand. "You're welcome, ma'am. Please be careful."

She was at the door before she remembered what she had wanted to ask. She turned and said, "What about Captain Frankel? Why did *he* wish me dead?" Of everything that had happened on this adventure, this one fact still perplexed her. He had seemed to genuinely like her.

The sergeant shook his head. "We may never know for certain," he said grimly. "But seein' as we never had a lick of trouble with the man before, I suspect Larssen threatened to kill Mrs. Frankel if the captain didn't do as he was told."

Violet swallowed. "Is she. . . ?"

"She is well," Willoughby assured her. "Or well enough, considering her husband is dead."

A moment later, she stood on the porch. Despite the blue sky and sunshine, it was still biting cold. Front Street faced the Klondike River, and there was very little protection from the wind that whistled off the frozen water. That didn't seem to stop anyone from going about their business. A sleigh drove by, horses blowing steam, the driver so bundled in furs and blankets that she couldn't tell if it was a man or a woman. The railroad followed the river into town, ending at the train station at the foot of the street.

A tall figure turned the corner and headed toward her.

"Miss Stanhope," said Mr. Aj'adde. "Are you ready?"

Violet came down the steps to meet him. "I am," she said, surprised once again by his extraordinary eyes. "Where are your dogs?"

He smiled. "You were right," he said. "The station master agreed to take them on as freight."

She smiled back. "Good. I'm glad you will have a stake with which to start your new life."

"Indeed. I expect I will get even more money from the gold I am bringing with me."

"What gold?"

"In the boxes," he said. "On the sled? If you'll recall, I was heading into town when I came across you."

Violet stared at him. "You mean those boxes are full of gold?" At his nod, she felt her heart speed up. "But you left the boxes at the station! I thought they were your possessions!"

"They are," he said equably.

If anyone guessed that those boxes contained gold. . . . But then, she hadn't and she had ridden on them. Another thought occurred to her. "Mr. Aj'adde! We left two boxes at the crash site!"

"We needed to make room for you."

After a moment, she closed her mouth and turned toward the hotel. It was a good thing she was small, or he might have left an even larger fortune behind. He fell into step next to her.

"Mr. Aj'adde," she said, "what did you do to my sister's ashes?"

He looked down at her, his breath puffing before him. "I sensed a great deal of metal in her ashes," he said softly. "I needed to make certain."

Violet dredged her memory. "Are we not composed of metals?" she asked. "At least in part?"

"You are. But not this much, and not this particular metal."

"Which one?" she asked. "Which metal?"

"Arsenic."

She stopped and stood staring at nothing.

Uncle George had murdered Felicity.

Violet knew now that she had suspected it all along. Had he murdered her parents, too? Or had the accident given him the idea to get rid of Felicity, and then her? No wonder he had wanted the locket as proof of her death: it contained proof of her sister's murder. She would turn the ashes over to the York constabulary for analysis.

Then, with Mr. Aj'adde's help, she would find the arsenic Uncle George had used to poison Felicity.

And then she would see him hang.

EMMA FARADAY (AKA Marcelle Dubé: marcellemdube.com) was born in New Brunswick, grew up in Québec, and lived all over the country before settling in the Yukon. "The Man in the Mask" is set in the same world as *Backli's Ford—Book One of the A'lle Chronicles*.

A Bunny Hug for Karl

MIKE RIMAR

My fingers probe under the brim of my beaten Massey Ferguson cap, the one my dad gave me before he went off to Flin Flon and never came back, and I wonder what the hell Lars Mackenna is doing on the roof of the old Pool elevator.

Lars and me go way back, getting into and out of trouble like only best friends can. When we were in grade ten, his hard-drinking old man got himself cut up fixing their combine. I'd helped Lars work the farm, and afterward, when his old man got back on his feet, he offered me a job. I didn't take it, of course—the last thing I wanted was to be like everyone else at the Liquor Board, sporting a permanent farmer's tan, always looking tired and worried waiting in line to buy beer.

No; we're more than friends, we are bros. So I'm in no way serious when I cup my hands to my mouth and call out, "You gonna jump, or what?"

Despite the great height, I see Lars smile. I barely have time to raise my hand and shout "No!" when the idiot steps off.

A more curious person would have wondered how Lars landed with no greater difficulty than if he'd jumped from the top step off his back porch. A more perceptive person might have wondered just how Lars got on that roof in the first place; grain elevators aren't exactly small or easy to climb. But I'm his best friend and see a bigger picture. Lars, you have to understand, isn't exactly a thinker. Oh, he isn't dumb; he did graduate high school, but let's just say his focus has always been limited.

I, on the other hand, have the ability to see opportunities where none normally exist, and Lars leaping unharmed from the top of a Pool elevator is a big opportunity. I know that as his friend—his best friend—it's my job to give Lars guidance, first by showing concern.

"You hurt, bro?" I say.

"Nah." Lars has that weird farmer's timbre to his voice, the kind you can barely hear inside an empty barn, yet understand every word over the rumble of a baler running full throttle. "But did you see me up there, Karl? What did I look like? Impressive?"

I squint up at the peaked roof of rusting corrugated steel. "To tell you the truth, I was wondering when they started putting up gargoyles on grain elevators."

"Very funny." Lars shoves me, the same friendly little push we've given each other since grade one, only this time he sends me flying some fifteen feet ass over tea kettle into the honeysuckle lining the dirt parking lot.

I poke my head up over the tall grass. "What the fuck, Lars!"

"Sorry, bro." In a single leap he is beside me, pulling me to my feet like a straw-filled scarecrow and dusting me off. "This stuff is new to me."

"I'm fine. I'm fine." I push him away and look around to make sure no-one sees him patting my body. Porcupine Corners is barely a pimple on the butt cheek of Saskatchewan, and rumours travel faster than cow shit on an autumn wind. "What exactly do you mean by 'stuff'?"

Lars shrugs. "Not sure, really, but it came on kind of gradual, starting around puberty, to tell the truth. It was easier to hide then, but I just got stronger and stronger until. . . ." He holds up his arms as if wanting me to behold his magnificence.

The thing is, he isn't all that magnificent to look at. Sure, he is tall, but not exactly muscular—no more than any farmer who worked the land all his life. Hell, if anything his back has started taking on that bowed look farmers get when too many crops fail and the government threatens to cut back subsidies. But something is different about the guy, that is certain.

"So," I say. "What are you gonna do?"

Lars lowers his arms and shrugs. "Be a superhero, maybe."

For as long as we've been friends, Lars has had only two expressions: a big dopey smile, and an all-encompassing shrug that means anything from "the barn is on fire" to "we're down to our last beer." Did I mention Lars isn't exactly a thinker? He never saw the big picture, which is why we make such good friends. The guy has some crazy luck, I'll give you that, but he never did know what to do with his good fortunes. Thankfully, I've been there to guide him and capitalize on favourable circumstances.

With that sheepish smile threatening to crack his wind-beaten face looking way older than his twenty-five years, I know we've hit the lottery. I just need Lars to see it my way before he sets his stubborn mind on some stupid course of action.

"You should think about this some," I say. "Sure, being a superhero is cool and all. You get into the comics and maybe even have your own television show, but think about it. Is this really what you want?"

That puts a flutter in his smile, and his shoulders rise in a shrug. "Superheroes are the good guys," he says. "They help people and stuff. I think I'd like to do that."

"Yeah, yeah. They help people," I say. Who doesn't want glamour and excitement? But I see a different reality, one that most overlook. "The thing is Lars, superheroes end up dead."

Lars grins. "Nah."

"Yeah," I say. "They do. Oh sure, they kick ass for years, but in the end they slip up, let the villain get too close. They fight and fight, the bad guy goes to jail, breaks out, gets caught, goes back in—but always there's that one last battle where he finally gets the upper hand."

I pause to let that bit of wisdom ferment. Before my dad fucked off to Manitoba we would watch Wrestling Cavalcade on the CBC out of Prince Albert. Once, the show was interrupted with a bulletin about some RCMP officer getting shot—the third cop that month—and my dad had looked over at me and said, "You should be a cop. There seems to be an opening."

That pearl of parental nurturing stayed with me, not because I wanted to be a cop, but because I knew I'd never want to be one. Cops get shot. They put their asses on the line every day and occasionally they get that ass shot off. Being a superhero is just like being a glorified cop, and I don't want to see my best friend pay the ultimate price—at least, not for nothing.

I continue, "You might be better off taking the other side. Be a villain." I hold my breath and wait for either that silly shrug or that idiotic smile. Instead, he turns and heads for the old rail line at the edge of town. I hurry to follow in step. "Look, bro, I know it's a lot to take in—"

Lars suddenly stops. "Want to see what it's like?"

"What what's like?"

"Flying."

That catches me by surprise. "You can fly, too?"

And there is that grin again, slicing across his suntanned face as he wraps his arm around my waist and jumps—just jumps—into the air.

We soar over cornstalks, so close I reach down and brush the silk-topped cobs. Then Lars arches back and we shoot straight for the clouds. At first it is exhilarating, but then I look down. Somewhere I hear a shrill alarm, like a siren and wonder what the hell an ambulance is doing way up in the sky, until Lars whispers in my ear to relax and I realize the siren is me, screaming.

"Don't you let me go, you bastard." I take hold of his arm, you know, for balance, and it is then I notice how unnatural his skin feels. It's not like we touch each other a lot, some play-wrestling when we were younger, high fives and handshaking, that sort of thing, but he definitely has changed. Overnight, practically. His skin is hard, almost like porcelain, and the hair on his arm has completely disappeared. His face, too, now that I really look, is hairless and smooth as a baby's butt. Along his forehead a bright white stretch of scalp shows where the hairline has begun to recede.

Lars is going bald! If I wasn't suspended a mile in the sky, I'd laugh my ass off.

But I don't. And I don't tell him either, since he probably already knows. Is this some aftereffect of his new powers? I groan inside. People are going to call him Mr. Clean, or Toilet Man, or some such thing. Everyone has a nickname for superheroes, but no-one ever disses the villain.

More than ever I need to get Lars back on track, but I can't think flying around like a helicopter. "Take me down, Lars."

"Don't be afraid. I got you."

"Screw you, I'm not afraid. I'm just getting a little airsick. You fly like a drunken goose."

Lars continues in a lazy circle. It's cold, and I have trouble breathing, but the altitude doesn't seem to affect him. "Look at it," he says. "Isn't it beautiful?"

From the air, Saskatchewan looks like an endless checkerboard. Acres and acres of land segmented into different crops, with only roads and the occasional lake to break up the monotony. "Lars, we need to go to Saskatoon, or Prince Albert—hell, even Tisdale. With this gift of yours, we can be rich."

"Rich?"

"Yeah. You know, performing maybe, or working as a bodyguard, that sort of thing. And there's other ways of making money. Hell, I bet you could pick up any ATM and just fly away with it."

We dip a little and something in the movement bothers me. I sense sadness and disappointment and realize Lars just gave an aerial shrug.

"You just don't get it," he says. "I'm not going to be some circus animal, or a thief. I've got to do some good, make a difference in this world. Wouldn't you, if you had the chance?"

I'm not sure what happens. Maybe oxygen deprivation, or the cold from being so high, or maybe it's the plain bullshit Lars is feeding me, but I've had enough. "No. I wouldn't. What is there to change? The world is crap. People, good and bad, have been trying to change the world since we were cavemen, but nothing ever happens. People are born, they live, they die, and the rest move on. Say you save a life. Big deal. Somewhere someone else dies. You can't stop it. You can't change anything. All you or me or anyone can do is do the best for ourselves before some safe falls on our heads and crushes our brains. And I say we start now by getting back on the ground."

Lars smiles at me, and I realize I've made a terrible mistake.

He lets me go.

For the first few seconds I look up at him, unable to believe he just did what he did. His body slowly shrinks in size until wind shear causes me to turn. The grand butt crack that is Saskatchewan rushes at me at terminal velocity. Directly below is the rusted tin roof of the Pool grain elevator. I figure I'll hit it dead on, probably burst through, my body shredding to pieces.

Would anyone care if I died?

Lars might, even if he were the one who'd killed me. He's the type of guy who'd feel enough guilt to turn himself in. Idiot. My mom died a couple years ago. My dad? I'm pretty much dead to him already.

I'm alone, and strangely I don't care. The world looms larger by the second, and I feel no fear. I don't scream, laugh, or cry. I face death with eyes wide open, daring fate to do its worst. Then everything slows like a bungee cord pulled taut.

Lars says, "I got you, bro," and I turn to look up into that stupid smiling face. Holding me by a fistful of my bunny hug, he lowers me safely to the ground. "There," he says, landing beside me. "I saved you. See? I made a difference."

"You tried to kill me!"

He waves a hand in the air. "Nah. You're my best friend. I'd never let you die. I needed you to see that I don't just want to be a superhero; I have to be. I can do good in this world, save people. Truth, justice, all of it. You can be my sidekick."

"So, you dropped me to teach me a lesson? What kind of idiot superhero does that?"

"A good one, I think," he says in that weird kind of soft voice you can hear over an idling John Deere tractor but barely understand alone in a wheat field. "See ya, Karl." He leaps into the air and, in a blink of an eye, is gone. Gone, and I know he'll never come back. Lars left me, just like everyone else.

I stare at the patch of sky for nearly an hour, not realizing I'm crying until a gust of wind chills my tear-damp bunny hug.

Sidekick. The word lies in my belly like a wad of swallowed gum, unwilling or unable to be digested. Was that all I'd meant to him after all these years? Lars was supposed to be my friend. But what kind of person drops a friend from a mile up? Sure, he saved me from hitting the ground, but I could've died from fright by then.

But I hadn't. In fact, I hadn't been afraid at all. An experience like that changes a person. Being fearless is a big opportunity.

Lars wanted a sidekick. I'll give him something better. A nemesis. An arch villain.

I walk to the main highway and head east, thumb out, away from Porcupine Corners. Flin Flon is a good place to make a name for myself. Not too big, not too small. Plenty of opportunities for a guy like me. First, I might look up my old man, find a nice tall building, and see if he screams before he hits the ground.

MIKE RIMAR (www.mikerimar.com) lives in Whitby, Ontario, with his two daughters and fondly remembers childhood summers visiting his grandparents in the village of Bjorkdale, Saskatchewan. He has been published in *Writers of the Future XXI*, *InterGalactic Medicine Show*, and *Tesseracts Fifteen: A Case of Quite Curious Tales*.

"Not a Dream! Not a Hoax! Not an Imaginary Story!"

~ THE LOST YEARS OF JOE SHUSTER ~

EMMA VOSSEN

Joe Shuster, the co-creator of Superman, was born in Toronto, Canada, 10 July 1914. Fame found him years later when he was living in Cleveland, Ohio, and by 1940 Superman was a household name. After a falling out with his friends and his publisher in 1948, Joe became depressed. Little is known about his life between 1950 and 1975, except that he had lost all his money to National Periodical Publications (as DC Comics was officially called then), his eyesight was failing, and he was working as a delivery boy to pay his bills. In 2009 comics historian Craig Yoe came across a box of 1950s fetish art with a few familiar faces. The publication known as *Nights of Horror* was, in the opinion of many, unquestionably drawn by Joe, and was arguably some of his best work. None of this can be confirmed, as the artist passed away in 1992, but his fans, friends, and family are left to wonder as to his motivations for drawing what was, at the time, very questionable content. Shuster was a virtuoso of the female form, and his erotic work is stunning. Some of the drawings are beautiful, some fear-inducing, and some funny, but for many fans it is undeniable that the work in *Nights of Horror* signed simply "Josh" belongs to the late, great Joe Shuster himself.

🍁

PART I: SECRETS

Joe's work was directed, unprettied, crude and vigorous; as easy to read as a diagram. No creamy lines, no glossy effect, no touch of that bloodless prefabrication that passes for professionalism these days.—Jules Feiffer (quoted in Craig Yoe, Secret Identity: The Fetish Art of Superman's Co-creator Joe Shuster, *p. 11)*

Yesterday I met a woman at the state fair.
Tall and lean
ten times more beautiful
than Miss Ohio herself.

Later that night,
as her head rammed into my mattress
and I bent her right leg
as close to her nose as possible,
I saw us sketched onto the white wall;
watched the ink shift.

She let out her muffled scream;
I faked a twitching fit.
White face, red lips,
she looked up,
said   *thank you*
fell asleep.

Pictures of Clark pour off my desk,
crumple and rip under
the weak legs of my wooden chair.

Automatic writing;
outlining extended limbs,
sweat droplets,
bulging veins.

I am
bearing over her with a whip;
I see the cityscape
outlined in red,
Toronto at night;
black and blue grand narrative.

The stars melt into planets,
no longer my own
but I keep moving
scribbling and scratching my way
into a deep sleep.

This morning,
I wake in a mess of cum
black as ink
stains the sheet
I wrapped myself in.
Glued to my forearms,
my thighs,
I peel it off slowly:
villains, spaceships,
Luthor bending Clark
over disassembled Metropolis. . . .

My kryptonite is also
my secret identity.

❦

I used to hide the pictures
under the floorboards,
at the bottom of my drawers,
in picture frames,
folded thick
behind snapshots of the family dog.

I ate a few once.
Ripped them up real small
tasted the inky zest,
washed them down with the water
Mom brought me before bed.
Vomited them up onto
my pillow in my sleep.
Flipped it over
and forgot about it.

My life is
showgirl after showgirl
I call them all babydoll
they make great models,
subjects.

Brought one home last night named Lucy
and thought
"I'd like to bring you to my mama"
  —haven't seen her in a long time.

If I stood in front of this beauty
I bet her chin would sit just right
on the top of my head.
Feet resting on the bed frame
I draw her
exactly as she's sleeping
ass-up across the bed

I try to dream up something dramatic,
I see her flying
circling tall buildings
searching for her lover.

I draw her naked breasts bouncing,
hair between her bounding legs
blown dark against her body

Soaring through an open window
She discovers him
breathless, drops to her knees.

Looking up;
dark innocent pools,
I pencil in her cum laden breath,
a whisper
  —*Joe*—

❄

My best sketches are drawn
between 5:30 and 6:30 a.m.
I am an early morning Superhero.

Fucking, cumming, pillow talk
penciling, inking, lettering
primary colours
blue, red, and yellow. . . .

130 dollars
was the price they paid me
for Sir Galahad himself.

PART 2: NIGHTS OF HORROR

> *Come, come boy don't go into another dream. We have work to do, remember?—Ellen, a writer, to Joe, a reporter, in* Nights of Horror *Issue No. 3*

> Nights of Horror *treats sexual perversion as a normal way of life. . . .—James B. Nolan, Deputy Police Commissioner and head of the Juvenile Aid Bureau (quoted in Craig Yoe,* Secret Identity, *p. 29)*

Living next door to my publisher
leaves me free to do what I want.
I sit in my room and draw
shamelessly
as the sun comes up
then go wander a while
worry about money.

Went out without a hat once
got picked up as a vagrant
cop brought me a sandwich.
As long as I put it on
and wear those damn thick glasses
they leave me alone.

No-one knows who I am
anymore.

Today in a coffee house
some kids were bugging me,
said I was too old to be reading comics.
So I said to them,
   Don't you know who I am!
I tore a napkin from their table
scribbled a quick drawing.
Hurt my eyes
drawing so viciously.
I showed it to them as proof!
They laughed and laughed.

I think I'll tell people
my name is something else
from now on.

🍁

Jerry keeps fighting
for something long gone.

Fucker's married to Lois
—the first Lois—
stole her right under my nose
at the Cartoonists Society's silly costume ball
back in '48.
It's okay though—
she wasn't tall enough anyway.

I think he should move on,
expand his horizons!
Fuck those assholes at National;
I wish they could see me now.

Today I drew a delightful piece about
Lex capturing old Duff and his girl
—oh the nasty things he did to her!—
reminded me of the old days.
I've been signing them "Josh":
JOe — SHuster .

I can't believe no-one's recognized us yet.

Drawing for Eugene and Clancy
isn't hard,
not much different than
drawing Superman really:
the villain captures some girl,
ties her up good,
holds her against her will,
then the hero comes in and pulls her away!

Hell, Clark tied up girls all the time!
the bad ones at least.
Like old Evelyn Curry back in issue one
murdered Jack Kennedy
so Clark hitched her up
gagged her good
while he tracked down the governor
told him what she'd done.

I've started helping with the stories,
I fill 'em with detectives,
writers, artists, reporters, showgirls.
Naming the characters
Jerry, Kent, Lucile, Lois.
The other day I had a girl named Ellen
captured and spanked by a Joe
and then later tortured by a Josh!

Still, no-one notices.

There's a girl who works in the diner downstairs
long drawn-out legs
wears high-heels her whole shift
  never slouches.
I sit and draw on place-mats.
She brings me coffee and toast.

The other day she leaned down on her elbows
got real close and said,
"I know you."
She smelled like french fries and maple syrup,
had freckles that looked like a little stream
running down into a pool in her cleavage.
She told me she'd read it *all,*
starting at *Action Comics* till they fired me—
I hadn't been recognized in almost two years.

She put one arm over the back of the booth
got close to my ear and said,
    —*I've even read those other ones.*
    Those dirty stories that you draw now
    I know you don't think we know it's you
    but Old Clancy from upstairs, he tells me all about it
    says you help him come up with some 'em ideas
    chains and whips and stuff—

She held the coffee pot in one hand behind me
but snuck the other right down to my thigh
her long red nails dug into me through my pants.
She filled up my cup,
walked away.

Clancy told me her name is Betsy.
She ain't no showgirl
but I'm getting too old for that anyway.
Strip clubs full of smoke;
it's hard to see in there.

Last night I dreamed she brought me coffee
poured it all over my hand
soaked my sketches into brown pulp.
I looked up and she smirked
so I bent her over a bar stool
and spanked her until her ass was red.

When she turned around she grabbed my shirt
ripped it apart with all her strength
hundreds of buttons flew across the restaurant
in every direction.
My shirt flapping open in the wind
she kissed me hard and said,
"A super-kiss for a super-man!"

PART 3: KIDS

*Virtually every child in America is reading color
'comic' magazines—a poisonous mushroom growth of
the last two years. Ten million copies of these sex-
horror serials are sold every month. The bulk of these
lurid publications depends for their appeal upon
mayhem, murder, torture and abduction, Superman
heroics, voluptuous females in scanty attire found on
almost every page. Badly drawn, badly written, and
badly printed, the effect of these pulp-paper night-*

mares is that of a violent stimulant.... — *Sterling North,* Chicago Daily News, *8 May 1940 (quoted in Craig Yoe,* Secret Identity, *p. 14)*

I hear these kids found
a coloured man
catching a few Zs on a bench,
burned him with cigarettes and
punched him when he screamed.

They drowned him in the river,
just for a thrill, they say!
Four little Jewish boys
beating girls in the park to get warmed up.

The papers say their leader,
he carries a whip and a switchblade
dresses in a vampire costume
does things he saw in my drawings.
They're called the Thrill Killers.
Saw their picture in the paper
pubescent mustaches
trimmed small rectangles
the words *Nights of Horror* right underneath!
It was the funniest damn thing I ever saw.

Kids these days are a far cry
from Jerry and me
cooped up in Maple Apartments—
me drawing on butcher paper
Jerry babbling about villains
and justice being served.
Jerry and I, well, we would have
dove right into the water
grabbed that coloured man
and flew off into the city night with him!

They say it's our fault
that these kids are so crazy.

Shut us down today
grabbing piles of freshly pressed comics
tossing them into the garbage
breaking pencils and calling us perverts
like I was nobody!
Like criminals.

When I was a kid
I would troll the newsstands
devour copies of *Weird Tales,*
hide them inside other, more acceptable pulps.
It wasn't easy to get your hands on those things in 1928!
I'd usually buy a copy of the less appealing
Amazing Stories—
not that I didn't like hearing about the power of flight
or what would happen if you swallowed nuclear sludge;
but it didn't have anything on the stuff in *Weird Tales*!
Girls chained up,
beaten and flogged by other girls,
touched in bad places.
I'd study the shape of their breasts
imagine what was under their skirts and panties.
When I got home I'd take out a pencil
scratch it down as good as I could.

But nothing ever looked quite right!
I hadn't examined enough breasts,
experienced the face-to-thigh proximity
that lets you sketch it out perfectly
like I can now
in under twenty careful lines.

Half the time I can't see the pen in front of me.

I got a better job:
doing sexy spy strips for *The Continental.*
Fancy magazine with fancy paper.

Annette, Secret Agent Z-4
much tamer than the last couple stories I wrote for *Nights*.

But, I can't see the same.
I'm afraid to tell them
that it hurts too much to squint at those fine lines.

I go home to Betsy
and work deliveries during the day.
We act out things I might have drawn
only a few months ago, because
I didn't bring my rickety desk to record them on.

I can barely sign my new lease
—Josh Kent

EMMA VOSSEN (www.getsomeactioncomics.com) is a sexuality and comics scholar originally from Clinton, Ontario. After living in Ottawa for the past six years, she now resides in Kitchener while pursuing her PhD at the University of Waterloo.

GIANT CANADIAN COMICS

PATRICK T. GODDARD

GIANT CANADIAN COMICS is proud to present . . .
"The Gathering of the Guardians of Canada!"

From all corners of the Dominion they came—
—to fight for **King and Country!**

ROLL CALL
(in alphabetical order)

CAPTAIN ZERO!
The CAT-GIRL!
The COACHWHIP!
The FIGHTING CANUCK!
The MOLECULE!
The MYSTERY MARVEL!
SUPER-SPEEDSTER!
and The WARLOCK!

Midnight at the elegant *Château Laurier* in the Nation's Capital . . .

. . . Where wait the **Fighting Canuck** and the **Warlock!**

150

—Are you sure your mystical summons was received? A *telegram* would be more *standard* . . .
—*Fear not!* Even now I sense the approach of *great heroes!*
Tap! Tap!

The *Canuck* opens the window . . .
—**The Mystery Marvel!**
—Hello! I just flew here from Vancouver! Am I the first?
—Indeed! Pleased to finally meet you!

Vibrating *through* the *wall!*
—**Super-Speedster!**
—Marvel, you rat! I thought we had a fair race!
—Fair enough, old friend—*as the crow flies!*
Ring! Ring!

Propelled by *electric current* down the *telephone wire*!
—**The Molecule!**
—Say, no-one told me this'd be a *party line!*
—*Ahem!* Forgetting someone, boys?

Stepping out of the shadows . . .
—**The Cat-Girl!** But how?
—Getting into locked rooms is my *specialty!*
—Hey, what's the ruckus outside?

Surrounded by flashing cameras . . .
—**The Coachwhip!** Woo woo!
—But did you have to bring the press corps?
—Can't be helped when you're a *star!* Now beat it, boys!

Soon . . .
—Well, according to my files, we're all *here* . . . except **Captain Zero!**
—*I'll* take care of that . . . in a *"cold snap!"*
Snap!

Instantly!
—*Blue Blizzards!* One second I'm in an arctic transport plane, and the next . . .
—. . . *at the first meeting of the* **Guardians of Canada!**

The heroes gather like *Knights of the Round Table!*
—The *Prime Minister* himself invited us all here . . .
—While we eat, let's get to know each other better!
—Why don't we tell our *origin stories?*
—Our secrets will never leave this room! *I command it!*
—*Marvellous!* And speaking of, I'll begin . . .

THE LEGEND OF THE *MYSTERY MARVEL!*

On the eve of the *Great War*, an orphan boy walks the lonely Saskatchewan prairie . . .
—Like my **Indian brothers** before me, I must perform my *Vision Quest.*

Suddenly! *The ground collapses!*
—Wh . . . what is this strange cave? *That glow!*

The young man is bathed in unearthly rays . . .
—**OH-H-H!**

A weird vision!
—Fear not, **Man of Earth!** If you have found this vessel, you are a *worthy champion!* We will grant you *great power!*

"The *strength* and *endurance* of the land . . .

"The ability to *fly* upon the winds . . .

"The *swiftness* of the river currents . . .

"The *power* of the sun!"

—Now *go* and use your power to bring *peace* and *justice* to the oppressed and downtrodden!
—*I swear!*

The cave collapses!
—**AH-H-H!**

Days pass. But then . . . !
—I made it! *Yippee!*

Miles above the Earth!
—*Flying!* But how . . . ?

In the distance . . .
—A train—heading right for that *washed-out bridge!*

In a flash!
—*So fast*—I'm already here!

He stops the train with his *bare hands!*
—It feels light as a feather!

The conductor is amazed!
—We're saved! But who was that ***mystery marvel?***

—That'll have to be a *secret* . . . for now!

Find out all about the ***Mystery Marvel*** in every issue of *GIANT CANADIAN COMICS!*

🍁

THE NIGHT OF THE NORTHERN LIGHTNING!

Night falls early at the *University of the North-West* . . .

. . . Where a scientist and his assistant **Ken Jones** burn the midnight oil!
—**Yawn** Are you sure it'll work, Dr. Kriegstein?
—*It must!* . . .

—. . . Canada's soldiers are *brave*—but *few*! With our formula, they will be able to remain *awake* and *vital* when the enemy is sleeping!
—I could sure use some now!

—*No!* It's not ready for human testing! Why don't you get some rest?

153

—Sorry, Doc. *Football practice* has tired me out . . .

But no sooner has he gone down the hall when . . .
Bang! Bang!
—*Shots!*

Back to the lab!
—Y-You've *killed* him!
—Ve must haf dot *formula!*
—Ja! **Heil Hitler!**

The *football star* fights valiantly! But . . .
—**OH-H-H!**
—Dot vill knock him out!
—Now ve *test* de formula!

A lethal dose!
—Vhat doesn't *kill* him . . .
—Makes *der Fuehrer* stronger!

Suddenly . . .
—De body!
—*Shaking!* **Zo fast!**

Amazingly!
—*Vas ist los? Vanished!*
—Disintegrated! Ein *failure!*
—Ach! Now ve must *radio* our *report* to Berlin!

But what *really* happened?
—N-Not dead! But I feel . . . so *strange!* Those *lights!*

Yes—the **Northern Lights!**
—A mortal, here on our plane?
—*The formula!* It must have *sped up* my internal *vibrations* to match your *frequency!*
—He *is* fast!
—And brave!
—*We find you . . . worthy!*
—We grant you the power of *super-speed!*
—Use it to bring the Axis scourge to *justice!*

Back at the lab . . .
—Awake! What a dream! But is it true?

In a *flash!*
—Back in my room! I'll need some *running* clothes . . . My *football uniform!* A few quick *stitches* and . . .

He dons the green and gold . . .
—I'll call myself . . . the **Super-Speedster!**

Vibrating at the speed of *sound* . . .
—Now to find that *Ratzi radio* . . .

Across the *river!*
—I'm running so fast I don't have time to sink!

Up the city's tallest building—*the transmitter!*
—So much for Otis Elevator!

Flashing fists!
—*Himmel!*
—*Ein blitzkrieg!*
—*Vas ist los?*

—"Vas" is me, *Herr Hitler*—the **Super-Speedster!**

Keep up with the exploits of **the Super-Speedster** (if you can!) in *GIANT CANADIAN COMICS!*

THE STRANGE CASE OF THE *CAT-GIRL!*

In a Montreal mansion, debutante **Cathy Starlin** listens to the radio . . .
—. . . *In yet another daring "cat" burglary, Chinese jade cat statues worth millions stolen!*
—**Father**, didn't the *museum* just acquire some priceless Egyptian artifacts?
—Why, yes, *Cathy*—of *Bast*, the *Goddess of Cats!*

—Let your *papa* worry about that, *chérie!*
—Why, of course, *maman!* My, it's getting late! I'd best be getting some *sleep* . . .

A lithe figure enters a museum window!
—Nothing like a little *excitement!* I'll catch the thief *myself!*

—Footsteps! I'll hide behind this strange *mummy!*

The "cat" burglar—a beautiful woman and two accomplices!
—*Bien!* I told you, I don't like stealing from my own husband!
—*Ferme ta bouche!* An' do what you're told!
—Or we tell your 'usband all about your *criminal past!*

—**M . . . MOTHER!**

—Qui? . . . *Non!* Non, Cathy, you mustn't know!
—*Vite,* Hélène! The getaway car's waiting!
—*My own mother!* But how? . . . Why? . . . Never mind, they're getting away!

An acrobatic leap onto the getaway car!
—*Allez-oop!* And a nice soft landing with none the wiser!

The thieves drive to a warehouse near the docks . . .
—*Le boss* is waiting!

The kingpin of Montreal crime—***Boss LeBlanc!***
—*Merci!* The other robberies were just a smokescreen . . . For the *Statue of Bast!* Legend says it has *strange powers!*
—I've held up my part of the bargain . . . Now it's your turn!

—Yes, you'll get what's coming to you, *ma belle!*
—**OH-H-H-H!**

A shocking sight to a devoted daughter!
—. . . *Maman* . . . **Dead!** *Monstre!*

The athletic young girl leaps into the fray!
—**OW!**
—**UH!**
—I'll take care of you, *ma petite!*

The statue glows with *strange power!*
—What? *Non! NO-O-O-ON!*

—I am *Bast,* goddess of those who *walk the night!* You are *brave* and *resourceful!* I will grant you the power of all **cats**—*to see in the dark—balance and agility—to enter and leave unseen!* Will you serve the cause of *justice?*

—By my poor mother's life, *I swear!*

—But *Father* must never know . . . I'll disguise myself, like a . . . a *Cat-Girl!*

Read the *Cat-Girl*'s adventures in *GIANT CANADIAN COMICS!*

THE SECRET OF THE *MOLECULE!*

Deep underneath the *Canadian Shield,* a top-secret demonstration . . .

Brad Nelson is a government scientist . . .
—*Imagine,* gentlemen—if we could reduce a *tank* to the size of a *toy!* We could ship them to England and our allies by the thousands—*and enlarge them again as needed!* Observe!

A strange ray reduces the tank!
—Incredible!

But . . .
POOF!

—Another *failure,* Nelson! Get out of my sight!
—But . . . *Major!*

That night, in his lab, Nelson talks to his beautiful assistant . . .
—I don't understand, *Brigid!* The calculations were *perfect!*
—You're still brilliant to *me,* Brad darling!

—*Ultra-X-Rays* . . . focused through a unique *Nickel-Uranium-Diamond* alloy . . . polished to glass . . .

—Wait! The apparatus . . . *sabotaged!*
—That's *right,* darling—*by me!*

—*Brigid!*
—Call me . . . **the Black Rose!**

—You? A *Nazi?*
—And *paid handsomely* for it, darling! Pity I had to *shoot* you . . .
BANG!

—Only wounded . . . but *out cold!* I'll dispose of him in the reducing ray! He'll be blasted to *molecules!*

The fatal ray *shrinks* the scientist! But . . .
—*Tiny—but alive!* All those months . . . exposed to the *Ultra-X-Rays!* They must've changed my *molecular structure!*

—*Brigid*—giving those MPs a sob story. The traitor!

—I'll just hitch a ride on her *shoelace. . . !*

Back in Brigid's room—*a secret radio . . .*
—I've *sabotaged* the ray! Now what about my *money?*
—You'll get what's coming to you, *"darling"!*

Like a *flea,* the scientist leaps many times his own height!
—*Brad!* But *tiny!*
—I may be *small,* but I still have normal *strength!*

A solid right hook!
—I never hit a lady . . . but you're no *lady!*

The effect of the ray wears off, and the scientist returns to normal size!
—I'll keep using my ray to fight . . . as the ***Molecule!***

The **Molecule** returns in every issue of *GIANT CANADIAN COMICS!*

❦

THE *COACHWHIP* AND THE COLD-BLOODED KILLER!

Chez Casablanca! Montreal's most glamorous nightclub . . . *and its most* **notorious!**
—*Hello, Suckers!*

"Texas" Diamond owns the club . . .
—Have we got a show for you tonight! Straight from the *Wild West . . .* ***"Coachwhip" Calhoon!***

—*Oh, I'm just a whip-crackin' cutie . . .*
Crack! Crack!
—WOO WOO!
—HUBBA HUBBA!

—Why, if it ain't *Roch Lapierre* of the Morality Squad! Come for your payoff?
—Aw, Texas, you know I'm clean! Say, isn't the *new gal* stealing your old act?

—I may be retired, Roch—but the old *whip act* ain't!
—Huh! Talk about a *cracker!*

Later . . .
—I'll just sneak *backstage* and introduce myself . . .

—OH! *Roch?*
—*Jane!* Y-You're "Coachwhip" Calhoon?

—Yes, but—please—*don't kiss me!*
—But why, *mon amour?* Don't you still love me, even after all these years?

—Yes—no—*I can't . . . I'm . . .* **Married!**

Meanwhile, in *Texas's* office . . .
—*Michael O'Connor!* You gangster—what do you want?
—I heard ye might know where to find me *wife, Jane!*

159

—There's nobody here by that name, you *two-bit crook!*

—*Talk!* Talk, or I'll *slap ye silly!*
—**OW-W-W!**

—She's *too good* for the likes of you! You'll never get her back *as long as I live!*
—*I'll fix that!*

POW! POW! POW!

In Jane's dressing room . . .
—*Gunshots!* Stay here, Jane! Stop! *Arrêtez! Police!*

—*Texas!*
—Jane—must tell you—*the coachwhip*—given to me by old medicine woman—it has *magical powers*—all yours now—take care of the club—*so long, suckers* . . .

Roch returns—*wounded!*
—Jane—darling—it was that gangster, *Michael O'Connor*—he got away! I'll—I'll call the *morgue* . . . I'm so sorry!

Later, alone in her dressing room . . .
—Is it true that this whip has *magical powers?* I'll use it to track down Texas's killer *as "The Coachwhip"* . . .

—. . . Even if the *killer* . . . is my *husband!*

Read the cases of the **Coachwhip** in every issue of *GIANT CANADIAN COMICS!*

THE ICY ORIGIN OF *CAPTAIN ZERO!*

At a lonely research station high above the Arctic Circle, near the *North Magnetic Pole* . . .

—Imagine! Me, lowly *Corporal Mamook*, guarding **Dr. Peter Barnes!** First Canadian to fly over the North Pole! Your supper, *"Captain Zero"*!

—*Leave me alone!* Blasted Ministry of War, saddling me with this *fool* . . . The Nazis will never invade us! The North is too *vast* and *cold!*

—But back to work! I've found a connection between *sub-zero temperatures* and the north pole's *magnetism* . . .

—This *isolation tank* should give a man the ability to survive in the Arctic *unaided!* I'll test it myself before that busybody *Mamook* can report it . . .

Into the strange apparatus!
— *S-s-so c-c-cold. . . !*

Meanwhile . . .
—*Nazis? Here? Impossible!*
—*Very* possible, Untermensch!
Whack!
— **UH-H-H!**

—Set de explosives! Ve must *destroy* dis station!
—*Jawohl*, Mein Herr!
—Den back to *"U-Boat Zero"!*

Soon . . .
BOOM!

Deep in the *sub-zero darkness* . . .
—Wake up! You must *help us!*
—W-what? . . .

A strange scene!
—A *polar bear* . . . a *seal* . . . a *killer whale* . . . a *snowy owl!* But how. . . ?
—*We guard the north!*
—Now *evil men* threaten us!
—We know of your *exploits*, Doctor!

—It is said that *ice water* runs through your *veins!* Now it is *true!* You control the *ice and cold!*

—We see all—*in air, land, or sea!*
—The men you call Nazis have a *special submarine!*
—You must *capture* it and *rescue* Mamook!

Soon, aboard "U-Boat Zero" . . .
—*Mein Herr!* Closing fast! *A torpedo . . . made of ice!*
—Vas ist? *Impossible!*
—*Very* possible, Heinie!

The ice torpedo strikes!
BOOM!
—One chance to *escape!*

Mamook dives out of the damaged U-Boat . . .
—The *U-Boat—frozen solid!* But how . . . ?

A *bathysphere* made of ice!
—Dr. Barnes!
—That's **Captain Zero** to you! All aboard!

Mamook is saved!
—But how did you survive the explosion?
—I'm not sure I believe it myself . . .

—But there's one thing I do believe—*now! The Nazi Menace!*
—Glad to hear it!

Captain Zero reports for duty in every issue of *GIANT CANADIAN COMICS!*

THE FIGHTING CANUCK vs THE SABOTEURS

"That's the man we want!"

On a fine spring morning, in the prairie city of Regina, Saskatchewan, a tall, thin, grey-eyed man in a Sergeant-Major's uniform talked to the head of the Royal Canadian Mounted Police. It was Graduation Day at the famed Mountie Academy.

"But Edward MacLeod's the finest cadet we've got!" exclaimed the Chief Inspector. "The Army can't just barge in here and take him away from the Mounties!"

"Do I have to remind you that we're at war? I'm here on orders from Prime Minister Mackenzie King himself!"

The Chief Inspector flushed with embarrassment. "Yes, Sir," he mumbled. "Cadet MacLeod! Front and centre!"

Cadet Edward MacLeod dismounted from his chestnut mare. "Whoa, Victoria. Wait here like a good girl!" He strode over to the two older men. Edward was six feet tall, with curly red hair cropped close and flashing blue eyes.

The grey-eyed man addressed him. "I am code-named Reynard. I'm here to recruit you to a top-secret military program. There are spies and saboteurs everywhere, and we need a man to root them out. Someone patriotic—who's ready to give his life for his country!"

"Sir, we MacLeods have been patriotic Canadians since we were United Empire Loyalists. I'm at the service of the King—and Canada!"

"Excellent—your training begins immediately!"

"Ah—MacLeod—come in!"

A year later, Edward entered the office of the mysterious Reynard.

"I have your final report here. It seems you've excelled in all of your training! You can drive any vehicle—fly any plane—fire any weapon—a master of personal combat—and a crack codebreaker!"

"I can also speak French, German, Italian, and Japanese!"

"I knew we'd picked the right man. Congratulations, son. You are the first secret agent of Department 'H'! Your codename will be . . . Canuck! Now—are you ready for your first mission?"

"Ready, aye, ready!"

"Good. You'll be going home—to *Halifax!*"

The Halifax shipyards were buzzing with activity when the new riveter arrived.

"No need to hide it from me, son," said the yard boss. "I'm fully briefed and happy to cooperate. It seems we have a saboteur in the yards! We'll put you to work on the night shift and let you find him!"

That night, dressed in coveralls and armed only with his rivet gun, the Canuck went to work . . . in an unusual way! No sooner had the whistle blown for the start of the shift when he went up to one of his comrades. "Say, I'm new here," he said lazily. "Where can a fellow go to take a nap? You know, we're getting paid just the same!"

"There's a quiet spot just over there. But don't tell anyone I said so!"

Edward crawled into one of the lifeboats and pulled his cap over his eyes. "Now to pretend I don't see anything!"

Hours later, in the deep of the night, Edward's ears were alerted to a strange sound—*CLANK! CLANK! CLANK!*

Three men with electro-magnets strapped to their boots were walking down the side of the battleship! They spoke to each other in German. "Vis zis acid, ve will soften und dissolve de steel of de bulkhead. Dis is vun ship dot vill never survive de Wolfpack!"

The Canuck sprung into action! He leapt out of the lifeboat and dove onto the first saboteur. Still attached to the ship by his magnets, he was a sitting duck for Canadian fists! The acid flew out of his hand—and onto the second Nazi saboteur, who let out a scream and fell into the cold water of the harbour. As for the third, the coward gave up without a fight—and revealed that he was following orders via radio . . . from *Montreal!*

The Canuck got off the train at Windsor Station and was met by a large man with a broken nose.

"I am Richthofen," lied Edward, in perfect German. "You are here to take me to 'the Baron,' ja?"

"Je ne comprends pas," said the giant, in Québec French. "Richthofen, you said?"

"That's right," said the Canuck, in French.

"Then come with me to 'the Room.'"

The car stopped outside a nondescript building on Ontario Street. The French giant led Edward down a hall and through a plain door into a plainer office ... but behind a coatrack lay a door painted the same colour as the wall. And behind the door was a beehive of telephone and radio operators!

"The whole building is full of wires," said the giant. "We report on the horse racing results and the sports scores for the gambling syndicates. But there's good money in forwarding orders for 'the war effort'—ha ha ha!"

"This is my kind of corruption," said Edward with an evil grin. "Now take me to le Baron."

Through another door was a well-appointed office, guarded by two twitchy young men with machine guns. Behind a desk was a suave man in a tailored three-piece suit: le Baron! The giant left Edward alone with them.

"What is the occasion, Richthofen?" inquired le Baron. "Come for a payoff?"

"No—a kiss-off!"

The Canuck twisted and, using a judo manoeuvre, threw one machine-gun-toting guard into the other, then, in the blink of an eye, had both guns trained on the gangster.

"Now—why are you working for the Nazis?"

"It's not me giving the orders! I'm only in it for the money! And the money's coming by wire—from *Winnipeg!*"

The Canuck landed his Bristol Beaufighter at the Royal Canadian Air Force base outside Winnipeg and met his old friend, mechanic "Gears" Godfrey.

"Gears! Be a pal and give me a lift into town. I could use some muscle on this job!"

Hours later, dressed like gangsters in pinstriped zoot suits, Gears and the Canuck pulled up to a jazz nightclub in the Exchange District. "Hi-di-hi," said Edward, getting out and slapping Gears's outstretched hand. "He-de-he," replied Gears, slamming the door behind him. They walked into the club with the club's guards none the wiser.

"This reminds me of the kind of place I grew up in," whispered Gears. To a cigarette girl with short blonde curls, he said, "Say, Fay Wray, where's a gorilla to go if he's looking for a buck on the side, Clyde?"

"You gotta see the boss, Hoss—he's in the back, Jack."

"Solid, Jackson. Have a ball, doll."

As Gears led Edward to the back of the club, the Canuck said, "They never covered jazz in my language classes!"

In the shadows of the back of the club sat an elegant man in a black tuxedo—Don Cesare of the Italian Mafia! The Canuck spoke to him in Italian. "We heard there's good money in blackmailing the Ministry of War," he said, "and we know planes."

"How did you know we're sabotaging planes?"

"We didn't—until now!" With that, Edward and Gears leapt upon the gangster and swiftly disarmed him. "Time to bring you in, Don Cesare!"

"But I'm just following orders—in code! Here are the latest, fresh from *Vancouver!* Do what you want, but don't send me to jail!"

"You're just as yellow as your grey-shirted Axis pals, Don. But the only grey shirt you'll be wearing is in the internment camp in Petawawa!"

🍁

The Avro X-4 experimental supersonic plane landed safely on the British Columbia coast mere hours later. "Are you sure you don't want to come with me, Gears?"

"Thanks, Eddie, but I want to take care of my plane—and I don't speak Japanese!"

The Canuck had broken the code and discovered the lair of the head of the coast-to-coast saboteur network, deep in Vancouver's Chinatown. "Pity," thought Edward as he applied his sallow-featured disguise. "There are so many loyal Japanese-Canadians! I guess it only does take a few bad apples to spoil the bunch!"

Now in the guise of a poor immigrant, Edward joined the ranks of a group of Japanese on the Vancouver docks—newly arrived and desperate! A beautiful Oriental woman clapped her hands and addressed the dirty mob. "You are looking for work? We will give you work! This group—to the munitions plant! This group—to the shipyard! You, young women—you will work the opium dens!"

"And what about one who wishes to see the Yellow Dragon?" said Edward, in Japanese.

"What do you know about the Yellow Dragon?"

"Only that he wishes to destroy our Anglo-American enemies in the name of the Emperor!"

"Come—you may be useful!"

Soon, he was being led through a typical laundry in Chinatown. The beautiful girl, Akiko, pressed a button—and a rack of pressed shirts was moved aside by a steel door! Steam appeared to rise from the darkness . . . but! "Welcome to the hall of the Yellow Dragon—one known to us as the Canuck!"

Powerful hands clutched his arms and dragged him through the hall. "I could resist," he thought, "but they're taking me exactly where I want to go!"

Feigning weakness, he let himself be thrown to the ground at the foot of an elaborate bamboo chair, where sat the master of the Japanese underworld . . . the Yellow Dragon!

"Welcome, Canuck," he said, putting his long fingers together and bowing, "You are our honoured guest . . . forever! Our spies are everywhere—yes, even in the halls of Parliament Hill! Soon this war will end—and the victory of the Axis will ensure that I, and my allies from coast to coast, will profit handsomely! You are brave—resourceful—strong! Remain here with us—be my samurai—take my beautiful daughter Akiko for a wife! Do not resist the inevitable! Bend as the bamboo bends in a storm—or be broken!"

"Never!" exclaimed the patriotic Canuck. He exploded into a storm of his own—a storm of kicks and punches, felling all of the Yellow Dragon's henchmen. Akiko looked on in amazement—"What a man," she breathed. "A true, red-blooded Fighting Canuck!"

Soon, only Edward was standing, his makeup running. He looked around the room. "Where is your father?" he asked Akiko.

"Escaped," she replied. "I have remained to tell you—*I am yours!*"

"I've destroyed your father's spy network, from here to Halifax," said Edward. "Turn yourself in to the authorities, and I'll make sure they go easy on you."

"Easy?" said the beautiful Japanese girl, dark eyes flashing. "No, handsome Edward—a Japanese prisoner-of-war camp is easy on no-one! We will meet again!" She threw a smoke bomb and vanished.

"And that's the last I saw of her, Reynard."

"Excellent work, MacLeod," said the tall, grey-eyed man. "It only goes to show that the Axis danger is, just as in the Canadian motto, *Ad mari usque ad mare.* I'll report it to the Prime Minister personally! You are a true Canadian hero!"

"But, sir, I'm only one man. Surely there are others we can find to help combat this scourge?"

"Indeed, MacLeod, you speak truer than you know. . . ."

Boys and girls! Join the **Fighting Canuck**'s Loyalists and follow his missions in *GIANT CANADIAN COMICS!*

THE WEIRD TALE OF THE *WARLOCK!*

Ottawa—*the Peace Tower* stands guard over a proud nation at war . . .
BONG! BONG! BONG! BONG!

The Prime Minister—*Mr. Mackenzie King!*
—*Midnight!* He said he'd be here!
BONG! BONG! BONG! BONG!

—*What? Thirteen* bells?
BONG! BONG! BONG! BONG! BONG!

From the crystal ball, a weird apparition!
—Here I am—the *Warlock*, at your service, sir!

—Is it true—everything they say—your *strange supernatural* powers?
—I'll show you!

In the *crystal ball*, a strange scene . . .

—Some years ago, I was a young *doctor* in search of *adventure.* I found it—*in Spain*—fighting the fascists with the *Mackenzie-Papineau Battalion!*

"It was the *Battle of Aragon*—the beginning of the end—that was the day I met . . . *Him!*"
—*Dead! All dead*—thanks to the dark mystical powers of **Aragon the Sorcerer!**

"I couldn't save my comrades . . . I retreated into the *shrine* of the *Black Madonna* . . .

". . . And that, Mr. Prime Minister, was where Dr. Lawrence Dublin *died!*"

The *Black Madonna* speaks!
—You are a good man . . . a *healer* . . . the world will soon be at *war* against the *wicked* men . . . *return! The forces of light* must stand against the *darkness!*

"Was it a dream? I awoke—*healed!*"
—I must study these *strange mystical powers!*

—And now you are Canada's foremost *Warlock!*
—Only for *Peace* and *Good!*

—Sir, the forces of *Evil* are on the move! I've come to *warn* you of a *gathering storm!*

—*Gathering,* eh? That's just what I wanted to discuss with *you!* . . .

—. . . A gathering of the *bravest heroes* in the land—of the **Guardians of Canada!**

Read the **Warlock**'s weird tales in *GIANT CANADIAN COMICS!*

Back at the hotel room . . .
—Quite the tales! I'll add them to my files!
—We could do a lot of *good*—*together!*

—Agreed!

—But wait—I'm not sure—our *country* is so *vast* . . .
—Maybe this will convince you, *Captain Zero!*

An apparition in the Warlock's *crystal ball*—the **Prime Minister!**
—Wow! Talk about a crystal radio!
—Good evening! . . .

—. . . I've been listening to you all . . . Now, more than ever, our country needs *brave men* and *women* like yourselves, from *sea to sea!* We will stand behind you with *every means at our disposal*—if you *agree!*

—What do you say, gang?
—All right then!

—From the North Pole to the Great Lakes—from Cape Breton to Vancouver Island . . .

—**WE STAND ON GUARD FOR CANADA!**

The **Guardians of Canada** return in the next issue of *GIANT CANADIAN COMICS!*

PATRICK T. GODDARD is the co-writer of the musicals *Johnny Canuck and the Last Burlesque* and *The Mid-Life Crisis of Dionysus* and the author of the chapbook serial *The Secret Roses*. An Army brat, he lived in Winnipeg, Regina, Edmonton, Borden, Calgary, Germany, Petawawa, and Ottawa before settling in Montreal.

Kid Wonder

A.C. Wise

When we last saw our heroes, that conniving Mistress of Crime, Lady Nordique, had left Kid Wonder tied to the tracks of the Great Canadian Pacific Railway. Will this be the end of the Terrific Twosome? Will Captain Polar arrive in time to save his young sidekick? Let's find out!

The blood pounding in his ears sounded like an oncoming train. It drowned the narration, brassy, loud, and full of declarative sentences. Pain split his skull. He blinked. The world spun—a whirl of colours, accompanied by loud, shrieking music.

Blink. Light, bright as the arctic sun, haloed faces that slid in and out of focus.

He couldn't move. His arms and legs were restrained. Maybe he *was* tied to the train tracks after all—it had happened before, hadn't it?

Pain made it impossible to focus. Mouth, cotton dry. A medicinal taste lingered on his tongue. Every limb ached. All his bones felt shattered. Maybe he'd already been hit by the train. Maybe he was dying.

He listened for the howl of a train over the pounding in his head. But there was only soft beeping, and the hiss-suck of a machine. A hospital? But superheroes didn't go to the hospital. They. . . .

Blink. More pain. He clenched his jaw around a scream. A voice. Not the brassy-loud narration of his dream or hallucination, but a woman's voice, clipped and efficient.

171

"He's coming out of it. Give him another dose. It's too soon."

He struggled to respond, but his mouth wouldn't cooperate. The faces around him dissolved in a four-colour, Sunday pages blur. He saw his face and Cap's in animated splendour against their trademark polar-bear silhouette. Another blare of music. Then, nothing.

♦

"Steady there, old pal. You gave me quite a scare. Easy does it."

A hand gripped Wonder's arm. He looked up, and familiar blue eyes looked back from behind the molded white mask covering the upper half of Cap's face. Below the mask, Captain Polar smiled.

"Gosh, Cap, what happened?" Wonder's voice cracked. It sounded strange, and his ears hadn't stopped ringing.

"It was touch and go there for a while." Cap helped him sit up. "Lady Nordique hit you with her new freeze ray. She lashed you to her sled, ready to whisk you off to the Frozen Fortress, where, no doubt, she would have tortured you for the secret location of the Polar Cave. Luckily, I got there just in time. I remembered to fill my bag with tasty treats to distract her sled dogs. While she tried to get them under control, I untied you."

"Gee, Cap. You saved my life again. I owe you big time!"

"Your safety is thanks enough, old pal. Can you stand?"

"I think so." Polar helped him to his feet. Wonder's legs were unsteady, but he didn't fall. "Wasn't there a train?" The words popped out, surprising Wonder, but now that he thought about it, he did remember a train. Maybe.

Cap let go of his arm. A frown so brief Wonder could have imagined it vanished from Cap's lips. "That must have been a dream, after Nordique knocked you out." Cap squared his shoulders and gave Wonder a bright smile. "Now, what do you say we head back to the Polar Cave? I'll bet we've got big mugs of hot chocolate waiting for us, full of marshmallows."

"Just the way I like it!" Wonder grinned, tension draining out of him. He was safe. Everything was okay. Cap had saved him again. When he thought hard, he *did* remember Lady Nordique levelling her freeze gun at him, and the sensation of being awake but unable to move. Just like Cap said; it'd been a close one.

There was no sign of Nordique now. Sergeant Flannigan must have already hauled her back to her cell at Meighen Penitentiary. The city was safe for another day.

Wonder followed Cap to the Polar Mobile. It sat, idling quietly, its shields up, keeping it secure. Wonder's breath hitched just a little. No matter how many times he saw the Polar Mobile, its beauty never ceased to amaze him. The car's lines were sleek, its body slung slow to the ground, and its paint was the most perfect, gleaming white anyone had ever seen. Just like fresh-fallen snow. The car looked fierce, too, its grille snarling. If a machine could be hungry, the Polar Mobile was— hungry, and ready to run.

Cap touched a switch; the shields slid back, revealing red bucket seats. Wonder's breath caught again, his stomach turning over on the moment of hope that rose every time. Cap climbed into the driver's seat, and Wonder's heart sank. It was stupid; he wasn't even old enough to drive, but, just once, maybe Cap would hand him the keys.

"Everything okay, old pal?" Cap squinted against the sun.

"Sure." Wonder shook himself. He vaulted over the door, and landed in the seat perfectly molded to him. Wonder buckled up, and Cap gunned the engine. They shot away from the scene of peril, back to the safety of home.

The speed of their passage stripped winter-pale leaves from the trees. Maple Leaf City blurred past. It was perfect. The school, the bank, the courthouse, neat homes surrounding the downtown core, all frosted in a gentle dusting of snow. Beyond the town lay idyllic countryside and the lake. On a vast estate bordering the lake sat majestic Dymond Manor and, hidden deep beneath it, the Polar Cave.

Maybe when Wonder was a bit older, Cap would let him change his name to something cool, like Arctic Fox. They'd still be a team, but Wonder would have his own fox cycle and a new uniform, with a mask like Cap's. His voice would change as he got older anyway, and then he could be a proper superhero instead of just being Kid Wonder, Captain Polar's sidekick.

He closed his eyes, letting the motion of the car soothe him. His body ached. Nordique's freeze ray really had done a number on him. Wonder tried to remember the circumstances of his capture, but all he could conjure was a kind of jump-cut montage, jumbled memories of their past encounters. Ice crunching underfoot as he and Cap infiltrated the Frozen

Fortress; the Snow Flake Flunkies throwing wide, roundhouse punches; Lady Nordique, disguised as a Mountie, joining the Musical Ride in order to kidnap the Prime Minister on Canada Day; Nordique's ice crystal lipstick, making her lips shimmer like frost in the sun. Wonder shifted uncomfortably in his seat, pushing away thoughts of Nordique and her deadly lipstick. He opened his eyes.

"I don't remember." He hadn't meant to speak aloud.

"Remember what, old pal?" Cap glanced at him sidelong. His gloved hands tightened on the steering wheel, white leather creaking.

"Anything. I mean. . . ." What was he trying to say? Wonder's stomach churned, no longer drawing comfort from the loping pace of the Polar Mobile. "I mean, I remember things, but it's all bits and pieces. It's like. . . ." Something tried to surface, gnawing its way up through Wonder's core. It was big. It had teeth and claws. And it terrified him.

Cap turned the car sharply, pointing its nose directly toward the frozen lake. He stomped the gas, and the car surged forward. Wonder didn't even flinch. At the moment the tires left the snow-slick shore, a hole appeared in the ice, and the Polar Mobile glided smoothly down into the vast, underground Polar Cave.

"It's been a long day, old pal. You should get some rest. You'll feel better in the morning." Cap pried his fingers from the wheel as he brought the car to a halt.

Wonder opened his mouth, and closed it again. He was thinking crazy. Maybe he'd hit his head when Nordique knocked him out, and he just needed some rest, like Cap said.

They climbed out of the car. Polar's boots clicked as he crossed the icy path leading to the cave's central platform and the Polar Computer. Sensors picked up the motion and lit the cave with its own aurora borealis. Green, blue, and violet light shifted across every surface. On a wheeled tray near the computer stood two steaming mugs of hot chocolate.

"Gosh! This is just what I needed." Wonder took a mug, inhaling deeply before taking a sip. Melted marshmallow clung to his upper lip. The temperature was just right. Another marshmallow melted on his tongue, leaving a sticky-sweet residue behind. Blinking heavy eyes, he watched Cap take a seat at the Polar Computer. Their battle with Nordique must be catching up with him, even if he didn't remember it. Sleep beckoned. Wonder yawned.

"I'm going to turn in. 'Night, Cap." The words emerged slurred, fuzzy around the edges.

"Sleep well, old pal."

Wonder wanted to reply, but the only sound that emerged was, "Hmmm."

The Polar Cave wobbled. The ripple of the aurora borealis across the walls made everything unreal. And he could no longer keep his eyes open.

❦

Wonder woke with his heart pounding. Sweat slicked his skin. His mouth was dry and tasted of burnt sugar.

A quick glance revealed nothing out of the ordinary. Except he was in his room, and he didn't remember leaving the Polar Cave. He threw back the covers and stared at his legs, his rumpled pyjamas—printed with maple leaves—and his feet sticking out of their worn-soft cuffs. He wiggled his toes. For an irrational moment, he expected the toes at the end of the bed wouldn't move.

He swung his feet to the floor. They met hardwood—solid, cold, and real. Careful not to let the boards creak, Wonder crossed the room to his dresser. On a red velvet pillow lay the key to the city. The Mayor had given it to him after he and Cap had foiled a particularly dastardly plan by the Moose Master. Beside it sat a medal, also awarded to him by the Mayor, for bravery, after he and Cap had rescued a group of schoolchildren from the Ignominious Igloo.

He scanned the walls, lined with framed photographs. Wonder and Polar, over and over again—shaking hands with the Mayor, the Prime Minister, the Queen. Wonder ran a finger along one of the frames. It came away dusty. The picture was unfaded, but the glass holding it looked dingy, weary.

Nothing seemed out of place. So why couldn't he shake the feeling of unease?

Books. Why didn't he own any books? There weren't even any textbooks. Fear prickled the base of his spine. One by one, he pulled open the dresser drawers, then opened the closet. Neat uniforms, all identical, hung within. The drawers were filled with clothing and with gadgets for fighting crime.

But there wasn't a single notebook, not a single test or school project. Now that Wonder thought about it, he couldn't remember the last class he'd attended, or even the name of his school. His pulse raced, quick as an arctic hare.

There were no personal objects in his room, either. No baseballs, or pictures of him with friends, or even a favourite teddy bear from when he was little. He'd had parents once, hadn't he? What happened to them?

He wiped clammy palms on his pyjamas, and tried to get his breathing under control. There was a dream he could almost remember, a memory trying to surface. The vast beast clawed at him, wanting to rise.

With trembling hands, he lifted his pyjama top and studied the smooth expanse of his chest in the mirror lining his closet. He wasn't sure what he was looking for, but it felt important. Wonder almost missed it, but even in the dim light he picked out a pale scar, just below his breast bone. He touched the mark. Phantom pain spread outward, leaving him dizzy and short of breath. His left arm tingled.

He dropped his shirt, hiding the scar. The back of his neck prickled now, and he looked to the door, half expecting Cap, or someone else, to be watching him through the crack. But the hallway was empty. Still making no sound, Wonder opened the door wider. Holding his breath, he crept down the stairs. The image of the scar lingered. He'd received his fair share of bruises during his and Cap's battles, but the scar was precise, deliberate. Like someone had cut him open and stitched him closed again.

In the library, Wonder opened the glass door of a grandfather clock taller and wider than he was. He turned the hands until the internal mechanism clicked and the clock's interior swung open, revealing a passage leading down to the Polar Cave.

At the bottom, Wonder paused, heart pounding. Until he crossed the bridge to the Polar Computer, the cave would remain in blue shadow. Lights blinked like constellations on the Polar Computer's terminal. A stuffed polar bear, a gift from the Redpath Museum in Montreal, loomed to Wonder's left. To his right, glass displays held different versions of his and Cap's uniforms, and trophies from their most famous cases.

He crossed the bridge, and the cave's false twilight was replaced by the boreal glow. The shifting green and blue light added an extra layer of unreality. Between the lights and the stillness, Wonder had the impression of being underwater, drifting peaceful.

Maybe he was being paranoid. Maybe he should go back to bed.

Wonder sat in the chair Cap had occupied earlier and keyed in his password. The screen lit up. Starting with the archives, he flipped through old case files. All the times they'd stopped Nordique or Moose Master; their team-ups with Timber Wolf and Bucky Beaver, and even the time they'd worked with Star Spangled, Union Jack, and the Sun King to stop an international caper dreamed up by the Villainous Five.

Fragments of newspaper articles and old photographs blurred past as Wonder scrolled through screen after screen. There were careful gaps and omissions, but Wonder couldn't piece together exactly what had been left out.

He skimmed the extensive background information on Nordique, and the rest of Cap's rogue gallery. There were files on allies, too, and a folder labelled Maple Leaf City. Opening it, Wonder found detailed maps, city plans, building schematics. There were subfolders labelled CP1, CP2, and KW.

He clicked the KW folder. A box popped up, asking for his password. He rekeyed it, and a message flashed across the screen: *invalid*. He tried again. The same message. Cap had never told Wonder his password. Blood thumping in his fingertips, Wonder guessed at a few—"Mack," Cap's nickname for the stuffed polar bear, after John A. MacDonald; "Niagara," after their most famous case, when Nordique had frozen the Falls; he even tried "Nordique."

Wonder used to suspect Cap had a thing for her. But it could have been his imagination. He hadn't seen any evidence recently. The spark between them was gone, if it had even existed in the first place.

The Polar Computer locked him out after the fifth try. Wonder dropped his hands into his lap. Footsteps behind him made him turn, jumping to his feet. He'd expected Cap, but his excuse for being up so late, and in the Polar Cave alone, died on his tongue.

Lady Nordique stood between him and the stairway leading back to majestic Dymond Manor. She had one hand planted on her hip; the other held a freeze ray, levelled at his heart.

"No sudden moves," she said.

Nordique's expression was grim in a way Wonder had never seen it before. Her suit, covered with a fine dusting of crystals, caught light from the cave's false aurora borealis and shimmered. But she wasn't wearing her mask, or her trademark fur-lined cape. And she looked tired.

"How did you. . . ?"

"Cut the crap, kid." Nordique stepped forward, her tone harsh, but her expression still weary.

Her boots echoed on the walkway; her freeze gun never wavered.

"Cap'll save me. He always does!" Wonder's voice broke. He backed up into the Polar Computer's behind him. He gripped the terminal until his fingers ached.

"Jesus Christ! Will you shut the fuck up for a second? I'm not going to hurt you."

Nordique's voice was different, less musical. She wasn't making any bad puns, either, or any grand, theatrical gestures.

Wonder's head ached. "Your freeze gun—"

"Oh, for fuck's sake. It's just for show."

Nordique tossed the weapon, and Wonder caught it—hollow plastic, glued with large, jewelled buttons. Up close the seams showed, as did the drips of hot glue. Wonder stared, open-mouthed. Nordique's expression changed. Her eyes went flat, a lake reflecting the winter sky.

"You really don't know, do you? You don't remember."

Wonder gripped the fake gun. The Polar Cave seemed to spin around him, the whole world tilting and sliding out from under him. "Your plan won't work! If you take me to the Frozen Fortress, Cap'll know it's a trap!"

His throat ached; his mind reached toward the emptiness where his memories should be. All he found was the vast, clawing thing.

"Will you just shut up and listen? I'm trying to help you, but we don't have much time." Nordique came closer, grabbing the second chair at the terminal. She sat, lacing her fingers, resting her arms on her knees, and leaned forward. "Look, kid. . . ."

"Leave him alone, Holly."

Wonder spun around. Captain Polar stood at the bottom of the second secret passageway leading to the Polar Cave. He wore silk pyjamas under a quilted dressing gown with matching fuzzy slippers. And no mask.

"Cap!"

Polar held up a hand. "It's okay, old pal."

Cap ran a hand through his blond hair, leaving it standing up erratically. In his other hand he held a glass of amber liquid. Wonder had never seen Cap touch alcohol before. But when Cap drew closer, Wonder could smell it on him. His eyes were glassy, surrounded by fine lines—not age, but something else.

Wonder's head pounded. Cap pressed his lips into a thin line, and Nordique glared at him. "He deserves to know," she said.

"You can't keep doing this to him." Cap's voice betrayed strain. He sipped his drink, ice rattling.

"Stop talking about me like I'm not here!" Wonder slammed a fist against the Polar Computer. His hand stung where he'd struck it. His eyes stung, too. He felt younger than ever, a kid throwing a tantrum while his parents argued above his head. Another wave of dizziness swept through him; his arm tingled, and it had nothing to do with hitting the computer console.

Cap and Nordique exchanged a look. Cap turned away, his stance rigid, as though tensed against a blow. Wonder had never seen his partner, his mentor, this way.

"Maybe you'd better sit down." Nordique spoke gently, as if calming one of her dogs.

Her soothing tone only jangled Wonder's nerves. Everything about the situation was wrong. Cap's turned back frightened him the most, as if he'd been abandoned—that and the expression in Nordique's eyes: pity.

Wonder let himself sink into the chair. He pressed his hands against his knees, trying to hold himself together.

"Do you remember the time I froze Niagara Falls?" Nordique asked.

Wonder nodded. He didn't trust himself to speak. Didn't trust his voice not to break, nor his stinging eyes not to spill over.

The pity in Nordique's gaze deepened, and she added a wistful smile. "I don't. Because it wasn't me. It was the Lady Nordique before me. Her hair was redder; she was more of a strawberry blonde."

Polar made a soft noise but said nothing.

"I don't think he's ever forgiven me for replacing her." Nordique gestured at Cap, the wistful smile twisting into something unreadable.

Ice clinked in Cap's glass, followed by a hard sound as he set it down.

"I don't understand." Wonder felt like a recording, played on an endless loop. The fine lines at the corners of Nordique's eyes reminded him of the lines around Cap's eyes, the lines their masks usually hid.

"Fix the poor kid a drink, will you, Gary?" Nordique spoke over Wonder's head again.

Wonder twisted around, surprised to see Cap sliding open a panel beneath the Polar Computer. He pulled out a crystal decanter, refreshing his own glass, and pouring a second, which he handed to Wonder.

"Sorry, no ice down here." Cap chuckled, a dry, humourless sound.

"But, Cap, I'm not old enough to drink!" Wonder took the glass anyway, his hand acting independent of his words. The amber liquid shivered.

"This is your idea, you explain it to him." Cap tilted his glass at Nordique.

"Be a fucking gentleman and offer me a drink at least." Nordique's tone broke, all gentleness gone.

Wordless, Cap poured her a glass and handed it over. She tossed half the contents back with a violent motion of her head. Wonder had seen Cap and Nordique trade blows dozens of times, but this was something different. Pain shadowed Cap's gaze, and animosity seethed in Nordique's. The punches and kicks were all a show compared to this. Whatever this was, it had nothing to do with stealing diamonds, or kidnapping the Prime Minster, or freezing Niagara Falls. And Wonder couldn't imagine *this* Nordique whispering her threats, silky smooth, in Cap's ear, or brushing his lips with her deadly ice-crystal frost, never meaning to kill him.

Wonder sipped from the drink Cap had handed him. The liquor burned, making his eyes sting even more, but he managed to swallow without coughing. Nordique leaned forward and put a hand on his knee. Under other circumstances, Wonder would have squirmed, but again he was reminded of the Lady calming her dogs, resting a reassuring hand on their heads to still their whining.

"I'm sorry," Nordique said.

Her eyes, free of their mask, found Wonder's gaze and held it. The words seemed genuine, the hurt real. Their arch nemesis, here in the Polar Cave, comforting him, and Cap turning his back like he wanted nothing to do with either of them.

"I really thought, after the last time, you'd remember, and it wouldn't be such a shock." Nordique took a deep breath. "There have been four Lady Nordiques, and three Captain Polars. He's the third." She took another, steadier sip of her drink. It left her voice hoarse, stripped raw. "There's only ever been one Kid Wonder. You."

Wonder stared, waiting for the joke, the punchline. None came. Every part of him ached. He was tied to the railway tracks again, a train bearing down on him, his bones waiting to shatter.

"Cap?" Wonder hated the smallness of his voice, echoing through the Polar Cave. Cap had saved his life a hundred times, maybe a thousand. He would make everything okay, he had to.

Cap swallowed, his throat working painfully. "I'm sorry, old pal. It's true." He turned. "Believe or not, kid, you're actually older than me."

Cap raised his glass, and downed the rest of his drink. Wonder mirrored the gesture, not meaning to. This time he did choke, and it turned into a coughing sob. His body heaved; his lungs ached; his ribs felt ready to snap and send splinters of bone straight to his heart. He gasped for breath, and Cap pounded him on the back.

"I hope you're happy now," Cap said to Nordique.

"It isn't right," she said. "He should know."

"How. . . ?" Wonder scrubbed the heels of his hands against his eyes, willing the tears away.

"Drugs, surgery, brainwashing." Cap shrugged. "They really did a number on you."

"There's a scar on my chest." Wonder touched the space below his breastbone. Memories struggled to surface again, things he could almost taste, touch, waiting at the edges of his mind.

"You had a heart attack." Cap's voice was flat. "Before my time. The strain of everything they'd done to you. They eventually had to do a full transplant. Your heart gave out, so they fixed you up with a shiny new one. Your liver's new, too. You half-killed it on this stuff a time or two."

Something jarred loose inside Wonder's mind, bringing the stale taste of vomit to his mouth; he nearly gagged. He'd tried to kill himself, but he hadn't had the guts to do it all at once. He'd run, holed up in a cheap motel where he could hear the Falls, but not see them. He'd thrown up almost as much as he drank, wrecking his stomach lining and throat. At the end, there'd been blood. Nothing the doctors couldn't repair. Cap had dragged him out of that place. Wonder had thrown a right cross, weak, but he'd hit Cap in the jaw. Cap had only grimaced, refusing to let go.

"Why?" The word snagged, hurting his throat. Wonder coughed again. An old man's lungs struggled in his chest, fighting to draw in enough air. His new heart kicked, rebelling against decaying flesh.

"The city needs heroes. And villains, too, I suppose." Cap gestured to Holly.

Nordique—Holly—covered Wonder's hands with her own.

"The powers-that-be hand-picked you and the first Captain Polar. There were hundreds of applicants; everyone wanted their chance to stand in the spotlight and receive the adoration of millions. None of them had a fucking clue what that meant." Cap raised his glass, and after considering it for a moment, set it aside with a look of distaste.

Nordique picked up his thread. "You were the only one without a mask. Everyone else they could replace and no-one would notice. Anyone could be Captain Polar, or Lady Nordique, but you were the only Kid Wonder.

"There wasn't a long term plan. Maple Leaf City was in the grip of an economic depression. The world was full of fear, uncertainty. There were rumours of another war brewing. People needed something to believe in, good guys and bad guys neatly defined—not faceless hunger, poverty, and despair they couldn't fight."

"You and the first Captain Polar, you became symbols," Cap said. His shoulders sagged, and he leaned against the computer console. "Your face became a beacon of hope. You were innocence, purity, standing up for truth and justice. Every kid, not just in Maple Leaf City, but all across Canada, wanted to be you."

"I still don't understand." Wonder's head felt ready to split wide open.

"There was an accident," Cap said.

"The train."

Cap nodded. "It was meant to be a stunt, but something went wrong. And, well, since they were patching you up anyway, one of the doctors got the brilliant idea of making a few tweaks here and there, tightening the suspension, buffing out the dents, as it were. Turning back the clock a few years." Cap picked up his glass, as though he'd forgotten setting it aside, and drank off the last of the alcohol. "You agreed to the plan. You were just a kid, what the hell did you know?"

He set the empty glass down so hard Wonder was amazed it didn't shatter. "As time went on, they had to go to greater extremes. Somewhere along the line, they started fucking with your head, too. They took old memories, used them to replace the new ones. It wasn't a lie, precisely, just an omission. When I took on the role of Captain Polar, I was given strict instructions on maintaining the facade, keeping you away from things like newspapers, calendars, making sure you didn't accumulate personal objects. You weren't supposed to have any exposure to anything that could trigger memories, or raise questions. Nothing to shatter the myth of Captain fucking Polar and Kid fucking Wonder, heroes eternal."

The montage of cases tried to creep into Wonder's mind, and he shut them down. They were his memories, but they weren't. They'd made an animated TV show of his and Polar's exploits, hadn't they? And they'd passed those off as memories, too, blurring the real and the unreal until his brain was such mush he believed every lie they fed him.

Wonder clenched his jaw; his teeth ached. It was an effort to speak. "Didn't anyone notice I never grew up?"

"Sure, a few people here and there," Cap said. "But most people wanted to believe the lie. That's the thing about superheroes. People want them to be real. Sometimes they want it badly enough they're willing to set logic aside, ignore the laws of physics, or even time."

"How long?" Wonder swallowed. "I mean. . . . How many times have I found out the truth?"

Cap and Nordique exchanged glances. After a moment, Nordique shook her head. "I don't know."

"You tried to help me once before, didn't you?"

"Yes, but Gary was right. I shouldn't have interfered." A look of genuine regret crossed her face.

Wonder took a deep breath. He held it until he felt as though his lungs would burst. When he let it out, he met Cap and

Nordique's gazes in turn. He almost felt steady, almost in control. "So, what happens now?"

"That's up to you," Cap said softly.

Age weighted Wonder's bones. He felt every one of his scars, even the ones he would never see. His whole being was scar tissue and myth. He didn't exist, not anymore. He'd had a family once, parents, but they'd be long dead by now. Had he ever been in love? He could almost conjure up the image of a girl with a bow in her hair, but could he trust it? What if it was another lie?

It hardly mattered; he'd given up whatever he was to become Kid Wonder. All his memories—they were ghosts of ghosts. Whatever had been real had been cut out long ago, replaced, like his heart and his liver.

It hurt. It hurt enough that he could imagine asking the doctors to wipe his memories, too. If he was going to be Kid Wonder, he would *be* Kid Wonder, and nothing else. At some point, he must have believed in Maple Leaf City enough to give his entire life for it. If he turned his back on it now, it would be like giving up that part of himself again. Except this time, it wouldn't mean anything.

"Let's go up to the roof," Cap said.

Wonder nodded, dazed. He stood, his legs moving automatically. He followed Cap to the elevator, and Nordique trailed behind them. They rode in silence. The doors slid open without a sound, and they stepped out onto a flat section of roof, surrounded by a wrought-iron railing.

The moon was full, as silver as Nordique's costume. Fat snowflakes drifted through the air. A dusting of white already glazed the roof. Their feet scuffed loose powder. Wonder realized he was barefoot, and he didn't care. He hugged his arms around his body against the chill. Cap followed him to the roof's edge, gripping the railing. Nordique stood a pace behind them. Their breath steamed in the air.

"It's beautiful," Wonder said.

And it was. From the rooftop of majestic Dymond Manor, they could see the frozen lake, the quiet houses, snow dusted, tucked tight and sleeping, and the distant glow of the city centre. Everything looked peaceful, unreal, like a toy town. Maple Leaf City, *his* city.

"The people still need heroes," Wonder said. He didn't look at Cap, afraid to, but he thought he saw Cap nod.

Nordique touched his arm. "You don't have to do this."

Wonder turned, looking her in the eye. "Yes, I do."

Lady Nordique pressed her lips together, and for a moment it looked like she would argue. But she nodded, her neck stiff. What else was there? He'd chosen Maple Leaf City, long ago, and, despite everything, he didn't think he regretted it now. The possibility that he might was too vast, too terrible to consider.

Wonder squared his shoulders and raised his chin. "Do what you have to do." He managed a half-smile, though it hurt all the way down to his core. "Make it convincing."

Nordique clenched her jaw. Then, before Wonder could blink, she hit him. Not a showy punch, but a quick blow that snapped his head back and folded his legs under him.

"You won't get away with this, Nordique!" Captain Polar shouted.

Wonder imagined his partner with his hands on his hips, chest puffed out, dressing gown fluttering in the chill breeze. The world flickered out of focus. Wonder tasted blood. Snow fell on his cheeks, his lashes, coming thicker now, and forming damp crystals in his hair.

"Just try to stop me, Captain!" Nordique shot back.

These were the theatrical tones he knew. Wonder closed his eyes. His lips cracked on a smile, and more blood flowed. The words washed over him, comforting. Against his closed eyelids Technicolor-bright images played, Cap and Wonder, Wonder and Cap, over and over again.

Is this the end of Kid Wonder?

Not by half, Wonder thought.

He let a blare of music pull him down, too deep for dreams. Above him, Captain Polar and Lady Nordique fought for his fate, the fate of Maple Leaf City.

A.C. WISE (www.acwise.net) was born in Montreal and currently lives in Philadelphia. Her work has appeared in *Clarkesworld*, *Best Horror of the Year Vol. 4*, and *Imaginarium 2012: The Best Canadian Speculative Writing*, among others. She co-edits the *Journal of Unlikely Entomology*.

LEAF MAN

RHEA ROSE

My Superhero Sidekick finally arrived as a bioluminescent blob, encased in a man-sized lava lamp. Two guys who looked like dockworkers lugged it up the narrow steps to my compact Kitsilano apartment and left it in the middle of my dining-living-kitchen-bedroom. I tipped them a joint each—which they didn't seem to appreciate.

After I got them out the door I studied my new toy. A small mailing sticker on the outer glass read: *Martin McKeel.* That was me, a recently unemployed postie for the Canadian government. Screw getting a job with UPS. With the abilities my own superpower pot instilled in me, I'd decided to make my lifetime hobby as a superhero my new fulltime career.

I studied the receptacle crowding my space. A brochure taped to the glass said the lifeform inside the lava lamp would be a transforming Pulchimmera—but my alien looked like a quietly undulating blob of cookie dough. I'd also expected something more attractive. The Sidekick brochure said these shapechanging aliens would conveniently transform into the opposite sex of their host, but my "she" blob hadn't yet noticed my manliness. I took a moment to pull up my red satin shorts tight so "she" could sense my machismo. Still no change. Dang! I thought an alien in the shape of a beautiful woman would be a much more exciting sidekick to run with in the backyards and lanes to rescue animals than was my Japanese blowup babe, Hiro. I had been using Hiro far too long for company in my

186

duties, but at least Hiro was faithful to me; more than I can say about Darala, my ex. She left me after one week.

I untied my homemade purple cape from around my neck and hung it on the hook by the door, making certain that the green leaf on the back faced outward. On a couple of my animal-saving gigs I'd had the leaf turned accidentally inward and people didn't know I was Leaf Man, which got me arrested. It amazed me how many people asked *why a green maple leaf?* I'd tell them, "It's not a maple leaf. I'm Leaf Man, and I protect the poor and downfallen—the tortured, the maimed, the imprisoned, the starved, the lonely. . . ."

Another animal rescue call was coming in on my police radio tracker. I didn't have time to figure out the alien in the giant Cola bottle right now; I had a mission.

When I arrived at the scene I found a menacing pit bull cornering a mother cat and her three kittens. The pit bull's owner was using the cats to train his dog for deadly savagery. I pulled my folded plastic sidekick, Hiro, out of my backpack. She'd certainly seen better days, and today was not one of them: her left arm and leg were badly frayed, and she was now permanently deflated. I doubted I'd be able to repair her.

Without Hiro's help I barely managed to save the puddy tats and rescue the dog (after blowing a little superpower pot up his snout).

By the time I got home again, I felt depressed, even though I'd once more saved the day. I dragged the deflated Hiro in behind me. She was ready for the recycling bin. Animal rescue was a lonely and mostly thankless job. Being a superhero didn't seem to impress the women—at least none that I'd met—so when I'd ordered my new sidekick I'd hoped that I'd at least have some kind of female company. At the moment I was dead tired. The massive container where the Pulchi appeared to sleep as a globby rainbow of red, pink, yellow, and green goo seemed more trouble than it was worth. I was about to reach in and Karate-chop the alien in frustration at her not being all that was advertised when bits of her goo began to pull apart into smaller lumps. These blobs floated upward within the tank then sank slowly, jelly-like, back to the mother blob, which presumably was too heavy to float.

I managed to push myself between the Pulchi's container and my bookcase. My Buddha belly rubbed gently against the warm smooth jar. A quick tingle passed through my loins. *Whoa, what the heck?* My longish, Gregg Allman-like blond hair filled with static and clung to the container, sliding across the glass like fine tentacles. The container, not quite six feet tall, permitted a rather disturbing bird's eye view of the tank's bottom; there, a large green eye, with a nice set of lashes and an iris with a lavender hue, blinked up at me..

I opened the messy drawer where I keep a paper bag full of superpower pot for this kind of occasion. Along with a pre-rolled reefer, I pulled out the official ten page brochure the AID (Alien Infiltration Department) authorities put out on how to live with a Pulchimmera.

The brochure outlined the responsibilities of having an alien exchange-student, but little did the authorities know that I'd ordered her from a shady mail-order ad I found on the last page of *Superman Comics* #9765, "Superman and the Flying Wombies," and that I planned a far more exciting and worthwhile existence for my companion than that of a mere home-stay visitor. I would make her my Robin, my Kato, my Rocky, my Sancho—my superhero sidekick. Now, upon rereading the fine print, which I had previously perused while under the influence of my superpower pot, I realized I had read incorrectly: it was not that a Pulchimmera needs a human host, but that it requires a *human body to host it*.

I put my small reefer back and reached for the mega-bong under my kitchen sink.

Turns out that this alien, in order to learn my male glandular properties and become my opposite, intended to squish herself up and live for about a week inside some *tiny space* inside me.

"No effing way!" I shouted. Crumpling the brochure, I threw it at the giant Coke bottle housing the creature. The paper ball ricocheted across the room, hit me in the forehead, and fell back into my hands.

My yell woke the Pulchi.

"Mar-Tin," she called to me from the jar, "don't afraid."

Don't afraid? Me very afraid.

I suddenly wanted very badly to back out of this deal.

I uncrumpled the paper ball, read on, and felt a bit sick: "Pulchimmera cocoon inside the human body, for an unspecified length of time, in one of three areas: the brain, the heart, or the genitalia. Failure to complete its cocooning cycle may result in death, or loss of genitalia."

Whose death? Whose junk?

I let out a groan. I looked over at the visitor—a face had now formed in the goo. It smiled eerily through the wavering solution. "It okay, Maaar-Tin. You seeee."

All I wanted was a sidekick to help me fight crime, not a parasite. I needed some superpower. I pulled my cape over my head, took a long drag from the mega bong, and held it in.

That night I relaxed on my futon, smoked a superpower fatty, meditated upon my predicament, and tried to forget the alien forming in the aquarium filling my space. After a while a strange orangey light filled my room. As I stared in the direction of the warm light, I realized that a woman stood there—an orange, naked woman. She glowed in the dark, her orange light reflecting in a groovy way off the walls. My mind boggled. She'd make an awesome sidekick: Glow Girl, or Orange Aide—nah, Glow Girl. I wondered what other powers she possessed.

The magnificent woman moved to the foot of my bed. This pale, traffic-cone coloured woman stared down at me. Then the glow from her naked body softened. She looked beautifully confused—as if something was happening to her that she didn't understand.

She moved her hands across her breasts, down her belly, between her legs, and I felt a stirring between my own. Feeling a little ashamed, I sat up, keeping the covers at my hips.

"He—hhhelp me," she said. The emotion in her voice literally turned her on. She lit up like a cool campfire. My heart raced with a combination of desire for her and a fear that a neighbour might think my apartment was on fire.

"Climb into bed with me," I urged. My motive was simply to get her under the covers so that the natural light of her body didn't disturb the neighbours.

But once she was under the covers, I forgot all about that. Her colour was amazing, now dissolving into a pale peach. Her strange, silver-white hair fell just below her breasts. I touched her out of curiosity, like a kid touching quartz crystal in a cave. My touch made her moan.

"Sorry," I said. "Does it hurt when I touch?"

She nodded *yes*, tears in her eyes. "Touch me, Mar-Tin," she said.

"But—" She rolled and pressed her body against mine. Her pain quaked through me like a rumbling train. She let out weird sounds—nails-on-chalkboard kinds of sounds—and it turned me on.

And then it was over. I thought she'd died. I shook her gently. She rolled away, as beautiful and as stiff as an ancient Greek statue. I whispered, "Are you okay? Does anything hurt?" She looked at me, but, if she was conscious behind those soft orange eyes, she'd closed shop. I guess the transition from alien to human had been too much for her. But that didn't seem to bother me; I was still turned on. "Can I call you Candy?" I asked, not knowing if she heard.

I reached for my fatty and lay back satisfied, puffing, dreaming of saving animals with Glow Girl at my side. Leaf Man and his sidekick Glow Girl, superheroes of the SPCA. . . .

Candy came to life suddenly, like some possessed marionette from *The Twilight Zone*. "Yes, Mar-Tin, me call Candy," she said, and put her hand on my buttock. She'd heard me name her. I didn't need a second invitation, but I'd toked one too many times and, try as I might, my lighthouse wouldn't rise to the occasion. I heard a strange rush, which turned into my own blood pumping past my eardrums. The darkness twinkled with dots of sparkling light. I felt as if I floated on a batch of illuminated bubbles that carried me to the ceiling of my room. If I didn't know better, I'd swear that joint was laced with something. Then beneath me the bubbles quickly disintegrated, like dishwater swirling down a sink.

Pop!

I was still in bed, hanging onto my penis for dear life when Candy became a cloud of rainbow-coloured smoke, which disappeared into my one-eyed snake like the chick in that old 60s show about the genie returning to her bottle.

She had vanished up my vessel. I felt as if something lodged in my lower belly—like I had just eaten an entire extra-large pie from Magdizzianola's—but I didn't hurt. In a way I was kind of glad to have a girl inside me—at least she hadn't booked. I guess I knew where she planned to spend her larval stages.

Suddenly her disembodied voice echoed inside my head, "I in your heart Mar-Tin."

"No, baby, you're not." I straightened my twisted cape and pulled it over my neither regions. *You are losing it, Martin,* I said to myself; *what kind of sidekick have you hooked up with?*

For the next few days I urinated more than I had in my entire life. I wanted her out of there, but nothing I did worked. I googled Pulchimmeras and discovered they were a dime-a-dozen as far as alien visitors to Earth went. They were poorly treated and even abused on their home planet, especially the "females," and that was why so many of them wanted to come to Earth as students or domestic workers, or whatever they could get. I learned that the Pulchis had a ninety-five percent rate of non-return. They seemed to disappear in large numbers after taking Earth hosts, even though their visas were usually only granted for one month. The authorities from both worlds were constantly hunting them as illegal aliens but could find few of them..

Not long after Candy's alien invasion, I lay half asleep in a dreamy lucid state. I hadn't had any animal rescue missions since the kitten episode. I imagined the Pulchimmera as she had been before she'd entered into our odd union. Glubb, glubb went my heart, almost painfully, as I remembered her hot orange body. I got warm, sweaty, uncomfortable. My skin got slick as sweat formed on my chest, lips, and palms. An orange glow spread across my ribcage. A steady pressure increased on my heart, then pain erupted in my chest and stomach. I convinced myself that a fully formed alien was about to burst forth.

Eventually she did reappear, but not instantly, and not from my heart—more as a lacy, saffron-coloured smoke, which blew out from my pee-pee. The smoke filled the room, settled like fog down around the bed, then solidified to form a cage of long fleshy orange bars.

The fleshy bars collapsed and wrapped me in their embrace like many warm Japanese towels, gently massaging. I reached out and touched her. Her body-bars felt like the firm but malleable texture of ripe bananas.

"Mar-Tin love," she said.

"Is that a question?" I asked, basking in her steamy and soothing rub. I relaxed and my forlorn feelings were extinguished by the flexible warm membranes that worked me over.

"No more, Mar-Tin. Candy go home," she said. I looked into her strange burning eyes. I knew she wanted to go home. She was leaving like all my other women—well, the one. But I couldn't blame her. . . .

I tried in my mumbling way to explain my idea of her role as a sidekick, working with me saving animals. Candy liked the idea of Glow Girl, but I wasn't sure she understood anything else I'd said. As I was wondering what to do, the police scanner burst out with an urgent call to rescue.

It was a call to a hoarder's house with a nest of homeless raccoons trapped in their garage and a warning of dangerous chemicals buried deep within: the perfect first job for Leaf Man and Glow Girl. "Candy," I said, "If you'll be Glow Girl with me this once, I promise I'll try to help you get home, even if technically I did buy you. I swear I won't hurt you, and I'll let you go."

She smiled. "I trust you Marr-Tin. I be here." She put a finger on my junk. I groaned faintly. Then she rose up from the bed, and in an instant transformed into the hottest spandex ass-kicking sidekick I had even seen. She was dressed in a neon orange body-suit. A huge "G" highlighted her popping breasts. Her silver-shiny hair sparkled down her back. Her green thigh-high boots led enticingly up to her crotch.

I grabbed my bong. Time for some animal saving!

I checked the position of the leaf on my cape, and out of habit almost grabbed Hiro, but quickly put her back in the bag, murmuring, "Sorry, Hiro, not today." And we were off, this time no stiff plastic figure beside me, but a flesh-and-blood (or flesh and whatever) bodacious sidekick babe.We worked hard to move the tonnage of debris in that garage. We'd rescued about five hundred rats and the same number of mice, but while preparing to capture and remove a family of raccoons, we were beset by a gang of drifters claiming the garage was their home.

Evil squatters! The old lady living deep inside the actual house had no idea of the variety of rodents collecting out here. It was then that Candy, I mean Glow Girl, discovered the true nature of her superhero sidekick prowess. She glowed until the threatening intruders had to cover their eyes. Then she wrapped them in that orange smoke thing she did, until they coughed so hard they fell to the ground. Then she became those soft spongy baton things she'd used to massage me with, but beat them about their tender parts, until the squatters crawled away on hands and knees, leaving behind their two-by-fours and sharpened sticks, which I guess they'd planned to use on us to make a point.

"You Glow Girl!" I was so proud of her.

I thought we could chalk up our first rescue as Leaf Man and Glow Girl, but as the orange dust settled I saw one last bad-ass drifter left standing, uglier than the Joker, the Penguin, and the Red Skull all rolled into one bad dude.

When he spoke his voice was low, gravelly, and accented: "Glow Girl goes home!"

My heart sank to the deepest regions of my baby toes. I recognized his accent; he was Pulchi! And he looked a lot like one of those delivery guys that had carried her tank up to my apartment.

"Mar-Tin?" she called out while she reassembled herself from the fight and once again became the gorgeous orange Glow Girl. She stepped toward the evil Pulchi facing us down. I stopped her.

"Get outta here. I'll get this one," I said, handing her a baby raccoon.

I took a huge draw off my hookah hose and stepped forward. I could feel my superpowers surge through me. The ugly Pulchi took that moment to throw a baseball sized glob of clear goo from his arm and hit me square in the face. I couldn't breathe through the clear, unshakeable goo, but I could see the nasty Pulchi drifter come toward me swinging a long object that looked a lot like the leg bone of an elephant. If I didn't get that goo off my face I was done for.

In that moment, while I was dying, all the goo monster movies I'd ever watched played out before me, and that's when I remembered *The Blob*. In that movie they dropped off the Blob in Antarctica, where it stayed frozen. I had to freeze this goo, quick. I remembered seeing some flasks of liquid nitrogen in the garage. I charged to the back of the shed, tripping on boxes and avoiding a dozen rakes but at last finding a flask of the vaporous substance. I poured it on the goo and in seconds I was free. I reached for a second flask and turned to face down the nasty Pulchi. He took two swings with his giant bone, and I threw the flask at him. While there wasn't enough liquid nitro to turn him into a complete ice sculpture, there was enough to give him some serious deepfreeze damage. The evil Pulchi fell onto his ass and sat stunned while the liquid nitro made icicles of his arms, half his face, and his chest and neck. Candy (who hadn't gone home like I'd told her to) ran in, grabbed the bone bat, and began chipping away those parts covered in liquid nitro. She pared him down to about the size of a fire hydrant. Then a little dog ran out from the garage and lifted a leg on the semi-frozen Pulchi.

We had made the news and missions began to really come in. Candy continued to live inside me, appearing long enough to become Glow Girl and help me rescue downtrodden animals, or to become peach-coloured girl and sleep with me—or meld with me, or whatever it was she did. All I knew is it felt like having sex ten times at once. After a while, I couldn't imagine life without her, but I knew I had to keep my word and send her back home.

Then one day there was a knock on the door. It was the two thugs who had delivered Candy. They wanted her back to resell her. Luckily, she was inside me at that moment. I could feel her jump like a kicking baby as they searched the house to no avail.

Over the next few days I tried to figure out how to get Candy back to her home planet, but couldn't. I didn't want to contact the shady operation that had sold her to me, and I couldn't contact AID, so I surfed the back alleys of the internet for help, but with no luck. I reread the government brochure countless times. I even examined the empty container. Candy grew increasingly despondent, until one day she just disappeared.

Days went by with nothing from her: no more conversations, no psychedelic manifestations of cascading lights, not even a glowing ember. I was worried. What if the authorities found out about us?

I knew she was deathly afraid of being captured and resold by the alien traffickers. Her fear seemed to have pushed her down deep inside me. I wondered how many of her kind were buried deep inside human hosts, like her, too terrified of the torture their kind endured.

After a while, I stopped sensing her; she had just petered out. I hoped she hadn't disintegrated; that would have been a terrible way to go. Many times I examined the empty container she'd arrived in. I unscrewed the bottom, pulled and wiggled anything I could wrap my fingers around, and then put it all back together. I found no clue as to how I could have gotten Candy back home. Finally, with some heave-ho, I pushed the container from the hall over to the side of the room, then into a coat closet, and tried to forget it was even there. I smoked my superpower pot and rescued ten animals from the confines of their owners' filthy yards and stables, single-handedly carrying a lame horse through a field of rocks. Well, actually I loaded the poor lame animal into a trailer and hauled him away. But it wasn't the same without Glow Girl, and eventually the news coverage faded, but those with hurt animals still called.

After one particularly long day of animal rescue, I walked into the bathroom, still wearing my purple cape with the leaf twisted around to the front, and there she was in the mirror: Candy, Glow Girl.

Only, I barely recognized her, because she was me. A mirror image of me. "Candy? What's going on?"

"I you Mar-Tin."

"I see that. I don't like it. Are you—are you taking me over?" In the mirror, Candy imitated my walk, the kind of schlep an overweight, flat-footed, ex-possible rock singer, now superhero fellow does when no-one's looking.

"I make you better Mar-Tin."

"But, Candy, I thought you liked me the way I was?" The pot lights in the bathroom seemed to brighten. I squinted. Shwish, shwish, my heart became hard, pushed forward in my chest, expanded. I staggered against the wall. Before me, Candy shimmered and wavered like she'd stepped out of a river of boiled air rising from a hot tar patch in the middle of summer. Her form—my form—stretched; I—she—we became taller, thinner, my arms erupted with sculpted biceps and triceps. Under my cape, my Hawaiian shirt, which she'd copied perfectly, ripped open like something out of a superhero movie and there, incredibly, was a six-pack. I goggled as my Sponge

Bob underwear split open and an impossible set of—well—tools thudded against my thigh.

Without thinking, I uttered a squeak.

"I for you Mar-Tin," she said, and walked from the mirror, her arms outstretched. She took hold of my shoulders, and I shuddered like an old car trying to start up after several years of sitting around on an acre of land.

"Candy, no," I managed. "I love you."

"Love you. *Two* Mar-Tins. Su-per-heroes."

Two Martin superheroes? And then I understood. She still needed me, to absorb, to copy, to study. It was the end of her larval stage—she was coming out of the cocoon. Her kind had to inhabit humans, then take on the mental self-images of their hosts. Candy was taking on my superhero image, making a better copy of what I was; we would form the ultimate Leaf Man together. From now on, we would be equal partners fighting animal crime.

I sighed.

The AID eventually came looking for Candy, but they were getting used to not finding Pulchimmeras. I knew some had come out of the cocoon as warped, sick forms of humanity, but I hoped a few had come out as at least good people—if not superheroes.

RHEA ROSE was born in Etobicoke, ON, and moved to Vancouver when she was twelve. She participated in the Clarion West writers' workshop and has been writing ever since. At the moment she's in her thesis year in UBC's Opt-Res MFA Creative Writing program.

OCTOPI BLEAKLY CORNERS

DAVID PERLMUTTER

I

You want to know about me and the thing with the octopus, don't you? You *do*? Okay, I'll tell. . . .

II

It was early afternoon, and Gerda Munsinger (i.e., me) had just returned home after a typically exhausting day in Bleakly Corners, Manitoba, one of the many small towns dotting the province, but one of the few dotting the rugged shores of that majestic body of water, Lake Winnipeg. Her parents were still at work, and she was looking forward to some time to herself before they did. Chiefly trying to catch some Zs. She had that— for about ten minutes.

Then the phone rang, and she was awakened abruptly, with a vicious urge to kill someone. Preferably the being at the other end of the line!

She—oh, all right, *I*—woke up and grabbed the nearest phone with the expected abruptness of someone faster than the speed of light and sound put together.

"Munsinger residence," I said in the feigned, overly "feminine" voice I use for my secret identity. "Gerda speaking."

"Well, hello there, Mun-*Singer*!" the all-too familiar voice at the other end said, purposely saying the name wrong to get my

197

goat. "Is your rough and tough *pal* in? Or did she *leave*—after beating you up again?"

Briefly, I took the phone away from my face and uttered some unladylike curses in my normal, slightly deeper voice. For I knew *exactly* who was on the other end, and also *exactly* what she wanted.

She was my nemesis: Petra O'Leum.

Petra is about the same age as me, and her family comes from the same corner of space as yours truly, so naturally she's got powers like me, too. She calls herself "the girl made of rock" 'cause of the origins of her name, and because she is supposedly as invulnerable as I am. I have a hard time dealing with her, seeing as how she's nearly my equal in size and strength. But there's another problem, too: her family is *loaded*, so she can easily afford to equip herself with enough dangerous weapons and things to prevent us having to even go toe-to-toe. A lot of times when we fight, she nearly kills me without even throwing a single punch. Add the fact that she's (only slightly) prettier than me, with flaming red hair and wild black eyes, to her muscle power, weapons, and sense of entitlement, and you can see why I want to wring her neck every time we meet.

I decided, however, that I'd just let Gerda take this message and let Muscle Girl deal with her later.

"She wouldn't beat me up," I said, as Gerda, to Petra. "She's my friend!"

"I *suppose* you're right," Petra answered snidely. "As her *enemy*, I see her a bit differently than you, of course. Listen, Gerd, can you give your bosom buddy a message for me?"

"Don't call me 'Gerd'!" I snapped, forgetting myself only briefly. "I *hate* that!"

"Too bad, *Gerd*," said Petra unrepentantly. "Just tell your *friend* that I'm gunning to turn Bleakly Corners into my own personal amusement park and, if she isn't as *yellow* as her *hair* is, she'll come and *try* to stop me!"

She hung up, leaving me stuck with the dial tone. I put the phone receiver down. I knew full well what I had to do.

I went to my room, shucked off the wool sweater, jacket, blouse, and skirt I wore as Gerda, and quickly donned the pink shirt and tights and the white shorts and cape I wore as Muscle Girl—complete with the "MG" monogram—along with MG's reinforced silver steel platform shoes. Then, after checking the velocity of the wind so I'd be flying in the direction and at the speed I wanted, I was off!

III

Given who I am and what I can do, it wasn't long before I spotted Petra O'Leum's dreadnought off the coast of Bleakly Corners. You'd recognize it if you saw it: a solid black steel Rubik's cube shape with a small, token sail attached. The thing was made out of a reinforced type of onyx available only on her—sorry, *our*—home planet. Naturally, it was something so strong that no Earthling's hands or weapons could penetrate it. But yours truly was and is no Earthling, so it didn't pose a problem to me. With my enhanced 3D vision, I searched for a way into the cube through the outer layer (there usually is one because the workmanship was shoddy in spite of the money Petra sunk into it). When I found it, it was simply a matter of throwing my fist forward and punching my way through, until I got into the plush interior of the cube. Soon, I was face to face with Petra O'Leum herself, and, as usual, she wasn't pleased to see me.

Petra was done up in a black leather catsuit and pumps plus an eye patch, an affectation designed chiefly to scare her underlings into doing her bidding. I just think it makes her look like a pirate—and an unthreatening one, at that! She had cut her hair short enough so it didn't get in her face, but it was still long enough for me to pull it if I needed to when and if the inevitable catfight between us resulted. As soon as I crashed through the ceiling and vaulted to the floor, her hand shot out and grabbed a black whip as protection—as if she *needed* that. Or as if it could *harm* me, which it *can't*. Anyway. . . .

"Well," Petra snarled as I advanced towards her, "if it isn't the *bull dagger* of Bleakly Corners! I *thought* you'd make an appearance sooner or later!"

"And a *good afternoon* to you, too—*BITCH*!" If she was going to cast aspersions on my sexuality, I had every right to tell her what she *really* was.

Furious, she forgot herself and brought the tail of the whip up, as if she intended to cut me in the face with it. However, I acted fast enough to grab the tail with both hands. With Petra clutching the butt and me the tail, we played tug-of-war with the whip. She nearly pulled me out of my shorts with a vicious tug that made me groan in pain before I gave her a taste of my strength at the same volume, which gave *her* some pain in turn. Then, the whip finally broken, we were thrown to opposing ends of the room like broken dolls.

"I got the biggest half, *Pet!*" I said, getting to my feet first. "That means I get my wish: that I get to take *you* to jail!"

"You won't *get* your goddamn 'wish,' you female *Charles Atlas!*" Petra snarled as she righted herself. "You forget we're from the same homeworld, so the things that can hurt *me* can hurt *you*, too!"

"What's your *point*, O'Leum?" I snapped, hands on hips. "It better be *good!*"

"*This*," answered Petra. Then she bellowed into an old-fashioned walkie-talkie: "OLIVER! Get in here! *Now!*"

I couldn't resist a chuckle at that one.

"*What* is so *funny*, BRAT?" Petra growled humourlessly.

"Do you really think a *boy* is going to stop *me*?" I said. "*You* forget that I'm *stronger* than any old *boy!* Especially *Earth* ones!"

"Oliver is *not* a boy," retorted Petra. "At least, not a *human* one! He is, in fact, my trump card over you. The one way for me to show you who *really* wears the *panties* in our relationship!"

"Okay . . . eeewww!" I said, with audible revulsion. "Even if I *liked* you, Pet, it wouldn't be *that* much! But you haven't answered my question yet. Who—or should I say *what*—is OLIVER?"

The floor shook beneath us as soon as I finished speaking.

"You're about to find that out *now*, MG, to your great *displeasure!*" Petra cackled.

I was, and I did. The cube's retractable roof opened, and, peering through the openings, dripping wet, was the largest and most vicious looking octopus I had ever seen in my life!

IV

Now, you can imagine that this was not your average Earth octopus. This was a giant breed only seen on my homeworld, a mammoth marine creature that made Moby Dick look like a leprechaun. I still remember seeing one of those suckers for the first time, in a book about my homeland, and how I yelled and screamed in my sleep for long nights afterward. My parents finally had to reassure me that, even though there were octopi on Earth, they were nowhere near as fearsome as the ones from the homeland. . . .

Until that moment. Because my parents didn't know about Petra. They also didn't know how rich Petra was, or to which lengths Petra would be willing to go to destroy me.

At that moment, I stopped being a superhero and retreated to being a scared little girl. I certainly remember screaming like one.

"Get away!" I shouted at the octopus, covering my face with my cape. "Get *away* from me! Don't *eat* me!"

"Hah!" Petra laughed. "The mighty Muscle Girl, afraid of a mere *octopus*! So *precious*!"

That hurt. I tried to get my composure back, although it wasn't easy with Oliver glaring down at me like that. "It's not like you're *not* afraid of anything, *Petra*!" I snapped back. "Remember how you *panic* every time you see a *spider*. . . ."

"You're grasping at straws, Muscle Girl!" she retorted. "This octopus can do far greater damage to *you* than one of those *creepy arachnids* could ever do to *me*, and you KNOW it! So— are you prepared to *surrender* now?"

"I don't surrender to evil," I replied, "and *you* know THAT!"

"Fine," she said. Snapping her fingers to get the beast's attention, she shouted at him: "Oliver! KILL her!"

There was a brief pause while the giant creature glowered at me menacingly and I trembled in my platforms. But he didn't actually *do* anything—yet.

"What are you WAITING for, you *retarded cephalopod*?" Petra fumed. "I said KILL HER!"

Another pause. I was thinking maybe the old boy hadn't heard her, given octopi don't have much in the way of hearing. But he heard the next thing she said for sure.

"Kill her," Petra ordered, pulling a gun out of her pocket, "or I kill *you*!"

She fired the gun in the air, like a robber first announcing her presence in the place she's going to rob. Oliver got the message.

He pulled his eight arms inside the opening in the roof, and launched himself into the cube, landing with a thud. Opening his gaping, toothless mouth, he uttered a keening screech that disabled my inner equilibrium and caused me to fall to my knees. Then, before I could make another move, Oliver roped one of his massive arms around my waist, making me his prisoner. I tried to free myself, but to no avail. Even I was helpless against this creature who hailed from the same part of space as I did.

"You see, Muscle Girl," said Petra, "whilst thou and I are invulnerable to any form of injury or illness on Earth, we are *not* to harm inflicted by those of our homeworld. It took me awhile to figure this out, but I did. I, as you know, was injured by one of these creatures before I arrived on this planet. And I reasoned that, if I could merely be *hurt* by one of these beasts, it would be the ideal thing to tear *you* apart! It can be done; I know what they can do to fish, and, to *him*, you're just another type of prey!"

"You won't get away with this, Petra!" I growled with what was left of my strength. "I. . . ."

But before I could finish, Oliver squeezed me and I screamed as pain engulfed me. Then I completely blacked out.

V

When I woke up, I was being held upside down by my platforms over water—because that slimy octopus still had me in his clutches! I could see what I thought was the soulless bestiality in his eyes. I also could see that the cube was gone, Petra having clearly abandoned me to my fate—which was to be alone with an octopus *clearly* intending to have his way with me, like some perverted King Kong of the ocean. But, even though I was still scared to death of him, I wasn't about to be anybody's toy.

"Put me *down*, you *jerk!*" I shouted. "I don't belong to you— or *anybody else!*"

Unfortunately, he was as unresponsive to me as he'd been to Petra, so I had to resort to force.

"Okay, buddy!" I snapped. "You *asked* for it!"

I squirmed and tried to free myself from his iron grip on my foot, but it was useless. Clearly puzzled at my actions, but knowing what I was trying to do, he whipped a suckered arm around my waist and actually *spanked* me with another one on my butt. (Bastard!) To "punish" me further, he let me fall, and, too weak to fly away, I crashed into the water with a giant splash. Though I surfaced immediately, he cornered me right away, with all of his arms poised to tear me apart!

VI

It was then that I figured out what I needed to do. I cursed myself for not thinking of it earlier.

Along with my physical powers, I'm also a telepath. This comes in handy when I have to deal with fellow aliens who don't possess the power of speech. And Oliver the octopus was about as alien as you can get. So, especially as he was about to kill me, and he obviously didn't respond to spoken English, it was the only chance I had to save my butt.

I put my hand to my head and thought what I needed to think, beaming it right at where I thought his brain was.

"Okay, pal," I "said" to him in my parents' native tongue through my brainwaves. "We need to talk. Let me know if you can hear me."

"You . . . understand me?" he "said" back to me in surprise.

"Of course I can, Oliver!" I said. "I can communicate with all the animals in the universe this way if I want to. Especially ones from my home planet, like you."

"So, you are from the homeland, too? The red headed girl said nothing to me of this. But then, she says nothing at all but her verbalized commands. She seems to lack your ability to communicate this way."

"That's not the *only* thing she lacks. My name is Gerda, by the way. But when I'm in this garb they call me Muscle Girl. Understand?"

"Yes. But why should I trust you and not the red headed one? It is because of her that I am here, after all. . . ."

"Because, even though we have the same powers, she uses hers for evil and I use mine for good. Often times, I have to use my good powers to counteract her evil ones. Understand?"

"What do you mean by "evil" and "good"? I do not understand. . . ."

That shocked me. But only for a moment. He was, after all, "just" a "dumb" animal (if you'll pardon the expression) and thus everything beyond basic things like getting his next meal, fighting sharks, and shacking up with a girl 'pus was beyond his thought processes. So I gave him a quick lesson in what good and evil were to humans, and how and why I came to be good and Petra evil. It wasn't anything that would have impressed any philosophical thinkers on the subject, but, for my purposes, it worked.

"You got it now, Olly?" I asked when I finished. (He didn't mind being called that, by the way.)

"I believe so, Muscle Girl," he said. "But I feel so . . . what is the word you would use?"

"Betrayed?" I suggested.

"Yes," said Oliver. "The red haired girl called you my enemy and trained me to destroy you. But I see now that you are not deserving of destruction. . . ."

"But *she* is," I said. Having regained my strength and agility, I flew up out of the water and toward his face. "Listen, I have an idea about how both of us can get revenge on Petra for what she did to us. But I'll need your help; I can't do this alone."

"I am indebted to you for showing me the error of my ways, so I will do as you command," said Oliver.

"Never mind that 'command' crap!" I responded. "I'm your *pal*, not your damned Queen! And Petra isn't your Queen, either. Remember that. From now on, Olly, you think for *yourself*. All I was doing was making some suggestions of what you *could* do—that's what pals do for each other."

"You are kind to me, Muscle Girl," he said.

"I always am—to my *friends*!" I said. "I only give hell to my *enemies*. Now *listen*, will ya?"

I put my hands to my head and started talking again.

VII

We parted temporarily, and I flew off to confront Petra O'Leum. This time, I wouldn't come in full throttle but take her by surprise instead. Make it easy on myself, for once.

The cube was a little farther up the harbour than last time. Once again, I found a weak spot in the cube's construction, but this time I manoeuvred my way through a convenient duct opposite from the way I came in. I snaked through it until I caught sight of Petra, getting some air on a deck between the cube's sides. I punched a hole in the duct, jumped down, and silently slunk up until I was directly behind her. With a barking cough, I commanded her attention, and she spun around in shock.

"*You!*" she snarled. "How did you escape from the. . . ?"

"By making him my *friend*," I answered.

"Your *friend*?" she repeated.

"Yeah, you know, somebody who *cares* about you and wants to see you do *well* in life. Something *you'll* never have!"

"I don't *need* friends to destroy *you*," she said. "Especially not that rotten aquatic *turncoat*!"

"Don't talk about him like that!" I said. "Not unless you want a punch in the face!"

"Don't think that's *not* what I want!"

"You asked for it, then!"

I threw a punch, and she blocked it. I threw another one, and she blocked that, too. Fed up with that, I reached for her hair and caught her arm. We wrestled, our muscle power shaking the deck to its foundations. It seemed like I would win, at first, but then Petra cheated, like I knew she would. She brought one of her big feet down on one of mine, making me yell in pain, and then used the other one to knock me off balance. Then, she pulled me up by my shirt close to her face. "Ready to *die* now?" she said, with a look of triumph.

"Not quite," I growled. Putting my hand to my head, I called out a command to Oliver, who, unknown to Petra, was under the water next to the cube. "NOW!" I thought.

Oliver jumped out of the water and, his power on full display, landed on the cube. With his strength concentrated in one arm, he swatted Petra and knocked her against the railing, making her drop me in the process. He picked her up and held her aloft, turning her around to face me so I could read her the riot act.

"Olly is my *pal* now," I said, "so you treat him with *respect*, you hear?"

"NEVER!" Petra snapped.

Olly wrapped an arm around her, trapping her like he had once done me.

"Remember," I said, needling her, "he comes from *our* homeworld, so he can wreck you—just like you tried to make him wreck *me*!"

"Like I care about. . . . AAARGGH!"

The octopus shot her away from the cube with an epic toss, while she vowed to gain her revenge against me for his actions. No matter. She's said that before, and it usually doesn't amount to much.

VIII

Olly and I teamed up to destroy the cube. With our combined power, it didn't take long. Then I asked him if he needed anything else.

"No," he said. "I believe I can sustain myself well in these waters. A lot of fish and other things of that nature are here."

"Okay," I said. "Just don't take too much. The other critters have to eat, too."

"Certainly. But do let me know if you need my assistance. Particularly against the red-haired one."

"Can do."

And so, after I gave him a hug that nearly strangled *him,* for once, we parted. But I knew I actually had something that, even with all of my powers, I never had before.

A friend.

DAVID PERLMUTTER lives in Winnipeg, Manitoba. His passions are American television animation (the subject of his MA thesis and a projected historical monograph), literature, and music. He is challenged with Asperger syndrome but considers it an asset more than a disability.

THE SEAMSTRESS WITHOUT A COSTUME

LISA POH

"Oh thank you, Madam Liu," said Andrew, a client, from inside the tiny changing room. "I love it!"

"Does it fit okay?" she yelled from the sewing machine.

"Yes," Andrew pulled the curtain apart and showed her his new Mr. Rust costume. "I can't believe I stuck to nylon and vinyl for so long."

Madam Liu had convinced Andrew to go for a redesign in gore-tex and carbon fiber, in deep shades of ochre and orange. Of course, there was still plenty of spandex for a snug fit in the right places.

"I told you to switch long ago, didn't I?" said Hiro, also known as the Zamboni Zap. His snowsuit wasn't new; Madam Liu had custom-made it for him a few years back, but he kept coming back to add newfangled features. He held it out to her. "Madam Liu, you didn't add on all these expansions that I wanted. Remember the side zip I wanted for my ice staff?"

"Oh. . . . I'm sorry." She didn't usually forget these things. "I've been busy lately."

"You look preoccupied today, Madam Liu," Hiro said with concern. "Are you feeling okay?"

"Bah! Don't worry about me," Madam Liu said. She might be seventy-two, but she was wiry and strong, never sick more than once a year, even with the notorious flu winters in Vancouver. "I'm just busy. . . . You know, summer coming. Everyone wants new costumes that show off skin."

"I guess you're no longer just a well-kept secret on the West Coast, eh, Madam Liu?" Andrew said, stepping out of the changing room in his regular clothes. "I met a guy from Charlottetown who said your rainproof costumes are now de rigueur in the Maritimes."

"I'm just surprised it took the rest of the country so long to catch on," Hiro said, putting the snowsuit back on her counter. "There's something special in your sewing. Something that makes the clothes fit better, work better. Have you thought about what I told you the last time? That you might have an ability?"

"Shoo, the two of you!" Madam Liu turned back to her sewing machine. "Don't bother me with your Western nonsense. There's enough of you to go around destroying and saving the world. I don't want to get involved."

"Just think about what I said, okay?" Hiro waved as he and Andrew left.

Think about what I said. That was exactly what Patrick Oldfield had said when he made her that offer to work exclusively for him. It was a lot of money, with the promise of a grand new studio with seamstresses working under her. But Madam Liu didn't know him well. She'd made only the one costume for him. She didn't even know his alignment.

Not that the alignment truly mattered. She sewed for both factions and prided herself on never taking sides, even if she did have favourite clients.

Worrying about him made her sew badly. The needle strayed off its path and made a mess of threads. Madam Liu cursed and cut the thread. It was a bad time to be making mistakes. But automatically, the instant she cut it the thread snaked backward through the fabric, undoing the stitches on its own. Then it poised itself over the right lines and reshot through the fabric as ramrod-straight stitches.

Madam Liu froze and got up from the machine. Normally, she was careful but today she was agitated. The offer had confused her. When she'd first opened the shop out of necessity, after her husband of thirty years had died, she would have been grateful for such an appointment.

But looking around her crowded little shop, at the piles of neon green tulle, metallic blue sequins, red PVC wings, and iridescent capes, she realized she'd gotten attached to her customers. Their once ludicrous demands for rainbow-coloured lizard suits or rocket-launcher-enabled ballgowns were now fun and creative exercises.

A voice interrupted her thoughts: "Thinking about how to design your new studio?" Patrick Oldfield stepped into her shop, impeccably dressed in a London-made business suit. His handsome bronzed face was devoid of wrinkles, and his smile was blinding.

"I'm sorry, Patrick," Madam Liu said briskly. "I'm an old woman, and I don't need much. I think I'm happy with things just the way they are."

"I was afraid you would say that," Oldfield said, his face hardening. "But fortunately I've already made some preparations."

A strange gas seeped into the room. Madam Liu gagged and grew faint. Everything went dark. She felt hands lift her up as though she was a feather, then she passed out.

❦

Madam Liu woke up on a bed in a windowless room. They'd taken her shoes. The room was bright, clinically white, except for splashes of opulence like the maroon velvet chaise Oldfield was sitting on.

Gone was the Saville Row suit. He was clad head-to-toe in the glittering black costume of the Druzy Drill. Madam Liu knew that costume well; she'd sewn it using element-coated Kevlar-iridium fabric and tungsten thread. It was the most expensive she'd ever made—and virtually indestructible.

"Good morning, Madam Liu," Oldfield said, stretching out his legs. "I'm glad to see you took the trip well."

"Where am I?" she demanded.

"Deep inside my lair in the Rockies. . . . You know, you could have chosen to live the good life as my chief designer, drinking champagne in my alpine chalet at Whistler, but since we went with Plan B, you'll have to settle for somewhat less of a view." Oldfield stood from the chaise. He opened the door. "Welcome to your new factory."

Madam Liu gasped. It was hard enough to blast through mountains for the railway, but Oldfield had managed to carve out a huge cavernous space! She stumbled out into the factory as he followed. The limestone was cold under her bare feet. Lit by hanging fluorescent tubes, the cavern was filled with row after row of machines—spinning, weaving. On one side, long corridors led off into darkness. A low mechanical hum filled the room.

Oldfield waved at the machines. "Why work for a regional crowd, when with this factory you can reach the world?"

"Take me home," Madam Liu demanded.

"Not until you finish production of these," Oldfield said, handing her a sheaf of design specifications. "This is my vision of The Canadian Superhero."

Madam Liu stared at the designs. Like Oldfield, they exuded power and sophistication. A stylish combination of red, white, and silver, the designs were sleek and heroic-looking. But they were completely identical.

"These aren't superhero costumes," she said. "They're *uniforms!*"

"We don't need a motley crew to change the world, Madam Liu," Oldfield said. "We need well-trained professionals who inspire confidence! We need a brand!"

Madam Liu looked at the designs again and tried to imagine her clients all wearing the same costume. Rani the Sari Girl, with her flowing silk chiffons and marigolds in her hair. Kogan in his iridescent rainbow Pride Warrior armour. Geena the Green, who lived in trees and only wore organic hemp.

"What makes you think anyone would want to wear these?" she asked.

"You'll be surprised," Oldfield said. "I've started a superhero academy. Training, advanced techniques, career management. I've got talents signing up from Asia, South America and Africa. They've all signed fifty-year contracts."

Madam Liu knew about superheroes. They didn't go to school; they were mentored by other superheroes. They didn't sign contracts, and they worked for themselves. "This is practically slave labour," she said. "You'll never succeed."

"You don't get to decide," Oldfield said. "You're just a seamstress."

"Not just any seamstress!" shouted a voice that echoed through the cavern. Cold air blasted through one of the corridors. The floors and steel froze over with a thick layer of ice, and Hiro rumbled into the room on his shiny blue zamboni. It was no ordinary zamboni—it slid over ice at the speed of lightning.

Andrew leapt from his seat behind Hiro. "She's *our* seamstress!"

Tears sprang to Madam Liu's eyes, and she felt a tingle in her fingers. For a brief moment, the sewing and weaving machines in the factory choked and spluttered, but then resumed production.

Oldfield laughed. "Mr. Rust and the Zamboni Zap! I shouldn't be surprised. You're two of the most meddlesome superheroes in BC."

"Druzy Drill!" Hiro pointed at him sternly. "You have no authorization to be drilling in the Rockies! You could be causing great environmental damage!"

"Madam Liu, are you okay?" Andrew asked. "We turned around ten minutes later because Hiro forgot another change he wanted to add to his costume. We've been tracking you ever since!"

"I'm fine." Madam Liu cleared her throat. "But Patrick is planning to train foreign superheroes here. And I'm afraid he's going to turn them into indentured servants!"

Andrew nodded at Hiro. Hiro's snowsuit glowed florescent. With his palms, he pushed out a wintry blast at the Druzy Drill, encasing him in ice. But sharp pointy drills shot out of the Druzy Drill's head, hands, and feet, and he began drilling his way out.

"I can't hold him for long!" Hiro shouted.

Andrew sucked in his breath and blew on one row of sewing machines. In seconds, the machines corroded. Shiny steel surfaces discoloured and flaked with rust. Hairline cracks turned into gaping holes, and the machines crumbled into crusty orange bits. Smoke rose from the debris, the fumes giving off a noxious sulphuric, yet floral, smell.

But perhaps the smell wasn't from the debris. Madam Liu recognized the floral scent as the gas that had knocked her out. Andrew gagged and staggered back before collapsing. Hiro got onto his zamboni, but he, too, collapsed before he could escape.

Oldfield drilled his way out of his ice prison. Shards of ice fell around him and melted. "Ah, Gassy Jack, thank you for that. Late, but better than never."

A fat man waddled from behind some machines. Madam Liu never made his costumes but she'd heard of him. Gassy Jack was a Vancouverite, known for breaking up bar fights. But instead of wearing his trademark saloon suit, he was dressed head in toe in red, white, and silver. Oldfield's design added padding in all the right places to simulate muscle and strength. But it didn't suit Gassy Jack and his side whiskers.

❧

"Why would a superhero like you want to work for the Druzy Drill?" Hiro asked as Gassy Jack tied him beside Madam Liu and Andrew in the storeroom, a smaller cavern carved out from solid rock and connected to the main factory. Stacked on the shelves were hundreds of bolts of the high-performance, elements-resistant fabric produced by the machines.

"You wouldn't understand, someone like you with commercial appeal." Gassy Jack shook his head as he knotted the rope. "You're always in need on the ski slopes or in the North. And you're even more popular in summer. Me, on the other hand? I'm a one-trick pony. My gas knocks out people only once. Then they become immune. Sure, I'm a hero because I quelled a Stanley Cup riot single-handedly. But no-one here wants to hire me because I can't do it again."

"You could travel around the world," Andrew pointed out. "There are riots everywhere."

"Yeah," Gassy Jack said. "But I'm getting on, you know? I just want a stable job. And Druzy Drill's rich. He offered a real good salary, with dental benefits and all."

Madam Liu found herself piping up. "Are you really happy dressed like that? Being a lackey?"

"Madam Liu, you wouldn't know," Gassy Jack said, hanging his head. "When I first discovered my gift, I thought I could change the world. But here I am, touching fifty, and the world's moving on without me."

Madam Liu felt something hard inside her heart crack and fall away. "When I was a little girl," she said, slowly, "it was just after World War II ended in Shanghai, and I saw the Allied superheroes helping with the liberation. I went home to my mother's sewing machine, and I sewed a superhero costume for myself. No-one taught me how to sew. It just came to me when I touched the threads."

"See? I always said that—" Hiro burst out and was hushed by Andrew.

"It was the first thing I ever made. I put it on and showed it to my mother. I told her that I was going to fight the Japanese demons. I don't mean you, Hiro; your people suffered enough during the internment. But in Shanghai we saw soldiers do horrible things."

"So what did she do?" Gassy Jack asked, forgetting he was on the other side.

"She watched me do my song and dance. Then she slapped me for my unseemly mannerisms. She forced me to strip the costume off, then she ripped it into pieces. She said it threw her face away. I never did that kind of thing again."

The burning shame had followed her long after her mother had died, long after she'd married a white man and moved to a foreign land. For forty years she lived a placid existence, keeping house for a husband, never touching a sewing machine. Then her husband died, and she found herself in need.

She fell back on her one talent. She bought a sewing machine and followed her mother's path into the seamstress's trade. But she kept away from what she knew she could do. Even surrounded by accepting and supportive superheroes daily, she was afraid.

The knots fell away from her heart. The knots fell away from around her wrists. If Andrew and Hiro could risk their necks to rescue an old lady like her, she had to reciprocate.

Madam Liu sat up in her chair, the ropes falling loose about her. She flicked a finger. Bolts of cloth unrolled themselves and flew off the shelves in the storeroom. They shot out at Gassy Jack and wrapped around him until he was swaddled up like a baby.

"Mmffghh!" Gassy Jack protested as the ends of the cloth stuffed themselves into his mouth.

"I'm sorry," Madam Liu said to him as she put his oversize boots on her bare feet. "I've instructed your bindings to unwrap you after we're gone. Meanwhile, think about what we've told you."

Mr. Rust and the Zamboni Zap sprang up from their chairs, their knots untied, and took their place at her side. They walked through the connecting tunnel, at her old lady's pace, back to the factory. Druzy Drill was not there, but the hundreds of automated machines rumbled away. The three of them made short work of the machines: Mr. Rust turned some into orange dust, the Zamboni Zap froze others into disrepair, while she mangled fabric and tangled threads, jamming the mechanisms.

Then the Zamboni Zap summoned his special blue zamboni and offered Madam Lui the best seat. They glided their way through a maze of tunnels toward the surface.

But the Druzy Drill was waiting for them at the entrance, between two deep chasms. He'd dug two yawning pits in the rock. One was full of red, glowing lava that gave off a sizzling heat. The other, he informed them, was filled with acid.

Standing in the middle, the Druzy Drill folded his sculpted arms. "Let's see how you get out now."

"Just let us go already," Mr. Rust said. "Don't be a sore loser."

"I haven't lost until you've escaped!" the Druzy Drill snapped back.

The Zamboni Zap summoned the best of his icy ability to try and freeze a path across the chasms. But the lava was so hot that it countered his arctic blast.

Mr. Rust had no effect on liquids, so he focused on the Druzy Drill instead. But no matter how hard he tried, nothing in the Druzy Drill's costume corroded.

"Didn't you learn anything from science class?" The Druzy Drill laughed. "Iridium and tungsten don't rust!"

It was Madam Liu's turn. She willed the bolts of fabric and threads from Druzy Drill's factory to come to her. And they did, rolling and snaking in masses on the ground.

She wove them together into a sturdy rope ladder, each end with multiple rope endings. Then she sent the rope ladder airborne across the chasms. On the other side, the ends of the rope ladder caught on rock face, and dug their ways into crevices, as deep as they could. On her side, the rope ends secured themselves around rocks.

"Madam Liu, you surprise me. I didn't know you had this kind of power!" the Druzy Drill shouted. "But I'm not afraid of a basic rope bridge!" The drills emerged from his costume as the Druzy Drill approached the bridge woven in the air. But Madam Liu was prepared.

"Call me The Seamstress from now on!" she shouted. "And you should be afraid of this!"

Madam Liu closed her eyes. This was more difficult than anything she'd tried so far. But she knew every seam and stitch. Mentally, she tugged and pulled and snapped at them.

The Druzy Drill shrieked mid-step. Bit by bit, thread by thread, his costume was unravelling. His drills retracted. His tights unspooled into black threads. Large holes appeared on his chestpiece developed as he clutched onto the fabric. His oversized codpiece clattered to the ground with nothing to hold it there.

Stark naked in a pool of threads, the Druzy Drill covered his privates with his hands. "That was an expensive costume!" he shouted. "I want my money back!"

By then Madam Liu was already being piggy-backed across the rope bridge by Andrew, while Hiro waited with his zamboni at the other end. As Hiro's zamboni raced down the mountainside with the three of them safely on board, Madam Liu reflected that the first thing she was going to do when she got home was to make The Seamstress a costume. She wondered what kind of design would look stylish on an old lady of seventy-two. . . .

Born in hot tropical Singapore, **LISA POH** now calls Canada home. Having lived on both sides of the country, she enjoys exploring East/West culture. Among the contrary things she likes are Montreal's long winters and Vancouver's constant rain.

THE KEVLAR CANOE

MARIE BILODEAU

The Voyager pulled hard on the reins, riding the night wind down, cutting clouds to shreds as he manoeuvred the modified bark canoe. He checked his weapons, edging the insides of the canoe, stuck to the Kevlar lining with basic Velcro.

Tested weaponry combined with new protection often worked best when dealing with old demons. He pulled the reins to the left, the canoe obeying.

The wind cut by his ears, and he heard his prey, booming, cracking against the air and slapping the sides of his canoe, which trembled in anticipation of the fight.

He rode the currents, following the small fissures in the ancient sky fabric, keeping a close eye out for demons that might break through. The veil was thin and each attack made it thinner.

Trees blurred by as he forced the canoe to move faster, until a village sprang up in front of him, surrounded by pines, houses blending into the dirt.

Another hit, and red waves rode the skies toward him. He grabbed his axe and stood tall, screaming as he brought it down against the first wave, the red shattering and crashing to the ground. The second wave erupted, and he struck again. His shoulders popped under the strain, and he screamed his fear.

He had failed to break the second wave.

The canoe shook and moaned as red flickers exploded around it. The Voyager threw himself to the bottom of the

216

canoe, covering his head with his arms. The third wave hit before he could stand.

It struck hard, but the canoe slid sideways to absorb some of the impact. The Voyager smelled burning and hoped the old canoe would hold together. There were so few of them left.

He stood and looked to his target, now visible against the shockwave of its own attack. The small northern Québec town was dominated by the steeple, still standing after centuries. From his vantage point, clutching the reins of the canoe, he could see the fissures in the stone, where the toll of the great bell had begun to rupture space.

The Voyager grinned. He loved this part. The steeple saw him approach, and the great bell sighed once before moving sideways. The Voyager grabbed his Taser and forced the canoe to go faster, but the bell struck before he could reach it.

The sky glowed with a hue he had never seen in this world. A type of green, maybe?

"That's not good," he mumbled.

The wave of colour highlighted hundreds of tiny rips, moans erupting from each of them as the encroaching demon dimensions smelled a new world to conquer.

"Faster," he implored, and the canoe slid on the currents, avoiding several fissures large enough to gobble them up. The canoe lined him up, passing left of the steeple.

He fired the Taser at the bell, but a nun jumped from the steeple and absorbed the blow. The Voyager swore and pulled back, letting her fall as gently as her garbs allowed. She floated silently to the ground. He ignored her—his battle was with the bell, not its servants.

He reloaded the Taser, the stench of burning flesh clinging to it. The bell struck as the canoe made a turn. Blue light, so electric it made The Voyager's eyes water, lashed out in bursts of lightning. He tried to counter the attack with his axe, but it came too strong. The canoe reacted and pulled up, protecting its rider from the direct hit, taking it fully itself. It shrieked over the sound of the bell and fell out of the sky, thundering against the ground.

The Voyager held on, the canoe loyally absorbing the shock, bouncing and skidding on the uneven terrain.

Before he could recover and get his bearings the bell struck again and snow streaked from the sky, pointed stars meaning to impale. The canoe flipped over, protecting The Voyager with its wounded flank. What the old bark could not stop the layers of Kevlar did, the sound of impaling wood hammering The Voyager. He whispered as he placed a hand on the side of the canoe, trying to make himself as small as possible.

"Hang on, old friend. I promise, if we make it through this, we'll get you some new toys. A new Kevlar lining. And a cannon. You'd like that, wouldn't you? Hang on, old friend."

The canoe did not respond. The attack ceased, and The Voyager didn't hesitate, cutting through his own thick breath and grabbing his favourite double-edged axe. He pushed the canoe aside and jumped up, screaming as he leapt to the bell, three stories cleared in one leap, and pierced it with his axe. The bell shifted sideways, but he was ready. This wasn't his first battle, and he didn't intend it to be his last.

Shifting sideways, he let the bell move into its upward swing, positioning himself under the metal behemoth. As soon as he was underneath it he jumped into its mouth, holding on to its clapper. He reached up to release it, but it was secured by a chain. He swore as the bell started its downward swing. He took a deep breath and wrapped his legs around the clapper to stop it from ringing and causing another rift.

The bell bit him, trapping him between the clapper and its great metal shell. Bones snapped. The Voyager grunted and spit out blood. His grip on his axe loosened.

The canoes were getting older and slower, but the bells only became more powerful with time.

The Voyager fought a gag, the stench of worn metal slamming his throat.

The bell shifted and cracked, ringing without its clapper. The Voyager's eardrums bled, but the bell was distracted now, just enough for him to shake free. Another ring—something was attacking the bell from *outside*.

The canoe!

He ignored the tearing in his gut and pulled himself up, grabbing his hunting knife and plunging it into the chain that held the clapper. The bell screamed as he plunged the knife deeper, a terrified shriek that turned to a guttural moan as the clapper fell. The Voyager slipped with it, and would have fallen had he not been caught by what remained of the canoe, shards of wood held together by glue and Kevlar.

The bell moaned for several minutes, and the silence that followed was accompanied by a gentle snowfall, illuminating the land. The canoe fell on the ground, letting The Voyager step out before shuddering once and lying still.

The Voyager dropped to his knees and clung to the canoe. He pulled off his gloves and placed his hands directly on its old wood, but he felt nothing. Not a whisper, not a sigh, not even a goodbye.

"Please wake up. . . ." Hot tears flowed down his cold cheeks. If only he had veered right, first. Or maybe used something stronger, like a bow. Maybe he should have called for help, but there were so few of them left. For years the canoe had been his only companion, they had only each other, and now. . . .

"Are you okay, monsieur?" A small voice perked up from nearby. The Voyager looked up, his vision blurred by grief. A child, wrapped in blankets and hope, stood near.

The Voyager took a step away from the canoe, toward the child. The canoe shuddered once, just a bit, and then a branch sprouted from its flank, and another, and another. They grew quickly, turned green, bore bright, red fruit. The canoe seemed to dance as it crumpled into branches, one after another, until there was nothing left of it but a large bush ripe with fruit and pieces of melted Kevlar. The Voyager leaned over and plucked a piece of the fabric, brought it to his nose, and smelled wood, which prevailed over the stench of melted chemicals. A final gift from the canoe.

He closed his eyes, said a silent prayer, and then turned to the child, who stared wide-eyed at the bush.

"If you eat those fruits," The Voyager said, recognizing the curiosity in the child, knowing what path now beckoned him, "your life will never be the same."

The child didn't look up to him, simply staring at that new bush, the grave of the old canoe, a gift from the land to the land. The Voyager watched the child take his first step toward the bush, called by the red berries to take on a mantle he did not yet understand but would soon enough.

The Voyager grabbed his axe and turned to the forest. This last bell had been strong and had probably summoned demons through the rifts. He could use the diversion until he found a new travelling companion. Maybe there was a canoe that needed a rider out there, still. Maybe something else would be sent to accompany him.

Movement caught his attention, swift and clunky. And fuzzy.

A Sasquatch had slipped through into this world. The Voyager gently pocketed the piece of fabric. He limped off into the forest, clutching his axe, tracking the invader.

He never once looked back, letting the whispers of the land guide him to his next battle.

MARIE BILODEAU (www.mariebilodeau.com) is an Ottawa-based SF writer and professional storyteller. Her short and novel-length fiction has been nominated for Canada's Aurora Awards. The native Montrealer enjoys running around Québec cemeteries in a mostly unsuccessful attempt to separate family legends from history.

Sea and Sky

RHONDA & JONATHAN PARRISH

In the beginning the people were scattered and scarce. They huddled alone or in small groups, hugging their ribs in the darkness of caves or primitive lean-tos. They watched the sun go down every night and spent the dark hours praying for its return. In the wastes of what we now call the Canadian Arctic there were months of darkness where the people feared the light would never return, that they'd never again feel soft heat upon their faces. They would wail, pull their hair, and beat their chests. They were alone, and they were afraid.

A boy was born into this place, a boy who was quick of thought but slow of action, so much so that his mother, when he had passed through but nine dark spells, abandoned his given name and simply called him "Glacier." As he grew, Glacier thought that if people weren't so alone perhaps their fears would not be so monstrous. After thinking this for many years he set out to bring the people together. With the speed of his namesake, groups came together in tens and eventually in hundreds. The heat of each other sustained them when that of the sun was absent.

Glacier settled with his family and several others on the northern shore of a great bird-shaped lake in the frozen north. It was there he met the woman who would later become his wife. She was large of body, strong of mind, and immovable once she'd set her mind to something. She was simply referred to as "Mountain." They were drawn to each other, and wed one year after they met. Once the ceremony was over and the feasting finished, Mountain and Glacier moved into an igloo together and kept one another warm during the darkest days of winter. When spring once more warmed the ground, Mountain's belly had grown round and heavy with the fruit of long dark nights.

When the days began to yet again grow short and the caribou started to mate and grow fat themselves, Mountain increased the size of the village by two. She and Glacier named the girl twin Sky and the boy Sea, and there was much rejoicing by the people, as the birth of twins was a great sign of approval from the Gods, a true blessing. For three nights the stars looked down on the revelry that marked the birth of the twins, and on the fourth the North Star reached down to touch the two infants—bestowing a gift upon each.

As time passed, the two grew very different personalities. Sky was boisterous and tumultuous. She would dash from one place to another like her bottom was on fire, and never paused to consider the consequences of an action before taking it. On a whim she'd dismantle a fish-drying rack to make a sword of one of the supports, or sneak out of their igloo late at night to hunt seals. Sea, on the other hand, was a quiet and introspective boy; he spent hours watching Glacier toss his bolo, drawing strange symbols in the snow, or simply cloaking himself in long, dark silences.

As different as they were from one another, the children were nearly inseparable. The elders in the village said the pair must share one soul, so close were they. Once the twins learned to talk, neither ever spoke a complete sentence in earshot of one another; one would begin to speak a thought and the other would complete it.

Then Glacier and Mountain began to notice strange things, and all of them tied to their children. First there was the pebble, smooth and black; Glacier discovered Sea playing with it. He would press it against his cheek, and, when he moved his hands away, the stone stuck in place as though frozen. Then, when Sky leaned to whisper to her brother, the stone leapt from his face to hers. One day, when Sky was racing through the igloo, the trio of iron fishing hooks Glacier had traded a missionary for jumped from the shelf and embedded themselves in Sky's thigh. There were many tears shed in their removal, and Mountain and Glacier both became very careful about all the goods they'd received in trade from the Europeans in case they too were easily affected by the power. Sometimes the effects were helpful, as fishermen learned that their spears and fishing rods would always point the way back to the village, but the villagers nevertheless became fearful of Sky and Sea.

It was always worse, more violent, when the children were together, and as they aged the power they shared grew stronger and stronger. When the twins turned eight years old, the village had a great gathering to discuss their fears of the children, and so Glacier and Mountain took the children and moved away. They travelled far from the village, off into the wilderness where they wouldn't have to fear harming anyone. They rid themselves of anything metal and went back to living as they had before the village existed.

For a time, it worked. Then the children reached puberty, and their power, which had been growing slowly and steadily, increased with the speed and strength of an avalanche. Rocks were ripped from the earth and pinioned themselves to the youngsters' bodies whenever they were too near one another. At first the family built their igloo in a place where no stones moved, and the youngsters never strayed far from home. That meant many miles of walking for Glacier to reach the hunting and fishing grounds, and Mountain's shoulders began to sag with the weight of her children's curse. Glacier began to think that something more would have to be done.

One day, Sky found a metal cup. As she reached for it, the cup leapt into her hand. She tried to put it down, only to discover her hands stuck to it. Sea, hearing her cries, came to help, and soon the twins were stuck, both to the cup and to each other. Their screams brought Glacier and Mountain, and it was only with great effort that the twins were detached from the cup and one other. That was when Glacier made the decision that would tear his family apart forever: the twins must be separated.

Mountain argued and wailed at this heartrending decision but finally accepted that there was no other solution; if the twin's powers continued to grow, they would become a danger not only to their own family but to the nearby village and to other families scattered across the tundra.

Sea and Sky were still too young to be sent off into the world alone, so Mountain took Sky south while Glacier and Sea travelled north. The idea was to walk as far as they could until they were at opposite edges of the world, or at least until the twins could no longer feel each other.

Glacier and Sea wended north until they found their way blocked by water, so they spent many weeks building a boat, and finally reached the shore of a great island.

Mountain and Sky walked for days and nights, the land extending on and on, and as they walked the days grew longer and the nights shorter. The weather grew warmer until one day it wasn't rock and ice beneath their feet but fields of green grass, with forests of more trees than either had ever seen.

Still they walked, for Sky could feel the tug of her connection to Sea. Sky and Mountain walked until there was no more land; being strong swimmers, they went into the water and swam until they reached the shores of a place as cold and barren as their homeland. Here the seals were different, and communities of clumsy-looking birds replaced the solitary bears they'd known before. Sky could feel only the barest of tugs toward Sea, and so they settled and, in time, grew comfortable. They were never truly happy, though, separated from their loved ones. Mountain missed Glacier, and it bowed her back and sapped her strength day by day.

Sky and Sea's powers, however, continued to grow and grow. Soon they were once again able to sense one another's thoughts and to finish each other's sentences though the length of the world separated them. Mountain and Glacier, on the other hand, felt their separation from each other keenly and found themselves feeling older and older each day.

Sky and Sea, owing to the North Star's gift, seemed to stop aging even as their parents approached their ends. They thought-spoke to each other and each resolved to visit the other parent one last time; they would swap places, travelling in opposite directions, with the width and breadth of the world always between them. The journey took many years, and when the twins arrived at their parents sides they found both of them still and peaceful.

Sky took Glacier out into the water and sank him in the north, while Sea piled stone after stone upon the body of Mountain. The two wept and consoled each other through their thoughts — both together and alone, as only they could be. They vowed to keep the memory of Glacier and Mountain close to their hearts, travelling back and forth to visit each parent's final resting place, two halves of the same whole separated by the entire world.

JONATHAN PARRISH, who immigrated to Canada from Hong Kong, and **RHONDA PARRISH**, who was born and raised in Alberta, live with their daughter in Edmonton. They quite like it there, even if politics sometimes inspire daydreams about leaving for another province.

A Face in the Wind

Chantal Boudreau

Only one thousand left to go.

Every time Sou'wester saved a life, he felt his burden lift ever so slightly from his soul. That was, if what he had was a soul—he assumed he did, but he couldn't quite tell. Actually, he wasn't sure what he was—hadn't known for almost a century. People used to call him a ghost or a fey if they caught sight of him, but nobody believed in those things anymore. Most considered him an urban legend, a story made up by overly imaginative or perhaps alcohol-addled minds. Those who swore they had seen him, or had even spoken with him, had taken to calling him Sou'wester, a fitting title since he was nine-tenths wind. It was the remaining one-tenth that made him different, though; the remaining one-tenth that drove him to seek out those in need in order to atone for a grievous misdeed that he could not remember committing. It was that one-tenth that made him self-aware.

He had fleeting memories of a past when he'd been as human as the people whom he attempted to save whenever he could. He had been a young man then, and he could not recall a wife or children, but occasionally the sight of a living little girl would briefly trigger the knowledge that he had been an older brother, with dear little sisters. He wished he could remember their names, but he couldn't even manage his own. Instead, all he had left to cling to from that past life were vague images. But he did cling to them, drawn to the slightest suggestion of something he once knew.

Sou'wester let the wind carry him along the beach, twisting and turning him in all directions. He could direct the wind if he chose, force it to carry him wherever he felt like going. When he had no goal in mind, he allowed the winds to follow their nature. Freeing them to do as they please was his only comfort besides the relief he drew from preserving souls, lessening his burden.

An odd scent in the air brought him back to the day he had been restored to consciousness. He remembered the last moment he had been human, alive and tangible, on a ship in the harbour. Then the incident that still caused him so much remorse had blasted its way into history, vaporizing him instantly, leaving behind only a handful of his sediment adrift in the wind. He had been partially responsible for that tragic circumstance—Sou'wester was sure of that—but "how" was another one of those things he couldn't remember. . . .

Sou'wester paused in his reveries, catching sight of a girl who struck him as close in appearance to one of his sisters—the youngest one. He had to get closer.

The girl on the beach was probably six or seven, here with her mother and father, along with a teenage couple, a girl and a boy. The mother sat, book in hand, the father and the teenagers tossing around a Frisbee. Sou'wester approached the little one, directing the wind to form tiny gusts to mould patterns in the sand: swirls, stars, flowers, and squiggles. His playmate's eyes widened.

"Mommy! Mommy! There was a face in the wind!"

Sou'wester hadn't meant to startle her. The mother tried to comfort her, thinking her daughter had had too much sun, or had lost herself in daydreams. The father jogged up as well, leaving the two teens to set out for a swim.

But the girl refused to settle.

Disturbed by her anxiety, Sou'wester prepared to withdraw and leave the family alone. At that moment the boy splashed to shore, calling out fearfully, "She swam too far out!" He gasped for breath, glancing helplessly out at the water. "The current has her and she can't fight it . . . it'll carry her out to sea!"

Sou'wester started pulling in all of the surrounding winds, wrapping them around the smattering of matter at his core. The air along the beach now still, he blasted seaward past the father, who had plunged into the waves, struggling toward his frantic daughter. Sou'wester blew past the drowning girl, then stopped and turned toward shore.

The winds fought Sou'wester with their great power and concentration, threatening to break away from him before he was done and scatter his fragments in all directions. If that happened, it might take him years to reassemble himself, delaying the progress of his tally. Although failure could prove to be a devastating blow toward his efforts to achieve release, Sou'wester could not let the girl drown.

He struggled more fiercely, bringing the air currents under control. With as much force as he could muster, he released the captive winds in one incredible gale. They attacked the water between Sou'wester and the beach. The result was a mini-tsunami, a great wave that lifted the girl up in its rippling grasp. Like a giant watery hand, it carried her most of the way back to the shore, picking her father up along the way and pushing him in that direction, too.

When Sou'wester finally dropped the winds and the wave collapsed, the father and daughter were left mere inches from dry land, coughing and gagging, propped on their hands and knees in the water. The man got to his feet quickly, but the girl, very shaky, crawled the last distance to collapse on the sand. Hoping not to startle her as much as he had her sister, Sou'wester condensed his sediment as he had done before.

"Are you well?" he breathed. The words caused what little physical mass he had to vibrate, a visual echo of the sounds. He knew the answer before she had spoken, as he felt the burden of one more life lifting from his conscience. He *had* saved her.

She nodded, staring up at him tearfully from where she lay in the sand. "You rescued me. I thought I was dead for sure," she finally managed to gasp. "Who are you? *What* are you?"

"They call me Sou'wester," he whispered.

Then he let go of the pretense of any physical form, fading into nothingness, and allowed the winds to carry him away.

Only nine hundred and ninety-nine lives left to go.

Accountant, author, and illustrator **CHANTAL BOUDREAU** was born in Toronto but has lived in Nova Scotia for most of her life. A Horror Writers Association member, she has five novels published between two series: Fervor and Masters & Renegades. Her website is writersownwords.com/chantal_boudreau.

THE CREEP

MICHAEL S. CHONG

I met her one of the first times I went out to help people. Maybe *meet* is not the right word here. I saw her, but she did not see me.

I can slow time. Not forever, but the harder I concentrate, the longer I can do it. My record so far is two hours, but after that exertion I was out for a few days, bedridden with no energy at all.

To an outside observer, I seem to be moving too fast to be seen, but in reality the rest of the world crawls. Racing cars barely seem to move, shot bullets are snails, raindrops hang in stasis.

The real world does not even see a blur, I believe, but I have never noticed anyone sense my presence until the creep stops. That's what I call it: *the creep.*

The first time I went out to stop trouble, save lives, feel good about myself, I saw her: Laura. I had started the creep in a mall, to stop a runaway shoplifter. I wanted to start small; baby steps.

After tripping the shoplifter, a young kid running with his jacket full of video games, I noticed a girl—Laura, I would soon discover—sitting at a fountain in the crowded chaos, watching the security guards give chase. Her eyes were red from crying, her hand clutching a damp tissue.

Looking at her, I knew something was wrong. I stood off to the side and let time start again, watching the rent-a-cops nab the kid.

Laura went back to crying. I wanted to go up and ask her what was wrong, but there were too many people around. A stocky jock came out of the nearby electronics store and started yelling at her.

"Laura, will you stop already," he said. "What the hell is wrong with you?"

"Just leave me alone," she said and got up, walking away from him.

He went after her, grabbed her arm. I slowed time, walked up to him, peeled his fingers off her and pushed him off his feet, walked back to the side and restarted time. He fell to the ground.

She didn't even look back. I put on the creep and kicked the guy in the side, then in the head a few times. I saw red and kind of lost count.

Starting time again, I followed Laura out to her car. Stopping time, I got in with her and looked in her handbag for some ID. She didn't live too far away. I wanted to check on her later to make sure the asshole wouldn't show up to hurt her. She was now under my protection. . . . Putting back her ID, I walked over to her apartment then let time start again.

She pulled up as I sat on a bench by a bus stop down the street. As she was getting into her apartment, I stopped time again, slipped by her standing statue-like at the door and looked around her place. It was simple, with old furniture that was either bought from thrift stores, inherited from family, or a combination of both. Her cat, a tabby, sat waiting for her, frozen.

Brushing past her, I paused to stroke the tears from her face, caressing the smooth, warm skin. I walked back to the bus stop, started time, and waited.

The asshole showed up in a cab, minutes later. He looked pissed. Stopping time, I looked at the guy close up and knew I had to do something drastic to protect Laura. He might kill her. So I shoved him in front of an oncoming bus. Starting time, I watched him get crushed.

Laura came out when she heard the sirens. She ran over but was stopped by a police officer. She seemed to cry hard for the asshole, but I knew it must've been more from shock than any feelings she could have for him.

While she sat on the curb with her head in her hands, I walked up and asked her if she was okay. She mumbled something unintelligible.

I left her there, not wanting her to link her shock and bad feelings to me. After that, I was her guardian angel. She had her protector. No matter where she went, I wasn't too far.

A few months later, as I did a perimeter check of her premises with the creep on, I noticed a man buzzing to get into her apartment. I still hadn't formally introduced myself to Laura because she had remained in a depressive, almost breakdown state, quitting her job and never leaving her apartment. I knew she needed time to heal from the asshole's abuse.

The man at her front door was a former co-worker who had been trying to email her but getting no response, since I was deleting them before she could be further disturbed by them. Laura wanted solitude. She knew that, and I knew that.

With time going, I tapped him on the shoulder. He turned around and seemed surprised. I told him Laura didn't live here anymore and there was no forwarding address. He asked who I was, and I said I was a friend. After he left, I heard Laura saying "Hello? Hello?" from the speaker at the door.

All she needed was me. Soon I would introduce myself, show my love for her by somehow knowing all her ways, then we would live as a loving couple.

Having made a copy of her keys, I put on the creep and let myself into her apartment. She lay on the couch, where she spent most of her days now. Her head was askew on a pillow, with her hair over her face.

I went to her, hugged her, lifting her up and wiping the hair from her face. She stared straight ahead with red eyes. "You'll be okay from now on," I said to the frozen Laura, and I knew she would be.

MICHAEL S. CHONG was born and raised in Toronto, having lived here all his life except for a few years in The Hague, Netherlands, waiting for the Milošević trial to end.

LONESOME CHARLIE JOHNSTONE'S STRANGE BOON

JASON SHARP

"Next!" called the barber.

The other two miners looked to Charlie. He nodded and stepped inside the barber's tent.

"It has been a while since your last trim," the barber noted, wrapping an old tablecloth around Charlie's neck and shoulders.

"Two years since it was done proper-like," Charlie said, "back in Seattle. This ain't the kind of place I'd have expected to find a barber."

The barber shook his head. "I came up here for the same reason you did, but I quickly learned that the miner's life is not for me. I intend to make my way back out to Skagway in the spring - but I have to earn my way in a manner better suited to me." The barber hacked off long clumps of hair, working in silence. When he'd reduced the matted mass to perhaps two inches in length, he inquired, "So, is today a special occasion?"

"I will be dining at the Majestic this evening, then buying a dance with the lady who owns it," Charlie said.

"Ah . . . you've encountered some paydirt?"

Charlie suppressed the urge to nod. "Two years of hard luck, and now I finally got some gold. Tonight I live like a real man."

Twenty or so minutes later, Charlie's grey-streaked hair was short and slicked back, his sideburns elegantly shaped, his face smooth and whisker-free. He reached into his pocket, found his poke, and produced a small nugget about the size of a pinhead. "Will this suffice?"

"Very much so." The barber quickly took the payment. "Thank you very much and have a marvelous evening."

"Thank *you*," Charlie said.

The sun had dropped behind the hills, leaving Dawson in shadow that would soon become night. A brisk breeze blew down the valley. While his canvas overcoat protected his body, the wind lashed at Charlie's freshly groomed head in a way he was unaccustomed to. Reluctant to muss his hair so soon, he grimaced and left his wool cap in the coat's outer pocket.

It was a good half-mile from the barber's tent to Front Street, where saloons, hotels, restaurants, and dance halls offered the district's thousands of bachelors an opportunity to dine, drink, and bask in the presence of women. Not all the miners would be out tonight—many could not afford it, did not wish to, or were simply too exhausted or ill to consider it—but there would be enough that latecomers risked being left out in the cold. None too keen to be one of those unfortunates, he picked up his pace until his footsteps were a drumbeat of crunching snow.

The Majestic was among the most impressive structures in all the Yukon—a long, two-storey edifice with sides of pine planking and a roof of corrugated tin. Charlie paused on the front stoop, listening to the muffled sounds of revelry coming from within, and then entered the coat room. He hung his coat up on a peg, confirmed that his poke remained in his trousers pocket, and passed through a pair of genuine French glass doors into the dining room.

The room was almost full, with a few faces he recognized but could not put a name to. The decor consisted largely of stuffed animals and some amateur artwork depicting miners at work. The host directed him to a setting for two along the outer wall, adjacent to a stuffed moose.

A waiter soon came by and introduced himself. Charlie said, "Evening. What have you got for drink?"

"We have a full bar, sir."

He could not help but grin. "Really?"

"Yes, sir."

"Oh my. Bring me a scotch, then."

He emptied his tumbler in the short time it took for the food to arrive, and ordered another drink as the waiter set the plate down before him. "If I may, sir, I could find a bottle of champagne that would complement your meal most satisfactorily."

He shrugged. "Okay, bring it, too."

The meal outlasted his second scotch and his first glass of champagne. He poured another glass, and swirled his bread around the plate, mopping up leftover tomato sauce and errant little bits of meat and vegetable.

"Best meal I had since I can remember," he said, as the waiter collected his plate.

"Would you care for a coffee and cigar?"

"No, I think I'll be over to the dance hall."

"Oh," the waiter said. "Dancing so soon after dinner may give you cramps and impair your enjoyment of the evening."

"Really?"

"Yes, sir."

"Huh. Then I guess I'll take you up on that offer after all."

The coffee and cigar came with a newspaper from Seattle—probably one from the summer, given the length of time it took anything to reach Dawson—and he breezed through it between sips of coffee and drags from the short, fat cigar. He couldn't read the text, but the pictures were tantalizing glimpses at life back in the civilized world.

Still, what he really wanted was a dance. To be near Ms. O'Donnell—to feel her hand and the small of her back, to smell her perfume, to see her smile—*that* was what he wanted. By the time the cigar was a smouldering stub in the ashtray, he was more than ready to finish off his champagne, settle his bill, and move along.

The dance hall was on the other side of the coatroom. There was no pause for contemplation at the door; if anything, he had to restrain himself to avoid running.

It was bedlam inside. Every seat was occupied by men in their dressiest clothes, and dozens more lined the walls, nursing drinks, smoking, or both. A gentleman in top hat and suit pounded on a baby grand piano while four comely women in long, frilly dresses circulated around the room, dispensing alcohol. In the middle of it all, on the dance floor, six miners and six girls stepped, spun, and wove. The miners were wide-eyed and whooping; the girls smiled and laughed and did their finest to keep up.

Charlie picked out Ms. O'Donnell within moments.

As on previous occasions, he noticed her face first—pleasantly round, flushed with exertion, and surrounded by tawny curls that bounced to the rhythm of the music. She wore a dark blue gown that complemented her tall, sturdy frame and heaved under the influence of concealed bosoms within. She grinned and whooped along with her partner as her skill and grace overcame the man's inebriation and clumsiness to produce something resembling an elegant waltz.

Charlie was smitten; had been since he'd spied her on his last visit. "Ms. O'Donnell. . . ." he said to the first serving girl to pass by.

"Martha?" she replied.

"Yeah. Martha. Is she busy?"

"Oh, yes—those gentlemen there are in line to dance with her," the girl said, gesturing toward eight or nine men in a file that reached from the edge of the dance floor to the wall on Charlie's left.

"Thank you." He pushed through the crowd to the end of the line. "This, er, Martha's line?" he inquired of the man before him.

"It is," the other fellow confirmed. "Best you have a generous poke at hand, friend—Martha is expensive."

Charlie patted his pocket. "I'm ready."

The downside of his decision to dance with Martha was that he had to wait his turn. Each song was no more than three minutes long, but that meant nearly half an hour of watching her dance with other men.

In each case, the procedure was much the same; the pianist concluded the tune, Martha and the partner parted ways (sometimes with a kiss on the cheek), and she sashayed to her line of admirers. She made a point of checking and taking the offered payment before accepting the arm of the prospective dance partner. Only then did she, and the other five girls operating in the same fashion, return to the floor for the next dance.

He could sense a man behind him, but pointedly refused to look back and see how long the line had grown. He wanted to imagine he would be Martha's final partner of the evening—which the sight of other men behind him would not facilitate.

As she concluded the pre-dance transaction with the man in front of Charlie, he caught the slightest hint of a floral perfume and heard her coo in delight as she took possession of the man's fee. That last dance lasted an eternity, but he made the most of it by watching carefully for useful information. It appeared that she liked to be dipped, and didn't mind being twirled, although he had doubts that, with his limited stature, he could correctly do that move. She was probably faster on her feet than he was, and was unquestionably a more skilled dancer in general. He'd hope for something slow and keep it simple.

The pianist wrapped up the song. Martha parted ways with her partner. Charlie took a deep breath and his fingers fumbled for his poke as she approached him.

"Evening, partner," she greeted him.

"Uh, hello, Ms. O'Donnell," he stammered. "I'm just a little lonesome and hoping to dance."

"You're in the right place, Lonesome. Call me Martha. Oh, is that for me?" she asked, eyes on his poke.

"Well, yes, of course," he replied quickly, and held it out for her to examine.

She looked at the last grains of gold dust in the little leather bag and blinked. Her laughter left him physically stunned and drew the eyes of many in the dance hall. "Oh, Lonesome," she said, lightly tapping his arm, "Seriously, now."

"But . . . that's what I got," he mumbled.

"Well, that's not nearly enough," she muttered in return. "Who's next?" she called, brushing past him.

He threw the poke to the floor and stormed out of the dance hall, plowing his way through snickering patrons and employees alike. It didn't occur to him to stop for his coat. He just shoved the main doors open and began running down the street, the heat of his growing rage and the alcohol in his blood drowning out the bitter chill of the night.

He didn't hear people telling him he'd catch pneumonia. He didn't smell the aromatic wood-smoke drifting out of five thousand wood stoves. He didn't see the northern lights, rippling slowly overhead. Without consciously thinking about it, he passed through the tent city and kept going, heading for his claim on Red Fox Creek.

She wanted more gold? Oh, he'd get her more gold, all right.

A light dusting of snow covered the trail up the creek. The only sounds he heard were his own crunching footsteps and his increasingly rapid breathing. Nobody would be out here working at this time of night; at this point in the season, most weren't even working during the day.

Upon reaching his claim, it occurred to him that all his equipment—shovel, pick, candles—was back at his tent in the city. No matter. He'd work in the dim light of the waxing moon and the northern lights. He'd kick loose a rock at the bottom of the shaft and use it as a hammer to dislodge other material. He knew what paydirt looked like, so he'd just pile up the frozen chunks of it in one corner and stack the waste in another. It would all work out.

At one side of the hole, he found the top-most rung of the ladder and climbed downward. The smooth-worn wood was cold and slick with frost, but experience won out and he was soon at the bottom of the twenty-three foot shaft.

The light wasn't as bright as he'd hoped, but he found a loose rock soon enough, a rounded grey cobble with an odd, waxy luster. He reached down and felt a strange sucking sensation as his hand grasped the rock and froze to it. He snorted. "Ain't gonna lose it now."

He pounded the rock into a wall of the shaft, over and over, releasing his anger. Bits of ice and gravel pelted him. Pebbles, cobbles, and frozen agglomerations fell, but it was all gangue, with no trace of the dark, heavy minerals that accompanied gold.

Eventually his swing was off and the tips of his fingers were smashed between the rocks. The sudden pain gave him pause. His exposed skin, other than that on the bleeding digits, felt numb. He was tired. The air quality was getting poor. And, since he had a damned rock stuck to his hand, climbing back out again was going to be well-nigh impossible.

He tried anyway. He got halfway up before his hand slipped and he fell down. His back scraped along the rough wall of the shaft, his head banged against a protruding boulder, and his collarbone took the brunt of the final impact on the irregular floor.

He lay on the cold rubble, pain throbbing through his body, and realized he was in trouble. This would be it. He would freeze to death, perhaps not to be found for days.

At least the northern lights were lovely this night. He watched the ribbons of pink-shot green swirling in the square of sky above the shaft as his arms and legs fell numb. He mumbled a short, slurred prayer, and waited for consciousness to end.

The last thing he noticed before blacking out was a dark rivulet oozing out of the rock, around his ring finger, and into the bloody knuckle.

🍁

When Charlie stirred again, somebody close by yelped, and so he yelped, too.

He cracked his eyes open to see the owner of a nearby claim, Samuel Harris, standing near the entrance to the shaft, barely recognizable under his thick coat and pants. "Jumping Jehosephat, Charlie! We thought you was dead!" Harris exclaimed.

Charlie was lying on his back in the snow, several feet away. He was apparently not dead, and there was no rock stuck to his hand. "What the blazes am I doing here?"

"We're wondering the same thing," Harris replied. "Rory spotted you on his way up to his claim. You were all cold, bloody, and stinking of liquor. Didn't see your breath or nothing." After a moment, he added, "Still don't, actually."

Charlie glanced down to confirm the observation. He wasn't sure what to make of it, so asked, "You found me here?"

"Rory did, yeah. What in tarnation were you doing, anyway? It's a miracle you ain't froze solid by now."

"Just a little keen, I suppose."

"Heh," Harris chuckled. "I heard you made a right fool of yourself last night at the Majestic."

"I don't want to talk about that," Charlie growled.

"Tried to dance on the cheap with—"

Charlie was on his feet in a heartbeat. He shoved Harris hard with both hands, figuring to knock him back a step and shut him up. The blows struck with loud, meaty thumps. Harris was flung a good twenty feet past the entrance to the shaft and tumbled end-for-end in the snow.

Charlie gaped.

Harris did not get up.

"Sam?"

Harris did not respond.

Uneasy, he trudged through the snow to Harris. "Sa—" his voice trailed off as he noticed the expression on Harris's face and the odd angle at which his head lay relative to his body.

He knelt down to look into Harris's lifeless eyes. "Oh Lord," he muttered. "I didn't mean for that to happen."

But it had happened. He'd killed a man. That was a hanging offense, and there was no practical way to escape the noose, save for running into the hills—not a feasible proposition given the frigid temperatures and his near-complete lack of clothing and equipment.

He stared at Harris, trying to think. He could blame somebody else. Make up a story—Harris had been dead when he woke up, slain by an unseen assailant.

Only, there were no tracks within fifty feet of Harris save for his own. He'd need to create a fake set somehow, lead it back to the main trail where it might get lost . . . then carefully return to this precise spot by stepping in his own tracks from minutes earlier. That could be done.

He'd taken four steps toward the trail when he spotted Rory Sampson and two Mounties—a constable and a sergeant—coming up from town. "Charlie?" Rory exclaimed as he caught sight of him. "You're alive?"

Hot panic surged through his veins, but Charlie couldn't make himself speak.

"I thought you said your friend's name was Samuel," said the sergeant, a grizzled veteran with a short beard.

"Yeah, Samuel's my buddy, but that there's Charlie, what we thought was dead."

"Clearly he isn't," the sergeant replied.

"I suppose he ain't," Rory agreed. "Jeepers, Charlie, you sure fooled us. Where's Sam?"

If Charlie could have made himself speak, he might've said "I don't know" or "Gone back to town" or *something* that would've caused Rory and the Mounties to stop before they caught sight of Harris's body. But he couldn't make sound come out of his mouth, and so the three drew closer.

"That your friend there?" the constable asked, pointing toward Harris's corpse.

"Yeah," Rory said. "But he don't look right. . . ."

"He looks dead," the sergeant observed. "You sure you didn't get these two mixed up, Rory?"

"No!" Rory protested. "Sam and I found *him* looking dead. Sam was just fine when I left to get you fellas!"

The sergeant stopped a few feet short of Harris and blocked Rory's progress with an outstretched arm. "Yeah, this one's dead. Broken neck." He turned to look at his colleague and Charlie.

"Accident," Charlie managed to blurt out at last. "Accident."

"At the very least, it's clear you've moved the body." The sergeant examined the tracks in the snow. "And this looks like evidence of a struggle," he added, pointing at the stretch through which Harris had tumbled.

"I believe we'll have to take you into custody, sir," said the constable, reaching into a pocket of his overcoat.

Charlie bolted.

The young Mountie was right behind him and caught up within seconds. He shoved Charlie in the back, sending him sprawling face first into the snow. Charlie rolled onto his side as the constable skidded to a stop and lunged at him, handcuffs dangling from one hand. Charlie lashed out with his left leg and caught the constable just below his right knee. Something cracked. The Mountie shrieked as his leg bent backward and gave out.

Charlie scrambled to his feet, sidestepping the fallen man, sparing not a moment to glance behind. There would be no turning back now. He was running for the hills and the meagre chance of freedom and survival that they offered.

Something cracked past his left ear. Something punched his back. He kept running.

An October day was still nine hours long at sixty-four degrees latitude, so running all day was no small feat.

Charlie's flight initially sent him east, away from town, but the occasional person collecting firewood or hunting had probably caught sight of him. When the Mounties crossed paths with them, they'd remember seeing the man with no coat.

So he turned north, following a valley parallel to the Yukon River. After encountering four men using the valley as a trail, he cut upslope and started following the ridgelines. There wasn't much concealment to be had, given how thoroughly it had all been logged out for timber and firewood. It was slower and more difficult travelling, but none of the men down in the valleys seemed to notice him above them.

The sun was plummeting out of the southern sky when he finally sat down on the exposed trunk of a fallen birch to rest.

His endurance was astonishing; he'd been on the move at a strong clip for hours, and while he was famished he was only barely winded.

Something wasn't right. Just looking at his hand told him this. He recalled having a leaky grey rock stuck to him, but it was gone now and hadn't taken any skin off with it. His flesh was warm, flexible, and pink despite having been continuously exposed to freezing temperatures for a good twelve or fifteen hours. His wounded fingers were completely healed. Factor in the strength with which he'd shoved poor old Harris . . . he had to conclude he was no normal man today.

"Like a grizzly in men's clothes. . . ." he mused aloud.

If he really was as strong and hale as a bear, and it was a lasting condition, then he had more options than just a quick death in the bush. At the very least, he could sneak back into Dawson, steal some grub and gear, and get out again. If he could avoid becoming predictable, he might last a while doing that.

Alternately, he could make a few raids in quick succession, build up a cache, grab a dog team, and strike out for Whitehorse and then Skagway. He'd be safe on American soil; he'd just need to wait for a steamship and get passage south. Of course, Skagway was four or five hundred miles away. When he'd done the trek coming in, it had taken months, and he'd been reasonably well supplied.

Perhaps a raid was a good starting point.

He backtracked south along the riverbank, scarcely concealed by the thin scrub and stumps. Around an hour after nightfall, he caught direct sight of Dawson again, a wide expanse of yellow candlelight and orange firelight that illuminated the snow around it. Overhead, the aurora had flared into existence and was rippling in waves of green, yellow, and white, as if pouring out of the Big Dipper. Their soft tinkle reminded him of candle ice breaking up in the spring, and he wondered why he'd never noticed the sound before.

His lower back twinged, and he reached to massage it. A fingernail snagged on a rip or hole in his shirt in the same spot as his backache. He picked at the rip for a moment; it hadn't been there earlier.

A strange thought crossed his mind. He unbuttoned the shirt and shrugged out of it. He was surprised to see a round hole, as wide as his pinky finger, in the lower back of the shirt. A smatter of frozen blood encircled it.

"That son of a bitch shot me," he muttered, remembering his flight from the Mounties. When he reached around and felt his back, it was certainly sore—but there was no open wound that he could determine, no wet or frozen blood, no scabs. At worst, he figured there might be a bruise.

So he was unnaturally strong, fast, weather-resistant, *and* bullet-proof? If so, why on God's green Earth was he thinking about running off to Skagway? Just a short distance away were both the source of his current humiliation and the richest gold placer on the continent.

The barber's turn of phrase came to mind. "I will try to earn a bit of gold in a manner better suited to me," he muttered.

Like on most Saturdays, the entertainment district was packed as miners sought to have fun and blow off steam before the Sabbath and its Mountie-enforced closures came into effect. For the most part, the people around him were chattering, laughing, and drinking. A few hapless souls, having over-indulged, were doubled over and vomiting into the snow, and one appeared to have passed out in a drift. Occasionally, he heard the sounds of fights, muggings, or sex taking place behind buildings.

Charlie drew curious glances as he approached the Majestic, probably due more to his lack of outerwear than because anyone recognized him as a wanted man. As he'd half expected, his coat was still hanging on the same peg in the establishment's coatroom. He left it; if he hadn't needed it for the past day, he wasn't going to need it later.

The dance hall was packed with miners standing shoulder to shoulder, several rows deep. From the entrance, Charlie couldn't see through or over them to the dance floor, but he had no doubt Martha was at the centre of it all.

He began forcing his way around the perimeter of the room. He earned no small number of hard looks from the patrons he shoved aside, but not one could hold his ground against him. He reached the piano without difficulty and leaned to speak into the pianist's ear. "Please stop a moment so I can talk to the crowd."

The pianist shook his head. His fingers continued to dance across the keys.

"I'm asking nice," Charlie said.

The pianist glanced up at him. "Sod off."

Charlie reached out, took hold of the back of his neck, and tossed him onto the dance floor.

The abrupt silence momentarily shocked the partygoers, but they quickly locked eyes on Charlie and began bombarding him with jeers and insults. As the pianist picked himself up off the planked floor, Charlie said, "I just want to say something."

The verbal abuse continued unabated.

He stamped his left foot, making less noise than he'd hoped, yet breaking through the floorboard. He swung his arms to maintain his balance, drawing laughter in addition to insults. He looked down as he yanked his foot free of the broken wood. As he looked up again, the pianist punched him square on the nose. The cheering of the crowd drowned out the impact, but there was no mistaking the expression of pain on the pianist's face; it wasn't Charlie's nose that had broken.

Charlie lifted the man by the waist and held him aloft despite his struggles and ineffectual blows. The crowd began to quiet. After a half minute, the pianist stopped fussing. The hall was finally silent.

"Thank you," Charlie said.

"Say your piece and get out, Lonesome!" Martha called. She wore a billowy, white lace gown and shoved aside a couple to confront him, hands on her hips.

"My name is Charlie, Martha."

She shrugged. "Lonesome. Charlie. Don't matter none. Set Rich down and clear out afore the Mounties arrive."

Charlie nodded, and set the pianist down. "You, sir, are a fool—you done broke your hand and now you can't earn your keep."

The pianist glared at him but kept his mouth closed.

"Okay," Charlie said. "Martha remembers me from last night, and some of the rest of you might, too. I been up here two long years, I came here last night to have a short dance with a pretty girl, and then I got *laughed* at when I offered her more gold than any girl would earn in a year down south. That was pretty darned humiliating, and I ran outta here with my tail between my legs." He paused to lock eyes with Martha.

She stared back until he broke eye contact again.

"But I'm all different now," he continued. "I'm strong enough to kill with my bare hands, tough enough to shrug off a Mountie's bullets, and hale enough that I can run round all day without a coat or gloves. I've decided I'm going to take ad—"

A two-by-four splintered across the top of his head. The crowd's roar of approval faded quickly as he slowly turned to face his assailant. It was a taller, younger fellow he didn't recognize, dressed in clean shirt and trousers. The jagged end of the board hung from his left hand.

Charlie grasped the man's wrist, and crushed it with an audible crackle. Raising his voice over the man's cries of pain, he said, "Now, look—I ain't keen to keep beating on people, but I promise you this: I will tear the head clean off the shoulders of the next man what interrupts me. That clear?"

Nobody contested the matter.

"Thank you," he said. "Now, as I was saying, I have decided to take advantage of my newfound . . . er, advantages, so I can get the gold I came here for. It ain't how I wanted to do it, but it seems I'm not much better at mining than the fellow what cut my hair yesterday. And since I ain't one for numbers or books, I'll make it real simple for everybody. Tomorrow, I want a pile of gold in front of my tent. And every day after that, I want it to get bigger. Who provides it and who brings it ain't my concern. If I'm happy with what I get, everything is swell. If I'm not, I will start breaking things, beginning with this particular establishment."

"That's preposterous," Martha said.

"Maybe, but you know what? Some fine day, when I know that there's no way any man will ever have a larger poke than mine, I will bring that pile of gold up this way, and I will buy a dance with one of your competitors."

She glared at him, and it drew a bit of a smirk to his face.

"Now, then—does anybody need any further demonstration of my seriousness, or can I retire to my tent for the evening?"

Nobody spoke.

"That's good. I will look forward to my earnings tomorrow." The crowd parted for him as he made his way out of the dance hall, ready to return to his tent and get some sleep.

❦

He didn't get as much shut-eye as he'd hoped. Without even a hint of dawn out east, he woke to a vaguely familiar voice shouting his name.

"This is Sergeant Hawke of the North-West Mounted Police! You are under arrest for murder, assault, public disorder, and resisting arrest! You come on out of that tent with your hands raised high!"

He blinked and rubbed his eyes. Silhouettes of armed men, backlit by the moon, played on the canvas around him.

"Charles Albert Johnstone! This is—"

"I heard you!" Charlie shouted. "Lord. . . ."

"You going to come out peaceful, Charlie?"

"Yeah, I'm coming!" Charlie tossed the wool blankets aside and slid off his cot. He stretched in the middle of the tent with his head just grazing the canvas, then opened the plank door set into the middle of the front end.

A number of Mounties stood in an arc aiming guns at him, including the sergeant from the day before. "Put your hands behind your head and stay where you are."

"No, I ain't surrendering," Charlie said. "Killing Samuel was an accident. So was injuring your man. I concede I resisted arrest, but I ain't prepared to stand trial for that."

"We have instructions to shoot you if you resist arrest."

Charlie nodded. "Go on then. Shoot me and be done with it. You ain't going to kill me, Sergeant. You already tried and failed at that. Here, look where you done shot me in the back." He turned around and lifted the back of his undershirt. "See a bruise or anything there? That's all there is."

"No doubt you got lucky, Charlie. Could be the cartridge didn't have a full powder charge."

"So shoot me again," Charlie said, turning to face the Mounties. "If you kill me, then you've saved me a date with a hangman. If you don't kill me, then you've proven I'm bulletproof. Just ask yourself if that's something better left unproven."

The constables on either side of Hawke holstered their revolvers and began to approach him. Charlie sighed.

When they were within reach, he carefully shoved the one aside, sending him sprawling into the snow. He took hold of the other man's forearm, trying not to crack the bones. He unbuckled the officer's holster and pulled out the heavy revolver.

He pushed the second constable down. Bullets and buckshot punched through his clothes, stung his face, chest, legs, and arms, drawing specks of blood in places. Nonetheless, he remained substantially unharmed when the Mounties ceased to fire.

"Jesus," one of the Mounties muttered.

"Well, I told you," Charlie snapped. "Here, let me make it crystal clear." He thumbed back the hammer on the stolen revolver, placed the barrel under his chin, and pulled the trigger. His jaw rocked upward with the report; the bullet ricocheted down into the snow. "Look, stand out there and keep watch if you want to. I'm going back to catch some more winks. You try getting me, and I'll bust you all up."

He didn't wait for a response; he just turned and ducked back inside.

❦

Come Sunday morning—in the proper sense of the word, with hints of daylight and everything—he rose again. It felt like he'd been in a fistfight; every place he'd been shot was tender, and a couple had given way to dark bruises. Moving gingerly, he stepped out of the tent and blinked.

There was a crowd watching him—perhaps fifty miners and a cluster of four Mounties. "Er . . . morning," he said.

None of the bystanders answered, though one Mountie nodded.

He padded around behind his tent, unbuttoned the flap on his trousers, and relieved himself, finding the process more challenging than usual, given the audience. "I guess you fellas are here to watch me," he said to the Mounties when he was done, "but what about you others?"

"Heard you killed a man up on Red Fox yesterday," one of the gathered miners remarked.

"It was an accident," Charlie said. "You wanting to dish out some justice?"

"Just curious," the man replied. "Heard you want people to give you gold, too."

"Like Martha O'Donnell," his neighbour piped up.

"Yeah," Charlie said.

"Think that'll happen?"

247

"Yeah," Charlie said, "or I'll have to go back and make some new arguments."

The miner chuckled. "Think I'll tag along. Martha ain't the kinda woman what takes crap from anybody."

"Heard she's hiring men for security," another stampeder interjected.

"And you didn't sign up?" Charlie asked.

"I heard the Mounties shooting at you earlier, yet here you are. So I reckon I'm content to just watch."

"That sounds mighty sensible of you," Charlie agreed. "You gonna contribute to my poke?"

The miner shrugged. "Ain't got nothing to give."

"'Course not," Charlie said. "What about the rest of you all?"

The miners shuffled or looked away.

"Well, don't that just figure."

He spent the morning on an empty wood crate beside the door to his tent. He nursed a cup of coffee and gulped down a pair of biscuits with bacon fat smeared across their tops. He made small talk with his audience. He tossed a few crumbs at a brazen raven that swooped down to land in the snow beside him.

As noon approached, the miners began trickling away, muttering and snickering as they headed back to their own camps. He couldn't make out what they said, but their collective refusal to give him so much as a grain of gold dust told him enough. They thought he was a joke.

He made himself a lunch of beans and bacon and another coffee. A bean slid off his spoon, and the raven darted in to snatch it from the snow. As the bird retreated, Charlie grinned. "Yeah, you get it. You want something, sometimes you got to take it. And it ain't like you took it all." He threw a few more beans to the bird as he ate.

Another quartet of Mounties arrived, and the two groups had a brief, muted discussion. The first set left without leaving any gold for him, and the newcomers didn't have look to have any heavy sacks on them. "Strange that you fellas are still here when all the other guys are gone home," he called out to the Mounties. "Unless it weren't them you was watching, of course."

He kept an eye on them as he repaired the bullet hole in his shirt with thread and needle. He washed his dishes and filled his pot with cleanish snow. He aired out his bedding and snow-washed his other set of clothes. He whittled a piece of birch and watched the sun begin to set.

The Sabbath was coming to an end. The town's entrepreneurs—their businesses closed by law—would have had no trouble coming up to his camp to give him the gold he'd asked for. They'd chosen not to.

"Goddammit it all anyway," he muttered, setting the wood and knife down on the edge of the crate. "Follow me, boys, 'cause I'm going back to town to make some new arguments."

The Mounties followed at a safe distance. Stampeders fell in behind them as they passed row after row of tents and shacks. A cry went up—"Lonesome's going to collect!"—and the retinue swelled. He could hear their chatter and sense their anticipation; they were looking forward to him getting his arse whooped. Well, he aimed to disappoint them.

As he reached the south end of Front Street, one of the Mounties split off toward their headquarters. Some of the Dawsonites ran out ahead of him, perhaps looking to secure good vantage points near the Majestic. Others poked their heads out of windows and doors or filtered out to join the parade.

Charlie stopped upon seeing two lines of men standing between him and the Majestic. The nearer line consisted of Mounties, hands clasped behind their backs. The second line was of ordinary Dawsonites holding boards or tools. A throng of hundreds or thousands stood on the periphery of it all, pushing and shoving for position.

Sergeant Hawke stepped forward from the front line. "Charlie Johnstone. Lonesome Charlie, they're starting to call you. This town doesn't need your trouble. If you won't surrender yourself, then turn around and walk back to your camp."

"Lonesome?" Charlie called back. "That really catching on?"

"It is. You don't care for it?"

"Sounds kind of pathetic, don't it?"

"No more so than Soapy or such," Hawke replied. "You'd hardly be the first criminal to acquire an unflattering nickname."

"I ain't a criminal!" Charlie shouted.

"Of course you're a criminal. On top of what you did yesterday, you're now extorting gold out of hardworking folk. What else would I call you?"

"Hardworking?" Charlie exclaimed. "Martha and her ilk steal every day and night they're open. Look what they charge for a meal, or cigar, or dance. They're fleecing fellas like me what do the hard work, and the law lets them get away with it. Anybody deserves to lose some gold, it's them. Ain't that right?" he called to the crowd.

Scattered cheers of encouragement echoed back.

Hawke ignored them. "Not one person is under any requirement to pay for an overpriced cigar or an old newspaper, Charlie. Fellas do it because they've got the gold and there's nothing else to do but spend it. Their choice."

"Well, I just want to get some gold, spend it on a dance, and get out of this shithole."

"If this is how you intend to do it, you'll have to go through us first," Hawke stated.

"Not gonna shoot me again?"

"Not yet. We'll take you down through weight of numbers."

Charlie counted the Mounties and the volunteers beyond them—fifty or more, easily. "We'll see about that," he called out, and sprang forward.

The crowd erupted as the Mounties and the volunteers surged toward him. He shoved the first Mountie to cross his path, sending the man hurtling away. A flailing fist knocked another to the ground. A third grimaced as his baton rebounded from Charlie's left forearm.

Blows rained down on him from behind, but he was through the Mounties. The first Dawsonite to come at him went down with broken ribs. He backhanded the next one, breaking his shoulder. Another would-be attacker stumbled back as Charlie locked eyes with him.

He twisted as somebody jumped on his back; a Mountie flew past him and took down two Dawsonites. Hands grasped at his clothes, his arms, his waist, and his legs. He realized that Hawke had been speaking literally; they were indeed trying to pile on to him, drag him down, and bury him under their collective weight. He started throwing wild punches. Those that landed did terrible damage, but his lack of fighting experience meant many didn't land at all.

His forward motion was coming to a halt. Three or four ranks of Dawsonites shoved and pushed at him, while Mounties leapt at his feet and his back, wrapped their arms around his shoulders and pulled at his ears.

His determination began to waver. They were going to stop him. They were going to beat him. He was going to be a laughing stock again.

Charlie bellowed his frustration, and the faces before him flinched at the intensity of the sound. Sensing less force against his body, he shouted again, shifted his weight to the right, then shoved left, taking down a couple of men. His left arm came free again. He swung in a wide arc, striking down two Mounties. He butted his head backward and struck flesh; the hands on his ears fell away. He squeezed his arms against his sides, and the arms around his shoulders cracked and disappeared. He spun, and more men fell or backed away.

The way to the Majestic's front entrance was no longer blocked. He kicked off two diehard Mounties and lunged forward, reaching the door in four long strides.

He flung the front door open. It crashed into the wall and rebounded, slamming into his side as he entered. He lashed out, and its hinges broke.

Flustered, he wrenched the handle off the door to the dining room with a crack of breaking brass. The door swung slowly open to admit him.

Martha O'Donnell stood in the empty room, arms crossed under her breasts.

"I told everybody yesterday that I wanted some gold," Charlie growled. "Ain't nobody brought it. So I'm here to take it."

"I sacrificed everything to get where I am," Martha growled back. "I left my husband and my babes behind in Boston. I travelled by steamer all the way around the Americas to get to Skagway. I climbed the Chilkoot Pass thirty-seven goddamned times to get my supplies over the top and nearly drowned in Miles Canyon. I risked every last cent I had to buy this place. Why would I give up my gold to you, Lonesome, just because you said so?"

"Because you were cruel to me, and if you don't make it right, I'm gonna rip this place apart," Charlie replied.

"I'll rebuild," Martha declared.

He stepped forward, grasped the edge of the nearest table and picked it up. Silverware crashed to the floor around his feet. Martha didn't waver, so he flung the table into the wall. Boards broke. The table crashed to the floor in fragments.

He kicked at an empty chair; it disintegrated as it struck the ceiling. "Are you really gonna make me do this?"

"You didn't take down all of the Mounties. More will be here shortly, and I expect they'll be bringing their Maxim guns this time," she said.

"You oughta see by now they can't stop me, guns or no." Charlie picked up another chair, pulled the legs off, and threw the pieces aside. He put his fist through a second table, spilling drink and food. He kicked away the chairs around it. Looking up, he saw Martha hadn't so much as shifted. He said, "I guess you can replace those."

"Carpenters will be lining up for the business as soon as your arse is out the door."

He glanced over to the side and smirked. "What about the piano?"

Her face fell, but she said nothing. The piano died in a horrible cacophony of breaking wood and screeching wire.

He started on the brass fittings of the bar, snapping them into pieces. Bottles of wine, champagne, and hard liquor flew in all directions. He looked up into a long mirror mounted on the wall above the empty wine racks and grinned at Martha's reflection.

"Enough!" she cried out. Tears were beginning to streak her rouged cheeks.

"Finally." He sighed. "I thought it would be the piano, honestly. Well, go get it, then."

"No, you get it yourself," she growled, pointing to the kitchen door. "The office is through there. I'm sure you can break into the safe easily enough."

"I expect so," he agreed. He stepped into the vacant kitchen and quickly spied a closed door off to the left. He tore the door off its hinges. Inside, he saw an iron safe behind a large desk.

It took him a few seconds to wrench the safe door open, but it yielded. He did not spare so much as a glance at the paper and cash stacked within. Only a large burlap sack caught his eye; he snatched it and grinned as he felt its weight: a good five or six pounds of gold in there, easily.

He knotted the top of the sack around his belt and whooped as his trousers sank on his right hip. He strode back through the kitchen, savouring the rhythmic bumping of the gold against his leg. He pushed open the door to the dining room, saying, "Thank you very much, my—" and had just enough time to comprehend that an object was flying at him before the lamp shattered against his chest.

Flaming kerosene engulfed him.

He screamed, lurched forward, and crashed through the wreckage of the dining room. Dripping oil ignited sawdust, splinters, and spilt spirits. The front wall of the Majestic burst outward as he smashed through it.

Staccato thunder erupted. He reeled and howled. His hair burned, his flesh bubbled. He dashed forward, unable to see or think beyond the need to reach the river.

His flight left slushy footsteps in his wake, and then he was tumbling into the blessed, black cold of the Yukon.

In his earliest lucid moments, face down on the river's edge, miles downstream from Dawson, Lonesome prayed for death. God did not see fit to take him, and Lucifer did not come to claim him.

He endured hours, days, and weeks, kept awake by the pain yet too weak to move except for desperate grabs at any organic matter within reach. Moss, leaves, sticks, fish, rodents—he could not shake a compulsive, almost animalistic urge to devour everything, however repulsive. What remained of his hair receded, and his fingernails seemed to absorb into his skin. The tattered remnants of his trousers and boots gradually dissolved, until he was naked in the freezing water.

Once the agony had receded to mere, ongoing pain, he could think clearly about what had happened; indeed, it was the only way he had to pass the time. He knew Martha had set him on fire and that the Mounties had—just as she'd predicted—fired on him with their Maxim guns.

In fits of nightmare-filled sleep, his mind played out fantasies of inflicting unspeakable horrors upon them all.

Eventually he woke from one such fit and felt not only hunger, but the energy to seek out sustenance. He shook free from the ice and snow binding him and crawled onto the frozen bank. Under a drab winter sky he observed that—though dangerously thin, and without hair—he was fully healed under a veneer of peeling scabs.

He stood and stretched, oblivious to the arctic wind flaying his bony, hairless body.

There would be no more politeness or half-hearted attempts at intimidation. There would be no turning back or slinking away after what had been inflicted upon him. While they forgot about him and prepared for Christmas, he'd be testing his strengths and his limits, and eating as much as he could. When he was ready, he'd start modestly—hitting the corporate mining operations, taking their gold. He'd learn to fight properly by ambushing the Mounties sent to apprehend him. He'd make sure Dawson—including the Mounties, and especially Martha—knew not only what he was doing but also that they were trapped, without prospect of escape or relief, for the rest of the winter.

He cleared his throat and rasped, "I will earn gold in a manner better suited to me."

JASON SHARP was born in Toronto, raised near Edmonton, and worked for several years as a geologist in Nunavut and the NWT. Currently a policy wonk by day, hobby farmer by night, and aspiring writer in between, he and his wife Valerie reside outside Ottawa.

THE SHIELD MAIDEN

ALYXANDRA HARVEY

It was Friday night, and as usual I was at work. I loved the sound the dirt made when it crumbled off a broken pottery sherd, or a rusted nail, or piece of bone. My best friend Poppy came by sometimes when I was working—okay, technically, since I wasn't getting paid, I was actually volunteering. Regardless, I loved archaeology way more than parties and watching Poppy flirt with some girl who didn't even know she was being flirted with. She got creeped out whenever she saw me clean human bone fragments. The truth was, the slivers and shards I get are so small you can't really tell the difference between animal and human.

Archaeology was all just story. That was the best part, imagining what someone was thinking as she drank out of that teacup, or if a guy used that hammer to build a cradle or a coffin. And if he ever hit his thumb, the way I always seem to.

I went back to cataloguing the seventeen bone fragments and iron nails from Newfoundland. Since archaeologists are neurotically possessive over artefacts, we must have had something they wanted more. You never can tell what people consider treasure.

I tensed at the scuff of a shoe on the concrete floor. I glanced at the clock. Damn. Time for Benedict's rounds. I usually timed it so I was in the bathroom.

"Hi, Val," he said, swaggering into the room and smiling his oily smile.

"Hi, Benedict," I said neutrally. To say there was absolutely nothing about this particular security guard that made me feel secure was an understatement. It was best to appear too busy to talk, even for a moment. "Just cataloguing," I said, grabbing the first tray I could reach. It was more unsorted items from the Newfoundland exchange. My thumb grazed something sharp and there was a bite of pain. I yanked it out, blood welling along the side of my nail. A long wooden splinter was lodged deep under the skin. I sucked at it, wincing.

"Shouldn't you be at a party or something?" He leered. He actually leered.

"No." I didn't even attempt a polite smile. "I have to get back to this."

"You work too hard," he said. "You should go out with me."

Before I could give in to a full-body shudder, my boss Ms. Radcliffe spoke quietly from the doorway. "Benedict, I thought we'd discussed you aren't to bother the staff."

"Thought I heard a noise," he said. "Just doing my job."

"I'll take that," Ms. Radcliffe reached for the Newfoundland tray before I could throw it at Benedict's head. "Why don't you go on home, Val." She smiled distractedly, staring into the tray. I knew the reason for that look; it was the same reason I always worked so late after school and wasn't actually looking forward to next week's vacation.

I grabbed my knapsack and eased around Benedict, who was taking up most of the doorway now. He leered again, sucking his teeth, knowing Radcliffe was now too distracted to notice.

I so prefer dead people.

Keira brought the axe to the barrow mounds. It could have been confused with any other weapon of its kind; brought back from a berserker raid, it was single bladed, the wooden handle wrapped with leather. But Vala, the priestess, said it shimmered and pulsed with magic she had never felt before.

Keira stood watch as Vala poured mead on the ground in offering to the ancestors and the gods. Keira struck a small fire with a jasper stone and sat quietly. The sun went down and the wind grew cold, and still she sat, to prove her worth. Keira tried not to shiver—if the old woman could sit so comfortably, a young shieldmaiden like herself could, too.

Eventually, the priestess nodded at Keira. Snow began to drift down as she swung the axe, driving the blade into the cleansing earth. At first the only reply was a faint blue glow, like fireflies gathering over the long frostbitten grass. Slowly, a figure emerged from one of the boat-shaped barrows: one of the ancient barrow-kings, long dead and slumbering in his wooden ship under the earth. He wore a fine embroidered tunic and gold at this throat and a sword at his hip. His beard was the colour of the setting sun on a misty summer night.

He did not look pleased.

"You carry a cursed axe, priestess," he said, the grass flattening all around at the sound of his voice. "And you bring it to our hall."

Vala bowed her head. "I was not sure."

"Take it as far from here as your ship will sail." He looked right at Keira. Ice travelled along the standing stones, glinting like knives. "Or the dead will rise."

I woke at dawn. The streets were empty, the only sound from the birds singing in the back garden. This time of day was always the same, no matter which city we lived in. My parents taught at a new college or university every year, which meant I also had to start at a new school every year. Nothing like being the new kid *all the time.* But at sunrise I could be anywhere at all, and nothing mattered but the slow unfurling of light and birdsong. I could perfectly imagine what it would have been like to wake up to a similar sky, the colour of marmalade, five hundred or even a thousand years ago. That was another thing I loved about archaeology; it made a stranger who died a thousand years ago as recognizable as my own reflection. I could see all the ways in which we were the same.

I could also see . . . a polar bear on the flagstones in the backyard.

I pushed the curtains aside. It was still there, lumbering slowly along, giant body swaying back and forth as it sniffed the ground. Its white fur glowed in the citrus light. I rubbed my eyes and the movement sent a jab of pain through the thumb I'd hurt at work. "Ow."

The polar bear jerked its head up, blue eyes meeting mine. It threw back its head and bellowed, sharp teeth exposed. I jumped, my heart thundering. I was wondering if I should call the police or the zoo, when it vanished, leaving only mist and dew and my heartbeat, too hard and too loud.

"Oh man," I muttered. "I have *got* to get more sleep."

I slept until noon, and when I woke up there was no polar bear in the yard and nothing in the news about a zoo breakout. That evening I decided to visit Poppy at work, a small artsy café called 1812 that didn't mind hiring a seventeen-year-old with tattoos and with fire-engine red streaks in her Anishinaabe black hair.

The walls of the 1812 were hung with local art, everything as brightly coloured as a carnival. In her red tutu, Poppy fit right in. She looked like she was made of sugar floss, when she actually made of sour jellies.

"I'm still mad at you for not going to the party last night," she said, but she was grinning manically. "It was lame. Justin threw up—" her words started to tumble together "—and then Simone started to cry and someone called the cops because it was too loud andweallrantothesubwaystation—" She stopped for a breath, and I could have sworn one of her eyeballs rolled back in her head. But just the one.

"How much coffee have you had today?" I asked her, laughing.

"Seven lattes. No, five—nine! Even my teeth are awake!"

"Then maybe you can make sense of the polar bear I saw this morning," I muttered.

"A polar bear?" she said dubiously over her shoulder as she steamed milk for my usual cinnamon cappuccino. "In Toronto?" The machine hissed and spat at her like a cat caught in a rainstorm. "I'm thinking that would've made the news."

"I know." I leaned on the counter. "I guess I imagined it."

"You don't sound convinced."

"It just looked so *real*." I picked at the sliver on my thumb. I'd finally worked it free with tweezers but it still throbbed.

"Let's get out of here," she said, tossing her apron on a hook.

I could smell the coffee on her clothes, even outside in the crisp April air. Litter danced along the sidewalk as we tucked our hands in our pockets and headed up Yonge Street.

"Let's cut through Mount Pleasant Cemetery," Poppy suggested. It was her favourite place, basically two hundred acres of lawns and trees. The dead people didn't bother either of us.

We made our way to the back where the old mausoleums still held court in their faded stone dresses, elegant as a black and white movie. The sounds of traffic and the ever-present sirens of a big city were muffled. Our parents would kill us if they knew we were here after dark; but it was still pretty early, and quiet.

The trees shivered. I could smell wet leaves, mud, and ... something else.

There was a crunch under my boot. "Please don't let that be a really big cockroach," I said. Poppy's boots were military, but mine were just old Doc Martens covered in multicoloured paint splatters—one of Poppy's art projects.

The street lamps were too far away to do us any good, but since we snuck in on a fairly regular basis Poppy had a flashlight in her bag. The beam chased moths and dust, to fall on leaf-strewn ground. I shifted my foot slowly; it wasn't a bug after all, just a chunk of crumbled rock.

"That's weird," I said.

She followed the grey powder to a headstone a few feet away. The top was cracked, one side crumbling off. The ground around it was uneven, with clods of dirt and turned up grass. "Someone vandalized it." Poppy scowled. "Uncool."

"It would take a hammer to do that kind of damage," I pointed out, frowning. "Maybe we should get out of here."

Poppy stiffened abruptly. "I've had a lot of coffee," she announced. "So I am not seeing what I'm seeing."

I followed her gaze and froze as a man in an old-fashioned pinstriped suit pulled himself out of a nearby grave. He wriggled like a decomposing worm, his blackened fingers clawing at the soil. His skin was grey and raw around his mangled lips. His eyes were bloodshot.

"Is this a performance art thing?" Poppy squeaked. "Please say yes."

We stepped closer to each other. I felt strange all over. The cut on my thumb pulsed hotly. "Zombie," I croaked. "That's a freaking zombie!"

The smell was appalling: rotten apples cores, dead flowers, and embalming fluid. I gagged. He shuffled toward us, joints creaking wetly. I didn't even want to know how that was possible. We whirled to make a frantic dash between the rows of stones, but another zombie shambled up on our left, hair crawling with worms.

You know when I said I preferred dead people?

Yeah, I totally take that back.

They were slow, but so unnatural—it was hypnotizing. It was difficult to move, though my leg muscles were twitching with the need to run. My brain was like a moth with glue on her wings: frantic, stuck, and about to beat itself bloody against a screen door.

And then it went from performance art to the surreal.

Salvador Dali, whose art I hate by the way but which Poppy loves, would have felt right at home.

"Bear!" Poppy shrieked, pointing, finally finding her voice even if it was squeakier than I'd ever heard it before.

"Zombies!" I shouted, also pointing, but in the opposite direction. Poppy's bear was the polar bear I thought I'd seen that morning. It was massive, thousands of pound of flesh and muscle and white fur. Its black nose was practically the size of my fist. It roared, and the sound shivered across the back of my neck.

Three zombies lurched toward us, half-leaning on each other for support. I thought I saw a finger fall into the grass. Bile burned in my throat. The bear charged at them, chomping with powerful jaws and swiping with paws like concrete blocks. The zombies fell into each other, bones snapping.

Poppy fumbled in her pocket. I was hoping she'd pull out a can of pepper spray or something sharp—not her phone. She wasn't even calling 911. "What are you doing?" I demanded as she lost her grip on the flashlight. I grabbed it before it could fall into the grass. Trapped in a graveyard at night with zombies, wildlife, and no light? No, thank you.

"I'm recording this!"

"We don't need YouTube!" I said as we stumbled backward. "We need a weapon."

My splinter flared so painfully my fingers cramped. It was like hot burning needles jabbing into my thumb. I dropped the flashlight after all. There was light everywhere. No, not everywhere; coming out of *me*.

It was just a flash, but it was so bright my eyes watered. When it faded, I was holding an axe. An actual axe with a sharply curved iron blade and nicks along the edge The wooden handle was wrapped with leather and carved with some sort of rune.

I was still wearing my jeans and Docs, but I was also now wearing some sort of apron-like tunic dress with straps over my black tee-shirt. It was grey-blue, with two bronze brooches linked with glass beads, and embroidered along the hem. There was a large brown leather belt around my waist, securing a curved horn and a cross strap with a holder for the axe. In my left hand I held a round wooden shield, painted red and white.

And I was spinning the axe around like I knew what I was doing.

"What? The? Hell?" I blurted out, thumb burning.

Poppy just stared at me. "Dude."

The bear was still tearing zombies apart. Its fur gleamed like exposed bone. It ripped and pawed at the bodies until the heads came off, stopping their attack. They didn't seem to feel pain.

Without even considering what a truly bad idea it was, I leapt into the fight. Poppy screamed at me but I knew only the axe in my hand, the strangely comfortable weight of it, and the whistle as it cut through the air. I held on tight and swung hard, cleaving a mostly decomposed head off rotten shoulders. Black blood oozed, sluggish, thickly congealed. The head rolled across the grass and bumped into a tree to lie staring at me.

A zombie had trapped Poppy against a pine. She was throwing branches and twigs at it, and whatever she could find in her bag—gum, pens, a bottle of water.

My body knew what to do. I ran and leapt over a tombstone, using another one as a launching pad. I was agile and strong.

Until I started thinking about it.

I stumbled, falling to one knee. The bear roared a warning. I'd practically landed on a zombie trying to crawl out of a grave. His arms were free, but the rest of him was still mired in soil. There was still dirt in his hair when I swung my axe and cut off his head.

My axe. For some reason, I knew it belonged to me. Or I belonged to it.

With my shield, I hacked at the zombie cornering Poppy until he fell. I decapitated him, his head like an overripe cabbage. I tried not to throw up. His body pitched forward and would have landed on Poppy if she hadn't leapt, shrieking, out of the way. The polar bear took care of the last zombie, blue eyes glowing, then blocked our path with a roar.

Poppy jumped. "Ohmygod, now were going to get eaten by a bear."

The bear plodded forward, immense paws slapping the ground. The axe felt suddenly heavy. It thunked to the ground of its own volition, like an anchor. The bear was close enough now that I could smell the musky animal scent of its fur. It swiped at me once, and I didn't have time to move my shield. I expected to feel its claws slicing through my exposed belly. Instead, one paw slapped the horn on my belt.

The bear disappeared, fading away into tendrils of frozen mist.

My tunic dress and shield followed, and lastly the axe shimmered away. I was left in my regular ripped jeans and peplum jacket. Poppy and I didn't waste any time; we raced down the road until my breath stuck in my throat. We scaled the fence, hands damp with sweat. On the other side, we bent over double, gasping. Cars drove by, their passengers blissfully ignorant.

"Dude." Poppy goggled at me. "You're a superhero."

I goggled back at her. "Shut *up*."

Keira was chosen to travel with the axe and given a guard of berserker warriors. Her brother tried to convince her to stay behind, but the priestess was too old for such a journey. A ship full of berserkers was not safe even for a shieldmaiden like Keira, but no-one could ignore a command from a barrow-king; the dead weren't to be trifled with, especially the Walkers who did not stay to their graves.

They sailed for weeks, passing the green islands and the icy ones, to a country called Vinland. The wind was cold and wet, and Keira's cloak was soaked through when the dragon prow at last neared the rocky shore.

"Far enough?" Bjorn asked her, shouting over the wind, his bear pelts crusted with ice. The other berserkers kept their distance, and Keira invoked Odin's protection each night. She wasn't frightened, not really. But Bjorn made her uneasy.

"If it's as far as we can sail," she replied, "then yes."

The subway was half full, carrying people around the city for Saturday night fun. It was still only just past nine o'clock even though it felt like the middle of the night. Poppy sat beside me, vibrating with the need to speak. We held hands so tightly it hurt, but neither of us let go.

I just stared out of the window at the passing platforms and then at my own reflection when the tunnel walls closed in again. My face floated in the glass. I looked normal. A little wild-eyed and dishevelled, but not like someone who'd just wielded an axe and fought zombies with a polar bear. What would that person look like, anyway? Besides batshit crazy? It was like some twisted Snow White game: *Mirror, mirror on the wall, who's the craziest of them all?*

"Shouldn't we get off?" Poppy asked when I just sat there as the doors to our stop opened.

"Can we ride the loop?" I whispered. "If I get off the train, it all becomes real. I need a minute."

"Okay," she said quietly as the signal sounded and the doors shut again. "But, dude. You were *fierce.*"

"I am freaking *out.*"

"Did you get bitten by any weird spiders lately?"

"Um, no."

"Have you been hanging out with aliens?"

"No."

"Just checking." She chewed on her lower lip. "Do you feel like an Amazon?"

I had to laugh. "No, not particularly. Not even a mutant."

"Okay, next theory: Thor is kind of a Norse God and also? Totally hot."

"I'm pretty sure I'd notice if I was a Norse god. And suddenly had abs."

"Good point."

"What about this theory: none of that was real," I suggested.

"So we're both nuts? Where's the fun in that?"

I groaned. "*This* is fun?"

"Yes! And you should be grateful." She beamed at me. "You're a superhero. So deal, already." Her eyes widened. "I got it! Archaeologists always find weird things that release demons or superpowers or some shit. Maybe that's what happened."

I went cold all over, except for my thumb, which was burning. "I did get a splinter."

She blinked, confused. "Sorry?"

"From an artefact." I held up my thumb to show her. "I thought it was infected."

"Infected with *awesome*."

"Do they make an ointment for that? And you're enjoying this way too much. Did you forget the part about the zombies?"

She shivered. "Yeah, those were gross. I think I got zombie goo on my boots."

"Let's get off here," I grabbed her hand suddenly and pulled her out of the train before the doors slid shut. "I need to know where in Newfoundland that artefact came from, and if we're cataloguing zombie-killing axes."

The combination of street lamps, shop lights, and car lights gave the night an electric glow. The neighbourhood was pretty quiet, mostly bordered with office towers. "Shh," I said sorting through my keys. "I'd rather not attract the guard's attention."

"That Benedict guy?" She grimaced. "Yeah, he's creepy. Is he still ogling you?"

"Kind of. And he's Radcliffe's nephew, so she can't even fire him."

"I can kick him in the balls."

"That might be excessive," I said on a half-laugh.

"I believe in being proactive," she said primly.

"You believe in being violent."

"That, too."

I punched in my code quickly, and we slunk down the back stairs. I didn't know if Benedict was doing rounds or sitting in the back room, but I didn't want to give him an excuse to come find us. I turned on the overhead lights and blinked, waiting for my eyes to adjust. Poppy dropped into a chair. "I'm already bored," she said, spinning the chair around. "I don't know how you can love it so much down here." She rolled along a line of shelves. "'Iron nail, stable, 1926' . . . 'Wedgewood pottery, 1901' . . . 'cast iron kettle handle, 1861' . . . *Snore*."

I ignored her, going through the trays of items I'd cleaned last night. Most of them were already tagged, bagged, and stored in bins. I located everything I'd catalogued except the collection Ms. Radcliffe had taken from me—she must have left it in her office. At least I had the printouts detailing each artefact. I skimmed them until I came to the right batch: Newfoundland, L'Anse aux Meadows. The back of my neck prickled.

"Hello, girls."

I sighed. "Benedict."

Poppy didn't say anything, just stood up and crossed her arms. Her scowl was impressive.

Benedict leaned in the doorway. "Work on a Saturday night? You two need to have some fun." He twirled his flashlight as if it was a gun and he thought he was in a western.

"We've had all the fun we can stand," Poppy said with a bright, fake smile. "In fact, I stepped in some." She walked close enough for him to smell the zombie blood on her boots. He recoiled. She stood there until he turned green, mumbled an excuse, and hastily left.

"Off you go," she said as we listened to his retreating footsteps.

I went straight to the laptop. "L'Anse aux Meadows was a Viking settlement in Newfoundland over a thousand years ago," I said slowly. "Before the whole Columbus thing."

"There was a Viking invasion?" Poppy glanced up from drawing on her tights with a magic marker. "Shouldn't they have mentioned that in class?"

"It wasn't an invasion," I corrected her. "Just one settlement on the north end of the island. Apparently it was uninhabited by anyone else at the time." I did a search for images. "Well, crap." I turned the screen to face her. "This is what Norse women wore in approximately 1000 C.E. It's called an apron-dress."

She looked up and her eyes widened. "You were wearing that! Anything about zombies?"

I shook my head. "Or axes either, beyond the usual. I'll keep searching at home." I stared harder at the photos of Norse dresses, battleaxes, and the turf houses of L'Anse aux Meadows.

Poppy just shook her head. "You're not just a superhero—you're a *Viking* superhero!"

Winter came suddenly. Snow fell, and mountains of ice drifted in the sea. They wouldn't be able to sail home again until spring. The warriors attacked the few trees as though they were the enemy, cutting them down and setting them into the earth to build huts. The first snow melted, and they cut turf to lay on the roof. But they knew the snows would come back; the air smelled like iron.

Keira wrapped the axe in fur and hurried from the makeshift settlement. She had to bury it before the earth froze, before it had a chance to call the spirits of this strange land. Vala had given her special rhymes, magical stones, and bindrunes to carve, but Keira had no way of knowing whether Odin or Hela would answer her plea to open their halls; she was a shieldmaiden, not a priestess.

Shivering, she used a spear to hack at the cold ground. It was slow, laborious work. Sweat gathered under her hair and her amber beads clicked together. By the time she had hacked a hole deep enough, her hands were cramped and red. She lay the axe into the ground, then poured mead over it and added the bindrune as Vala had instructed.

Behind a rocky outcropping, Bjorn watched her in silence.

"This is the worst idea ever," I said. "Just so we're clear."

"I know," Poppy agreed. "But we have to start somewhere."

We stood on the sidewalk and stared at the cemetery gates for another five minutes. "Did you turn on your phone GPS?" I asked. She nodded. If we were going to be the idiots who went into a cemetery possible full of zombies, we'd be the idiots who did it prepared.

I hadn't been able to find anything about possessed axes on the internet. At least nothing that didn't lead me to a gaming site. The Ancient Norse used horns as drinking cups, only mine had a hole cut out in the pointy end, so it was clearly meant for something else. I found a few references to hunting horns, which you blew into, but I hadn't exactly had the time to experiment.

"Ready?" Poppy asked.

"Not even a little."

She was wearing a bright blue tutu skirt tonight—to match my superhero tunic. I felt like we were going to the undead prom and she was wearing a cummerbund to match my dress. All I needed was a corsage.

We took a deep breath and stepped through the gates together. We both waited.

Nothing happened.

I should have felt relief. If anything I felt more tense. And stupid. Lots more stupid.

It was just before twilight—we'd wanted enough light to see by but not enough to call the attention of innocent bystanders. The local news had mentioned the defamation of the a few grave sites in Mount Pleasant. If we weren't careful we'd have cops to deal with as well as the walking dead.

"I shouldn't feel disappointed, right?" Poppy whispered.

We forced ourselves to walk down the road and across the grassy hills. We were haphazardly armed with Swiss army knives, kitchen knives, and even a barbecue fork slipped into the side of my boot. I picked up a thick branch, holding it like a baseball bat—which might have been more helpful if I'd ever actually played baseball.

We followed our usual route, past the Eaton memorial, with its columns like a Greek temple, then toward less frequently visited areas. Everything was quiet and peaceful, with grey stones poking through the lawn and trees budding a hundred shades of green. It was like all the other times we'd walked this way.

"Nothing."

"Uh, Poppy?"

"Yeah?"

"Look behind you."

Zombies in various stages of decomposition shuffled toward us, a few broken stones and mounds of dirt behind them. Another zombie still had her foot caught in the grave.

"Okay," Poppy tugged my arm. "Power up!"

"I don't know how!" We stumbled back, half-running. I waved my thumb at them.

"I don't think a thumbs-up is going to help!"

"This is how it happened last time," I said, pressing hard on my thumb, along the side of the nail the axe fragment had pierced. "Splinter, remember?"

"Well, it's not working!" She squawked. "Why isn't it working?"

"I don't know. This was *your* idea!" I reached for the barbecue fork out of my boot. It was pointy and sharp and might buy us a few minutes. My thumb pulsed, sending waves of hot pain into my hand. "Something's happening," I gasped. The heat gathered and gathered, until there was a flash of searing light.

I was holding the axe again. The horn was at my belt, and the red- and white-striped shield was strapped to my back. Poppy whooped with joy. I swung the axe, refamiliarizing myself with the weight of it. It felt right. I jumped forward and hacked at the nearest zombie. Black blood oozed onto the grass. I swung again. A head rolled toward Poppy's foot, and she jumped higher than I'd thought possible, especially after seeing her in gym class. "This superhero stuff is disgusting," I said.

And then, of course, it got, much, much worse.

I didn't see where he came from, but all of a sudden there was a man charging at us. He was huge, both tall and broad, and wore a metal helmet that covered his face. The bear and wolf pelts draped over his shoulders made him look like a shaggy mountain. He held a long spear, and his dented shield had bite marks along the top edge. His eyes rolled wildly.

"Give me the axe!" he commanded, his voice rough and jagged. "It is *mine*, Keira."

"My name is not Keira!"

"You can't trick me again. You carry the axe."

"Who are you?" I asked, trying not to look at the zombie gore on my blade. I felt queasy already. Zombies were closing in, and this guy wasn't making a single move against them. He was entirely mesmerized with my axe.

"We need backup!" Poppy yelled, swinging the branch around. "Call the bear!"

"I don't think it has a phone." I shot back, leaping aside as the man made a grab for me.

He howled in frustration and shrieked, spit and blood bubbling on his lips. His voice grew even hoarser. "Give me the axe!"

When the man took a step closer, the axe became suddenly light, as if it could move by itself in my hand. As if I didn't already know not to trust someone literally foaming at the mouth. It had done that before, growing heavy when I'd thought I'd need to use it against the polar bear. It knew its enemies, even if I didn't. It hadn't twitched when the bear hit the horn.

The horn.

I fumbled to unhook it from the loop on my belt. I blew hard into the smaller curved end until it sounded out, ringing and shivering loud enough to send the roosting birds from the trees. The zombies paused, screeching. The polar bear materialized, already charging and bellowing. As it tore through a zombie's neck with its huge claws, the demented warrior stabbed at the bear with his spear.

"Hey!" I felt suddenly very protective of my giant scary polar bear. I threw the barbecue fork at the warrior. It bounced off his pelt-draped arm. So much for being a superhero.

The bear clamped its mouth around the warrior's thigh. The warrior screamed, hacking down with his shield, infuriated as though he recognized it. And my axe—he definitely recognized *it*. He was still shooting it burning glances, trying to dodge teeth and claws to reach me. He dispatched a zombie, pulling its arms off with his gauntlet-covered hands, but only because it had stumbled between us.

"Not good!" Poppy shouted. "Not good!"

I swung the axe, grazing the warrior. He made a weird guttural sound and clutched his wounded throat. It was a deep scratch but not life-threatening. He shot me a glare of such boiling hatred, I took a step back. Poppy tripped on a headstone and fell on her backside. The warrior loped away, limping on his bad leg. I broke into a run to follow him, but three more zombies shuffled out of the shadows. The sun had completely set, leaving the light blue and smoky. One zombie grabbed Poppy by the hair.

I slipped the shield free and whirled back around, slicing through the other two zombies as my momentum brought me to Poppy. She was struggling and kicking, wedged against a headstone. I jumped, using another stone to get more height. As I landed, I brought the axe down hard on the back of the zombie's neck. He collapsed, his head severed.

"Thank you," Poppy gasped, scrambling to her feet. "God, I'm the worst sidekick ever," she groaned. "The bad guy got away because of me."

"It's not y—"

"On your left!" She kicked out with her combat boot, cracking a zombie in the knee. He dropped as I turned, axe like a natural extension of my arm. The tiny splinter in my thumb seared, like I was bring branded. I decapitated the zombie and then kept swinging.

Finally, after what felt like years, it was just Poppy and me and the sound of our ragged breaths. And body parts littered all around us.

The axe glowed faintly, along the nicked edge. "Take a picture," I urged. "Quick, it's fading!"

"Are we scrapbooking our defeat of evil now?" She snapped a picture with her phone, sweat running down the side of her face. "'Cause that's an awesome art project idea."

"I want to research it," I explained, leaning weakly against a tree. "Just as soon as I catch my breath." I was myself again, no longer an axe-wielding, shield-slinging superhero.

"Val, look." Poppy pointed her flashlight near my foot. The grass gleamed wetly. "Blood."

I felt queasy again. "I like my old job much better than this superhero thing. Artefacts aren't gooey." I grimaced and stepped aside, nearly slipping on the blood. "That's not from a zombie," I said after a closer look. "Maybe we can track that warrior."

"Tracking." She shook her head, grinning. "Give the girl a magic axe, and she starts with the lingo."

I grinned back as we limped along. My legs ached and my lungs felt like sandpaper. The trail led us to the fence and then onto Yonge Street. We followed it north, until it turned down an alley. Without the cover of trees, it wasn't quite as dark as it had been in the cemetery. "Let's hurry," I said. "I'm pretty sure smart girls, even superheroes and sidekicks, shouldn't walk down dark alleys."

Poppy paused . "Crap. I'm your sidekick." She looked at me. "I'm not wearing spandex for you."

We hurried between dumpster bins behind the restaurants, out onto a side street.

"You know what's weird?" Poppy said.

"Zombies? Magic axes? Big-ass warrior?"

"Besides that."

"I'm scared to ask."

"Well, the news reported on the broken headstones. They said it was vandals."

"So?" I asked as we cut through the back parking lot of a store.

"So that means they didn't find any body parts. The zombies must have . . . what, crawled back into their holes?"

I frowned. "And none of this happened in any other cemetery. So what's special about Mount Pleasant?"

"I don't think it *is* Mount Pleasant," Poppy said. "I think it's *you*. Think about it."

I really, really didn't want to.

The trail of blood led us to the back lot of an empty shop. There were no cars. The apartment upstairs was dark. "I don't see an alarm," Poppy murmured, peering into the dusty window. "Keep an eye out," she added before using the end of her heavy flashlight to break the glass. We froze as the shattering window pierced the silence. When no-one yelled and cops didn't burst out of the dumpster to arrest us, Poppy turned the door handle.

The door creaked open, and we slipped inside. The room was empty except for cardboard boxes stacked in one corner. Another door led down into what was no doubt the basement. And I was just me now. No axe, no shield, no special moves. We were just two girls with Swiss army knives, a barbecue fork, and a flashlight.

We eased down the stairs. I could feel my pulse in my throat and in my ears. I heard scratching sounds and moaning. My palms went damp. Poppy's flashlight trembled in her hands.

We poked our heads around the corner. The blood trail ended, but there was no warrior. There was, however, a cage with zombies locked inside, repeatedly banging into the bars. Congealed blood and substances I didn't want a closer look at stained the concrete floor around the cage.

"Someone's keeping them as pets," Poppy blurted.

"Or as weapons," I said grimly. "What happens if there's a zombie invasion?"

"More zombies." Poppy raised her eyebrows. "And you have a zombie-killing axe and a zombie-killing polar bear. That's your mission!"

"My mission was to be Indiana Jones," I muttered. "Or Schliemann."

"Who?"

"He discovered Troy."

"Whatever. If that big warrior guy wants the axe, and he's keeping zombies. . . ."

"Yeah, not good," I agreed. I nodded to a hunk of fur from a pelt, caught on a broken nail. "He was definitely here."

When they saw me, the zombies started to rattle the bars.

. "I was right," Poppy said as we turned and fled. "It *is* you."

♦

The sea had turned against them. They were stuck in a strange land where there were no villages to loot, no food to steal. When their stock ran out they would be left with nothing to eat but seal and tree-bark tea.

Even the bears were different here, white and massive, the colour of ice in a place with nothing but ice. What was the use in being oathed to the bear, when there were no battles to wage? They were building turf huts and gathering like farmers, like women.

Bjorn wasn't afraid of an axe, no matter what the spirits said. There was no weapon he couldn't bend to his will. He missed the rage, the red haze of war.

He looked forward to a battle, even one slippery with magic.

He began to dig.

I wanted to skip school on Monday; I couldn't face the possibility of turning into a Viking superhero in class. On the other hand, if Poppy was right about zombies being strangely fond of me, at least there were no dead bodies to be zombified at school.

I couldn't have a mystical axe that summoned puppies?

Poppy wanted to skip as well, but mostly because she always wanted to skip. We compromised by missing first class and meeting at a café across the street from where we'd found the zombie cage. The night before, I'd called the cops from a payphone and left an anonymous tip about a gas leak in the basement of the building. I figured if I said there was a cage of zombies they'd just hang up on me. Poppy and I drank our mocha lattes and stared at the empty storefront. There was no police warning tape, nothing in the papers—I wondered if they'd even bothered to investigate.

"So much for that plan," I said. I grabbed my cup. "Let's go look."

"But it's so early to be eaten by zombies," she said, following me reluctantly. "And what if we run into that warrior guy?"

"I think he was a berserker."

"A what-what?"

"They were Viking warriors who wore bear pelts and went all crazy with bloodlust and bit at their shields." I remembered the warrior's shield in the cemetery. "You know what? I've got an axe and apron dress, but my jeans aren't historically accurate."

"Seriously? That's what you're complaining about?"

We crossed at the corner and went down a side street, cutting through to the parking lot. There were a lot more cars than there had been last night. We tried to look nonchalant as we hovered near the door with the broken window. It was already boarded up. Clearly, someone had come by.

"Careful back there, girls," an old man called out as he walked his two dogs through the alley.

I jumped, positive I looked as guilty as I felt. "Just lost my bus pass!" I said loudly and as cheerfully as a birthday clown.

"Dude, your smile is freaking me out," Poppy muttered.

"I'm trying not to look guilty," I muttered back under my breath.

"Looking psychotic is better?"

"The cops were here last night," the old man continued. "Something about a gas leak, even evacuated the neighbours. Didn't find anything though."

Poppy and I exchanged a glance. "Nothing at all?" I asked.

"No, but if you feel dizzy or smell something funny, clear out."

"We will," I promised. "Thanks." We walked away quickly, heading back out to the side street. "So they went in," I said. "And didn't find a cage of zombies."

"They must have been moved or, you know. . . ." She slid a finger across her throat and made a dead face. She looked like a constipated fish. "So what are you gonna do now?"

"I don't know. Why *me*?"

Poppy shrugged. "Accident. Destiny. Pick one."

"Shouldn't I have a guide or something?" I asked, feeling very lost and suddenly very cranky. "Let's go look at the artefacts again."

Poppy sighed. "I knew you were going to say that. You know, most people skip class to go to a movie or something. We're doing this delinquent thing all wrong."

"And at least at work we're used to dead things." I spent a few minutes enjoying the mental image of Benedict's reaction if he came face to face with a zombie on his rounds. Benedict. . . . "He's the Berserker!"

"Who?"

"Benedict."

Poppy snorted. "Please, that other guy was like six foot five and buff. Benedict, not so much."

"I don't usually have a glowing axe and a pet polar bear either," I pointed out. "But he was there when I got the splinter, and again after the first zombie attack. Coincidence?"

When we got there, I couldn't find the L'Anse aux Meadows artefacts anywhere. My notes were wiped off the laptop. "He must know we're onto him," I said, adrenaline shooting through me. "We have to find him." We didn't have to look far.

"I saw you come in," he drawled, his hands hooked onto his belt loops. "You're here an awful lot lately."

"Benedict," I narrowed my eyes. "We know it was you. How did you turn into a berserker?"

"And what did you do with the zombies?" Poppy demanded.

"Zombies?" He looked confused.

"Don't play dumb with—" I cut myself off. "Oh, crap."

Something rattled in the back. The smell of rotten apple cores and mildew wafted toward us. A thin, eerie moan lifted the hairs on my arms.

"Not fair," I said, shivering as more adrenaline flooded my system. "There aren't even any bodies here!"

"But there are body *parts*," Poppy said. "I *told* you cleaning bone fragments was a gross pastime."

Several zombies emerged from the back storage, knocking over artefacts and equipment as they shuffled through the tight space. The stench intensified. The flash of light seared through me; suddenly I was armed with shield and horn and axe. I leapt at the closest zombie, swinging. Black blood splattered the laptop.

"I don't think it's Benedict," Poppy said, using one of the desk chairs like a lion tamer. She hit a zombie over and over until his leg buckled. He tried to grab her ankle, but I cut off his hand. "Wouldn't he be berskering right about now?"

Instead, he was about to throw up on the decapitated head. Then he grabbed me suddenly and jerked hard. I yanked out of his grasp as he crumpled, the gash on his head already matting his hair with blood.

He wasn't the Berserker. He'd actually tried to save me. From my boss. Because she'd been aiming for my head, not his.

"I needed those Walkers!" Ms. Radcliffe was furious.

I was confused. "It was *you*?"

Ms. Radcliffe already had me by the wrist, squeezing hard. My hand hurt, blood leaking from around the splinter. There was the familiar flash again. Only this time I was in someone else's body.

The wind was howling and full of ice pellets. Snow crunched under my fur-lined boots and it was stained with blood. Someone was shrieking, "Keira!"

"Bjorn, what have you done?" I yelled, my cloak whipping at my legs in the winter storm. The morning sun was a hazy indistinct glow. We'd had been fighting the restless dead since just past midnight. At first, it was only the bloated corpses of dead seals washing up on shore. The white bears followed, drawn by the scent of blood.

"They will be my army!" He shouted. "With the Walkers at my command, none will be able to stop me!"

He had taken the axe from the mound I'd dug; I had failed. The axe woke the dead, even when the dead were far away. And I was surrounded by mad berserker warriors who had killed hundreds while under the battle rage. They carried the bones of their victims in their shields, as knife handles, or charms around their necks. They wore bear pelts and wolf fur.

When the dead walked, they returned with the fury of vengeance beating in their black blood.

Bjorn hacked at them, laughing and bloody-toothed. He swung the cursed axe. A Walker fell, his head rolling from his corpse. Two of Bjorn's sword-brothers were already dead, their lips black with ice-burn. A white bear ambled between them, lapping at the snow.

I couldn't undo this. I could only try to stop Bjorn. If he survived to sail home again with the axe, our people would know no peace. The Walkers contaminated anyone they bit, and he would call them all out of the earth.

I spoke the rhymes Vala had taught me. More warriors fell, like wheat on harvest day.

The bear charged, maddened by the blood dripping from the axe and the bear-magic Bjorn carried twisted up inside him. Bjorn struck with the axe, and the beautiful white fur turned red. The bear bellowed, stumbling, then fell like a giant rock, close enough that its breath ruffled the fur of my hood. It had managed to wound Bjorn, tearing a raw gash into his leg. The axe fell within my reach.

"You can't stop me," Bjorn crowed. "In this life, or the next. The queen of the dead herself cannot stop me!"

Poisoned with battle-rage, Bjorn ground his boot into my stomach, pinning me to the ground, next to the white bear. He thought he'd won.

I uttered the words the priestess had taught me: "To use the axe for the good of all is the only way to be in its thrall." I couldn't stop the decent of his spear. I didn't try. Some magic needed a willing sacrifice. Some battles needed to be lost.

"What have you done? He raged, voice hoarse from screaming. "What does that mean?"

I smiled, even as I choked on my own blood.

"It means this isn't the end of the story."

❦

I was Keira.

And Bjorn was Ms. Radcliffe, enraged and hateful, even without the bear pelts and the axe.

"It wasn't easy moving that cage," she said, grinding her teeth. "You caused me a long troublesome night, little girl." She stabbed at me with her spear. I jumped out of the way. "They were going to be my sacrifice. With enough of their blood on my hands, I can be Bjorn again, strong again. And I can finally reclaim my axe!"

"You were the one who brought it back from a raid," I said slowly. Bjorn's image kept superimposing itself over her. I felt lightheaded and oddly calm. If I was Keira, then I had to stop Bjorn. Keira had worked some kind of magic to make sure she'd always be able to stop him. And the polar bear had gotten caught in the crossfire. Now we were all together again.

Ms. Radcliffe blurred, then swelled. Her blouse shifted into pelts. Her spear whistled toward me. I blocked it but only barely; the force of the blow reverberated through the shield and up my shoulder.

She wasn't Ms. Radcliffe anymore. She wasn't even Bjorn, not really. She was a berserker, demented with bloodlust. And she was stronger than I was. I hacked at her with my axe. I sliced a gash in her arm, just under the pelts. Blood trickled, but she didn't even blink—maybe she wasn't even capable of feeling pain. I thought I'd read that somewhere about bererkser warriors; they fought as if in a trance, like maddened bears.

She bashed at my shield until I slammed into the side of the desk. Her chainmail- and pelt-draped arm knocked me down. I sprawled, trying to catch my breath. I didn't feel like a shieldmaiden. I felt like a history geek about to get pummelled to death by a piece of cranky history.

Poppy tried to knock her down with the rolling desk chair. The spear shaft caught her across the stomach, tossing her into the shelves.

The Berserker stomped down, and I felt something crack in my wrist. The axe fell out of my grasp. A boot pinned me to the ground, heel digging into my stomach. I had nowhere else to go. I was pinned down by Radcliffe, as Keira had been pinned down by Bjorn. But I had one weapon left, created from the very land he'd desecrated. The Berserker reached for the axe—

I blew the horn with my free hand.

The metal shelves crackled with electricity as the polar bear materialized. It roared viciously, thousands of pounds of angry spirit-bear. It charged, tackling the warrior who'd spoke an oath to the spirit of the bear as a berserker.

There was the snap of bones, and they both vanished.

Poppy sat up, groaning. "Did we win?"

"I don't know," I cradled my injured wrist. "They're gone. For now."

"For *now*? You mean, we have to do this again?" She rubbed her stomach. "Ouch."

"Well, it wasn't the first time, so it might not be the last. And we don't know where they actually *went*."

"But they're gone. And so are the zombies?"

"Yes."

"Good enough for me." She pushed to her feet. "Can I tell you I'm glad I'm the sidekick and not the Viking superhero?"

"I'm not *just* a Viking superhero," I grinned wearily. "I'm a reincarnated shieldmaiden, too."

"Now you're just showing off."

"And the jeans?" I glanced down at my pants and shot her a smile. "Still not historically accurate."

ALYXANDRA HARVEY was born during an ice storm in Montreal. She lives in Ontario with her husband, dogs, and a few resident ghosts who are allowed to stay as long as they keep company manners. She is the author of The Drake Chronicles, *Haunting Violet*, *Stolen Away*, and *Briar Rose*.

THE MANY LIVES OF THE XUN LONG

MICHAEL MATHESON

Wei Jia watched his granddaughter's granddaughter, Xinhua, from a second-storey window of their row house home overlooking Kensington Avenue; watched the young woman make her way through crowds browsing the street market; watched Xinhua thread through them like the waters of a swiftly flowing river. Like her mother, and all the daughters of his line, she had taken quickly to his training.

Xinhua's mother, Lin, coughed at Jia from the adjacent room. "The neighbours," she said.

He sighed and moved away from the window, slipping around the doorjamb and drifting down the stairs, the fog of his feet trailing slowly after his translucent form. He was at the front door when Xinhua unlocked it from the other side. He could hear her talking to someone. Laughing. She said her farewells as she opened the door, her friend's footsteps fading.

"Welcome home," Jia said in Mandarin, smiling at his great-great-granddaughter as she slipped inside and closed the door quickly behind her.

"Xianxian Jia," she reproached, slipping into English in the space of a single breath: "What are you doing?"

"Must we, in English?" Jia asked, working the memory of his lips around words still uncomfortable nearly a century after he had learned them. Death did not make them easier to say.

"Yes, in this house we must," Lin said from the top of the stairs, her hands on her hips as Jia whirled slowly in midair like

279

a leaf caught on the wind. Wisps of his form trailed after him in a lazy circle. "What are you doing near the front door? What if someone had seen?"

"Someone nearly did," Xinhua whispered, frowning at Jia.

"Can I not even greet my line-daughter in my own home?"

"We've discussed this, Xianxian Jia." Lin descended the stairs in quick two-steps. At the bottom, she looked into Jia's eyes and, as though talking to a recalcitrant child, said, "You must not be seen by others."

Jia harrumphed and stood straighter, putting his hands on his hips, his self-image still lithe and muscular—the image of a man in his prime: the image of his body at the time of his death. "And who was it who taught you both of stealth?" he began.

Both women groaned and turned toward the kitchen, Jia drifting after. "Did you remember the milk?" Lin asked Xinhua.

Xinhua nodded. "And the bak choi, and the duck," Xinhua rattled off, tapping her full backpack for emphasis.

"—Who was it," continued Jia, slipping into Mandarin, "who first fought for our people in this strange land?"

"How was the interview?" Lin asked her daughter as they moved into the kitchen.

"I think it went well," Xinhua said, pursing her lips and slipping her backpack off. "I'm not sure I'm what they're looking for though."

"—Who first woke Tianlong to our plight, and begged him whisper of it to the Celestial Bureaucracy, that it might make its way to the Jade Emperor?"

"Do *they* know what they want?" Lin asked, leaning on the wooden table in the centre of the kitchen.

"Probably not," laughed Xinhua, unpacking her backpack and handing the items one by one to her mother.

"—Who was it who was granted the blessing of the Jade Emperor himself and was made the first Xun Long, defender of our people against the violence of the Canadian gweilo?"

"I will *not* have you using that word in my house," Lin said, finally acknowledging Jia's presence in the kitchen, "divinely appointed Swift Dragon, or no."

Xinhua watched them both, leaning back against the table.

"You have gone soft, line-daughter." Jia said in slow English, and shook his head, frowning. "It is good your daughter has taken up the mantle of the Xun Long. She is still fierce," he said proudly, looking to Xinhua to support him.

"Actually, I've been meaning to talk to you about that," Xinhua said, offering an apologetic smile to Jia.

He raised an eyebrow, his gaze flitting between Xinhua and Lin. "Talk to me about what?"

"Well, I—" began Xinhua.

"—Xinhua has found work," interjected Lin.

"Mom!"

"She won't be able to patrol anymore," Lin said.

"Is this true?" Jia asked Xinhua, bewildered. "You are abandoning the mantle of the Xun Long?"

"Well, I don't know for sure if I have the job yet, but. . . ." Xinhua shrugged, seeking the right words. "Well, between college and the new job I do need to cut back on the patrolling."

Now Lin looked bewildered. "You said you wanted to drop it entirely."

"No," said Xinhua, putting up one finger to ward off her mother's words. "I said I wanted to cut back on patrolling, I didn't say I was giving up the mantle. I want this in my life, I just . . . I don't know exactly how it fits right now." She looked to Jia, then to Lin. "I wasn't going to bring this up now. I. . . . You know what, I'm just gonna go be in my room for a while."

Lin opened, then closed her mouth. "Will you be back down for dinner?"

Xinhua ran a hand through her hair, short black strands waterfalling around her fingers, as she turned back to her mother. "Maybe. I don't know yet."

Jia watched Xinhua go, his youngest line-daughter disappearing up the stairs as Lin unpacked Xinhua's bag. "You cannot let her do this," he said.

"She needs to have a life." Lin paused between the table and the fridge, one hand clutching a plastic bag of milk. "Other heroes have risen where once the Xun Long stood alone," she said to Jia. "And we are no longer a community of strangers, of outsiders. We are citizens of a different land, protected by its laws and by heroes who will fight for us as well as their own people."

"You are still so naïve, line-daughter. I never could train it out of you."

"No, not naïve. . . ." The refrigerator made a soft sucking noise as she pulled it open to slip the milk into its empty plastic container. ". . . Hopeful."

She smiled at the ghost of Jia.

✤

Xinhua stood in her room, half undressed with her shirt tossed on the bed and the door closed, when Jia's voice spoke from behind her. "Your mother makes an interesting argument," he said in Mandarin.

"What the hell are you doing?" Xinhua jumped, snatching up her shirt from the bed and holding it across her chest.

"Talking to you?" Jia said, switching to English.

"It was sort of okay that you randomly showed up in my room when I was six, awkward when I hit puberty, and now it's just incredibly creepy."

Jia shrugged his spectral shoulders and made a face of disinterest. "I am indifferent to the pleasures of the flesh."

"*So* not the right answer," said Xinhua, moving past Jia without looking at him. "What *do* you want?"

"To talk to you about your decision to ... suspend ... or scale back, or ... I do not know what you are planning on doing with your activities as the Xun Long," Jia finished awkwardly, watching Xinhua open her closet, hang up the formal shirt she had worn to her interview, and pull out a faded tee-shirt.

"I'm not giving it up if that's what you're afraid of." Xinhua's words were muffled as she slipped into the change of clothes. "Do you mind turning around?" she asked as she reached for a pair of skintight leggings.

"I did not think you were," Jia said, turning his back on Xinhua and studying the soft rug of her room. "But your mother said something that. . . ."

Xinhua listened, changing her pants, then said, "Yes?" when Jia didn't continue.

"Xinhua, what do you see as the role of the Xun Long?" Jia asked, turning around as his line-daughter pulled the leggings up to her waist.

"To protect others," she answered without hesitation.

"Yes, but who are those others?"

"I don't understand," Xinhua said as she ruffled her short hair and bound it back with a thin hairband.

"When I first called upon Tianlong," Jia said, passing a hand through the air, a furl of his chi flowing after it, "our people were still new to this city. We had been in Toronto in number little more than a generation. We were feared because of who we were when we came to this country, and I sought to protect the young communities we had made in this city from that fear. From that ignorance. I did it for our people."

"You sought to save them from the hatred of others," Xinhua said, asking *And, so?* with a shrug of her shoulders.

Jia thought for a moment, drifting past Xinhua. He used his chi to pull back the hidden panel at the back of closet to reveal the costume of the current Xun Long: the figure-conforming black polymer fibre with its breathable face covering, so different from Jia's own original shenyi and mask. "Spirits live in the past, Xinhua. That is all that we know. The world passes us by because we are no longer a part of it. *Cannot* be a part of it." Jia turned to his line-daughter. "I am beginning to wonder if I have done you all a disservice through what I taught you."

"What was it Mom said to you?"

"That the Xun Long is no longer needed," Jia said, scrutinizing the carpet beneath the mist trailing from the hems of his pant legs.

Xinhua crooked an eyebrow up. "What? Seriously?"

"Not in so many words," Jia said. "But she wants you to have a life, and I cannot deny that she is right in that. No, your mother said that there are others who can do now what once only we could. And that they protect *our* people as well. So what need is there for us now?"

"Maybe," said Xinhua, reaching into the back of the closet to retrieve her costume from the hidden recess. "But just because other people can do it doesn't mean I don't have an obligation to do so as well," said Xinhua, slipping into the bodysuit one limb at a time. She stopped when she reached the mask, leaving it hanging in bunched folds at the back of her neck. "I don't just protect our community, xianxian. I use our gifts to help everyone, because I can't imagine doing otherwise." Xinhua closed her closet behind her and opened the door of her room. "Once," she said, glancing at Jia and leaning half out of the open door, "our community needed a protector for its own people, when no-one else would stand up to help them. Now we are in a position to help other communities; people who need protection just as much as we did, and still do." Xinhua leaned fully out of her doorway. "Mom! I'm heading out. You don't have to wait dinner for me. I'll grab something on the way back!"

"Be careful!" Lin called up from the kitchen, her voice ringing off walls and around corners.

"Always!" shouted Xinhua. She turned to Jia as she pulled her door half-closed. "I don't know how I'm going to balance everything yet, but I will." She walked to the window and opened it. Xinhua closed her eyes and breathed in and out, the visible expansion and retraction of her focused chi flexing on the air. She drew the cowl of her costume up and over her head, stretching it down across her face and securing the material to seal at the front of her neck. "There are too few heroes as it is," she said, and climbed over the lip of the open window and was gone.

Jia watched his line-daughter fade into the gathering dark. He felt the weight of time passing—a slow river dragging him along in its currents.

Eventually, Lin came up to join him, and together they stood watching out the window, waiting for Xinhua's return.

A native of Toronto, **MICHAEL MATHESON** is a writer, editor, and book reviewer. His reviews have appeared at *ChiZine*, *Innsmouth Free Press*, and *The Globe and Mail*. His fiction is featured in, among others, *Future Lovecraft, Chilling Tales 2,* and *Dead North*.

REVENGE OF THE IRON SHADOW

~ A TALE OF KINGSTONIA ~

JASON S. RIDLER

AN ACCOUNT OF THE PHANTOM BILL GANG
EXCLUSIVE TO *LIBRE KINGSTONIA PRESS*
October 15, 1891
by Mutt Wilford
as told to and confirmed by Frederick Grant

I share this tale as a warning, to what I witnessed in the caverns beneath this damned city, a warren of spider holes and wolf dens that the Queen of Kingstonia has yet to tame, where other kinds of vermin have lived and hid as they built their little empires like ants.

Vermin like me, who witnessed what can be done if vengeance against the cruel is given shape and form. Vermin like me, who remain alive solely because such an instrument of vengeance saw fit to leave a witness.

It is true that I ran with Phantom Bill, terror guard of Kingston Pen before the sky rock crashed into the den of thieves and turned this city into a nightmare. I, too, was a guard, junior in rank, and saw firsthand the collection of wild damnations caged for society's protection. Phantom Bill was Captain of the Guard, ran his ship with barbed discipline, and when the chaos reigned after the impact of the sky rock, he took to the transformed city to start his own law and order, hunting down those who'd escaped. Justice, he said, justice has no mercy. Bill certainly had none as master of corrections. And he had less now.

But his gang was being whittled. Through the limestone streets, into the shifting walls of the city's heart, called Arcadia, and even at the outskirts where the green mist that emerged from the sky rock covers us like an impenetrable cloud, Phantom Bill's gang and associates were being slaughtered.

Rumours filled the din. Of a madman with iron hands. Of a shadow that could not be stopped. In Kingstonia, one is quick to believe such creatures exist, what with the walking dead called Lurchers who serve Queen Charlotte like slaves, and the Copper Knights, made of railway junk, that run mad through Arcadia. Anyone who tasted the green mist that emerged from the sky rock was changed in ways vile and unnatural. My own small taste cursed me with a memory like a book that can never be lost, whose pages I recall without desire, a perfect reflection of the past stamped in my head, filled to the brim with monsters.

Though his gang was reduced from twelve to four, Phantom Bill was no fool. A veteran of the Indian Wars, he began a reconnaissance, gathered intelligence, pieced together the scraps about what thing had bested his men.

And it led us to the *Libre*.

This very paper held accounts of the creature and the slaughtering of Bill's crew. Every man had been a guard of the Pen, men who'd stood at Phantom Bill's side as he kept the savage inmates from breaking loose, until the sky rock undid all his work. The articles had such details that Phantom Bill came to believe the author had himself witnessed the attacks and was turning this murderous shadow into a hero.

So he sent his last squadron to the home of the author, one Frederick Grant, living above the secret and transient office of the *Libre* at the Broken Beard Tavern. I led the attack, having gathered and remembered all the stray facts about Grant's whereabouts from the vendors at the market square and the other old gossips who milled about in daylight before the fangs of the city emerged to feast.

My squad was all that remained of Bill's mighty gang, two of the best Kingston Pen had to offer. Lieutenant Martin Jones, a graduate of the Royal Military College, had hands as cold as a witch's heart, and a curdled reputation for cruelty. The other was Badger Collins, a former circus strongman with black eyes whose blood and bone might as well have been made of iron ore, as no man could tear him down.

And me, Mutt Wilford, a third-rate soldier who turned in his Enfield for the baton and irons of a jailer rather than dig an early grave along the All Red Route and find his death in some malaria-strewn scrap of the Empire.

We surprised Grant in his cot. Badger's gut shot took out his screams, and Jones's frosted finger silenced his lips before the sackcloth covered his face and we made our escape. Not one of the guzzling thugs in the main room stopped us.

Which should have made me suspicious.

Our lair was below ground. How the great tunnels of Kingstonia were built is a coat of myth stretched so thin the colour of truth has all but bled out, and I've heard tall tales of everything from magical worms to supernatural hares the colour of old dead blood. No matter, it's where much of Kingstonia lives who wish to avoid the gaze of Queen Charlotte and her Lurchers. So it was with Phantom Bill.

We thrust the sacked head of Mr. Grant into the orange flutter of gaslight that illuminated the interrogation chamber. He landed before Phantom Bill.

In his day, Bill had been the most fearsome thing in Kingston Pen. A soldier during the first Riel rebellion, he'd parlayed his dirty fists into bare-knuckle brawls and rough and tumble championships before hunting scalps for Washington during the war with the Sioux. I'd not heard much else of his exploits until he came to the Pen, ordered by the Warden to establish "peace and order" to this nest of cretins. So he did. And the inmates called him the King of Beasts, though never to his visage. Tall, hard, and with the only hair on his head being his jagged sideburns, Bill's arms were as tough as the rhino-hide whip that he took from the Pen and wrapped around his waist. Miles of truth and blood have been spilt by that serrated hide. And our room would likely go red again.

"Let's see him," Phantom Bill said, and I took off the hood.

"Gash!" Lieutenant Jones said, covering his mouth with spidery white fingers. "He looks like fresh shit!"

The mangled, ruined countenance of Mr. Grant looked up. Nose crunched into his skull-like face, one eye swollen black, the other pleading. But worst was the mouth. It was as if someone had cut a wound in a swollen man's guts, yet words came out past cracked teeth. "Puh-please, no more, I . . . told 'em . . . I told 'em all I knew—"

"This your handy work?" Phantom Bill said to Badger Collins, who shook his head.

"I carried 'em after one blow to the gut. That's all," said Badger. "Must have been like this when we bagged him."

Phantom Bill leaned down at the quivering dishevelled man in poorly matched breeches and shirt. "Who did this to you? Be quick and true, and I'll be the same." He gripped his belt where his irons hung. Irons that had tasted the green mist. Irons that never ran out of bullets. Never jammed. The whip, the iron, and Bill's ... talent made him the most feared underlord of Kingstonia. "Speak."

"T'was Ruby Jacks."

Ruby was one of our own, gone missing a day ago.

Bill's boot cuffed Mr. Grant's head, sending a single jagged tooth through the gloom. "Ruby Jacks is dead. We found his body this morning and burned it so Queen Charlotte would not turn him Lurcher." He gripped his iron in its holster. "Last chance."

"I saw him die!" Mr. Grant screamed. "I will tell you what happened. Just let me live."

The rotten man still oozed with the beating he took, kneeled before Phantom Bill as if in confession. "You got one chance of leaving my domain alive," said Phantom Bill. "Answer every question I ask. I smell deceit dripping on the floor, and we'll toss your innards before a Copper Knight and see if it walks away wearing your skin."

Mr. Grant sighed, lips red and wet. "Honestly, sir, once you hear what I've seen, that might be a blessing."

So it rolled out of him. How Ruby Jacks had found Grant last night while we hunted dead ends. But Grant was not alone.

"Jacks worked me over, saying I need to share what I knew of the creature who tore your gang to threads. But when I tried ... *he* showed up."

"Who?"

Grant's eye spied around, as if he feared to speak the creature's name, lest it pop from the shadows like Athena from the skull of Zeus. Finally, he whispered, "The Iron Shadow."

Phantom Bill cackled, as did Jones and Badger. "Worthy of a dime novel! And the Iron Shadow bested Ruby Jacks?"

Mr. Grant closed his eyes and shuddered. "You saw him, didn't you?"

What was left, anyway. Ruby Jack's face had been mangled as bad as Mr. Grant's. But his heart . . . it had been torn from the body like the pit from an overripe cherry.

Bill shot us hard gazes, wrist twisting, warming his whiphand. "You weren't followed, were you?"

"No, sir," Badger said. "Mutt said to run through Arcadia, so none could follow, as the walls were shifting. You'd have to have been a louse in my beard to have followed us into the city's undergut."

Phantom Bill nodded at me. "At least one of you had brains while mine were here. Now, Mr. Grant. To business. Who is he?" Phantom Bill said, stalking around Mr. Grant, walking from light to darkness while the gas light flickered. Badger stood by the chamber entrance with arms crossed, Jones tapped his dead-white fingers next to him, and I leaned against the wall with a hand on my iron, watching things I can never unsee. "Who is the Iron Shadow?"

Mr. Grant's head rolled forward. "He was a prisoner."

"Ha! That narrows it down, eh, boys?" Phantom Bill said, and pulled the handle of his rhino-hide whip, uncoiling that snake of agony from his guts. "How about we get more specific."

Mr. Grant gurgled. "He was the only innocent man in the Pen."

The whip cracked as loud as our laughter. "My ribs are aching! Oh, Mr. Grant, you should have been in vaudeville." Bill stalked around Grant, the whip slithering behind him until he stopped and prepared to unleash it. "And who might be the only innocent man in Kingston Penitentiary?"

Mr. Grant's eyes opened. "Mercer Donnelley. Of the Black Donnelleys."

All we heard was the hiss of lamps.

The Donnelleys. Land-thieving Irish. They'd been massacred by a Vigilance Committee a decade before the sky rock fell. Men, women, children, broken and beaten and killed in an orgy of mob violence in the name of the law. Their name was blood in Ontario.

"But he died in solitary. The place collapsed in on itself when the sky rock hit us like an artillery barrage," I said, having been guard on watch that night. Badger and Jones looked away and Phantom Bill's mouth twitched.

Mr. Grant's voice hardened. "No, that last relation survived. He was an innocent man, but surrounded by the drunken Vigils with the blood of his family still bright on their boots he was goaded. No man alive could quell the desire to lash out, and so he did, and the mob near beat him half to death before a real lawman arrived and dragged the last Donnelley to jail for fighting for his life. A few dozen assaults were pinned on him, while the Vigils walked free. So it was that the last of the Donnelleys was silenced behind the grey walls of the Stony Lonesome. But I suppose you all know that." Badger and Jones held their heads low, though Phantom Bill was steady as the pillars of heaven. "The boy had been weak and stupid. Had not thought more than one step ahead of his angry firsts, so it was life in the Pen, under the watchful eye and red right hand of the King of Beasts." Grant sucked in air through his frostbit and gashed lips. "But, when the boulder from heaven rammed the Earth, he tasted green mist. Like all of you. And he changed. His hate, his desire for vengeance, well it bled into the walls, and they bled into him, that limestone soaked in the screams of the damned. Those iron manacles around his fists melted into his flesh, and his goal in life turned cold and true. He would kill his tormentors. And those who killed his family."

"How in the hell do you know any of this?" Jones said, iced hands like claws. "Are you in league with that bastard Donnelley?"

Grant smiled, "You could say we share a life sentence."

Bill cracked back his whip.

Of all the impossible things locked in my mind's vault, the nightmare that fuels my dread is what happened next.

Grant tore his shirt, revealing the empty space where his heart used to be and the tattoo of a scorpion on his arm, the only one I'd ever seen was on Ruby Jacks, from his time in Cairo with the constabulary.

"Hell's gate," Phantom Bill said, teeth clenched. "We . . . we burned you clean." Every man took a step back. The smell of blood and iron filled the room. It was is if the skin of the creature before us had molted and where his hands once sat there emerged iron fists, manacles the likes we use for those in solitary.

The kind worn by Mercer Donnolley.

But this was no beaten Irishman on the bloodstained stones of the corrections room. It was a stone grey monster, built of brick and mortar, skin akin to the walls that held him. But unlike the prison, Donnelley moved like wildfire. His face was a brick of hatred with tombstones for teeth. His hands snapped his bonds like we'd made them of braided paper.

The rest was a bloody whirlwind. Phantom Bill called for an attack, and I reached for my irons while Badger and Jones attempted their one-two special: Jones's iced hands went like claws for Donnelley's throat. Normally the shock of cold would freeze a man so hard that Badger could then maul his paralyzed form into kindling. I held my fire, fearing to cut them down.

But Donnelley's prison skin was colder than Judas's soul. He clamped his iron hands around Jones's wrist. A sick crunch followed before he rammed those arctic talons onto Badger's chest. The giant froze, skin gone a paler shade of death.

I fired. All six shots. The room swarmed with ricochets. Gripping both men by the necks, Donnelley tossed Badger and Jones at me like two money sacks. They hit me so hard the rest is a fuzzy dream, though it came back sharp when I clawed myself through my unconscious patrons.

There was a crack, and the whip wrapped around Donnelley's neck. Bill yanked, but the monster stood unmoved. "No more whips, William," said Donnelley's hoarse voice, like gravel broken under the hammer of a chain gang. "No more nights of blood and scar in the lonesome cell. It's retribution, William. On you and your Vigils. I am your reckoning." He gripped the rhino hide and yanked the weapon free from Bill, who went for his gun. "Fire all you want. Mosquitoes do worse."

"Ain't no normal iron, you Black Irish shit!"

Bill fired and fired, and Donnelley smiled . . . but as the shots kept coming, the smile died. Pieces of him broke off and black ooze fell from the wounds that emerged from his grey skin. "You ain't the only one made fresh and terrible, you bastard! This gun was in my hand when I tasted green mist!"

Donnelley covered his face and charged with the thunder of a locomotive, aiming straight for Bill . . . and learned firsthand how Bill got his nickname in Kingstonia.

Donnelley passed through Bill, whose body had gone blue and shiny. The monster crashed into the cavern wall and shook the lamps so bad it was hard to see. Bill took a deep breath, the blue hue gone, and laughed. Donnelley screamed and tried again and fell on his face near the cavern's mouth, the whip still in his metal hands.

"Mercer Donnelley," Bill said, taking another deep breath, spinning his iron's chamber, "I find this rich. When we goaded you to fight you were as namby-pamby weak as your kin, screaming under our heels as we brought justice by snuffing out their thieving lives. And when fortune frees you, gives you the means for vengeance, where do I find you? On your knees, broken and leaking as before." He spun the chamber again. "You've been killing my crew. You've been sneaky and backstabbing as only your kind can be. And tonight, you Irish dog, I will finally end what we started in your family's stolen home. Would the very last Donnelley have any parting words?"

Donnelley pulled himself to his knees, grey arms before him, one hand holding the whip. But the holes in his arms shook and bled black across the floor. "Yes, Phantom Bill. I do."

He clocked the hammer. "Then say your peace."

Wheezing, Donnelley raised his head to find the terrible iron before him. "It is a question I have longed to ask you."

"You're stalling, and I'm bored. So long, Mercer. When you get to hell, tell your bastard family the King of Beasts says hello."

Donnelley gripped the whip in his shaking hand. "I held my breath each time you skinned me. Held in the pain, too. Each scar a mark of pride on my hide. Because I learned not to scream, thanks to you, William. I keep my screams inside. So I must ask you." His lip twitched. "How long can you hold your breath?"

Bill's eyes went wide.

There was a short burst of gunfire as Donnelley charged, chest exploding, gunshot on rock, suffering wounds that should have killed a rampaging bear. Then the gunfire stopped. Donnelley had slashed the air with the whip; it gripped Bill's wrist as he held his breath and became a phantom.

But the whip already had him, and the ghostly blue hue covered Donnolley, as if he were in the intangible realm with Bill. Bill raised his pistol, mouth puckered, but Donnolley yanked, tearing Bill down and toward him as his iron right hand swung with the merciless strength of an executioner's ax, and nailed Bill's chin so hard his jaw broke off, flying into the dark, while his immortal iron flew in the other direction.

Bill gasped, ghostly blue hue gone, his form returned to the land of the living, but on his hands and knees. His cleaved skull looked up, red and rushing.

Donnelley's limestone face grinned. "When you get to hell, tell Old Scratch the last of Donnelleys sent you!"

Choking on redness, Bill could not turn phantom. An iron hand was raised high, and the punch that Donnelley brought down drove Bill's face three feet into the rock, and shook out all but one lamp.

Then, Donnelley ... changed. His skin lightened and the wounds healed quicker than dirt rinsed off skin, bullets popping out of his skin like corn kernels from a fire. And there before me was the picture perfect visage of Phantom Bill, jaw intact.

I uttered a curse, and Donnelley tore me away from the two slumbering sods. "You. . . ." he said with Bill's sadist tone. "You were not there. At our home. With the Vigils."

I shook. "No," I said, for it was true.

He dropped me, then retrieved Bill's immortal iron and holstered it. "You see what price I pay. I wear the face of those I kill. For a day, their skin is mine, and I can walk among the living, before I go back to being an iron shadow." So it was that he killed Ruby Jacks, and took his form the day before.

For it was all part of a cunning ruse.

Donnelley and the journalist Grant were partners in justice here in Kingstonia. When Phantom Bill's gang became feared and powerful, Donnelley hunted them down and Grant seeded the *Libre* with tales that would lead Bill's men to Grant's whereabouts. When Ruby found Grant, Donnelley was waiting and dispatched him with such violence that his heart was never found. He tossed the body where it would be discovered, had Grant spread rumours he was hiding above the tavern, and then Donnelley asked Grant to work him over so we would not recognize the face of Ruby Jacks.

I know this because Donnelley and Grant told me, and, because my hands were clean of his family's massacre, I lived to tell it. Jones and Badger were not so lucky. Ex-Vigils both, the Iron Shadow wore their hides for a day before vanishing into Kingstonia.

There is the truth of it. What comes of me is of little account. This is a mad city at the best of times, and my flawless memory will soon drive me madder still.

So I leave you with a warning. Think twice of committing ills on the streets of Kingstonia, be you inmate or jailer, because for one man those who wreak harm on the innocent are all the same and are to be accorded no quarter. For those who glory in suffering, for those who seek the joy of pain, for those who prey on families in rough times, an Iron Shadow waits.

Jason S. Ridler

JASON S. RIDLER (www.jridler.com) was born in Pointe-Claire, Québec, raised in Toronto, and spent ten years in the prison capital of Canada, Kingston (though as a student). He holds a PhD in War Studies and has published three novels and more than fifty short stories.

AFTERWORD

Claude: Superhero fiction is my favourite genre; I've been addicted to it for as long as I can remember. I've wanted to compile an anthology of original Canadian super stories for years, so this book, my eleventh volume as editor or co-editor, is a dream come true.

But, as much as I've been chafing to put such a book together for what seems like forever, waiting turned out to be a great thing. First, I've become a better editor with time, and I think experience helped make this—my dream anthology—better. Second, I've grown to prefer putting together original anthologies with a co-editor. That way, the editing process is more passionate, more involving, more stimulating . . . simply put: better for the book. And the co-editor who came along with me on the journey of creating *Masked Mosaic: Canadian Super Stories*, Camille Alexa, brought more passion and energy to it than I could have dared hope. We argued and fought for the stories we each loved until those left standing were our absolute favourites, stories we couldn't bear not to publish. One of the most fun side-effects of this process was having to sometimes defend and define the outer limits of the genre. I was delighted, surprised, intrigued, and even challenged by how broadly writers tackled the idea of the Canadian superhero (or -villain). More than once, Camille, your passion and conviction changed, focused, and/or expanded my thinking about the book's shape, tone, and content. And I loved that fluid, interactive process.

Camille: Claude, I hope you haven't ruined me forever for other co-editors, because I had the most amazing time compiling this anthology with you. The magazine slushing and editing I've done in the past—much as I loved it—simply doesn't compare. And once things really got rolling with *Masked Mosaic*, certain stories only got better and better every time I read them. The diversity in approaches to superherodom and supervillainy, the scope of what we were getting to consider, started to become very exciting. I even adored some of the stories we had to let go! Particularly toward the end when we realized the sheer volume of pieces we loved, and how much Canadian lore and geography and history and setting we were gathering together in one volume.

Claude: It was a challenge to whittle it down. In the end, the publisher offered to up our word count for the book, allowing us to squeeze in a few more stories. I was surprised by some of the motifs that propped up regularly; for example, the Yukon Gold Rush, which is barely a blip on my own consciousness, ended playing a major role in a startling number of submissions—so we included a couple of the best ones. And then some stories stretched even the concept of *story*. And I was very happy that we selected a few of those as well.

Camille: We did get some great settings and unusual narrative structures, but it's the voices in these final pieces that won me over in the end, especially now they're all woven together in the finished anthology. Remember how many permutations and iterations we went through, figuring out the order? I started unconsciously thinking of stories as light or heavy, as chewy or pithy ... as though they were things I was consuming rather than simply reading, stuff I could sink my teeth into. It was more like cooking a complex meal or whipping up a magic potion with a bunch of ingredients.

I'm particularly pleased about the range we achieved in tone. I think both you and I, as writers and as editors, tend to gravitate toward characters and stories that are neither Good nor Evil, but a complex and organic combination. There's a tendency to think of superheroes and supervillains as either/or, but the best ones are neither/both.

That said, no matter how rich and interesting these pieces are on their own, their textures change when envisioned together; the creepiest villain genesis tale and the brightest hero genesis tale each get more textured, more vibrant, when they bounce off each other. Like varied colours in a mosaic.

Claude: In the end, the writers really came through. When soliciting for a thematic anthology, there's always the risk that submissions will adhere too closely to a template. But the writers who sent their stories to us, through the diversity of their imaginations, took the idea of the mosaic—culturally, stylistically, regionally, and more—to heart, gifting us with a breadth and scope that more than fulfilled what we were hoping for. In 1938, Canadian cartoonist Joe Shuster's co-creation, Superman, was first published, defining the concept of the superhero. Now, seventy-five years later, I'm happy that we get to showcase two dozen uniquely Canadian takes on the superhero idea, informed by those seventy-five years of exploration and experimentation.

CAMILLE ALEXA (camillealexa.com) is a dual Canadian/American currently splitting her time between Vancouver, BC, and Portland, Oregon. Her stories appear in *Ellery Queen's* and *Alfred Hitchcock's* mystery magazines, *Fantasy*, and *Imaginarium 2012: The Best Canadian Speculative Writing*. Her collection, *Push of the Sky*, earned a starred review in *Publishers Weekly* and was shortlisted for the Endeavour Award.

CLAUDE LALUMIÈRE (lostmyths.net/claude) is the author of *Objects of Worship* and *The Door to Lost Pages*, the editor or co-editor of eleven other anthologies, including *Super Stories of Heroes & Villains* and the Aurora Award finalist *Tesseracts Twelve: New Novellas of Canadian Fantastic Fiction*, and the co-creator of Lost Myths (lostmyths.net). Originally from Montreal, he's recently been enjoying the West Coast.